FIC
Day, Sylvia.
One with you.
c2016

Discarded by
Santa Marja Library

JUN 0 2 2016

FROM ~~BESTSELLIN~~

The final chapter in th~~e~~ ~~Santa Mar~~

Gideon Cross. Falling in love with him was the easiest thing I've ever done. It happened instantly. Completely. Irrevocably.

Marrying him was a dream come true. Staying married to him is the fight of my life. Love transforms. Ours is both a refuge from the storm and the most violent of tempests. Two damaged souls entwined as one.

We have bared our deepest, ugliest secrets to each other. Gideon is the mirror that reflects all my flaws . . . and all the beauty I couldn't see. He has given me everything. Now I must prove I can be the rock, the shelter for him that he is for me. Together, we could stand against those who work so viciously to come between us.

But our greatest battle may lie within the very vows that give us strength. Committing to love was only the beginning. Fighting for it will either set us free . . . or break us apart.

Heartbreakingly and seductively poignant, *One with You* is the breathlessly awaited finale to the Crossfire saga, the searing love story that has captivated millions of readers worldwide.

D0950766

By Sylvia Day

THE CROSSFIRE NOVELS

Bared to You
Reflected in You
Entwined with You
Captivated by You
One with You

THE MARKED SERIES

Eve of Darkness
Eve of Destruction
Eve of Chaos
Eve of Sin City (e-book)

One with You

SYLVIA DAY

St. Martin's Griffin ▲ New York

This is a work of fiction. All of the characters, organizations, and events portrayed in this novel are either products of the author's imagination or are used fictitiously.

ONE WITH YOU. Copyright © 2016 by Sylvia Day, LLC. All rights reserved. Printed in the United States of America. For information, address St. Martin's Press, 175 Fifth Avenue, New York, N.Y. 10010.

www.stmartins.com

Designed by Steven Seighman

The Library of Congress Cataloging-in-Publication Data is available upon request.

ISBN 978-1-250-10930-9 (trade paperback)
ISBN 978-1-250-10931-6 (e-book)

Our books may be purchased in bulk for promotional, educational, or business use. Please contact your local bookseller or the Macmillan Corporate and Premium Sales Department at 1-800-221-7945, extension 5442, or by e-mail at MacmillanSpecialMarkets@macmillan.com.

First Edition: April 2016

10 9 8 7 6 5 4 3 2 1

*This one is dedicated to Hilary Sares,
who has been caught in the Crossfire with
me from the first word to the last.*

1

⤜⤛⤚

NEW YORK WAS THE CITY that never slept; it never even got sleepy. My condo on the Upper West Side had the level of soundproofing expected in a multimillion-dollar property, but still the sounds of the city filtered in—the rhythmic thumping of tires over the well-worn streets, the protests of weary air brakes, and the nonstop honking of taxi horns.

As I stepped out of the corner café onto always-busy Broadway, the rush of the city washed over me. How had I ever lived without the cacophony of Manhattan?

How had I ever managed living without *him*?

Gideon Cross.

I cupped his jaw in my hands, felt him nuzzle into my touch. That show of vulnerability and affection cut right through me. Just hours before I'd thought he might never change, that I would have to compromise too much to share my life with him. Now, I stood in the face of his courage and doubted my own.

Had I demanded more of him than I had of myself? I was shamed by the possibility that I'd pushed him to evolve while I had remained obstinately the same.

He stood before me, so tall and strong. In jeans and a T-shirt, with a ball cap pulled low over his brow, he was unrecognizable as the global mogul the world thought it knew but still so innately compelling he affected everyone who walked by. In the corner of my eye, I noted how the people nearby glanced at him, then did a double take.

Whether Gideon was dressed casually or in the bespoke three-piece suits he favored, the power of his leanly muscular body was unmistakable. The way he held himself, the authority he wielded with faultless control, made it impossible for him to ever fade into the background.

New York swallowed everything that came into it, while Gideon had the city on a gilded leash.

And he was mine. Even with my ring on his finger, I still sometimes struggled to believe it.

He would never be just a man. He was ferocity sheathed in elegance, perfection veined with flaws. He was the nexus of my world, a nexus of *the* world.

Yet he'd just proven that he would bend and yield to the breaking point to be with me. Which left me with a renewed determination to prove I was worth the pain I'd forced him to face.

Around us, the shop fronts along Broadway were reopening. The flow of traffic on the street began to thicken, black cars and yellow cabs bouncing wildly over the uneven surface. Residents trickled onto the sidewalks, taking their dogs out or heading toward Central Park for an early-morning run, stealing what time they could before the workday kicked in with a vengeance.

The Benz pulled up to the curb just as we reached it, Raúl a big shadowy figure at the wheel. Angus slid the Bentley into place behind it. My ride and Gideon's, going to separate homes. How was that a marriage?

Fact was, it was *our* marriage, though neither of us wanted it that way. I'd had to draw a line when Gideon hired my boss away from the advertising agency I worked for.

I understood my husband's desire for me to join Cross Industries, but trying to force my hand by taking action behind my back? . . . I couldn't allow it, not with a man like Gideon. Either we were together—making decisions *together*—or we were too far apart to make our relationship work.

Tilting my head back, I looked up into his stunning face. There was remorse there, and relief. And love. So much love.

It was breathtaking how handsome he was. His eyes were the blue of the Caribbean, his hair a thick and glossy black mane that brushed his collar. An adoring hand had sculpted every plane and angle of his face into a level of flawlessness that mesmerized and made it hard to think rationally. I'd been captivated by the look of him from the moment I first saw him, and I still found my synapses frying at random moments. Gideon just dazzled me.

But it was the man inside, his relentless energy and power, his sharp intelligence and ruthlessness coupled with a heart that could be so tender . . .

"Thank you." My fingertips brushed over the dark slash of his brow, tingling as they always did when they touched his skin. "For calling me. For telling me about your dream. For meeting me here."

"I'd meet you anywhere." The words were a vow, spoken fervently and fiercely.

Everyone had demons. Gideon's were caged by his iron will when he was awake. When he slept, they tormented him in violent, vicious nightmares that he'd resisted sharing with me. We had so much in common, but the abuse in our childhoods was a shared trauma that both drew us together and pushed us apart. It made me fight harder for Gideon and what we had together. Our abusers had taken too much away from us already.

"Eva . . . You're the only force on earth that can keep me away."

"Thank you for that, too," I murmured, my chest tight. Our recent separation had been brutal for both of us. "I know it wasn't easy for you to give me space, but we needed it. And I know I pushed you hard. . . ."

"Too hard."

My mouth curved at the quick bite of ice in his words. Gideon wasn't a man used to being denied what he wanted. But as much as he'd hated being deprived of access to me, we were together now because that deprivation drove him forward. "I know. And you let me, because you love me."

"It's more than love." His hands banded my wrists, tightening in the authoritative way that made everything inside me surrender.

I nodded, no longer afraid to admit that we needed each other to a degree some would consider unhealthy. It was who we were, what we had. And it was precious.

"We'll drive to Dr. Petersen's together." He said the words with unmistakable command, but his gaze searched mine as if he'd asked a question.

"You're so bossy," I teased, wanting us to leave each other feeling good. Hopeful. Our weekly therapy appointment with Dr. Lyle Petersen was only hours away, and it couldn't have been more opportunely scheduled. We'd turned a corner. We could use a little help in figuring what our next steps should be from here.

His hands circled my waist. "You love it."

I reached for the hem of his shirt, fisting the soft jersey. "I love *you*."

"*Eva.*" His shuddered breath gusted hot on my neck. Manhattan surrounded us but couldn't intrude. When we were together, there was nothing else.

A low sound of hunger left me. I yearned for and craved him, shivering with delight that he was once again pressed against me. I breathed him in with deep inhalations, my fingers kneading into the rigid muscles of his back. The rush sliding through me was heady. I was addicted to him—heart, soul, and body—and I'd gone days without my fix, leaving me shaky and off-balance, unable to function properly.

He engulfed me, his body so much bigger and harder. I felt safe in his embrace, cherished and protected. Nothing could touch or hurt me when he was holding me. I wanted him to feel that same sense of security with me. I needed him to know he could drop his guard, take a breath, and I could protect us both.

I had to be stronger. Smarter. Scarier. We had enemies, and Gideon was dealing with them on his own. It was innate to him to be protective; it was one of his traits I deeply admired. But I had to start showing people that I could be as formidable an adversary as my husband.

More important, I had to prove it to Gideon.

Leaning into him, I absorbed his warmth. His love. "I'll see you at five, ace."

"Not a minute later," he ordered gruffly.

I laughed despite myself, infatuated with every rough-edged facet of him. "Or what?"

Pulling back, he gave me a look that made my toes curl. "Or I come get you."

❧

I should have tiptoed into my stepfather's penthouse with my breath held, since the time—a little after six A.M.—meant getting caught sneaking back in was likely. Instead, I strode in with purpose, my thoughts occupied with the changes I needed to make.

I had time for a shower—barely—but I decided not to take one. It had been so long since Gideon had touched me. Too long since his hands had been on me, his body inside mine. I didn't want to wash the memory of his touch away. That alone would give me the strength to do what had to be done.

An end-table lamp clicked on. "Eva."

I jumped. "Jesus."

Pivoting, I found my mother sitting on one of the living room settees.

"You scared the crap out of me!" I accused, rubbing a hand over my racing heart.

She stood, her floor-length ivory satin robe shimmering

around her toned, lightly tanned legs. I was her only child, but we looked like we could be sisters. Monica Tramell Barker Mitchell Stanton was obsessive about maintaining her looks. She was a career trophy wife; her youthful beauty was her stock-in-trade.

"Before you start," I began, "yes, we have to talk about the wedding. But I really have to get ready for work and pack up my stuff so I can go home tonight—"

"Are you having an affair?"

Her curt question shocked me more than the ambush. "*What?* No!"

She exhaled, tension visibly leaving her shoulders. "Thank God. Will you tell me what the hell is going on? How bad was this argument you had with Gideon?"

Bad. For a while, I worried that he'd ended us with the decisions he made. "We're working things out, Mom. It was just a bump in the road."

"A bump that had you avoiding him *for days*? That's not the way to deal with your problems, Eva."

"It's a long story—"

She crossed her arms. "I'm not in a hurry."

"Well, I am. I have a job to get ready for."

Hurt flashed across her face. I felt instantly remorseful.

Once, I had wanted to grow up to be just like my mother. I spent hours dressing up in her clothes, stumbling around in her heels, smearing my face with her expensive creams and cosmetics. I tried to emulate her breathy voice and sensual mannerisms, certain my mother was the most gorgeous and perfect woman in the world. And her way with men, how they looked at her and catered to her . . . well, I'd wanted that magic touch of hers, too.

In the end, I had matured into her spitting image aside from the style of our hair and the color of my eyes. But that was just on the outside. Who we were as women couldn't be more different and, sadly, that was something I'd come to take pride in. I'd stopped turning to her for advice, except when it came to clothes and decorating.

That was going to change. Now.

I'd tried a lot of different tactics in navigating my relationship with Gideon, but I hadn't asked for help from the one person close to me who knew what it was like to be married to prominent and powerful men.

"I need your advice, Mom."

My words hung in the air, and then I watched comprehension widen my mother's eyes with surprise. A moment later she was sinking back onto the sofa as if her knees had failed her. Her shock was a hard blow, telling me how completely I'd shut her out.

I was hurting inside when I took a seat on the couch opposite her. I'd learned to be careful about what I shared with my mom, doing my best to withhold information that might start discussions that drove me crazy.

It hadn't always been that way. My stepbrother Nathan had taken my warm, easy relationship with my mother away from me, just as he'd taken my innocence. After my mom learned of the abuse, she had changed, becoming overprotective to the point of stalking and smothering me. She was supremely confident about everything in her life, except for me. With me, she was anxious and intrusive, sometimes bordering on hysterical. Over the years, I'd forced myself to skirt around the truth far too often, keeping secrets from everyone I loved just to maintain peace.

"I don't know how to be the kind of wife Gideon needs," I confessed.

Her shoulders went back, her entire posture shifting to one of outrage. "Is *he* having an affair?"

"No!" A reluctant laugh escaped me. "No one is having an affair. We wouldn't do that to each other. We couldn't. Stop worrying about that."

I had to wonder if my mother's recent infidelity with my father was the true root of her concern. Did it weigh on her mind? Did she question what she had with Stanton? I didn't know how to feel about that. I loved my dad so much, but I also believed that my stepfather was perfect for my mom in just the way she needed a husband to be.

"Eva—"

"Gideon and I eloped a few weeks ago." God, it felt good to put that out there.

She blinked at me. Once, twice. "What?"

"I haven't told Dad yet," I went on. "But I'm going to call him today."

Her eyes glistened with welling tears. "*Why?* God, Eva . . . how did we grow so far apart?"

"Don't cry." I got up and went to her, taking a seat beside her. I reached for her hands, but she pulled me into a fierce hug instead.

I breathed in the familiar scent of her and felt the kind of peace only found in a mother's arms. For a few moments, anyway. "It wasn't planned, Mom. We went away for the weekend, and Gideon asked me if I would, and he made the arrangements. . . . It was spontaneous. Spur of the moment."

She pulled back, revealing a tear-streaked face and fire in her eyes. "He married you without a prenup?"

I laughed, I had to. Of course my mother would zero in on the financial details. Money had long been the driving force of her life. "There's a prenup."

"Eva Lauren! Did you have it looked at? Or was that spontaneous, too?"

"I read every word."

"You're not an attorney! God, Eva . . . I raised you to be smarter than this!"

"A six-year-old could've understood the terms," I shot back, irritated by the real problem in my marriage: Gideon and I had way too many people meddling in our relationship, distracting us so that we didn't have time to tackle the things that really needed work. "Don't worry about the prenup."

"You should've asked Richard to read it. I don't see why you wouldn't have. It's so irresponsible. I just don't—"

"I saw it, Monica."

We both turned at the sound of my stepfather's voice. Stanton entered the room ready for the day, looking sharp in a navy suit and yellow tie. I imagined Gideon would be much like my stepfather at the same age: physically fit, distinguished, as much an alpha male as ever.

"You did?" I asked, surprised.

"Cross sent it to me a few weeks ago." Stanton crossed over to my mother, taking her hand in his. "I couldn't have argued for better terms."

"There are always better terms, Richard!" my mom said sharply.

"There are rewards for milestones such as anniversaries and the birth of children, and nothing in the way of penalties for Eva, aside from marital counseling. A dissolution would have a more than equitable distribution of assets. I was tempted to ask if Cross had his in-house counsel review it. I imagine they argued strenuously against it."

She settled for a moment, taking that in. Then she pushed to her feet, bristling. "But you knew they were eloping? You knew, and you didn't say anything?"

"Of course, I didn't know." He pulled her into his arms, crooning softly like he would with a child. "I assumed he was looking ahead. You know these things usually take a few months of negotiating. Although, in this case, there was nothing more I could've asked for."

I stood. I had to hurry if I was going to get to work on time. Today of all days, I didn't want to be late.

"Where are you going?" My mother straightened away from Stanton. "We're not done with this discussion. You can't just drop a bomb like that and leave!"

Turning to face her, I walked backward. "I've seriously got to get ready. Why don't we get together for lunch and talk more then?"

"You can't be—"

I cut her off. "Corinne Giroux."

My mother's eyes widened, then narrowed. One name. I didn't have to say anything else.

Gideon's ex was a problem that needed no further explanation.

It was the rare person who came to Manhattan and didn't feel an instant familiarity. The skyline of the city had been immortalized in too many movies and television shows to count, spreading the love affair with New York from residents to the world.

I was no exception.

I adored the Art Deco elegance of the Chrysler Building. I could pinpoint my place on the island in relation to the position of the Empire State Building. I was awed by the breathtaking height of the Freedom Tower that now dominated downtown. But the Crossfire Building was in a class by itself. I'd thought so before I had ever fallen in love with the man whose vision had led to its creation.

As Raúl pulled the Benz up to the curb, I marveled at the distinctive sapphire blue glass that encased the obelisk shape of the Crossfire. My head tilted back, my gaze sliding up the shimmering height to the point at the top, the light-drenched space that housed Cross Industries. Pedestrians surged around me, the sidewalk teeming with businessmen and -women heading to work with briefcases and totes in one hand and steaming cups of coffee in the other.

I felt Gideon before I saw him, my entire body humming with awareness as he stepped out of the Bentley, which had pulled up behind the Benz. The air around me charged with electricity, the crackling energy that always heralded the approach of a storm.

I was among the few who knew it was the restlessness of Gideon's tormented soul that powered the tempest.

Turning to him, I smiled. It was no coincidence that we'd arrived at the same time. I knew that before I saw the confirmation in his eyes.

He wore a charcoal suit with a white shirt and silver twill tie. His dark hair brushed his jaw and collar in a sexy, rakish fall of inky strands. He still looked at me with the hot sexual ferocity that first scorched me, but there was tenderness in the brilliant blue now and an openness that meant more to me than anything else he could ever give me.

I stepped toward him as he approached. "Good morning, Dark and Dangerous."

His lips curved wryly. Amusement warmed his gaze further. "Good morning, wife."

I reached for his hand, felt settled when he met me halfway and gripped mine firmly. "I told my mother this morning . . . about us being married."

One dark brow arched in surprise, and then his smile curved into one of triumphant pleasure. "Good."

Laughing at his unabashed possessiveness, I gave him a soft shove to the shoulder. He moved lightning quick, catching me close and kissing the corner of my smiling mouth.

His joy was infectious. I felt it bursting inside me, lighting up all the places that had been so dark the past few days. "I'm going to call my dad at my first break. Let him know."

He sobered. "Why now, and not before?"

He spoke softly, his voice pitched low for privacy. The office-bound crowd continued to flow by, paying very little attention to us. Still, I hesitated to answer, feeling too exposed.

Then . . . the truth came easier than it ever had. I'd been hiding so many things from the people I loved. Little things, big things. Trying to maintain the status quo, while also hoping for and needing change.

"I was afraid," I told him.

He stepped closer, his gaze intense. "And now you're not."

"No."

"You'll tell me why tonight."

I nodded. "I'll tell you."

His hand curved around my nape, the hold possessive and tender at once. His face was impassive, giving nothing away, but his eyes . . . those blue, blue eyes . . . they raged with emotion. "We're going to make it, angel."

Love slid warmly through me like the buzz of a fine wine. "Damn straight."

❧

It was strange walking through the doors of Waters Field & Leaman, mentally counting down the number of days I'd be able to claim I worked at the prestigious advertising agency. Megumi Kaba waved from behind her reception desk, tapping her headset to let me know she was on a call and couldn't talk. I waved back and headed toward my own desk with a determined stride. I had a lot to get done, a new start to get rolling.

But first things first. I dropped my purse and bag into the bottom drawer, then settled in my chair and surfed to my usual florist's website. I knew what I wanted. Two dozen white roses in a deep red crystal vase.

White for purity. For friendship. For eternal love. It was also the flag of surrender. I'd drawn battle lines by forcing a separation between Gideon and me, and in the end, I had won. But I didn't want to war with my husband.

I didn't even try to come up with a clever tie-in note for the flowers, like I'd done in the past. I just wrote from the heart.

You are miraculous, Mr. Cross.
I cherish you and love you so much.
Mrs. Cross

The website prompted me to finalize the order. I clicked submit and took a moment to imagine what Gideon would think of my gift. One day, I hoped to watch him receive flowers from me. Did he smile when his secretary, Scott, brought them in? Did he stop whatever meeting he was commanding to read my notes? Or did he wait until one of the rare lulls in his schedule for privacy?

My mouth curved as I considered the possibilities. I loved giving Gideon gifts.

And soon I'd have more time to pick them out.

⤙�⤚

"You're quitting?"

Mark Garrity's incredulous gaze lifted from my resignation letter and met mine.

My stomach knotted at the expression on my boss's face. "Yes. I'm sorry I can't give more notice."

"Tomorrow is your last day?" He leaned back in his chair. His eyes were a warm chocolate shades lighter than his skin, and they registered both surprise and dismay. "Why, Eva?"

Sighing, I leaned forward, setting my elbows on my knees. Yet again, I went with the truth. "I know it's unprofessional to cut out like this, but . . . I've got to rearrange my priorities and right now. . . . I just can't give this my full attention, Mark. I'm sorry."

"I . . ." He blew out his breath and ran a hand over his dark, tight curls. "Hell . . . What can I say?"

"That you'll forgive me and won't hold it against me?" I huffed out a humorless laugh. "It's asking a lot, I know."

He managed a wry smile. "I hate to lose you, Eva, you

know that. I'm not sure I've ever really expressed how much you've contributed. You make me work better."

"Thank you, Mark. I appreciate that." God, this was harder than I thought it would be, even knowing it was the best and only decision I could make.

My gaze went beyond my handsome boss to the view behind him. As a junior account manager, he had a small office and his view was blocked by the building across the street, but it was still as quintessentially New York as Gideon Cross's sprawling office on the top floor above us.

In a lot of ways, that division of floors mirrored the way I'd tried to define my relationship with Gideon. I knew who he was. Knew *what* he was: a man in a class by himself. I loved that about him and didn't want him to change; I just wanted to climb to his level on my own merits. What I hadn't considered was that by stubbornly refusing to accept that our marriage changed the plan, I was pulling him down to mine.

I wouldn't be known for earning my way to the top of my field. For some people, I would always have married into success. And I was just going to have to live with it.

"So, where are you going from here?" Mark asked.

"Honestly . . . I'm still figuring that out. I just know I can't stay."

My marriage could only take so much pressure before it broke, and I had allowed it to slide to a dangerous edge, trying to find some distance. Trying to put myself first.

Gideon Cross was as deep and vast as the ocean, and I had feared drowning in him from the moment I first saw him. I couldn't be afraid of that anymore. Not after realizing that what I feared more was losing him.

By trying to stay neutral, I'd been shoved from side to side. And as pissed off as I'd been about that, I hadn't taken the time to comprehend that if I wanted control, I just had to take it.

"Because of the LanCorp account?" Mark asked.

"In part." I smoothed my pinstriped pencil skirt, mentally brushing away the lingering resentment over Gideon's hiring of Mark. The catalyst had been LanCorp coming to Waters Field & Leaman with a specific request for Mark—and therefore me—a maneuver Gideon viewed with suspicion. Geoffrey Cross's Ponzi scheme had decimated the Landon family fortune, and while both Ryan Landon and Gideon had rebuilt what their fathers had lost, Landon still hungered for revenge. "But mostly for personal reasons."

Straightening, he set his elbows on the desk and leaned toward me. "It's none of my business and I won't pry, but you know Steven, Shawna, and I are all here for you, if you need us. We care about you."

His earnestness made my eyes sting with tears. His fiancé, Steven Ellison, and Steven's sister, Shawna, had become dear to me in the months I'd been in New York, part of the new network of friends I had built in my new life. No matter what, I didn't want to lose them.

"I know." I smiled through my sorrow. "If I need you, I'll call, I promise. But it's all going to work out for the best. For all of us."

Mark relaxed and returned my smile. "Steven's going to flip. Maybe I should make you tell him."

Thinking of the burly, gregarious contractor chased any sadness away. Steven would give me a hard time for bailing out on his partner, but he'd do it with a good heart. "Aw, come on," I teased back. "You wouldn't do that to me, would you? This is hard enough as it is."

"I'm not opposed to making it harder."

I laughed. Yeah, I was going to miss Mark and my job. A lot.

‿◦‿

When my first break came around, it was still early in Oceanside, California, so I texted my dad instead of calling.

Let me know when you're up, k? Need to tell you something. And since I knew that being a cop as well as a father made Victor Reyes a worrier, I added, *Nothing bad, just some news.*

I'd barely set my phone down on the break room counter to get a cup of coffee when it started ringing. My dad's handsome face lit up the screen, his photo showing off the gray eyes I had inherited from him.

I was suddenly struck with a case of nerves. When I reached for my phone, my hand was shaking. I loved both of my parents a lot, but I'd always thought that my dad felt things more deeply than my mother. And while my mother never hesitated to point out the ways I could fix my flaws, my dad didn't seem to realize I had any. Disappointing him . . . hurting him . . . it was brutal to think of it.

"Hey, Dad. How are you?"

"That's my question, sweetheart. I'm doing the same as usual. How 'bout you? What's going on?"

I moved over to the nearest table and took a chair to help myself calm down. "I told you it wasn't bad and you still sound worried. Did I wake you up?"

"It's my job to worry," he said, with warm amusement in his deep voice. "And I was gearing up for a run before I head in for the day, so no, you didn't wake me. Tell me what your news is."

"Uh . . ." Choked by tears, I swallowed hard. "Jesus, this is tougher than I thought it would be. I told Gideon it was Mom I was worried about, that you'd be okay with it, and here I am trying to—"

"Eva."

I took a deep breath. "Gideon and I eloped."

The line went eerily quiet.

"Dad?"

"When?" The scratch in his voice killed me.

"A couple weeks ago."

"Before you came to see me?"

I cleared my throat. "Yes."

Silence.

Ah, God. Totally brutal. Only weeks ago I'd told him about Nathan's abuse and that nearly broke him. Now this . . .

"Dad—You're freaking me out. We were on this island and it was beautiful, so beautiful. The resort we were staying at does weddings all the time, they make it easy . . . like Las Vegas. There's a full-time officiant and someone who handles the licenses. It was just a perfect moment, you know. The perfect opportunity." My voice cracked. "Dad . . . please say something."

"I . . . I don't know what to say."

A hot tear slid down my face. Mom had chosen wealth over love, and Gideon was a prime example of the type of man my mother had picked instead of my dad. I knew that created a bias my father had to overcome, and now we had this hurdle.

"We're still having a wedding," I told him. "We want our friends and family with us when we say our vows. . . ."

"That's what I was expecting, Eva." He growled. "Damn it. I feel like Cross just stole something from me! I'm supposed to give you away, I was working up to that, and he just runs off and takes you? And you didn't tell me? You were here, in my house, and you didn't say anything to me? It hurts, Eva. It hurts."

There was no way to stop the tears after that. They came in a hot flood, blurring my vision and closing my throat.

I jolted when the door to the break room opened and Will Granger walked in. "She's probably in here," my colleague said. "And there she—"

His voice trailed off when he saw my face, his eyes losing their smile behind his rectangular glasses.

A darkly clad arm shot in and brushed him aside.

Gideon. He filled the doorway, his eyes zeroing in on me and chilling to arctic. He was suddenly like an avenging angel, his fine suit making him look both capable and dangerous, his face hardened into a beautiful mask.

I blinked, my brain trying to process how and why he was there. Before it did, he was in front of me and my phone was in his hand, his gaze dropping to the screen before he lifted it to his ear.

"Victor." My father's name came out as a warning. "You seem to have upset Eva, so you'll be talking to me now."

Will backed out and shut the door.

Despite the cutting edge to Gideon's words, the fingertips that brushed my cheek were infinitely gentle. His gaze was focused on me, the blue filled with icy fury that nearly made me shiver.

Holy fuck, was Gideon *angry*. And so was my dad. I could hear him shouting from where I sat.

I caught Gideon's wrist, shaking my head, suddenly panicked that the two men I loved most would end up disliking—maybe even hating—each other.

"It's okay," I whispered. "I'm okay."

His gaze narrowed and he mouthed, *No, it's not.*

When he spoke to my father again, Gideon's voice was firm and controlled—and all the more scary because of it. "You've got a right to be angry, and hurt, I'll give you that. But I won't have my wife twisted up over this. . . . No, obviously without children of my own, I can't imagine."

I strained to hear, hoping that reduction in volume meant my dad was calming down instead of getting more worked up.

Gideon stiffened suddenly, his hand dropping away from me. "No, I wouldn't be happy about it if my sister eloped. That said, she's not the one I'd take it out on. . . ."

I winced. My husband and my father had that in common: They were both incredibly protective of those they loved.

"I'm available anytime, Victor. I'll even come to you, if that's what you need. When I married your daughter, I accepted full responsibility for both her and her happiness. If there are consequences to be faced, I have no problem facing them."

His gaze narrowed as he listened.

Then Gideon took the seat opposite me, set the phone on the table, and turned on the speaker.

My dad's voice filled the air. "Eva?"

I took a deep, shaky breath and squeezed the hand Gideon held out to me. "Yeah, I'm here, Dad."

"Sweetheart . . ." He took a deep breath, too. "Don't be upset, okay? I'm just . . . I need to let this sink in. I wasn't expecting this and . . . I've got to put it together in my head. Can we talk later tonight? When I get off my shift?"

"Yes, of course."

"Good." He paused.

"I love you, Daddy." The sound of my tears came through my voice and Gideon slid his chair closer, his thighs bracketing mine. It was amazing how much strength I drew from him, what a relief it was to have him to lean on. It was different from having Cary's support. My best friend was a sounding board, cheerleader, and ass kicker. Gideon was a shield.

And I had to be strong enough to admit when I needed one.

"I love you, too, baby," my dad said, with an aching note of pain and grief that stabbed me in the heart. "I'll call you later."

"Okay. I—" What else could I say? I was at a loss for how to fix things. "Bye."

Gideon killed the call, then took my trembling hands in his. His eyes were locked on me, the ice melting into tenderness. "You will not be ashamed, Eva. Is that clear?"

I nodded. "I'm not."

He cupped my face, his thumbs brushing away my tears. "I can't bear to see you cry, angel."

I forced back the lingering heartache, shoving it into a corner where I would deal with it later. "Why are you here? How did you know?"

"I came to thank you for the flowers," he murmured.

"Oh. Do you like them?" I managed a smile. "I wanted to make you think of me."

"All the time. Every minute." He caught my hips and tugged me closer.

"You could've just sent a note."

"Ah." His ghost of a smile made my pulse skip. "But that wouldn't cover this."

Gideon pulled me into his lap and kissed me senseless.

We still heading home tonight? Cary texted as I waited for the elevator to take me back down to the lobby at noon. My mom was already waiting for me there and I was trying to pull my thoughts together. We had a lot of ground to cover.

God, I was hoping she could help me deal with it all.

That's the plan, I replied to my beloved pain-in-the-ass-sometimes roommate, typing as I stepped into the car. *I have an appt. after work, though, then dinner with Gideon. Might be late.*

Dinner? U have to catch me up.

I smiled. *Of course.*

Trey called.

I exhaled in a rush, as if I'd been holding my breath. I guess in a way I had been.

I couldn't blame Cary's on-again, off-again boyfriend for taking a big step back when he'd learned that Cary's booty-call girl was pregnant. Trey had already been struggling with Cary's bisexuality, and now a baby meant there would always be a third person in their relationship.

There was no question that Cary should have committed

to Trey sooner, instead of keeping his options open, but I understood the fear behind Cary's actions. I knew all too well the thoughts that ran through your mind when you'd survived the things Cary and I had, yet still somehow found yourself faced with an amazing person who loved you.

When it was too good to be true, how could it possibly be real?

I sympathized with Trey, too, and if he called it quits, I'd respect that decision. But he was the best thing to happen to Cary in a long time. I was going to be extremely bummed if they didn't make it. *What did he say?*

I'll tell u when I see u.

Cary! That's cruel.

It took him until I was walking through the lobby turn-stiles to reply. *Yeah, tell me about it.*

My heart sank, because there was no way to interpret that as good news. Stepping aside to allow others to pass me, I typed back, *I love you madly, Cary Taylor.*

Love u 2, baby girl.

"Eva!"

My mother crossed the space between us on delicately heeled sandals, a woman impossible to miss even amid the lunchtime crush of people heading in and out of the Cross-fire. As petite as she was, Monica Stanton should've been lost in the sea of suits, but she drew too much attention for that to ever happen.

Charisma. Sensuality. Fragility. It was the bombshell combination that made Marilyn Monroe a star, and it exemplified my mother. Dressed in a navy blue sleeveless jump-suit, Monica Stanton looked younger than her years and more confident than I knew her to be. The Cartier panthers hugging her throat and wrist told the observant she was expensive.

She came straight to me and wrapped me in a hug that took me by surprise.

"Mom."

"Are you okay?" Pulling back, she studied my face.

"What? Yes. Why?"

"Your father called."

"Oh." I looked at her warily. "He didn't take the news well."

"No, he didn't." As she linked her arm with mine, we headed out. "But he's dealing with it. He wasn't quite ready to let you go."

"Because I remind him of you." To my father, my mom was the one who got away. He still loved her, even after more than two decades apart.

"Nonsense, Eva. There's a resemblance, but you're much more interesting."

That startled a laugh from me. "Gideon says I'm interesting."

She smiled brightly, making the man passing her stumble over his own feet. "Of course. He's a connoisseur of women. As gorgeous as you are, it would take more than beauty to get him to marry you."

Slowing to a halt by the revolving doors, I let my mother go out first. A blast of muggy heat hit me when I joined her on the sidewalk, bringing an instant mist of perspiration to my skin. There were times when I doubted I'd ever get used to the humidity, but I considered it one of the costs of living in the city I loved so much. Spring had been beautiful and I knew fall would be, too. The perfect time of year to renew my vows with the man who owned me heart and soul.

I was thanking God for air-conditioning when I spotted Stanton's head of security waiting by a black car at the curb.

Benjamin Clancy greeted me with an easy, confident nod. His demeanor was so business-as-usual, while I felt such gratitude for him it was hard to restrain myself from grabbing and kissing him.

Gideon had killed Nathan to protect me. Clancy had made sure Gideon would never pay for it.

"Hey, you," I said to him, seeing my smile reflected in his mirrored aviator shades.

"Eva. It's good to see you."

"I was just thinking the same about you."

He didn't smile outwardly; it wasn't his way. But I could feel it nonetheless.

My mom slid in first, and then I joined her in the backseat. Before Clancy even rounded the trunk of the car, she was shifting to face me and reaching for my hand. "Don't worry about your father. He's got that quick Latin temper, but it never lasts long. All he really wants is to make sure you're happy."

I squeezed her fingers gently. "I know. But I really, really want Dad and Gideon to get along."

"They're two very headstrong men, honey. They're going to clash occasionally."

She wasn't wrong. I wanted to dream about the two of them hanging out the way guys did, bonding over sports or cars, with all the playful ribbing and backslapping that usually accompanied that sort of thing. But I had to work with reality, whatever that turned out to be.

"You're right," I conceded. "They're both big boys. They'll figure it out." Hopefully.

"Of course they will."

With a sigh, I glanced out the window. "I think I've come up with a solution for Corinne Giroux."

There was a pause. "Eva, you have got to put that woman out of your mind. By giving her any thought at all, you're giving her power she doesn't deserve."

"We allowed her to become a problem by being so secretive." I looked back at my mother. "The world has a tremendous appetite for all things Gideon. He's gorgeous, rich, sexy, and brilliant. People want to know everything about him, but he's guarded his privacy to such an extreme degree that they know next to nothing. That's given Corinne this opening to write her biography about her time with Gideon."

She gave me a wary look. "What are you thinking?"

Digging into my bag, I pulled out a small tablet. "We need more of *this*."

I flipped the screen around, showing her the image of Gideon and me that had been taken just hours before as we'd stood in front of the Crossfire. The manner in which he gripped me by the nape was both tender and possessive, while the way my face tilted up to him revealed my love and adoration. It made my stomach turn to see such a private moment spread out for the world to ogle, but I had to get over it. I had to give them more.

"Gideon and I need to stop hiding," I explained. "We need to be *seen*. We spend too much time shut in. The public wants the billionaire playboy who's finally becoming Prince Charming. They want fairy tales, Mom, and happy endings. I need to give people the story they want and by doing so, I'm going to make Corinne and her book look pathetic."

My mother's shoulders went back. "That's a horrible idea."

"No, it's not."

"It's terrible, Eva! You don't trade hard-earned privacy for *anything*. If you feed that public hunger, it will just get larger. For God's sake, you don't want to become a tabloid fixture!"

My jaw set. "It won't play out that way."

"Why would you risk it?" Her voice rose and became shrill. "Because of Corinne Giroux? Her book will come and go in the blink of an eye, but you'll never get rid of the attention once you invite it!"

"I don't get you. There's no way to be married to Gideon and *not* get attention! I might as well take control and set the stage myself."

"There's a difference between being prominent and being a TMZ headline!"

I growled inwardly. "I think you're taking the drama to the extreme."

She shook her head. "I'm telling you, this is the wrong way to handle the situation. Have you discussed this with Gideon? I can't see him agreeing to this."

I stared at her, truly startled by her response. I'd thought she would be all for it, considering how she felt about marrying well and what that entailed.

That was when I saw the fear tightening her mouth and shadowing her eyes.

"Mom." I softened my voice, mentally kicking myself for not putting it together sooner. "We don't have to worry about Nathan anymore."

She returned my stare. "No," she agreed, not the least bit soothed. "But having everything you've done . . . everything you've said or decided dissected for the entertainment of the world could be its own nightmare."

"I'm not going to allow other people in the world to dictate how I and my marriage are perceived!" I was tired of feeling like a . . . victim. I wanted to be the one to go on the offensive.

"Eva, you're not—"

"Either give me an alternative that doesn't involve sitting around doing nothing or drop the subject, Mom." I turned my head away. "We're not going to agree and I'm not changing my mind without a different game plan on the table."

She made a frustrated noise, then fell silent.

My fingers flexed with the need to text Gideon and vent. He had once told me I would excel at crisis management. He'd suggested I lend my talents to Cross Industries as a fixer.

Why not start with something more intimate and important instead?

2

"More flowers?" Arash Madani drawled as he strolled into my office through the open glass double doors.

My lead attorney walked over to where Eva's white roses decorated the main seating area. I'd had them placed on the coffee table in my direct line of sight. There, they had been successfully drawing my attention away from the stock tickers streaming on the wall of flat screens behind them.

The card that accompanied the flowers sat on the smoked glass of my desk and I fingered it, rereading the words for the hundredth time.

Arash pulled a rose out and lifted it to his nose. "What's the secret to getting sent some of these?"

I sat back, absently noting that his emerald-hued tie matched the jeweled decanters decorating the bar. Until his arrival, the brightly colored carafes and Eva's red vase had been the only spots of color in the monochromatic expanse of my office. "The right woman."

He returned the flower to its vase. "Go ahead, Cross, rub it in."

"I prefer to gloat quietly. Do you have something for me?"

Approaching my desk, he grinned in a way that told me he loved his job, although I never doubted it. His predatory instincts were nearly as highly developed as my own.

"The Morgan deal is coming together nicely." Adjusting his tailored slacks, he settled into one of the two chairs facing my desk. His style was slightly flashier than mine but couldn't be faulted. "We've ironed out the bigger points. Still finessing some clauses, but we should be ready to proceed by next week."

"Good."

"You are a man of few words." Casually, he asked, "You up for getting together this weekend?"

I shook my head. "Eva may want to go out. If so, I'll try to talk her out of it."

Arash laughed. "I gotta tell you, I expected you to settle down at some point—we all do, eventually—but I thought I'd have some warning."

"So did I." Which wasn't quite the truth. I never expected to share my life with anyone. I'd never denied that my past shadowed my present, but I saw no need to share that history with anyone before Eva. It couldn't be changed, so why rehash it?

Standing, I walked to one of the two floor-to-ceiling walls of windows framing my office and took in the urban splendor sprawling beyond the glass.

I hadn't known Eva was out there, had been afraid to even dream of finding the one person in the world who would accept and love every facet of me.

How was it possible that I'd found her here, in Manhattan, at the very building I'd had built against sound advice and at great risk? Too expensive, they'd said, and unnecessary. But I'd needed the Cross name to be memorable and mentioned in a different way. My father had dragged our name through the mud; I'd lifted it to the heights of the most relevant city in the world.

"You showed no sign at all you were leaning that way," Arash said behind me. "If I remember correctly, you tagged two women when we blew out Cinco de Mayo, and a few weeks later you're telling me to draft an insane prenup."

I surveyed the city, taking a rare moment to appreciate the hawk's-eye view afforded me by the height and position of my office in the Crossfire Building. "When have you known me to delay sealing a deal?"

"It's one thing to expand your portfolio, another to reboot your life overnight." He chuckled. "So what are your plans, then? Breaking in the new beach house?"

"An excellent idea." Taking my wife back to the Outer Banks was my goal. Having her all to myself had been heaven. I was happiest when I was alone with her. She revitalized me, made me anticipate living in a way I never had before.

I'd built my empire with the past in mind. Now, thanks to her, I would continue to build it for our future.

My desk phone flashed. It was Scott, on line one. I pressed the button, and his voice came through the speaker. "Corinne Giroux's at reception. She says she needs just a few minutes to drop off something for you. Because it's private, she wants to give it to you personally."

"Of course she does," Arash chimed in. "Maybe it's more flowers."

I shot him a look. "Wrong woman."

"If only my wrong women looked like Corinne."

"Keep thinking that while you head up to reception to get whatever it is she has."

His brows shot up. "Really? Ouch."

"She wants to talk, she can talk to my attorney."

He pushed to his feet and headed out. "Got it, boss."

I glanced at the clock. Quarter to five. "I'm sure you heard that, Scott, but to be clear, Madani will handle."

"Yes, Mr. Cross."

Through the glass wall separating my office from the rest of the floor, I watched Arash round the corner on his way to reception, and then I mentally brushed the whole thing aside. Eva would be with me shortly, the very thing I'd been waiting for since the workday started.

But of course, it couldn't be that easy.

A flash of crimson in the corner of my eye just a few moments later had me looking back out at the work floor and seeing Corinne marching toward my office with Arash hot on her heels. Her chin lifted when our eyes met. Her tight smile widened, transforming her from a beautiful woman to a stunning one. I could admire her the way I would admire anything except Eva—objectively, dispassionately.

Now happily married, I could fully grasp what a horrible mistake it would have been to marry Corinne. It was unfortunate for all of us that she refused to see it.

I stood and rounded my desk. The look I swept over both Arash and Scott called them off from any further action. If Corinne wanted to deal with me directly, I'd give her one last opportunity to do the right thing.

She glided into my office on red stilettos. The strapless

dress she wore was the same hue as the shoes and showed off both her long legs and pale skin. She wore her hair down, the black strands sliding around her bare shoulders. She was the polar opposite of my wife and a mirror image of every other woman who'd passed through my life.

"Gideon. Surely you can spare a few minutes for an old friend?"

Leaning back into my desk, I crossed my arms. "And extend the courtesy of not calling security. Make it quick, Corinne."

She smiled, but her eyes, the color of aquamarines, were sad.

She had a small red box tucked under her arm. When she reached me, Corinne offered it to me.

"What is this?" I asked, without reaching for it.

"These are the photos that will appear in the book."

My brow arched. I found myself unfolding and accepting the box, driven by curiosity. It hadn't been too long ago that we'd been together, but I scarcely remembered the details. What I had were impressions, big moments, and regret. I'd been so young, with a dangerous lack of self-awareness.

Corinne set her purse on my desk, moving in a way that brushed her arm against mine. Wary, I reached over and hit the button that controlled the opacity of the glass wall.

If she wanted to put on a show, I'd make sure she didn't have an audience.

Taking the lid off the box, I was confronted with a photo of Corinne and me entangled in front of a bonfire. Her head was nestled in the crook of my shoulder, her face tilted up so I could press a kiss to her lips.

The memory assailed me immediately. We'd taken a day

trip to a friend's house in the Hamptons. The weather had been cool, fall giving way to winter.

In the picture we looked happy and in love, and in a way, I suppose we were. But I'd refused the invitation to spend the night, despite Corinne's obvious disappointment. With my nightmares, I couldn't sleep beside her. And I couldn't fuck her, though I knew that was what she wanted, because the hotel room I reserved for that purpose was miles away.

So many hangups. So many lies and evasions.

I took a deep breath and let the past go. "Eva and I were married last month."

She stiffened.

Setting the box down on the desktop, I reached for my smartphone and showed her the picture wallpapering my screen—Eva and I sharing the kiss that sealed our vows.

Turning her head, Corinne looked away. Then she reached into the box, flipping through the top few photos to pull out one of us at the beach.

I was standing waist deep in the surf. Corinne was twined around me from the front, her legs wrapped around my waist, her arms draped over my shoulders and her hands in my hair. Her head was tossed back on a laugh, her joy radiating from the image. I gripped her fiercely, my face upturned to watch her. There was gratitude there and wonder. Affection. Desire. Strangers would see it and think it was love.

Which was Corinne's goal. I denied that I ever loved anyone before Eva, which was no less than the truth. Corinne was determined to prove me wrong in the most public way possible.

Leaning over, she looked at the picture, then at me. Her expectation was tangible, as if some monumental epiphany was supposed to strike me. She toyed with her necklace and I realized it was one I'd given her, a small gold heart on a simple chain.

For fuck's sake. I didn't even remember who took the damn photo or where we were at the time, and it didn't matter.

"What do you expect these photos to prove, Corinne? We dated. We ended. You married, and now I have. There's nothing left."

"Then why are you getting so upset? You're not indifferent, Gideon."

"No, I'm irritated. These only make me appreciate what I have with Eva more. And knowing that they'll hurt her sure as hell doesn't make me feel sentimental about the past. This is our final good-bye, Corinne." I held her gaze, making sure she saw my resolve. "If you come back here, security won't let you through."

"I won't be back. You'll have to—"

Scott beeped through and I picked up the phone. "Yes?"

"Miss Tramell is here for you."

I leaned over the desk again, tapping the button that opened the doors. A moment later, Eva walked in.

Would the day ever come when I would see her and not feel the earth shift beneath my feet?

She came to an abrupt halt, giving me the pleasure of taking in the sight of her. Eva was a natural blonde, with pale streaks framing a delicate face and accentuating stormy gray eyes that I could spend hours looking into—and had. She was petite but dangerously curved, her body deliciously soft to roll around with in bed.

I might've called her angelically beautiful, if not for the

lush sensuality that always made me think of and crave wickedly raw *sex*.

Without volition, my mind filled with the memory of her scent and the feel of her beneath my hands. The throaty laugh that brought me joy and the fiery quick temper that rocked me on my feet were visceral recollections. Everything in me thrummed to life, a surge of energy and awareness I felt at no other time than when I was with her.

Corinne spoke first. "Hello, Eva."

I bristled. The urge to shield and protect the most valuable thing in my life overrode any other consideration.

Straightening, I tossed the photo back in the box and went to my wife. Compared to Corinne, she was dressed demurely in a black pinstriped skirt and a sleeveless silk blouse that gleamed like a pearl. The surge of heat I felt was all the proof I needed as to which woman was sexier.

Eva. Now and forever.

The pull I felt drew me across the room in long, quick strides.

Angel.

I didn't say the word aloud, didn't want Corinne to hear it. But I could see that Eva felt it. I reached for her hand, felt a tingle of deep recognition that tightened my grip.

She shifted to look past me and acknowledge the woman who was no rival. "Corinne."

I didn't turn to look.

"I have to run," Corinne said behind me. "Those copies are for you, Gideon."

Unable to take my gaze off Eva, I spoke over my shoulder. "Take them with you. I don't want them."

"You should finish going through them," she countered, approaching.

"Why?" Aggravated, I glanced at Corinne when she stopped next to us. "If I have any interest in seeing them, I can always flip through your book."

Her smile tightened. "Good-bye, Eva. Gideon."

As she left, I took another step toward my wife, closing the final bit of distance between us. I caught her other hand, leaning over her to breathe in the scent of her perfume. Calm drifted through me.

"I'm glad you came." I whispered the words against her forehead, needing every connection I could manage. "I miss you so much."

Closing her eyes, she leaned into me with a sigh.

Feeling the lingering strain in her, I tightened my grip on her hands. "You okay?"

"Yeah. I'm good. I just wasn't expecting to see her."

"Neither was I." As much as I hated to pull away, I hated the thought of those photos even more.

Returning to my desk, I put the lid back on the box and tossed the whole thing into the trash.

"I quit my job," she said. "Tomorrow's my last day."

That decision was one I'd wanted her to come to. I believed it was the best and safest step for her to take. But I knew what a difficult conclusion it must have been for her to make. Eva loved her job and the people she worked with.

Knowing how well she could read me, I kept my tone neutral. "Did you?"

"Yep."

I studied her. "What's next for you, then?"

"I've got a wedding to plan."

"Ah." My mouth curved. After days of fearing she had second thoughts and wanted out of our marriage, it was a relief to hear otherwise. "Good to know."

I beckoned her closer with a crook of my finger.

"Meet me halfway," she shot back, with a glint of challenge in her eyes.

How could I resist? We met in the middle of the room.

That was why we were going to get past this and every other hurdle we faced: We would always meet each other halfway.

She wouldn't ever be the docile wife my friend Arnoldo Ricci had wished for me. Eva was too independent, too fierce. She had a jealous streak a mile wide. She was demanding and stubborn, and she defied me just to drive me crazy.

And that friction worked in a way it never could have with any other woman, because Eva was meant for me. I believed that as I believed in nothing else.

"Is this what you want?" I asked her quietly, searching her face for the answer.

"*You're* what I want. The rest is just logistics."

My mouth was suddenly dry and my heartbeat too quick. When she lifted a hand to brush my hair back I caught her wrist and pressed her palm to my cheek, my eyes closing as I absorbed her touch.

The past week melted away. The days we'd spent apart, the hours of silence, the crippling fear . . . She'd been showing me all day that she was ready to move ahead, that I'd made the right decision to talk to Dr. Petersen. To talk to *her*.

Not only didn't she turn away, she wanted me more. And she called *me* miraculous?

Eva sighed. I felt the last of her tension drift away. We

stood there, reconnecting with each other, taking the strength we needed. It shook me to the core to know that I could bring her some measure of peace.

And what had she brought me?

Everything.

∞

The way Angus's face brightened when Eva exited the Cross-fire Building moved me in ways I could never explain. Angus McLeod was quiet by nature and by training. He rarely showed any emotion at all, but he made an exception for Eva.

Or maybe he couldn't help himself. God knew I couldn't.

"Angus." Eva flashed him her bright, open smile. "You're looking especially dapper today."

I watched as the man I loved like a father touched the brim of his chauffeur's hat and smiled back with an amusing touch of embarrassment.

After my dad's suicide, my entire life was upended. In the messy years that followed, the one point of stability had been Angus, a man hired to be a driver and bodyguard but who turned out to be a lifeline instead. At a time when I felt isolated and betrayed, when even my own mother refused to believe I'd been repeatedly raped by the therapist who was supposed to help me adjust, Angus had been the one to anchor me. He never doubted me. And when I struck out on my own, he'd come with me.

As my wife's sleek, toned legs slid out of view into the backseat of the Bentley, Angus spoke. "Let's not muck it up this time, lad."

My mouth twisted ruefully. "Thanks for the vote of confidence."

I joined Eva, settling in as Angus rounded the car to reach the driver's seat. I set my hand on her thigh and waited for her to look at me. "I want to take you to the beach house this weekend."

She held her breath a moment, then released it in a rush. "My mom invited us up to Westport. Stanton's asked his nephew, Martin, to come, and Martin's girlfriend, Lacey—she's Megumi's roommate, I don't know if you remember. . . . Cary will be there, too, of course. Anyway, I said we'd come."

Wrestling with disappointment, I considered my options.

"I want us to do some family things," she went on. "Plus, my mom wants to talk about this plan I have."

I listened as she related her lunchtime conversation with Monica.

Eva studied my face as she finished. "She said you wouldn't like the idea, but you've used the paparazzi before, when you dipped me on the sidewalk and kissed me until I couldn't think straight. You wanted that picture out there."

"Yes, but the opportunity presented itself, I didn't seek it out. Your mother's right—there is a difference."

Her lower lip curved downward, and I revised my strategy. I wanted her involved and actively participating. That meant encouragement and acknowledgment, not roadblocks. "But you're also right, angel. If there's an audience for Corinne's book, there's a market void that needs to be filled and we should address that."

The smile she beamed at me was its own reward.

"I was thinking we could ask Cary to take some candid

photos of us this weekend," she said. "Some moments that are more personal and casual than red carpet photo ops. We can sell the ones we like best to the media and donate the proceeds to Crossroads."

The charitable foundation I'd established had plenty of funding, but I understood that raising money was a side benefit to Eva's plan to mitigate the impact of Corinne's tell-all book. Because I regretted the pain the situation was bound to cause my wife, I was prepared to support her in whatever way she needed, but that didn't mean I wouldn't fight for a weekend alone with her.

"We can make it a day trip," I suggested, beginning the negotiation at the extreme, which gave me room to whittle down. "We can spend Friday night through Sunday morning in North Carolina, then spend Sunday in Westport."

"Go from North Carolina to Connecticut to Manhattan in a day? Are you nuts?"

"Friday night through Saturday night, then."

"We can't be alone like that, Gideon," she said softly, setting her hand over mine. "We need to follow Dr. Petersen's advice for a while. I think we need to spend some time dating, going out in public, figuring out how to take care of . . . issues without using sex as a crutch."

I stared at her. "You're not saying we can't have sex."

"Just until we're married. It won't be—"

"Eva, we're already married. You can't ask me to keep my hands off you."

"I am asking."

"No."

Her mouth twitched. "You can't say no."

"*You* can't say no," I countered, my heart beginning to pound. My palms grew damp, a low-grade panic beginning to set in. It was irrational, infuriating. "You want me as much as I want you."

She touched my face. "I sometimes think I want you more, and I'm okay with that. But Dr. Petersen's right. We moved so fast and we've been hitting all the speed bumps at a hundred miles per hour. I feel like we have this little window of time when we can slow down. Just for a few weeks, until the wedding."

"A few *weeks*? Christ, Eva." I pulled away, running my hand through my hair. Turning my head, I looked out the window. My mind was racing. What did this mean? Why would she ask?

How the fuck was I going to talk her out of it?

I felt her slide closer, then curl up against me.

Her voice lowered to a whisper. "Weren't you the one who brought up the benefits of delayed gratification?"

I shot her a look. "And how well did that turn out?"

That night was one of the bigger mistakes I'd made in our relationship. The evening started out so strong, and then Corinne's unexpected appearance threw everything off, spurring one of the worst arguments Eva and I ever had—an argument made more volatile by the seething sexual tension I'd deliberately stoked and held off on satisfying.

"We were different people then." Eva drew back, her gray eyes clear as they held mine. "You're not the same man who ignored me at that dinner."

"I didn't ignore you."

"And I'm not the same woman," she pushed on. "Yes,

seeing Corinne today made me a little twitchy, but I *know* she's not a threat. I know you're committed. . . . *We're* committed. That's why we can do this."

The spread of my legs widened as I stretched out. "I don't want to."

"I don't either. But I think it's a good idea." Her mouth softened with a smile. "It's old-fashioned and romantic to wait 'til the wedding night. Think how hot the sex will be when we do it."

"Eva, we don't need our sex life to be any hotter."

"We need it to be something we do for fun, not because we're counting on it to hold us together."

"It's both, and there's nothing wrong with that." She might as well have asked me not to eat, which I would've been more inclined to agree to, given the choice.

"Gideon . . . we have something amazing together. It's worth the effort to make us rock solid in every way."

I shook my head. It pissed me off that I was feeling anxious. It was a loss of control and I couldn't have that with her. It wasn't what she needed.

Leaning forward, I put my lips to her ear. "Angel, if you're not missing the feel of my cock inside you, I need to step it up, not hold back."

Her shiver made me smile inwardly. Still, she whispered, "Please try. For me."

"Fuck." I dropped back into my seat. As much as I wanted to say no to her, I couldn't. Not even about this. "Damn it."

"Don't be mad. I wouldn't ask if I didn't think it was important to try. And it's such a short time."

"Eva, five minutes would be a short amount of time. You're talking weeks."

"Baby . . ." She laughed softly. "You're pouting. It's so adorable." Leaning forward, she pressed her lips to my cheek. "And really flattering. Thank you."

My gaze narrowed. "I'm not agreeing to make this easy for you."

She trailed her fingers down my tie. "Of course not. We'll try to make it fun. A challenge. See who breaks first."

"Me," I muttered. "I've got no fucking incentive to win this."

"How about me? Wrapped up in a bow—and nothing else—as your birthday present?"

I scowled. Nothing was capable of making this more palatable. Even the thought of her bursting out of a cake naked couldn't make this better. "What does my birthday have to do with anything?"

Eva dazzled me with her smile, which only made me want her more. She was sunlight and warmth at any time, but when she was beneath me, writhing in pleasure and moaning for harder . . . deeper . . .

"That's when we're getting married."

It took a second for that to sink into my lust-addled brain. "I didn't know that."

"I didn't either, until today. On my last break, I went online, trying to see if there was anything happening in September or October that I should consider when setting a date. Since we're getting married on the beach, we don't want it to be too cold, so we've got to get it done this month or next."

"Thank God for winter," I grumbled.

"Fiend. Anyway . . . I got a Google alert about you—"

"You're still doing that?"

"—and there was a post about us on this fan site. There was—"

"Fan site?"

"Yep. There are whole sites and blogs dedicated to you. What you're wearing, who you're dating, events you're attending."

"Jesus."

"The one I went to had all your stats: height, weight, eye color, birth date . . . everything. To be honest, it freaked me out a little that some total stranger knew other details about you that I don't, which is another reason why I think we need to date each other and talk more—"

"I can recite stats while we're fucking. Problem solved."

Her grin was delighted. "You slay me. Anyway, having the wedding on your birthday is a good idea, don't you think? You'll never forget our anniversary."

"Our wedding anniversary is August eleventh," I reminded her dryly.

"We'll have two to celebrate." She ran her hand through my hair, tripping my pulse. "Or better yet, we'll celebrate straight through from one to the other."

August 11 through September 22—a full month and a half. The thought of that was almost enough to make the next few weeks bearable.

❧

"Eva. Gideon." Dr. Lyle Petersen stood and smiled as we walked into his office. He was a tall man, and his gaze lowered a noticeable distance to take in our linked hands. "You're both looking well."

"I feel good," Eva said, sounding strong and sure.

I didn't say anything, extending my hand to shake his.

The good doctor knew things about me I'd hoped never to share with anyone. Because of that, I wasn't entirely comfortable with him, despite the soothing blend of neutral colors and comfortable furniture that made up his office. Dr. Petersen himself was a comfortable man, easy in his own skin. His neatly groomed gray hair did much to soften his appearance but couldn't distract from how incisive and perceptive he was.

It was hard to rely on someone who knew so much my vulnerabilities, but I dealt with it as best I could because I had no other choice—Dr. Petersen was a pivotal player in my marriage.

Eva and I took seats on the sofa, while Dr. Petersen settled into his usual wingback chair. He left his tablet and stylus sitting on the arm and studied us with dark blue eyes that were sharp with intelligence.

"Gideon," he began, "tell me what's happened since I saw you on Tuesday."

I settled back and got to the point. "Eva's decided to follow your recommendation to abstain from sex until we marry publicly."

Eva's low, husky laugh broke out. She leaned into me, hugging my arm. "Did you catch the note of accusation?" she asked the doctor. "It's all your fault he's not going to get any for a couple weeks."

"It's more than two weeks," I argued.

"But less than three," she shot back. She smiled at Dr. Petersen. "I should've known he'd bring that up first."

"What would you start with, Eva?" he asked.

"Gideon told me the details about his nightmare last night." She glanced at me. "That was huge. It's a really big turning point for us."

There was no mistaking the love in her eyes when she spoke, or the gratitude and hope. It tightened my throat to see it. Talking to her about the fucked-up shit in my head was the hardest thing I'd ever had to do—even telling Dr. Petersen about Hugh had been easier—but it was all worth it just to see that look on her face.

The ugliest things about each other brought us closer. It was crazy and it was wonderful. I pulled her hand into my lap, cupping it with both of mine. I felt the same love, gratitude, and hope that she did.

Dr. Petersen picked up his tablet. "Quite a few revelations for you this week, Gideon. What brought them on?"

"You know."

"Eva stopped seeing you."

"And speaking to me."

He looked at Eva. "Was that because Gideon hired your boss away from the agency you work for?"

"That was the catalyst," she agreed, "but we'd been building up to a breaking point. Something had to give. We couldn't keep going in circles, having the same arguments."

"So you withdrew. That could be considered emotional blackmail. Was that your intent?"

Her lips pursed as she weighed that. "I'd call it desperation."

"Why?"

"Because Gideon was . . . drawing lines to define our relationship. And I couldn't imagine living within those lines for the rest of my life."

Dr. Petersen made some notes. "Gideon, what do you think about how Eva handled this situation?"

It took me a minute to answer. "It felt like a goddamned time warp, but a hundred times worse."

He glanced at me. "I remember when you first came to see me, you and Eva hadn't spoken for a couple of days."

"He cut me off," she said.

"She walked out," I countered.

Again, it had been a night when we'd really opened up to each other. She told me about Nathan's assaults, let me see the source of what had unconsciously drawn us together. Then I'd had a nightmare about my own abuse and she pushed me to talk about it.

I couldn't and she left me.

Eva bristled. "*He* broke it off with *me* via interoffice memo! Who does that?"

"I didn't break it off," I corrected. "I challenged you to come back. You walk away when things don't—"

"*That's* emotional blackmail." She released my hand and shifted to face me. "You cut me off for the express purpose of making me accept your status quo. I don't like the way things are? Well, then, you'll shut me out until I can't take it anymore."

"Didn't you just do that to me?" My jaw clenched. "And you seem to take it just fine. If I don't change, you don't budge."

And that killed me. She'd proven so many times that she could leave and not look back, while I couldn't breathe without her. That was a fundamental imbalance in our relationship, which gave her the upper hand in everything.

"You sound resentful, Gideon," Dr. Petersen interjected.

"And I don't?" Eva crossed her arms.

I shook my head. "It's not resentment. It's . . . frustration. I can't walk away, but she can."

"That's not fair! And it's not true. The only leverage I've got is to make you miss me. I try talking it out with you, but in the end, you do what you want. You don't tell me things, don't consult me."

"I'm working on that."

"*Now* you are, but I had to pull away to make you do it. Be honest, Gideon, I came along and you realized you had a void in your life that I could fill, and you wanted to put me there and leave the rest of your life as it was."

"What I wanted was for you to let us—be us. Just enjoy each other for a while."

"My right to decide, to say yes or no, is fucking important to me! You've got no business taking that away from me or getting pissed when I don't like it!"

"Jesus." Reality check. It felt like I'd taken a punch to the gut. Considering her history, to have her feel—for even a moment—that I'd taken her choices away was a brutal blow. "Eva . . ."

I knew what she needed, had recognized it from the first. I'd given her a safeword that I respected at all times, in public or private. She said the word and I stopped. I reminded her often, made sure she always knew that the choice to cease or continue rested entirely with her.

But I'd failed to make the connection when it came to her job. It was inexcusable.

I turned toward her. "Angel, I didn't mean to make you feel powerless. I would never. *Ever.* I didn't think of it that way. I'm . . . I'm sorry."

The words weren't enough; they never were. I wanted to be her fresh start, her new beginning. How could I be when I was acting like the assholes in her past?

She looked at me with those eyes that saw everything I'd rather keep hidden. For once, I was grateful that she could.

Her combative posture relaxed. Her gaze softened with love. "Maybe I haven't been explaining myself well."

I sat there, unable to express what was churning through my mind. When we talked about being a team and sharing our burdens, I hadn't related it to her needing the power to agree or disagree. I thought I could shield her from the troubles we faced and make things smoother for her. Eva deserved that.

She poked my shoulder. "Didn't it feel good, even a little bit, to talk to me about your dream last night?"

"I don't know." I exhaled harshly. "I just know you're happy with me because I did. If that's what it takes . . . then that's what I'll do."

She sank back into the sofa cushions, her lips trembling. She looked at Dr. Petersen. "And now I feel guilty."

Silence. I didn't know what to say. Dr. Petersen just waited with that maddening patience.

Eva took a deep, shaky breath. "I was thinking if he'd just try it my way, he'd see how much better it could be between us. But if I'm just pushing him into a corner . . . if I'm just blackmailing him . . ." A tear slid down her face, cutting into me like a blade. "Maybe we have different ideas about what our marriage should be. What if that's not going to change?"

"Eva." I put my arm around her and pulled her closer, grateful when she leaned into me and put her head on my shoulder. Not surrender. More like a momentary truce. Good enough.

"That's an important question," Dr. Petersen said. "So let's explore it. What if the level of disclosure you want from Gideon isn't something he will ever feel comfortable with?"

"I don't know." She swiped at her tears. "I don't know where that leaves us."

All the hope she'd had when we entered the room was gone. Stroking her hair, I tried to come up with something to say that would take things back to the way they'd been when we arrived.

Lost, I told her, "You quit your job for me, even though you didn't want to. I told you about my dream, even though I didn't want to. Isn't that how this works? We both compromise?"

"You left your job, Eva?" Dr. Petersen asked. "Why?"

She curled into my side. "It was starting to cause more trouble than it was worth. Besides, Gideon's right—he gave a little, so it seems only fair to give a little, too."

"I wouldn't say what either of you compromised was 'little.' And both of you chose to open our session with other things first, which suggests neither of you are completely comfortable with the sacrifice." He sat back, setting his tablet in his lap. "Have either of you asked yourselves why you're in such a hurry?"

We both looked at him.

He smiled. "You're both frowning, so I'll take that as a no. As a couple, you have a lot of strengths. You may not be sharing everything, but you're communicating and you're doing so productively. There's some anger and frustration, but you're expressing them and validating each other's feelings."

Eva straightened. "But . . . ?"

"You're also both pushing personal agendas and manipulating each other to make them happen. My concern is that they're issues and changes that would naturally present themselves and be resolved in time, but neither of you wants to wait. You're both driving your relationship forward on an accelerated schedule. It's only been three months since you two met for the first time. At this point, most couples are deciding to date exclusively, but you two have been married for nearly a month."

I felt my shoulders going back. "What's the point in delaying the inevitable?"

"If it's inevitable," he responded, his eyes kind, "why rush it? But that's not my point. You're both jeopardizing your marriage by forcing each other to act before you're ready. You each have ways of coping with adverse situations. Gideon, you disassociate, as you've done with your family. Eva, you blame yourself for why the relationship isn't working and start subverting your own needs, as you've demonstrated with your previous self-destructive romantic relationships. If you continue to maneuver each other into situations where you feel threatened, you will eventually trigger one of these self-defense mechanisms."

As my pulse began to race, I felt Eva stiffen. She'd said as much to me before, but I knew hearing it from a shrink would validate that worry for her. I pulled her closer, breathing her in to calm myself. The hatred I felt for Hugh and Nathan in that moment was vicious. They were both dead and buried, but they were still fucking up our lives.

"We're not going to let them win," Eva whispered.

I pressed a kiss to the top of her head, fiercely grateful for her. Her thoughts were like mine and that filled me with a sense of wonder.

Her head tilted back, her fingertips drifting along my jaw, her gray eyes soft and tender. "I can't hold out against you, you know. It hurts too much to stay away. Just because you cross the battle lines first doesn't mean I'm less invested. It just means I'm more stubborn."

"I don't want to fight with you."

"So let's not," she said simply. "We started something new today—you talking, me quitting. Let's stick with it for a while and see where it takes us."

"I can do that."

<hr />

I'd originally planned to take Eva someplace quiet and tucked away for dinner, but I changed the venue to the Crosby Street Hotel instead. The restaurant was popular and the hotel was known to often have paparazzi nearby. I wasn't prepared to go to any extremes, but as we'd discussed with Dr. Petersen, I was open to meeting her halfway. We would find our middle ground.

"How pretty," she said, as we followed the hostess to our seats, her gaze taking in the pale blue walls and subdued pendant lighting.

When we reached our table, I scanned the space as I pulled the chair out for her. She was attracting attention, as she always did. Eva was a stunner by any measure, but her sex appeal was something you had to witness firsthand. It was there in the way she moved, the way she carried herself, in the curve of her smile.

And she was mine. The glance I spared the other diners made that patently clear.

I took the seat opposite her, admiring the way the light of the candle on the table gilded her golden skin and hair. The gloss on her lips invited long, deep kisses, as did the look in her eyes. No one had ever looked at me the way she did, with total acceptance and understanding blended in with the love and desire.

I could tell her anything and she would believe me. Such a simple gift, but so rare and precious. Only my silence could push her away, never the truth.

"Angel." I took her hand. "I'm going to ask you again, and then I'll let it go. Are you sure you want to quit your job? You won't hold it against me twenty years from now? There's nothing we can't fix or undo, if you just say the word."

"Twenty years from now, you might be working for me, ace." Her husky laugh floated through the air and stirred my hunger for her. "Don't worry, okay? It was actually kind of a relief. I've got a lot on my plate: packing, moving, planning. When that's all behind us, I'll figure out what's next."

I knew her well. If she'd had doubts, I would have sensed them. What I picked up on instead was something different. Something new.

There was a fire inside her.

I couldn't take my eyes off her, even as I ordered wine.

After the server walked away, I lounged back, enjoying the simple pleasure of staring at my gorgeous wife.

Eva wet her lips with a teasing swipe of her tongue and leaned forward. "You are so insanely hot."

My mouth quirked. "Am I now?"

Her calf rubbed mine. "You are—by far—the hottest

man in the room, which makes this really fun. I like show-ing you off."

I gave an exaggerated sigh. "You still just want me for my body."

"Totally. Who cares about your billions? You've got better assets."

I trapped her wandering leg between my ankles. "Like my wife. She's the most valuable thing I own."

Her brows rose with amusement. "Own, huh?"

She smiled at the server when he returned with our bottle. As he poured, Eva's foot drifted up to tease me, her eyes heavy-lidded and hot. I pushed the glass toward her, watched her swirl the dark red wine, lift the glass to her nose, then take a swallow. The hum of pleasure she made as she approved my choice sent a surge of heat through me, which was certainly her intent. The slow stroking along my leg was maddening. I grew harder by the minute, already more than primed by days of deprivation.

I hadn't known sex could quench a deeper thirst, until Eva.

Taking a sip out of my freshly poured glass, I waited until the server walked away. "Have you changed your mind about waiting?"

"No. Just keeping things interesting."

"Two can play," I warned.

She grinned. "That's what I'm counting on."

3

"WHERE WILL YOU GO from here?" I asked Gideon as he escorted me into the lobby of my apartment building. The Upper West Side was my home—for now. Gideon's penthouse was on the Upper East. The vast green expanse of Central Park divided us, one of the few things between us that was easily crossed.

I waved at Chad, one of the night staff at the front desk. He smiled back at me and gave a polite nod to Gideon.

"I'm going up with you," Gideon replied, his hand pressed lightly against the small of my back.

I was hyperaware of that touch. It conveyed possession and control effortlessly, and made me so hot. Which only made it harder for me to deny us both when we reached the elevator. "We need to say good-bye right here, ace."

"Eva—"

"I don't have the willpower," I confessed, feeling the pull of his need. He'd always been able to lure me in just by the force of his will. It was one of the things I loved about him, one of the ways I knew we were meant to be. The connection we had, it was soul-deep. "You and me with a bed nearby is a bad idea."

He stared down at me with a wry curve to his lips that was sexy as hell. "That's what I'm counting on."

"Count down instead—to our wedding. That's what I'm doing. Minute by minute." And it was excruciating. My physical connection to Gideon was as vital to me as our emotional one. I loved him. Loved touching him, soothing him, giving him what he needed . . . My right to do so meant everything to me.

I gripped his forearm, gently squeezing the rock-hard muscle beneath his sleeves. "I'm missing you, too."

"You don't have to miss me."

Pulling him aside, I lowered my voice. "You say when, you say how," I murmured, repeating the basic tenet of our sex life. "And part of me really wants you to say *when* right now. But there's something I want more than that. I'll call you later tonight, after I talk to Cary a bit, and tell you what that is."

The smile faded. His gaze turned avid. "You can just come next door and tell me now."

I shook my head. When Nathan had been a threat, Gideon had taken up residence in the apartment directly beside mine, watching over me and ensuring I was safe, even though I didn't know it. He could do that sort of thing because he owned the building, one of many that belonged to him in the city.

"You need to go to the penthouse, Gideon. Just relax and enjoy that beautiful place we'll be sharing soon."

"It's not the same without you there. It feels empty."

That hit me hard. Before I'd come along, Gideon had structured his life so he could be alone in every way—work interspersed with occasional hookups and avoidance of his family. I'd changed that, and I didn't want him to regret it.

"Now's your chance to get rid of all the things you don't want me to find when I move in," I teased, still trying to keep things light.

"You know all my secrets."

"Tomorrow, we'll be together in Westport."

"Tomorrow's too far away."

Pushing up onto my tiptoes, I kissed his jaw. "You'll sleep through some of it and work through the rest." Then I whispered, "We could sext. You can see how creative I can be."

"I prefer the original over reproductions."

I dropped my voice to a purr. "Video, then. With sound."

He turned his head and caught my lips, taking my mouth in a long, deep kiss. "This is love," he murmured. "Agreeing to this."

"I know." I smiled and pulled back to hit the button for the elevator. "You could send me naughty pics, too, you know."

His eyes narrowed. "You want pictures of me, angel, you'll have to take them yourself."

Backing into the elevator, I wagged a finger at him. "Spoilsport."

The doors started to close. I had to grip the handrail to stop myself from dashing back out to him. Happiness came in so many forms. Mine was Gideon.

"Miss me," he ordered.

I blew him a kiss. "Always."

❧

When I opened the door to my apartment, I was hit with two things at once: the smell of recent cooking and the sounds of Sam Smith.

It felt like home. But I was abruptly struck with sadness that it wouldn't be home for much longer. Not that I doubted the future I'd accepted when I married Gideon, because I didn't. I was so excited about the thought of living with him, being his wife in private and public, sharing my days—and nights—with him. Still, change was harder when you were happy with the pre-change version of your life.

"Honey, I'm home!" I called out, dropping my bag on one of the teakwood bar stools at the breakfast bar. My mom had decorated the entire apartment in a modern traditional style. I probably wouldn't have gone with some of her choices, but I liked the result.

"I'm right here, sweet cheeks," Cary drawled, drawing my attention across the open floor plan to where he lay sprawled on our living room sofa in board shorts and no T-shirt. He was lean and tanned, his abs as beautifully defined as Gideon's. Even off duty, he looked like the super hot male model he was. "How was dinner?"

"Good." I headed over to him, kicking off my heels on the way. I figured I should enjoy doing that while I could. I couldn't picture myself leaving shoes strewn around Gideon's penthouse. I thought it might drive him a little crazy. And since I was sure there were other things I'd drive him crazy with, it was probably best to pick my vices carefully. "How was yours? Smells like you cooked."

"Pizza. Semi-homemade. It's what Tat was craving."

"Who doesn't crave pizza?" I said, plopping gracelessly onto the couch. "Is she still here?"

"Nah." He glanced away from the TV to look at me, his green eyes serious. "She left all pissed off. I told her we wouldn't be moving in together."

"Oh." To be honest, I didn't like Tatiana Cherlin. Like Cary, she was a successful model, although she hadn't yet attained his level of recognition.

Cary had met her on a job. Their purely sexual relationship had shifted drastically when she'd found out she was pregnant. Unfortunately, she'd discovered she was expecting around the same time Cary found a great guy he wanted to work on a relationship with.

"Big decision," I said.

"And I'm not sure it's the right one." He ran a hand over his gorgeous face. "If Trey weren't in the picture, I'd be doing the right thing by Tat."

"Who says you aren't? Being a good parent doesn't mean you have to live together. Look at my mom and dad."

"Fuck." He groaned. "I feel like I'm choosing myself over my child, Eva. What does that make me, if not a selfish bastard?"

"It's not like you're cutting her off. I know you'll be there for her and the baby, just not in that way." Reaching over, I twirled a lock of his chocolate brown hair around my finger. My best friend had suffered through so much in his life. The twisted way he'd been introduced to sex and love had left him with a lot of baggage and bad habits. "So Trey's going to stick?"

"He hasn't decided."

"Did he call you?"

Cary shook his head. "No. I broke down and called him before he forgot about me altogether."

I gave him a little push. "As if that could ever happen. You, Cary Taylor, are utterly unforgettable."

"Ha." He stretched out with a sigh. "He didn't sound too happy to hear from me. Said he's still working some stuff out in his head."

"Which means he's thinking about you."

"Yeah, thinking he dodged a bullet," Cary muttered. "He said it was never going to work for us if I was living with Tat, but when I told him I'd fix that, he said that would just make him feel like an asshole for getting in the way. It's a no-win, but I laid it all out for Tat anyway, because I have to try."

"It's a tough spot to be in." I couldn't imagine it myself. "Just try to make the best decisions you can. You have a right to be happy. That's the best thing for everyone around you, including the baby."

"If there is a baby." His eyes closed. "Tat says she's not doing this alone. If I'm not going to be there, she doesn't want to go through with it."

"Isn't it getting a little late for her to say that?" I couldn't keep the anger out of my voice. Tatiana was a manipulator. It was impossible not to look ahead and see that being a source of misery for an innocent kid.

"I can't even think about it, Eva. I lose my shit. It's all so fucked up." He huffed out a humorless laugh. "And to think

I once said she was easy to deal with. She's never cared that I'm bisexual, and she didn't care if I slept around. . . . Part of me feels good that she cares enough now to want to be exclusive, but I can't help how I feel about Trey."

He turned his troubled gaze away. It tore me up to see him so down.

"Maybe I should talk to her," I offered.

He tilted his head back to look at me. "How is that supposed to help? You two don't get along."

"I'm not a fan," I admitted. "But I can work around that. A woman-to-woman talk—if it's done right—could help. It really couldn't make things worse, right?" I hesitated before saying more. I meant well, but my good intentions did sound naïve.

He snorted. "There's always worse."

"Way to look on the bright side," I chastised. "Does Trey know that you talked to Tatiana and she's not moving in?"

"I texted him. Got nada back. But I really didn't expect to."

"Give him a little more time."

"Eva, at the end of the day, he wishes I were totally gay. In his mind, being bisexual means I have to sleep around. He doesn't get that just because I'm attracted to men and women doesn't mean I can't be faithful to one person. Or maybe he just doesn't want to get it."

I blew out my breath. "I don't think I helped with that. He brought it up to me once and I didn't explain things well."

That had been eating at me for a while. I needed to reach out to Trey and set that straight. Cary had been in the hospital recovering from a vicious assault when Trey approached me. My mind hadn't been at its sharpest at the time.

"You can't fix everything for me, baby girl." He rolled

over onto his stomach and looked at me. "But I love you so much for trying."

"You're part of me." I struggled to find the right words. "I need you to be okay, Cary."

"I'm working on it." He scooped his hair back from his face. "I'm taking this weekend in Westport to deal with the possibility that Trey might be out of the mix. I have to be realistic about that."

"You be realistic, I'll be hopeful."

"Have fun with that." He sat up and put his elbows on his knees, his head hanging. "Which brings me back to Tatiana. I guess I am clear about that. We can't be together. Baby or not, it wouldn't work for her or me."

"I respect that."

It was hard not to say more. I would always give my best friend the support and reassurance he needed, but there were some hard lessons to be learned here. Trey, Tatiana, and Cary were all hurting—with a baby on the way to join them—because of Cary's choices. He pushed those who loved him away with his actions, daring them to stay. It was a test rigged for failure. Facing the consequences might just get him to make a change for the better.

His grin was wry, one beautiful green eye peeking through the fall of his long bangs. "I can't pick and choose based on what I'm going to get out of it. Sucks, but hey . . . I gotta grow up sometime."

"Don't we all?" I gave him an encouraging smile. "I quit my job today."

Accepting what I'd done got easier every time I said it aloud.

"No shit?"

Looking up at the ceiling, I replied, "No shit."

He whistled. "Should I break out the bourbon and some shot glasses?"

I shuddered. "Ugh. You know I can't stand bourbon. And really, Cristal and flutes would be more appropriate for my resignation."

"Seriously? You want to celebrate?"

"I don't need to drown any sorrows, that's for sure." I stretched my arms out over my head and let the last of my tension go. "I've been thinking about it all day, though."

"And?"

"I'm good. Maybe if Mark had taken the news differently, I'd have second thoughts, but he's leaving, too, and he's been there way longer than the three months I've been there. It wouldn't make sense for me to be more upset about moving on than he is."

"Baby girl, things don't have to make sense to be true." Grabbing the remote, he turned the speaker volume down.

"You're right, but I found Gideon at the same time I started at Waters Field and Leaman. Practically speaking, there's no comparison between a job you've had three months and a husband you're going to spend the rest of your life with."

He shot me a look. "You went from sensible to practical. This just keeps getting worse."

"Oh, shut up." Cary never let me get away with the easy explanation. Since I was often good at deluding myself, his no-bullshit policy was a mirror I needed.

My smile faded. "I want more."

"More what?"

"More of everything." I looked his way again. "Gideon's

got this presence, you know? When he walks into a room, everyone straightens up and pays attention. I want that."

"You married that. You get it de facto with the name and the bank balance."

I sat up. "I want it because I've earned it, Cary. Geoffrey Cross left behind a lot of people who want some payback from his son. And Gideon's made his own enemies, like the Lucases."

"The who?"

I wrinkled my nose. "The bat-shit Anne Lucas and her equally insane husband." Then it hit me. "Oh my God, Cary! I didn't tell you. About the redhead you messed around with at that dinner a few weeks back. *That* was Anne Lucas."

"What the hell are you talking about?"

"Remember when I asked you to run a search on Dr. Terrence Lucas? Anne is his wife."

Cary's confusion was obvious.

I couldn't go into how Terry Lucas had examined Gideon as a child and lied about finding signs of sexual trauma. He'd done so in order to shield his brother-in-law, Hugh, from prosecution. I would never understand how he could do that, no matter how much he loved his wife. As for Anne, Gideon had slept with her to get back at her husband, but her physical resemblance to her brother had led to sexual depravity that haunted Gideon. He'd punished Anne for the sins of her brother, leaving both himself and her mentally warped in the process.

That left Gideon and me with two very vicious enemies to contend with.

I explained as much as I could. "The Lucases have this whole twisted history thing with Gideon that I can't get into, but it's no coincidence that you two ended up together that night. She planned it that way."

"Why?"

"Because she's nuts and she knows it'll fuck with my head."

"Why the hell would you care who I tangle with?"

"Cary . . . I always care." I heard my mobile phone start ringing. The "Hanging by a Moment" ring tone told me it was my husband calling. I stood. "But in this case, it's the calculation behind it. You weren't just some random hot fling. She targeted you specifically because you're my best friend."

"I'm not seeing how that accomplishes anything."

"It's flipping the bird at Gideon. Getting his attention is what she wants more than anything."

Cary arched a brow. "The whole thing sounds loopy, but whatever. I ran into her again not too long ago."

"What? When?"

"Last week, maybe." He shrugged. "I'd just wrapped up a shoot and my Uber was waiting outside the studio. She was stepping out of a café with a girlfriend at the same time. It was totally out of the blue."

I shook my head. My phone stopped ringing. "No way. Did she say anything to you?"

"Sure. She kinda flirted a little, which isn't surprising considering the last time we saw each other. I shut her down, told her I was working on a relationship. She was cool about it. Wished me luck, said thanks again for a fun time. She took off down the street. End of story."

My phone started ringing again. "If you ever see her, walk the other way and call me. Okay?"

"O-kay, but you're not telling me enough for this to make any sense."

"Let me talk with Gideon." I hurried toward my phone and answered it. "Hey."

"Were you in the shower?" Gideon purred. "Are you naked and wet, angel?"

"Oh, God. Hang on a minute." I dropped the phone to my shoulder and walked back to Cary. "Was she wearing a wig when you saw her?"

Cary's brows shot up. "How the hell would I know?"

"Was it long like when you first met her?"

"Yeah. Same."

I nodded grimly. Anne wore her hair cropped and I'd never seen a picture of her otherwise. She'd worn a wig when she pursued Cary at the dinner, which had thrown me off and hidden her from Gideon.

Maybe it was a new style for her.

Or maybe it was another indication that she had special plans when it came to Cary.

I put the phone to my ear. "I need you to come back over, Gideon. And bring Angus up with you."

~∾~

Something in my tone must have relayed my concern, because Gideon showed up with both Angus and Raúl. I opened the door and found the three men filling the hallway, my husband front and center, with both bodyguards flanking him. To call the sight of them intense would be an understatement.

Gideon had loosened his tie and unbuttoned his collar

and vest but was otherwise dressed as he'd been when we parted earlier. The slight dishevelment was sexy as hell, sending an instant tingle of arousal through my blood. It was a temptation, an enticement for me to finish taking off those expensive, elegant layers and reveal the powerful, primal male underneath. As smoking hot as Gideon was with clothes on, there was nothing like the sight of him purely nude.

My gaze locked with Gideon's and gave me away. One darkly winged brow arched upward, and the corner of his mouth lifted in amusement.

"Hello to you, too," he teased, in reply to my heated look.

The two men behind him stood in contrast with their bespoke but starkly basic black suits, white shirts, and unembellished black ties all perfectly arranged.

I'd never really noticed before how superfluous Angus and Raúl appeared when standing beside Gideon, a man who could clearly manage a hand-to-hand confrontation without any help.

Raúl stood stone-faced, as per his usual. Angus, too, was stoic, but the mischievous glance he sent my way told me he'd caught me eye-fucking his boss.

I felt my face get hot.

Stepping back and out of the way, I let them in. Angus and Raúl headed into the living room where Cary waited. Gideon hung back with me as I shut the door.

"You're giving me that look, angel, but you wanted Angus with me. Explain."

That made me laugh, which was just what I needed to break the tension. "How can I help it when it looks like you were stripping when I called you?"

"I can finish here."

"You realize I may have to burn all your clothes after the wedding. You should always be naked."

"Would make for interesting meetings at work."

"Umm . . . maybe not, then. For my eyes only and all that." I leaned into the door and took a deep breath. "Anne's made contact with Cary since the dinner."

All the warmth and lightness left Gideon's eyes, replaced by a chill that warned of bad things ahead.

He started toward the living room. I raced to catch up, linking our hands to remind him that we were in this together. I knew it was a concept that was going to take some getting used to. Gideon had been standing alone for so long, fighting his own battles and those of the people he loved.

Taking a seat on the coffee table, he faced Cary and said, "Tell me what you told Eva."

Gideon looked ready to tackle Wall Street while Cary looked ready to tackle a nap, but that didn't seem to impact my husband at all.

Cary ran through it all again, his gaze darting occasionally toward Angus and Raúl, who stood nearby. "That's it," he finished. "No offense, guys, but you seem like a lot of muscle for a redhead who's maybe a hundred twenty pounds soaking wet."

I would've pegged Anne at a hundred thirty, but that was neither here nor there. "Better safe than sorry," I said.

He shot me a look. "What can she do? Seriously. What's everyone all anxious about?"

Gideon shifted restlessly. "We had an . . . affair. That's not the right word. It wasn't pretty."

"You fucked her," Cary said bluntly. "I figured that much."

"Fucked her over," I elaborated, stepping closer so I could rest my hand on Gideon's shoulder. I supported my husband, even though I couldn't condone what he'd done. And truthfully, the part of me that was obsessed with Gideon pitied Anne. There had been times when I believed I'd lost Gideon forever, and I had gone a little crazy myself.

Still, she was dangerous in a way I could never be, and that danger was directed at people I loved. "She's not taking it well that he's with me."

"What? Are we talking *Fatal Attraction*–type stuff?"

"Well, she's a psychologist, so *Fatal Attraction* meets *Basic Instinct* would be more accurate. It's a Michael Douglas marathon wrapped up in one woman."

"Don't joke, Eva," Gideon said tightly.

"Who's joking?" I shot back. "Cary saw her in that long wig she wore to the dinner. I'm thinking she wanted him to recognize her so they could chat."

Cary snorted. "So she's crazy town. What do you want me to do? Let you know if I run into her again?"

"I want a protection detail on you," I said.

Gideon nodded. "Agreed."

"Wow." Cary rubbed at the five o'clock shadow on his jaw. "You guys are hard-core about this."

"You've got enough going on," I reminded him. "If she's got an agenda, you don't need to deal with it."

His lips twisted wryly. "Can't argue with that."

"We'll take care of it," Angus said. Raúl nodded, and then both men headed downstairs.

Gideon stayed behind.

Cary looked back and forth between us, then stood. "I don't think you two need me anymore, so I'm hitting it. I'll catch you in the morning," he said to me, before sauntering down the hall to his bedroom.

"Are you worried?" I asked Gideon when we were alone.

"You are. That's enough."

I took the spot on the sofa directly across from him. "It's not so much worry. More like curiosity. What does she think she can accomplish through Cary?"

Gideon exhaled wearily. "She's playing head games, Eva. That's all."

"I don't think so. She was very specific in her comments to me at the dinner, warning me away from you. Like I don't know you and wouldn't want you if I did."

His jaw tightened and I knew I'd struck a chord. He'd never really gotten into what they had talked about when he went to her office. It was possible she'd said something similar to him then.

"I'm going to talk to Anne," I announced.

Gideon pierced me with his icy blue gaze. "The hell you are."

I laughed softly. My poor husband. So accustomed to having his word be law and then choosing to marry a woman like me. "I know we've covered a lot of ground over the course of our relationship, but somewhere in there we did discuss working as a team."

"And I'm open to doing that," he said smoothly, "but Anne is not the place to start. You can't reason with someone who's completely irrational."

"I don't want to reason with her, ace. She's targeting my friends, and she thinks I'm a weak spot for you. She needs to know I'm not helpless, and that by taking you on, she's taking on both of us."

"She's my problem. I'll deal with her."

"If you've got a problem, Gideon, it's my problem, too. Listen. Operation Gideva is in full effect now. My inaction is only making this situation with Anne worse." I leaned forward. "In her mind, either I know what's happening and I'm too weak to do something or you're hiding everything from me, which suggests that I'm too weak to handle it. Either way, you're making me a target and that's not what you want."

"You don't know what's in her mind," he said tightly.

"Things are a little twisted up there, sure. But she's a woman. Trust me, she needs to know I have claws and am prepared to use them."

His gaze narrowed. "What would you say?"

A little flare of triumph had me holding back a smile. "Honestly, I think it's enough if I just pop up somewhere unexpected. An ambush, so to speak. That'll shake her a little, to find me lying in wait. Will she go on the defensive or take the offense? We'll get insight from her reaction, and we need it."

Gideon shook his head. "I don't like it."

"I didn't think you would." I stretched out my legs between his. "But you know I'm right. It's not my strategy that's bugging you, Gideon. More like your past won't go away and you don't want it in my face."

"It *will* go away, Eva. Let me handle it."

"You need to be more analytical about this. I'm a member of your team, like Angus and Raúl, but obviously I'm not an employee and I'm sure as hell not a dependent—I'm your better half. It's not just Gideon Cross anymore. It's not even

Gideon Cross and wife. We are Gideon and Eva Cross, and you need to let me live up to that."

He leaned forward, his gaze hot and intense. "You don't have anything to prove to anyone."

"Really? Because I feel like I have to prove something to you. If you don't believe I'm strong enough . . ."

"Eva." Gideon's hands cupped the back of my knees and pulled me closer. "You're the strongest woman I know."

He said the words, but I could see he didn't truly mean them. Not in the way we needed him to. He saw me as a survivor, not a warrior.

"Then stop worrying," I countered, "and let me do what I have to do."

"I don't agree that you have to do anything."

"Then you'll have to agree to disagree." I leaned into him, draping my arms across his broad shoulders and pressing my lips to the corner of his stern mouth.

"Angel—"

"To be clear, I wasn't asking permission, Gideon. I'm telling you what I'm doing. You can either participate or stand back—your choice."

He made a noise of frustration. "Where's the compromise you're always pushing me for?"

Pulling back, I shot him a look. "The compromise is letting me try it my way this time. If it doesn't work, we try it your way next time."

"Thanks."

"Don't be like that. We'll sit down together to work out the logistics of when and where. We'll need Raúl to get a handle on her routine. By definition, an ambush is unexpected, but it should happen somewhere she feels safe and comfortable, too. Give her a nice jolt." I shrugged. "She's laid down the ground rules. We're just taking her cue."

Gideon took a long, deep breath. I could practically *see* him thinking, his agile mind trying to find a way to get the result he wanted.

So I distracted him from that. "Remember this morning, when I said I'd explain why I decided to tell my parents about our marriage?"

His focus instantly shifted, his gaze watchful and alert. "Of course."

"I know it took a lot of courage for you to tell Dr. Petersen about Hugh. Especially considering how you feel about psychologists." And who could blame him for that distrust? Hugh had come into Gideon's life under the guise of therapeutic help and had become an abuser instead. "You inspired me to be equally brave."

His gorgeous face softened with tenderness. "I heard that song today," he murmured, reminding me of the time I'd sung the Sara Bareilles anthem to him.

I smiled.

"You needed me to tell him," he said quietly. The words were phrased as a statement but were really posed as a question.

"Yeah, I did." More than that, Gideon had needed it. Sexual abuse was private and personal, but in some way, we had to put it out there. It wasn't a dirty, shameful secret to shove into a box. It was an ugly truth, and truths—by nature—needed to be aired.

"And you need to confront Anne."

My brows rose. "I actually wasn't swinging the conversation back to that, but yeah . . . I do."

This time, Gideon nodded. "All right. We'll figure it out."

I indulged in a mental fist pump. Score one for Gideva.

"You also said there was something you wanted more than having sex with me," he reminded me dryly, the look in his eyes calling my bluff.

"Well, I wouldn't put it quite like that." I ran my fingers through his hair. "Banging you is literally my favorite activity. Ever."

He smirked. "But?"

"You're going to think I'm silly."

"I'll still think you're hot."

I kissed him for that. "In high school, most of the girls I knew had boyfriends. You know how it is, raging hormones and epic love stories."

"So I heard," he said wryly.

My words caught in my throat. So stupid of me to forget how it must have been for Gideon. He'd had no one until Corinne in college, too damaged by Hugh's exploitation to have the normal teenage-love-affair angst I was thinking of.

"Angel?"

I cursed silently. "Forget it. It's lame."

"You know that's not going to work."

"Just this once?"

"No."

"Please?"

He shook his head. "Spit it out."

I wrinkled my nose. "Fine. Teenagers talk on the phone at night for hours because they have school and parents and can't be together. They spend all night chatting with their boyfriends about . . . whatever. I never had that. I never . . ." I bit back my embarrassment. "I never had a guy like that."

I didn't have to explain. Gideon knew how I'd been. How sex had once been my twisted way to feel loved. The guys I'd fucked hadn't called me. Not before or after.

"Anyway," I finished, my voice rough, "I had this idea that we could have that for now . . . while we're waiting. Late-night calls where we talk just to hear each other's voice."

He stared at me.

"It sounded better in my head," I muttered.

Gideon was quiet for a long minute. Then he kissed me. Hard.

I was still reeling from that when he pulled away and spoke in a voice that was more than a little hoarse.

"I'm that guy for you, Eva."

My throat tightened up.

"Every milestone, angel. Every rite of passage . . . *Everything*." He swiped at the tear that leaked out of the corner of my eye. "And you're that girl for me."

"God." I gave a watery laugh. "I love you so much."

Gideon smiled. "I'm heading home now, because that's what you want. And you're going to call me and tell me that again, because that's what I want."

"Deal."

I woke before my alarm the next day. Lying in bed for a few minutes, I let my brain wake up as much as it was going to without coffee. I forced myself to focus on the fact that it was the start of my final day at work.

Surprisingly, I felt more than good about that. I felt . . . impatient. It really was time to shake things up.

And now the really big question. What to wear?

I rolled out of bed and hit my closet. After rifling through pretty much everything, I decided on an emerald green sheath dress that had an asymmetrical neckline and hemline. It showed a little more leg than I would normally consider for work, but why end the way I began? Why not take the opportunity to transition from the former to the future?

Today was Eva Tramell's last. On Monday, Eva Cross would have her debut. I could picture her. Short and blond against her husband's tall and dark but as dangerous as him in a very similar way.

Or maybe not. Maybe, play up the differences. Opposite sides of the same, sharp blade . . .

With a final glance at my cheval mirror, I headed into the bathroom to put on my makeup.

A short time later, Cary poked his head in. He whistled. "Lookin' good, babe."

"Thanks." I dropped my lipstick brush back into its stand. "Can I talk you into helping me with a chignon?"

He sauntered in wearing nothing but Grey Isles boxer briefs, looking not so different from the billboards of him presently gracing phone kiosks and buses around the city. "Translation: Do it for you. Of course."

My best friend got to work, expertly brushing and twisting my hair into a sleek, elegant bun.

"That was pretty intense last night," he said, after pulling the last hairpin out of his mouth. "Having a living room full of black suits like that."

My eyes met his in the mirror. "Three suits."

"Two suits and Gideon," he shot back, "who can fill a room by his damn self."

I couldn't argue with that.

He flashed his megawatt smile. "If anyone gets wind that I've got a private security detail, they'll think either I'm bigger shit than they knew or I've got an inflated sense of my own importance. Both of which are true."

Standing, I lifted onto my tiptoes and kissed his chin. "*You* won't even know they're around. They'll be in super stealth mode."

"Betcha I can spot 'em."

"Five bucks," I said, skirting around him to get a pair of heels from the bedroom.

"What? How about five big ones, Mrs. Cross?"

"Ha!" I snatched my phone off the bed when it chimed with an incoming text. "Gideon's on his way up."

"Why didn't he spend the night?"

I answered over my shoulder as I rushed toward the hallway, "We're abstaining until the wedding."

"Are you fucking kidding me?" Cary's long strides easily overtook mine, even with him strolling and me scrambling. He swiped my heels right out of my grasp, freeing me to grab my travel mug of coffee off the breakfast bar. "I figured the honeymoon period lasted longer than that. Don't most husbands get laid at least a few years before they get cut off?"

"Shut up, Cary!" I grabbed my bag and yanked the front door open.

Gideon stood on the other side, his hand lifted with key at the ready. "Angel."

Cary reached around me and pulled the door open wider. "I feel for you, man. Put a ring on it and *bam*, the legs slam shut."

"Cary!" I glared. "I'm going to punch you."

"Who's going to pack your overnight bag if you do that?" He knew me too well.

"Don't worry, baby girl, I'll be ready with your bag and mine." He looked at Gideon. "Can't help you, I'm afraid. Wait 'til you see her in that blue La Perla bikini I'm packing. You'll have the balls to match."

"I'm going to punch you, too," Gideon drawled. "You'll have bruises to match."

Cary gave me a soft push out the door and slammed it shut.

It was nearing noon when Mark leaned over the top of my cubicle and gifted me with his crooked smile. "Ready for our last workday lunch?"

I clasped a hand over my heart. "You're killing me."

"Happy to give your resignation letter back."

Shaking my head, I stood, my gaze sliding over my workstation. I hadn't packed my few personal items yet. When five o'clock rolled around, I expected to feel closure. But for now, I wasn't quite ready to give up my claim to my desk and the dream it had once represented.

"We'll have other lunches." I grabbed my purse out of the drawer and walked with him to the elevators. "I'm not letting you off the hook that easily."

I had a wave ready for Megumi when we hit reception,

but she'd already taken off for lunch and her relief was busy manning the phones.

I was going to miss seeing her, Will, and Mark every weekday. They were my own little piece of New York, a part of my life that belonged to me alone. That was something else I'd feared giving up by leaving my job—my personal social circle.

I would work hard to keep my friends, of course. I'd make time to call and plan things for us to do together, but I knew how it was—already I'd gone months without touching base with my San Diego pals. And my life would no longer resemble those of my friends. Our goals, dreams, and challenges would be worlds apart.

The elevator car that picked up Mark and me held only a few people, but the space filled quickly as it made more stops. I made a mental note to ask Gideon for one of his magic elevator keys that allowed him to glide straight up or down with no interruptions. After all, I'd still be coming to the Crossfire, just heading up to a different floor.

"What about you?" I asked, as we shuffled closer together to make room for more passengers. "Have you decided whether you're staying or going?"

He nodded and shoved his hands in his pants pockets. "I'm taking your cue."

I could tell from the set of his jaw that he was firm in his decision. "That's awesome, Mark. Congratulations."

"Thanks."

We exited on the ground floor and made our way through the security turnstiles.

"Steven and I talked it out," he went on, as we crossed the gold-veined marble of the Crossfire lobby. "Hiring you was a big step up for me. It was a sign that my career was moving in the right direction."

"There's no doubt about that."

He smiled. "Losing you is another sign—it's time to move on."

Mark gestured me through the revolving door first. I felt the heat of the sun before I finished the rotation that ushered me outside. Fall weather couldn't come quick enough. I was looking forward to the change of seasons. It felt appropriate for there to be some outward shift to match the one happening within me.

My gaze slid over Gideon's sleek black limousine parked at the curb, and then I turned to face my boss when he joined me on the sidewalk. "Where are we headed?"

Mark gave me an amused glance before he began scouting for an available taxi amid the surging sea of cars. "It's a surprise."

I rubbed my hands together. "Yay."

"Miss Tramell."

I turned at the sound of my name and found Angus standing beside the limo. Dressed in his usual black suit and traditional chauffeur's hat, he looked dapper and expensive yet blended in so easily that only a trained observer might suspect his MI6 background.

It always tripped me out to think about his history. It was so James Bond. I'm sure I romanticized it way too much, but I was comforted by the knowledge, too. Gideon was in the best of hands.

"Hey, you," I greeted Angus, allowing affection to color my voice.

I couldn't help but feel special gratitude for him. His past with Gideon spanned years and I would never know the whole of it, but I knew he'd been the one support in Gideon's life after Hugh. And Angus had been the only person from our daily lives who'd witnessed our elopement. The look on his face when he talked to Gideon afterward . . . the tears that had shined in both of their eyes . . . There was an unbreakable bond there.

His pale blue eyes sparkled at me as he pulled open the limo door. "Where would you both like to go?"

Mark's brows shot up. "This is what you left me for? Hell. I can't compete."

"You never had to." I paused before I slid into the back and looked at Angus. "Mark doesn't want me to know where we're headed, so I'll just climb in and try not to eavesdrop."

Angus tapped the brim of his hat in acknowledgment.

A few minutes later we were on our way.

Mark sat on the bench seat opposite me, taking in the interior. "Whoa. I've rented limos before, but they never looked like this."

"Gideon has great taste." It didn't matter what the style was—modern and contemporary like his office or classic and old world like his penthouse—my husband knew how to present his wealth with class.

Looking at me, Mark grinned. "You're a lucky lady, my friend."

"I am," I agreed. "All of this"—I waved my hand—"is amazing, of course. But he's the catch all by himself. He's just genuinely a really great guy."

"I know what it's like to have one of those."

"Yes. You sure do. How's the wedding planning coming along?"

Mark groaned. "Steven's killing me. Do I want blue or periwinkle? Roses or lilies? Satin or silk? Morning or evening? I tried to tell him that he can do what he wants, I just want him, but he chewed me out. Said I damned well better care because I didn't have a chance of ever getting married again. All I can say is thank God for that."

I laughed.

"How about you?" he asked.

"I'm starting to get into it. In this crazy world filled with billions of people, we managed to find each other. As Cary would say, we should celebrate that."

We talked about first dances and seating arrangements as Angus maneuvered us through the traffic that seemed to always clog Midtown. Looking past Mark out the window, I watched a cab come to a stop at the light beside us. The passenger in the back pinched a phone between her shoulder and ear, lips moving a mile a minute and hands furiously flipping through a notebook. Behind her, on the corner, a hot dog cart vendor did brisk business with a waiting line of five people.

When we finally arrived and I stepped out onto the sidewalk I knew right where we were. "Hey!"

Tucked below street level, the Mexican restaurant was one we'd been to before. And it just so happened to employ a server I was very fond of.

Mark laughed. "You quit so suddenly Shawna didn't have time to request the day off."

"Aww, man." My chest felt tight. It was starting to feel like an ending I wasn't ready for.

"Come on." He caught me by the elbow and directed me

inside, where I quickly spotted the table that held a party of familiar faces and Mylar balloons that said GREAT JOB and BEST WISHES and CONGRATS.

"Wow." My eyes burned with a sudden wash of tears.

Megumi and Will sat with Steven at a table set for six. Shawna stood behind her brother's chair, their bright red hair impossible to miss.

"Eva!" they shouted in chorus, drawing the attention of everyone in the room.

"Oh my God," I breathed, my heart breaking more than a little. I was suddenly filled with sadness and doubt, faced with what I was giving up, even if only in one way. "You guys are so *not* getting rid of me!"

"Of course not." Shawna came over and gave me a hug, her slim arms strong and fierce around me. "We've got a bachelorette blowout to plan!"

"Woot!" Megumi wrapped me in a hug the second Shawna stepped back.

"Maybe we could skip that tradition," interjected a warm, deep voice behind me.

Turning in surprise, I faced Gideon. He stood beside Mark with a single, perfect red rose in hand.

Mark flashed a big smile. "He touched base earlier to see if we were doing anything and said he wanted to come."

I smiled through my tears. I wasn't losing my friends, and I was gaining so much more. Gideon was always there when I needed him, even before I realized he was the integral piece that was missing.

"I dare you to try their diablo salsa," I challenged, holding my hand out for my rose.

His lips curved faintly with a subtle smile, the one that did me in every time—and every other woman in the room, too, I couldn't help but notice. But the look in his eyes, the understanding and support for what I was feeling . . . That was all mine.

"It's your party, angel mine."

4

THE TWO-STORY HOUSE that sprawled along the coastline glowed with golden warmth spilling from every window. Lights embedded in the curving driveway glittered like a bed of stars in the gloaming, while hydrangea bushes the size of small cars burst with petals around the edges of the wide lawn.

"Isn't it pretty?" Eva asked, her back to me as she knelt on the black leather bench seat and stared out the window.

"Stunning," I replied, although I was referring to her. She was vibrating with excitement and a childlike delight. I took that in, needing to understand it and the cause. Her happiness was vital to me. It was the wellspring of my own contentment, the weight that balanced my equilibrium and kept me steady.

She glanced over her shoulder at me as Angus slowed the limo to a halt by the front steps. "Are you checking out my butt?"

My gaze dropped to her ass, cupped so perfectly by the shorts she'd changed into after work. "Now that you mention it . . ."

She plopped down onto the seat with a huff of laughter. "There's no help for you, you know that?"

"Yes, I knew there was no cure the first time you kissed me."

"I'm pretty sure *you* kissed *me*."

I held back a smile. "Is that the way it went?"

Her gaze narrowed. "You better be joking. That moment should be seared into your brain."

Reaching over, I ran my hand down her bare thigh. "Is it seared into yours?" I murmured, pleased by the thought.

"Hey, now," Cary interrupted, pulling his ear buds out. "Don't forget I'm sitting right here."

Eva's roommate had been unobtrusively watching a movie on his tablet during the nearly two-hour drive through evening traffic, but I could never forget he was there. Cary Taylor was a fixture in my wife's life and I accepted it, even if I didn't like it. While I believed he loved Eva, I also believed he made bad choices that put her in tough situations and even posed a risk.

Angus opened the door. Eva was out and running up the steps before I put my tablet away. Monica opened the front door just as her daughter hit the top landing.

Surprised by my wife's enthusiasm, considering she barely tolerated her mother most of the time, I stared after her curiously.

Cary laughed as he gathered his things and shoved them into a small messenger bag. "One whiff. That's all it takes."

"Excuse me?"

"Monica usually bakes these crazy good cookies with peanut butter cups. Eva's making sure she stashes some before I get in there and eat 'em all."

Making a mental note to get that recipe, I looked back toward the two women on the porch, catching them exchanging air kisses before they both turned to look my way. At that moment, with Monica dressed in capris and a casual shirt, the similarities between them were striking.

Cary hopped out and took the steps two at a time, barreling directly into Monica's open-armed embrace and lifting her off her feet. Their laughter rang out through the gathering dusk.

I heard Angus speak to me from where he stood by the open door. "You can't spend the weekend in the limo, lad."

Amused, I left my tablet on the seat and stepped out.

He grinned. "It'll be good for you to have family."

I set my hand on his shoulder and squeezed. "I already have one."

For years, Angus had been all I'd had. And he'd been enough.

"Come on, slowpoke!" Eva came back to me, grabbing my hand and dragging me up the steps after her.

"Gideon." Monica's smile was wide and warm.

"Monica." I held out my hand and was startled to be hugged tightly instead.

"I'd tell you to call me Mom," she said, pulling back. "But I'm afraid I'd feel old."

Awkwardness morphed into a prickling that ran down my spine. It struck me then that I'd miscalculated to a wide degree.

Marriage to Eva made her mine. It also made me hers, and connected me to her loved ones in a very personal way.

Monica and I had known each other for a while, our paths crossing occasionally because of the various children's charities we both supported. We'd established particular parameters for our interactions, just as every association followed known protocols.

Abruptly, that was all blown to hell.

I found myself glancing back at Angus, at a loss. Apparently my predicament was entertaining, since he gave me a wink and left me to my own devices. He rounded the trunk to greet Benjamin Clancy, who waited by the driver's-side door of the limo.

"The garage is over there," Monica said, pointing at the two-story building across the road that was a small replica of the main house. "Clancy will make sure your driver gets settled and your bags are brought in."

Eva tugged on my hand and led me inside. Cary had guessed right. I was inundated with the smell of buttery vanilla. Not candles. Cookies. The homey and comforting scent made me itch to turn around and step back outside.

I wasn't prepared. I'd come as a guest, Eva's plus-one. To be a son-in-law, a true member of the family, was a possibility I hadn't anticipated.

"I love this house," Eva said, taking me through the archway that framed the opening to the living room.

I saw what I expected. An upscale beach house with white-slipcovered seating and nautical-themed accessories.

"Don't you love the espresso hardwood floors?" she asked. "I would've gone with bleached oak, but that's so predictable, right? And the green, orange, and yellow accent colors over the usual blue? Makes me want to go rogue when we get back to the Outer Banks."

She had no idea how much I wanted to get back there now. There at least I'd have more than a second to myself before I had to deal with a houseful of brand-new relatives.

The expansive living area flowed directly into the open kitchen, where Stanton, Martin, Lacey, and Cary all gathered around a large kitchen island with seating for six. The entire space shared the view of the water afforded by a row of sliding glass panels that opened onto a wide veranda.

"Hey!" Eva protested. "You better save me some cookies!"

Stanton grinned and approached us. Dressed in jeans and a polo shirt, he looked like a younger version of the man I knew from our dealings in New York. He'd shed the corporate vibe along with his suit, and I felt like I faced a stranger.

"Eva." Stanton kissed Eva's cheek, then turned to me. "Gideon."

Accustomed to being addressed by my last name, I wasn't braced for the hug that followed.

"Congratulations," he said, giving me a firm pat on the back before releasing me.

Irritation simmered. Where was the natural evolution? The gradual shifting from business colleague to social acquaintance. And from there, from friend to family?

I abruptly thought of Victor. He'd understood what my marriage meant in a way I hadn't.

While I stood stiffly, Stanton smiled at my wife. "I think your mother stashed some cookies in the warming drawer for you."

"Yes!" She rushed into the kitchen, leaving me with her stepfather.

My stepfather-in-law.

My gaze followed her. In doing so, I caught the wave

Martin Stanton sent my way, and I acknowledged it with a nod. If he tried to hug me, he was going to get a fist in the face.

I'd once told him he could count on seeing me at family gatherings. It felt surreal now that it was actually happening. Like I was being punked.

Eva's husky laugh carried across the room to me and drew my eye. She held her left hand out to the blonde standing by Martin, showing off the ring I'd given her when I made her my wife.

Monica joined Stanton and me, sliding into place at her husband's side. Her youthful beauty aged him, drawing attention to the stark whiteness of his hair and the lines etching his face. It was evident, however, that Stanton didn't care about the decades that separated him and his wife. He lit up when he looked at her, his faded blue eyes softening with affection.

I searched for something appropriate to say. In the end, all that came out was, "You have a beautiful home."

"It didn't look this good before Monica got her hands on it." Stanton wrapped an arm around her slender waist. "Same can be said for me."

"Richard." Monica shook her head. "Can I give you a tour, Gideon?"

"Let's give the man a drink first," Stanton suggested, eyeing me. "He's been in the car awhile."

"Wine?" she offered.

"Maybe scotch," Stanton said.

"Scotch would be great," I replied, chagrined that my unease was apparently obvious.

I was out of my element, something I should be used to

since meeting Eva, but she had been an anchor of sorts, even as she sent me reeling. As long as I held on to her, I could weather any storm. Or so I'd thought.

Looking for my wife, I turned and felt a rush of relief to find her coming toward me with a bounce in her step that had her ponytail swaying.

"Try this," she ordered, lifting a cookie to my lips.

I opened my mouth but snapped my teeth shut a split second too soon, deliberately nipping her fingers.

"Ow." She frowned, but the literal bite of pain had the intended effect of focusing her attention on me. The frown faded as understanding dimmed the light in her eyes. She saw me, saw what was happening inside me.

"Want to go outside?" she murmured.

"In a minute." I jerked my chin toward the bar in the living room where Stanton was pouring my drink. I also caught her by the wrist, keeping her close.

It rankled, holding her back from the group. I didn't want to be one of those men who smother the women who love them. But I needed time to adjust to all this. The usual distance I maintained from others, including Cary, wouldn't be acceptable with Monica or Stanton. Not after seeing how much joy Eva took in being with those she considered family.

Family for her was a safe place. She was as relaxed and easy as I'd ever seen her. For me, gatherings like this sent up red flags.

I told myself to chill as Stanton returned with our drinks. But I didn't let my guard down completely.

Martin came over and introduced his girlfriend, both of them offering congratulations. That went as expected, which soothed me a little, although not as much as the double scotch I polished off with one swallow.

"I'm going to show him the beach," Eva said, taking the empty glass from me and setting it on an end table we passed on the way to the glass doors.

It was warmer outside than it was in the house, summer lingering this year to the very end. A strong salt-tinged breeze washed over us, whipping my hair across my face.

We walked to the edge of the lapping surf, her hand in mine.

"What's going on?" she asked, facing me.

The concern in her voice had me bristling. "Did you know this was some sort of family celebration because we're married?"

She recoiled from the snap in my tone. "I didn't think about it like that. And Mom didn't call it that, but I suppose it makes sense."

"Not to me." I turned my back to her and began walking into the wind, letting it blow my hair away from my heated face.

"Gideon!" Eva hurried after me. "Why are you mad?"

I rounded on her. "I wasn't expecting this!"

"What?"

"The assimilation-into-the-family crap."

She frowned. "Well, yeah. I told you they knew."

"That shouldn't change anything."

"Uh . . . Why tell them, then? You wanted them to know, Gideon." She stared at me when I didn't say anything. "What did you think would happen?"

"I never expected to get married, Eva, so forgive me if I didn't think about it."

"Okay." She held up both hands in a gesture of surrender. "I'm confused."

And I didn't know how to make things clear. "I can't . . . I'm not ready for this."

"Ready for what?"

I waved an impatient hand toward the house. "For that."

"Can you be more specific?" she asked carefully.

"I . . . No."

"Did I miss something in there?" Her voice held a sharp note of anger. "What did they say, Gideon?"

It took me a moment to understand that she was rising to my defense. That only goaded me further. "I came here to be with *you*. It just so happens you're spending time with your family—"

"They're your family, too."

"I didn't ask for that."

I watched as understanding sifted across her face. When pity followed, my fists clenched at my sides. "Don't look at me like that, Eva."

"I don't know what to say. Tell me what you need."

I exhaled roughly. "More liquor."

Her mouth curved. "I'm sure you won't be the first groom who feels the need to drink around his in-laws."

"Can we not call them that, please?"

The faint smile faded. "What would that change? You can call them Mr. and Mrs. Stanton, but—"

"I'm not the one who's confused about where I fit here."

Her lips pursed. "I'm not sure I agree with that."

"Two days ago, they would've shaken my hand and called me Cross. Now, it's hugs and 'call me Mom' and smiles that expect something!"

"Actually, she told you *not* to call her Mom, but I get it. You're their son by marriage and it's freaking you out. Still, is it so terrible that they're happy about it? Would you prefer it if they were like my dad?"

"Yes." I knew how to deal with anger and disappointment.

Eva took a step back, her eyes dark and wide in the light of a waning moon.

"No," I retracted, shoving a hand through my hair. I didn't know how to deal with disappointing *her*. "Damn it. I don't know."

She stared at me for a long minute. I looked away, out over the water.

"Gideon . . ." She closed the gap she'd put between us. "Honestly, I get it. My mom's been married three times. Every time it's a new instant father figure that I—"

"I have a stepfather," I interrupted tersely. "It's not the same thing. No one gives a shit whether a stepparent likes you."

"Is that what this is about?" She walked into me and hugged me tight. "They already like you."

I gripped her close. "They don't fucking know me."

"They will. And they're going to love you. You're every parent's dream."

"Cut the bullshit, Eva."

She shoved away from me, her temper flaring. "You know what? If you didn't want any in-laws, you should've married an orphan."

She marched back toward the house.

"Get back here," I snapped.

She flipped her middle finger at me over her shoulder.

I caught her in three strides, grabbing her arm and spinning her back around. "We're not done."

"I am." Eva pushed up onto her tiptoes to get in my face, which still left her tilting her head back to glare at me. "You're the one who wanted to get married. If you're having cold feet, it's all on you."

"Don't make this my problem!" Fury sizzled through my blood, ratcheting up my frustration.

"Sorry you didn't realize the commitment involved more than a convenient piece of ass!"

"Conveniently unavailable," I countered, feeling a muscle twitching in my jaw.

"Screw you."

"Excellent idea."

She was flat on her back in the sand before she knew what hit her. I pinned her down, pressing hard, my mouth on hers to shut her up. She arched, struggling, and I gripped her ponytail to hold her in place.

Her teeth sank into my bottom lip and I pulled back with a curse.

"Are you fucking kidding me right now?" Her legs tangled with mine and I found myself beneath her, staring up at her furious, beautiful face. "*This* is exactly why you're not getting any, ace. Sex is your go-to solution for everything."

"You've got to make this worth my while," I taunted, wanting a fight.

"*I'm* worth your while, asshat. Not my vagina." She pushed down on my shoulders. "I'm sorry you feel ambushed. I'm *really* sorry that being welcomed with open arms makes you lose your damn mind. But you're going to have to get used to it because it's all part of the package you got with me."

I knew that. Knew I had to make it work, because I had to have her. It trapped me, my love for her. Pushed me into corners I couldn't back out of. Forced a family on me when I'd gotten by just fine without one.

"I don't want this," I said tightly.

Eva stilled. She sank back onto her knees, her thighs bracketing my hips. "Think about what you're saying," she warned.

"I don't know how to play this role, Eva."

"Jesus." Her temper left her on a sigh. "Just be yourself."

"I'm the last thing they'd want for their daughter."

"You really think that?" She studied me. "You do. God, Gideon . . ."

I gripped her thighs, holding her in place. She couldn't leave me now. Whatever happened, I wasn't letting her leave me.

"Okay." Her eyes took on a calculation that made me wary. "So be yourself. If they find out what a terrible guy you are and hate you, you'd like that better anyway, right?"

"Leave the mind games to the shrinks, Eva."

"I'm just working with what you're giving me, ace."

A whistle drew our gazes to where Martin, Lacey, and Cary were stepping onto the sand from the edge of the slate-covered patio.

"You guys are totally newlyweds," Lacey called out, almost too far away to hear. She laughed as she struggled to balance on the shifting sand, spilling half the contents of her wineglass in the process.

Eva looked back at me. "Do you want to fight in front of them?"

I took a deep breath. Let it out. "No."

"I love you."

"Christ." My eyes closed.

It was a goddamned weekend. A couple days. Maybe we could leave early on Sunday. . . .

Her lips brushed mine. "We can do this. Just try."

What choice did I have?

"If it starts driving you crazy," she went on, "just imagine some terribly wicked thing you want to do to me on our wedding night as payback."

My fingers flexed into her flesh. I wasn't ashamed to admit that sex with my wife—even just the *thought* of sex with my wife—took precedence over damn near everything else.

"You can even text me all your nefarious plans," she suggested. "Make me suffer, too."

"Keep your phone on you."

"You're evil." She bent down and pressed her lips to mine in a quick, sweet kiss. "You're so easy to love, Gideon. Even when you're impossible. One day, you're going to see it."

I dismissed that. What mattered was that I see her, that she was right there with me even after I fucked it all up.

❦

Dinner was simple—salad and spaghetti. Monica cooked and served, and Eva glowed. Wine flowed freely, bottle after bottle opened and emptied. Everyone relaxed. Laughed. Even me.

Lacey's presence was a welcome buffer. She was the newest addition to the group and got the most attention. That gave me some breathing room. And as time passed, Eva became flushed and bright-eyed with intoxication. She slid her chair closer and closer to my own, until she was pressed against my side, her body soft and warm.

Beneath the table, her hands and feet were busy, touching me often. Her voice grew huskier, her laugh became lusty. Eva had once confessed that drinking made her horny, but I would know the signs anywhere regardless.

It was nearing two in the morning when Lacey's yawn turned everyone's thoughts to ending the night. Monica walked with us to the stairs.

"Your things are already in your room," she said, speaking to both Eva and me. "Let's all plan on sleeping in and having brunch."

"Um . . ." My wife frowned.

I caught her by the elbow. Clearly Eva hadn't considered that we'd be sharing a room and a bed, but that inevitability had never been far from my mind. "Thank you, Monica. We'll see you later today."

She laughed and cupped my face in her hands, kissing my cheek. "I'm so happy, Gideon. You're just what Eva needs."

I managed a smile, aware that her sentiments would change if she knew how dangerous it was for her daughter to share a bed with a man whose violent nightmares posed a serious risk of harm.

Eva and I started up the stairs.

"Gideon—"

I cut her off. "Where are we going?"

She glanced aside at me. "All the way up."

Eva's room was indeed at the top, taking up the entirety of what was once probably a large attic. The low-pitched gabled roof made for a comfortable ceiling height and would offer an impressive view of Long Island Sound during daylight.

The king-size bed sat in the middle of the room, facing the wall of windows. Its brass headboard formed a divider of sorts, with a couch placed against the back to anchor a small seating area. The en suite bathroom filled the other side of the space.

Eva faced me. "How is this going to work?"

"Let me worry about that." I was used to worrying about sharing a bed with my wife; it was something I did daily. Of all the things that jeopardized our relationship, my atypical sexual parasomnia—as Dr. Petersen called it—topped the list. I had no defense against my fucked-up mind when I was sleeping. On rough nights, I was a physical danger to the one I loved most.

Eva crossed her arms. "Somehow, I don't think you're as invested in waiting till the wedding as I am."

I stared at her, realizing we were thinking of two entirely different things. "I'll take the couch."

"Take *me* on the couch, you mean. You've—"

"I'll fuck you there, given the chance," I said tightly, "but I'm not sleeping with you."

Her mouth opened to retort, then closed as comprehension hit her. "Oh."

The entire mood changed. The challenge in her eyes and voice altered to subdued caution. It killed me to see it, to know that I could be the source of any unhappiness in her life.

Still, I was too selfish to walk away. One day her family would see that about me and hate me for it.

Aggravated, I looked for my duffel bag and found it atop a luggage rack by the bathroom. I went to it, needing to do something other than see Eva's disillusionment and regret.

"I don't want you sleeping on the couch," she called after me.

"I wasn't planning on sleeping."

I grabbed my grooming kit and went into the bathroom. The lights came on as soon as I entered, revealing a pedestal sink and freestanding tub. I turned on the taps in the floating glass shower and took off my shirt.

The door opened and Eva stepped in. I glanced at her, pausing with my hand on the fly of my slacks.

Her hot gaze slid all over me, missing nothing, touching everything. She took a deep breath. "We have to talk."

I was aroused by her admiration and furious with my own shortcomings; talking was the last thing I wanted to do. "Go to bed, Eva."

"Not until I say what I have to say."

"I'm taking a shower."

"Fine." She pulled her tank top up and over her head. Everything roiling inside me coalesced into a single driving need.

I straightened, every muscle tense and straining.

She reached behind her back to unsnap her bra.

My dick hardened painfully as her lush, firm tits bounced into view. I'd never been a breast man before Eva. Now . . .

God. They made me lose my mind.

"Talking isn't what's going to happen if you take your clothes off," I warned, my cock throbbing.

"You're going to hear me out, ace, whether it's out here or in the shower. Your choice."

"Tonight isn't the night to push me."

She dropped her shorts.

I had my pants opened and on the floor before she finished stepping out of the silky triangle she wore as underwear.

Despite the building humidity that fogged the room, her nipples tightened into hard points. Her gaze fell to my cock. As if she imagined tasting me, her tongue slid along her lower lip.

My hunger for her rumbled up from my chest in a near growl. Eva shivered at the sound. I wanted to touch her . . . to put my hands and mouth all over her . . .

Instead, I let her look her fill.

Her breathing picked up. Seeing the effect I had on her was painfully, undeniably erotic. What I felt when she looked at me . . . it moved me.

She remained by the door. Steam drifted over the top of the shower, encroaching on the edges of the mirror and misting my skin. Her eyes dropped to my throat. "I haven't been completely honest with you, Gideon."

My hands fisted reflexively. She couldn't say those words to me and not redirect my attention. "What are you talking about?"

"Just now, when we were in the bedroom. I could sense you pulling away and there was this panic I felt . . ."

Eva fell silent for a long moment. I waited, reining my lust back with a deep breath.

"Holding off until the wedding . . . It's not just about Dr. Petersen's advice or the way you cope with fights." She swallowed. "It's about me, too. You know how I was—I told you. Sex was all twisted up for me for a long time."

She shifted on her feet, shame bowing her head. It made

me sick to see it. It struck me then that I'd been too wrapped up in my own reactions to the events of the last week without thinking about what my wife was going through.

"It was for me, too," I reminded her gruffly. "But it's never been that way between us."

She caught my gaze. "No. Never."

My clenched fists relaxed.

"But that doesn't mean I can't still twist things up in my head," she went on. "You walked into the bathroom and my first thought was that I should fuck you. Like if we have sex, it'll fix everything. You won't be mad anymore and I'll have your love again."

"You always have it. You always will."

"I know that." And from the set of her jaw, I could see that she did. "But that didn't stop the voice in my head from telling me I'm risking too much. That I'm going to lose you if I don't put out. That you're too sexual to go so long without it."

"God." How many times and ways could I fuck this up? "The way I talked to you on the beach . . . I'm an asshole, Eva."

"Sometimes." She smiled. "You're also the best thing that's ever happened to me. That voice has been screwing me up for years, but it doesn't have the same power anymore. Because of you. You've made me stronger."

"Eva." Words failed me.

"I want you to think about that. Not your nightmares or my parents or anything else. You're exactly what I need, just the way you are, and I love you so much."

I walked toward her.

"I still want to wait," she said quietly, even as her eyes betrayed how I affected her.

She grabbed my wrist when I reached for her, her gaze holding mine. "Let me do all the touching."

I inhaled sharply. "I can't agree to that."

Her mouth curved. "Yes, you can. You're stronger than I am, Gideon. You have more control. Greater willpower."

Her other hand reached up to graze my chest. I caught it and pressed it against my skin. "Is that what you need me to prove? My control?"

"You're doing fine." She pressed a kiss over my pounding heart. "I'm the one who needs to figure things out."

Her tone of voice was soft, almost crooning. I was raging inside, burning with lust and love, and she was trying to gentle me. I almost laughed at the impossibility of that.

Then she stepped into me, her plush body fitting tightly against mine, her arms hugging me so hard there wasn't any space between us.

I crushed her close, my head bowing over hers. I didn't know until that moment how badly I'd needed to feel her like that. Tender and accepting, bared in every way possible.

She leaned her cheek against my chest. "I love you so much," she whispered. "Can you feel it?"

It overwhelmed me. Her love for me, my love for her. Every time she said the words, they hit me like blows.

"You said once," she whispered, "that there's a moment while we're making love when I open and you open and we're together. I want to give you that all the time, Gideon."

The suggestion that there was something missing in what we had stiffened my spine. "Does it really matter how and when we feel it?"

"You could argue that." Her head tilted back. "I won't

disagree. But if you're on the other side of the world when you need reassurance from me, I need to know that I can give it to you."

"You'll be with me," I muttered, frustrated.

"Not always." Her hand cupped my cheek. "There will be times when you need to be in two places at once. Eventually, you'll trust me to fill in for you."

I studied her, looking for cracks in her resolve. What I saw was determination. I didn't totally understand what she hoped to achieve, but I wasn't getting in the way. If she was going to change or evolve, I needed to be part of that process if I expected to keep her.

"Kiss me." The words left my throat as a low command, but she must have sensed the yearning behind it.

She offered her mouth and I took it hard, too hard, my hunger violent and greedy. I lifted her off her feet, wanting her to wrap her legs around me, to open to me so I could push inside her.

She didn't. She hung there, her hands stroking through my hair, her body trembling with the same unquenchable desire I felt. The flicks of her tongue against mine were maddening, taunting me with the memory of that tongue stroking over the rest of my body.

I struggled to pull away when everything inside me was goading me to push further. "I need to be inside you," I said hoarsely, hating that I had to voice what was so obvious. Why make me plead?

"You are." She nuzzled her cheek against mine. "I want you, too. I'm so wet for you right now. I feel so empty it hurts."

"Eva . . . Christ." Sweat slid down my back. "Let me have you."

Her lips touched mine. Her fingers raked through my hair. "Let me love you another way."

Could I handle that? Hell. I had to. I'd vowed to give her whatever she needed, to be the beginning and end of everything for her.

I set her down and went to the shower, shutting the taps off. Then I moved to the tub, stopped the drain, and started filling it.

"Are you mad?" she asked in a low voice I barely heard over the rush of water.

I looked at her, saw the way her arms crossed her chest and gave away her vulnerability. I told her the truth. "I love you."

Eva's lower lip trembled, then curved in a beautiful smile that took my breath away.

I'd once told her I would take her any way I could get her. That was even more true now than it was then. "Come here, angel."

Her arms dropped to her sides and she came.

The shifting of the bed woke me. Blinking, I registered the sunlight flooding the room. Eva's face came into focus, haloed by the light and bright with a wide grin.

"Morning, sleepyhead," she said.

The night came flooding back to me. The long bath with my wife's soapy hands running through my hair and over my skin. Her voice as she talked about the wedding. Her sensual laugh as I tickled her in bed. Her sighs and moans as we kissed until our lips were sore and swollen, making out like teenagers who weren't ready to go all the way.

I won't lie—sex would've taken things to another level. But the night was memorable all the same. It ranked right up there with other all-nighters we'd shared.

Then I remembered where I was and what that meant.

"I slept in the bed." The realization was like a bucket of cold water dumped over me.

"Yep." She gave a happy little bounce. "You did."

To have done so was irresponsible in the worst way. I hadn't even taken the medicine prescribed to help mitigate the risk.

"Don't scowl like that," she chastised, bending down to kiss the space between my brows. "You slept *hard*. When's the last time you had a good night's sleep?"

I sat up. "That's not the point and you know it."

"Listen, ace. We've got enough to be stressed about. We don't need to get worked up over things that go right." She stood. "If you want to be mad about something, be mad at Cary for packing this."

She shrugged out of the short white robe she was wearing, revealing a tiny dark blue bikini that hugged what little it managed to cover.

"Jesus." All the blood in my body rushed to my dick. It waved beneath the sheet in hearty appreciation.

Eva laughed, her eyes dropping to where my erection tented the luxuriously thick cotton. "You like."

Holding her arms out, she turned, showing off the Brazilian cut of the bikini bottom. My wife's ass was as voluptuous as her tits. I knew she thought she was too curvy, but I couldn't disagree more. I'd never been one to appreciate overly generous assets on a woman, but Eva changed that for me, as she'd changed so many other things.

I hadn't a clue what kind of material the bikini was made of, but it was seamless and hugged her skin so perfectly it looked painted on. Thin straps at the neck, hips, and back brought to mind thoughts of tying her up and taking what I needed.

"Come here," I ordered, reaching for her.

She danced out of reach. Tossing the sheet back, I surged to my feet.

"Down, boy," she teased, darting around the sofa.

I fisted my cock, stroking it hard from root to tip as I stalked her into the seating area. "That's not going to work."

Her eyes sparkled with laughter.

"Eva—"

She snatched something off the back of the chair and ran to the door. "See you downstairs!"

I lunged for her and missed, finding myself facing the back of the slammed door instead. "Damn it."

I brushed my teeth, threw on swim trunks and a T-shirt, and followed her down. I was the last one to make an appearance, discovering the rest of the group already seated at the kitchen island and eating heartily. A quick glance at the clock told me it was almost noon.

I looked for Eva and found her sitting on the patio with a phone to her ear. She'd covered herself in a strapless white skirt thing. I noted that Monica and Lacey were both dressed similarly, with bathing suits partially hidden by barely-there cover-ups. Like me, Cary, Stanton, and Martin had on trunks and T-shirts.

"She always calls her dad on Saturdays," Cary said, following my gaze.

I watched my wife for a long minute, looking for any

signs of distress. She wasn't smiling anymore, but she didn't look upset.

"Here you go, Gideon." Monica set a plate of waffles and bacon in front of me. "Would you like coffee? Or maybe a mimosa?"

I glanced at Eva again before answering. "Coffee—black—would be great, thank you."

Monica moved toward the coffeemaker on the counter. I joined her.

She smiled at me, her lips painted the same pink as the halter tie of her swimsuit. "Did you sleep well?"

"Like a rock." Which was true, though that was pure luck. The entire household might've been woken up by a fight between Eva and me, with her struggling to fight me off while my dreams imagined she was someone else.

Glancing over my shoulder at Cary, I caught his grim gaze. He'd seen what could happen. He didn't trust me with Eva any more than I trusted myself.

I grabbed an extra mug out of the cupboard Monica reached into. "I can get it," I told her.

"Nonsense."

I didn't argue with her. I let her pour my coffee, then followed suit by pouring a cup for my wife. After adding Eva's preferred amount of half-and-half, I grabbed the handles of both mugs in one hand. Then I picked up the plate Monica had served me and headed out to the patio.

Eva glanced up at me as I set everything on the table beside her and took the seat on the other side. She'd left her hair down. Blond tendrils fluttered around her bare face as the breeze ruffled through it. I loved her this way, earthy and natural. Here and now, she was my own piece of heaven on earth.

Thank you, she mouthed, before snatching up a piece of bacon. She munched quickly while Victor said something I couldn't hear.

"Eventually, I'll focus on Crossroads," she said, "which is Gideon's charitable foundation. I hope to be active in that. And I've been thinking about maybe going back to school."

My brows rose.

"I'd like to be a sounding board for Gideon," she continued, looking straight at me. "Obviously, he's managed well enough without me and he's got a great team of advisors, but I'd like him to be able to talk shop with me and at least understand what he's saying."

I tapped my chest. *I'll teach you.*

She blew me a kiss. "In the meantime, I'm going to be crazy busy trying to pull off a wedding in less than three weeks. I haven't even picked out invitations yet! I know it's going to be hard for some of the family to get time off. Could you send out an e-mail in the meantime? Just to get the ball rolling?"

Eva bit into the bacon while her father talked.

"We haven't discussed it," she replied, swallowing quickly, "but I'm not planning on inviting them. They lost the right to be part of my life when they disowned Mom. And it's not like they've ever reached out to me, so I don't think they'd care anyway."

I looked across the span of sand to the water beyond it. I wasn't interested in meeting Eva's maternal grandparents, either. They'd rejected Monica for becoming pregnant with

Eva out of wedlock. Anyone who found my wife's existence distasteful was better off not crossing paths with me.

I listened to Eva's side of the conversation for another few minutes, and then she said good-bye. When she set her phone on the table, she gave a big sigh that sounded like relief.

"Everything good?" I asked, studying her.

"Yeah, he's better today." She glanced inside the house. "You didn't want to eat with the family?"

"Am I being antisocial?"

She smiled wryly. "Totally. I can't hold it against you, though."

I gave her an inquiring look.

"I realized I haven't included your mother in the wedding planning," she explained.

Settling deeper into the chair to conceal the stiffening of my spine, I told her, "You don't have to."

Her lips pursed. She reached for another piece of bacon, then handed it to me. True love.

"Eva." I waited until she looked at me. "It's your day. Don't feel obligated to do anything but enjoy yourself. And have sex with me, which should fall under enjoying yourself."

That brought her smile back. "It's going to be wonderful no matter what."

I voiced what was left unsaid. "But?"

"I don't know." She tucked her hair behind her ear and shrugged. "Thinking about my mom's parents has me thinking about grandparents, and your mother is going to be our children's grandmother. I don't want that to be awkward."

I bristled. The thought of my mother and a child I created with Eva together in any way filled me with a riot of emotions I couldn't deal with now. "Let's cross that bridge when we come to it."

"Isn't our wedding the place to start?"

"You don't like my mother," I snapped. "Don't pretend you do for the sake of children who don't exist yet."

Eva jerked back slightly. She blinked at me, then reached for her coffee. "Did you try the waffles?"

Knowing it wasn't in my wife's nature to steer away from sensitive topics, I still let her do it. If we were going to get into the subject of my mother, we could do it later.

She set her mug down and tore off a piece of waffle with her fingers. She held it out to me. I took it for what it was: a peace offering.

Then I stood and took her hand, leading her out to the beach for a walk to clear my head.

～◌～

"You're welcome."

Turning my head, I saw Cary grinning at me from where he lay on the sand a few feet away.

"I know you appreciate my packing that bikini," he elaborated, jerking his chin toward Eva, who was standing thigh-deep in the water.

Her hair was damp and slicked back from her face. Over-size aviator sunglasses shielded her eyes from the sun as she threw a Frisbee back and forth with Martin and Lacey.

"Did you help her pick that out?" Monica asked, smiling from beneath an elegant wide-brim hat.

I'd watched her slather sunscreen all over Eva, a job I wanted for myself, but I didn't press the point. Sometimes,

Monica mothered Eva as if she were still a child. While my wife rolled her eyes at me, I could see that she basked in the attention. It was a very different relationship from the one I had with my own mother.

I couldn't say that my mom didn't love me, because she did. In her own way—within boundaries. Monica's love, on the other hand, had no limits, something Eva found stifling at times.

Who could say which was better or worse? To be loved too much or too little?

God knew I loved Eva beyond all reason.

A sudden sea breeze snapped me out of it. Monica hung on to her hat as Cary turned his head toward her.

"I did," Cary replied, rolling over onto his stomach. "She was looking at one-pieces and I had to intervene. That bikini was made for her."

Yeah. Hell yeah. I had my arms crossed over my bent knees so I could take in my fill of her. She was wet and nearly naked, and I was hot for her.

As if she sensed we were talking about her, Eva crooked her finger at me, beckoning me to come to her. I nodded but waited for a few moments before rising from where I'd been sitting in the sand.

The chill of the water made me suck in a sharp breath, but I was grateful for it a moment later when she surged toward me and plastered herself against me. Her legs wrapped around my waist, her smiling mouth puckering into a heated kiss against my lips.

"You're not bored, are you?" she asked.

Then she twisted in a way that sent us both tumbling into the water. I felt her hand cup my cock and give it a gentle squeeze. She wriggled away as I came up for air, laughing as she pulled her sunglasses off and tried to run onto the beach.

I caught her by the waist and took us both down, absorbing the fall onto the sand on my back. Her squeal of surprise was my reward, as was the feel of her cool, sleek body writhing against my own.

Turning, I pinned her down. My hair hung around my face, dripping water onto hers. She stuck her tongue out at me.

"The things I'd do to you if we didn't have an audience," I told her.

"We're newlyweds. You can kiss me."

Looking up, I saw all eyes on us.

I also spotted Ben Clancy and Angus closing in on a house two lots down. Even at this distance, the glint of light from the patio betrayed a camera's lens.

I started to sit up, but Eva's legs tangled with mine and held me down.

"Kiss me like you love me, ace," she challenged. "I dare you."

I remembered saying those words to her and how she'd kissed my breath away.

Lowering my head, I sealed my mouth over hers.

5

I'D BEEN DOZING more than sleeping when I heard my bedroom door open. After spending a weekend at the beach, the sounds of energetic Manhattan filtering into the apartment had both soothed and excited me. I had a long way to go before I could call myself a New Yorker, but the city already felt like home to me now.

"Rise and shine, baby girl!" Cary shouted. A moment later, he bounded onto my bed, nearly bouncing me off.

Sitting up, I shoved the hair back from my face. Then I shoved him. "I'm sleeping in, if you hadn't noticed."

"It's after nine o'clock, lazybones," he drawled, settling on his stomach with his heels kicked up behind him. "I know you're unemployed, but don't you have a shit-ton of stuff to get done?"

As I drifted in and out of sleep, I'd been thinking about everything on my to-do list. There was so much to scratch off, it was overwhelming. "Yeah."

"Such enthusiasm."

"I need coffee for that. What about you?" I looked at him, noting that he was dressed in olive cargo pants and a charcoal V-neck T-shirt. "What's on your agenda today?"

"I'm supposed to take it easy, so I can be ready to hit the catwalk tomorrow. For now, I'm all yours."

Reaching behind me, I propped my pillows up and scooted back against them. "I need to call the wedding planner, the interior designer, and get the invitation thing sorted out."

"You also need a dress."

"I know." I wrinkled my nose. "That's not on my list today, though."

"Are you kidding? Even if you bought a dress off the rack—which we both know you can't—if it needs any alterations whatsoever, Mrs. Big Boobs and Voluptuous Ass, you're pushing it timewise."

Cary was right. I'd realized I had to find something custom after photos of Gideon and me kissing on the beach had spread all over the Internet on Sunday. The number of "steal this look" blog posts on my beachwear boggled my mind. Since the bikini I'd worn had been discontinued, prices for used ones on resale sites were staggering.

"I don't know what to do, Cary," I admitted. "It's not like I have any designers on speed dial."

"Lucky for you, it's Fashion Week."

That woke me up and sent my thoughts racing around in circles. "No shit? How did I miss that?"

"You've been mostly wallowing in misery," he reminded dryly. "You know your mom will be hitting a few shows, rubbing elbows and spending thousands. Go with her."

I rubbed the sleep out of my eyes. "I'm afraid to talk to her about anything after she flipped out yesterday."

He made a face. "Yeah, she had a full-on Monica Melt-down."

"I swear we just had a conversation about her turning my wedding into a publicity op and now she's acting like any press is a nightmare."

"Well, to be fair, she was specific about tabloid coverage."

"Is there any other kind nowadays?" I sighed, knowing I was due for another talk with my mother. That wouldn't be fun. "I don't know what she's so upset about. I couldn't have asked for a better picture of Gideon and me if I'd tried. It's perfect for making Corinne Giroux look desperate."

"True." His grin faded. "And honestly, it's good to see Gideon so into you. He had a stick up his ass most of the weekend. I was starting to think he was cooling off."

"Too late for that." I kept my tone light, but it had torn me up to see how uncomfortable Gideon was with any sign of affection. Friendship seemed to be the closest connection he could tolerate outside our marriage. "It wasn't personal, Cary. Remember how he acted at the Vidal Records party at his parents' house?"

"Vaguely." He shrugged. "Not my problem anyway. Do you want me to reach out to some friends and see if we can't put the word out while we're strutting our stuff this week? Your bikini blew up the Internet. I can't imagine any designer turning down the chance to design your wedding dress."

I groaned. How amazing would it be to knock Gideon's socks off with a glamorous, made-just-for-me dress? "I don't know. It would suck royally if word got out about how soon it's all going down. I don't want a media circus. It's bad enough we can't even go out of town for the weekend without some creepy photographer following us."

"Eva. You have to do something."

Wincing, I confessed, "I haven't told Mom about the September twenty-second date."

"Get on it. Now."

"I know."

"Baby girl"—he blew his bangs out of his face—"you could have the best wedding planner in the world, but your mom is the only woman who can pull off an epic wedding—an Eva-worthy wedding—in a matter of days."

"We can't agree on style!"

Cary hopped off the bed. "Hate to point it out, but Momma knows best. She decorated this place and buys you clothes. Her style *is* your style."

I glared at him. "She likes shopping more than I do."

"Sure thing, sweet cheeks." He blew me a kiss. "I'll fix you a cup of coffee."

Throwing back the covers, I got out of bed. My best friend had a point. Sort of. But I pulled outfits together my own way.

I reached for my phone on the nightstand to call my mom when Gideon's face lit up my screen. "Hey," I answered.

"How's your morning so far?"

It tickled me to hear his clipped, businesslike tone. My husband's head was in the game, but he was still thinking of me.

"I just rolled out of bed, so I can't really say. How's yours? You finish buying up everything in Manhattan?"

"Not quite. Have to leave something for the competition. Otherwise, where's the fun?"

"You do love your challenges." I headed into the bathroom, my gaze sliding over the tub before pausing on the shower. Just thinking about my husband naked and wet made me hot. "What do you think would've happened if I hadn't resisted you to begin with? What if I'd just fallen into bed with you when you asked?"

"You would've blown my mind, just as you did. That was inevitable. Have lunch with me."

I smiled. "I'm supposed to be planning a wedding."

"I hear a yes in there. It's a business lunch, but you'll enjoy it."

Looking in the mirror, I saw wildly tousled bedhead and creases in my cheeks from the pillow. "What time?"

"Noon. Raúl will be waiting for you downstairs shortly before."

"I should be responsible and say no."

"But you won't. I miss you."

My breath caught. He tossed that out there nonchalantly, the way some men would say *I'll call you*. But Gideon wasn't the type of man to say anything he didn't mean.

Still, I craved to feel the emotion behind the words. "You're too busy to miss me."

"It's not the same," he said. There was a pause. "It doesn't feel right not having you here in the Crossfire."

I was glad he couldn't see me smile. There was an unmistakable trace of perplexity in his voice. It shouldn't make a difference to him that I wasn't working floors below his office, where he couldn't see me. But it did.

"What are you wearing?" I asked.

"Clothes."

"Duh. A three-piece suit?"

"Is there any other kind?"

Not for him, there wasn't. "What color?"

"Black. Why?"

"It makes me hot thinking about it." Which was true, but not why I was asking. "What color tie?"

"White."

"Shirt?"

"Also white."

Closing my eyes, I pictured him. I remembered that combination. "Pinstripes."

He'd go with a pinstriped suit to keep the business look with that shirt and tie combination.

"Yes. Eva . . ." His voice lowered. "I have no idea why this conversation is making me hard, but it is."

"Because you know I'm seeing you in my head. All dark and dangerous and sexy as hell. You know how much it turns me on to look at you, even if it's only by memory."

"Meet me here. Early. Come now."

I laughed. "Good things come to those who wait, Mr. Cross. I'll be cutting it close as it is."

"Eva—"

"I love you." I hung up and faced myself squarely in the mirror. With the picture of Gideon freshly in my mind, I found the sleepy mess looking back at me totally insufficient. I'd changed my look when I'd thought Gideon had left me for Corinne. I had dubbed the result "New Eva." In the time since, my hair had grown past its former shoulder length and my highlights had grown out with it.

"You decent?" Cary called from the bedroom.

"Yes." I faced him when he strolled into the bathroom with my coffee in hand. "Change of plan."

"Oh?" He leaned into the counter and crossed his arms.

"I'm hopping in the shower. You're going to find me a fabulous hair salon that can fit me in about thirty minutes from now."

"Okay."

"Then I'm going to lunch and you're going to make a few calls for me. In return, I'm taking you out to dinner tonight. You pick the place."

"I know that look you've got," he said. "You're on a mission."

"Damn straight."

❦

I showered quickly, since I didn't wash my hair. Then I hurried over to my closet, having spent the time in the bathroom thinking about what I wanted to wear. It took a few minutes to locate the right dress. Bright white, with a built-in bra and fitted tulip skirt, it draped beautifully across the bust and thighs. The color and cotton fabric kept it casual, while the fit was both elegant and sexy.

It took a little longer to find the right pair of shoes. I considered nude for a long time. In the end, I went with a pair of strappy heeled sandals in aqua blue that matched Gideon's eyes. I had a clutch that matched, and a set of opal earrings that had the same bright blue fire.

I laid it all out on the bed to make sure it worked, standing back in my bathrobe to eye the ensemble carefully.

"Nice," Cary said, as he came up behind me.

"I bought those shoes," I reminded him. "And the clutch and jewelry."

He laughed and tossed an arm around my shoulders. "Yeah, yeah. Your hairstylist is here. I told the desk to send him up."

"Really?"

"I can't see you going into any old salon without making a scene. You'll have to find someone you trust to style you in private appointments. In the meantime, Mario can rock a haircut."

"How about color?"

"Color?" His arm dropped and he faced me. "What are you thinking?"

I caught his hand and started out of the room. "Stick with me, kid."

Mario was a compact bundle of energy with a stylish flop of purple-tipped curls. Shorter than me and hard with muscle, he set up shop in my bathroom while gossiping with Cary about people they knew, dropping names I sometimes recognized.

"A natural blonde," he gushed when he first got his hands on my hair. "You, my dear, are a rare breed."

"Make me blonder," I told him.

Taking a step back, he stroked his goatee thoughtfully. "How much blonder?"

"What's the opposite of black?"

Cary whistled.

Mario sifted my hair through his fingers. "You've already got platinum highlights."

"Let's take it up a notch. I want to keep the length, but let's do something edgy. More layers. A little spiky on the tips. Maybe some bangs to frame my eyes." I sat up straighter. "I'm sassy, sexy, and smart enough to flaunt it."

He glanced at Cary. "I like her."

My best friend crossed his arms and nodded. "Me, too."

❧

Stepping back from the mirror, I took in the full effect. I loved what Mario had done with my hair. It fell in piecey, choppy layers around my shoulders and face. He'd heavily foiled my crown and around my face, creating an overall look of lighter hair without altering the dark gold strands underneath. Then he'd teased the roots just enough to give me some sexy volume.

My weekend tan only made my hair look lighter. I'd gone a little wild with a smoky-eye look, using grays and blacks to play up my gray irises. To balance that, I'd kept the rest of my makeup neutral, including my lips, which were glossed in a nude tint. When I juxtaposed my reflection with the image of Gideon in my mind, I saw just the result I was looking for.

My husband was the definition of tall, dark, and gorgeous. His hair was pure black, as dark as ink and just as lustrous. He wore dark colors more often than not, which focused attention on the chiseled planes of his face and the striking color of his eyes. I'd pulled off being a complementary opposite. The yang to his yin.

Bam. I looked *good*.

"Whoa. Hotness." Cary raked me with an appreciative glance as I rushed through the living room. "What kind of lunch is this that you're going to?"

I glanced at my phone, cursing silently to see that ten

minutes had passed since Raúl texted that he was waiting downstairs. "I don't know. Something to do with business, Gideon said."

"Well, you're spectacular arm candy."

"Thanks." But I wanted to be more than that. I wanted to be a weapon in Gideon's arsenal. I'd have to earn it, though, and I relished the challenge. If I could manage to contribute something—*anything*—to the conversation today, I'd be happy. If I was out of my depth, though, I could at least make him proud to be seen with me.

"He's going to be hobbled by his blue balls by the time the wedding comes around," he called after me. "You can only prime a pump so many times before it has to blow."

"Gross, Cary." I opened the front door. "I'll text you the numbers of the designer and wedding planner. And I'll be back in a couple hours."

I was lucky to catch the elevator without a wait. When I stepped out onto the sidewalk outside the lobby and Raúl climbed out from behind the wheel of the Benz, I knew I was on the right track when he gave me the once-over. He kept it professional, but I could tell he liked what he saw.

"Sorry I lagged," I told him as he opened the rear door for me. "I wasn't quite ready when you texted."

There was almost a hint of a smile on his stern face. "I don't think he'll mind."

During the ride, I texted Cary the phone numbers of Blaire Ash, the interior designer working on the penthouse renovations, and Kristin Washington, the wedding planner, and asked him to arrange meetings with them. By the time I was done and glanced out the window, I realized we weren't headed to the Crossfire.

When we arrived at Tableau One, I wasn't totally surprised. The popular restaurant was a co-venture between Gideon and his friend Arnoldo Ricci. Arnoldo had been unknown when Gideon discovered him in Italy. Now, he was a celebrity chef.

As Raúl pulled into the valet area, I scooted forward in the seat. "Could you do me a favor while we're having lunch?"

He turned his head to look at me.

"Can you find out where Anne Lucas is right now? Today's as good a day as any for me to rattle her." I was dressed to impress. Might as well get as much mileage out of that as possible.

"It's possible," he said carefully. "I'll have to discuss it with Mr. Cross."

I almost backed off. Then I remembered that Raúl technically worked for me, too. If I wanted to step up my game, wasn't it best to start at home? "No, *I* have to. And I will. Just find her for me. I'll take care of the rest."

"All right." He still sounded reluctant. "You ready? They're going to take your picture as soon as they see you." He jerked his chin forward and I followed the gesture to where a half-dozen paparazzi stood outside the entrance.

"Oh boy." I took a deep breath. "Got it."

Raúl got out and rounded the car to open my door. The moment I straightened, camera flashes lit up the already bright day. I kept my face straight and walked briskly into the restaurant.

The place was packed and buzzing with the multitude of loud conversations taking place. Still, I found Gideon almost immediately. He spotted me, too. Whatever he'd been saying before I arrived died on his lips.

The hostess said something to me, but I didn't hear her. I was too focused on Gideon, whose stunning face took my breath away—as it always did—but gave me no clue to his thoughts.

Pushing his chair back, Gideon stood with powerful grace. The four men seated with him glanced my way, then stood as well. There were two women with them, both of whom swiveled in their seats to look at me.

I remembered to smile and started toward their large round table situated near the center of the room, making my way carefully over the hardwood floors, trying to ignore the stares I garnered as the focus of Gideon's dark gaze.

My hand shook a little as reached for his arm. "I apologize for being late."

He slid his arm around me and brushed his lips over my temple. His fingers flexed into my waist with near-painful pressure and I pulled back.

He looked at me with such heated intensity and ferocious love that my pulse skipped. Pleasure rushed through me. I knew that look, understood I'd given him a little buzz he was struggling to process. It was nice to know I could still do that. It made me want to try my hardest to find just the right dress to walk down the aisle in.

I looked at everyone at the table. "Hello."

Gideon pulled his gaze away from my face. "It's my pleasure to introduce you to my wife, Eva."

Startled, I turned wide eyes toward him. The world thought we were only engaged. I hadn't realized he was making the fact that we were married known.

The heat in his gaze softened to warm amusement. "These are the board members of the Crossroads Foundation."

Shock turned into love and gratitude so fast, I swayed with it. He held me up, as he always did, in all ways. At a time when I was likely to feel a little adrift, he was giving me something else.

He introduced everyone to me, then pulled out my seat for me. Lunch passed in a whirl of excellent food and intense conversation. I was happy to hear that my idea for adding Crossroads to Gideon's bio on his website had ramped up traffic to the foundation's site, and that my suggested overhauls to the Crossroads site—now in place—had increased applications for assistance.

And I loved how close Gideon sat to me, holding my hand beneath the table.

When they asked me for input, I shook my head. "I'm not qualified to offer anything valuable at this point. You're all doing an amazing job."

Cindy Bello, the CEO, gave me a big smile. "Thank you, Eva."

"I would like to sit in on board meetings as an observer and get up to speed. If I can't contribute ideas, I hope to find another way to lend a hand."

"Now that you mention it," Lynn Feng, the VP of operations, began, "many of our recipients want to acknowledge and thank Crossroads for its support. They hold luncheons or dinners, which also act as fund-raisers. They would love to have Gideon accept on behalf of the foundation, but his schedule precludes that most of the time."

I leaned briefly into Gideon's shoulder. "You want me to nudge him some more for you."

"Actually," she smiled, "Gideon suggested that you might

step in and handle those. We're talking about you representing the foundation in person."

I blinked at her. "You're kidding."

"Not at all."

My gaze turned to Gideon. He tilted his head in acknowledgment.

I tried to wrap my brain around the idea. "I'm not much of a consolation prize."

"Eva." Gideon conveyed a wealth of disapproval in that one word.

"I'm not being modest," I countered. "Why would anyone want to hear me speak? You're accomplished, brilliant, and a wonderful orator. I could listen to you give a speech all day. Your name sells tickets. Offering me up instead just creates . . . an obligation. That's not helpful."

"Are you done?" he asked smoothly.

I narrowed my eyes at him.

"Look at the people in your life and how you've helped them." *Like me.* He didn't say it, but he didn't have to. "If you put your mind to it, you could deliver a powerful message."

"If I can add," Lynn interjected, "when Gideon can't make it, one of us goes instead." She gestured at the rest of the board members. "Having a member of the Cross family personally attend would be wonderful. No one would be disappointed."

The Cross family. That had me sucking in a sharp breath. I didn't know if Geoffrey Cross had left any other family members behind. What was indisputable was that Gideon was the most visible reminder of his infamous father.

My husband didn't remember the man who was known

as a fraudster and coward. What he remembered was a father who had loved and nurtured him. Gideon worked so hard and had achieved so much, driven by the need to change what people associated with the Cross name.

Now I had the name, too. One day in the future, we would have children who carried it. I had the same responsibility as Gideon to make our surname something our kids would be proud of.

I looked at Gideon.

He held my gaze, unwavering and focused. "Two places at once," he murmured.

My heart felt like it was squeezed inside my chest. This was more than I'd expected, sooner than I had expected it. Gideon had gone straight to something personal, something intimate and essential to who he was. Something that meant a great deal to me, as well, and that I could put my own stamp on.

He had been waging the war to clear the stain on his name all alone, as he'd had to fight all of his battles. That he trusted me to join him in this, of all things, was a declaration of love as wonderful to me as the ring on my finger.

My grip on his hand tightened. I tried to show him, with just a look, how touched I was. He lifted our joined hands to his lips, his gaze saying the same thing back to me. *I love you.*

Our server came by to clear our plates.

"We'll talk about it," he said aloud. Then he looked at the others. "I hate to cut this short, but I have an afternoon meeting coming up. I could be generous and leave Eva with you, but I won't."

Smiles and laughter went around the table.

He looked at me. "Ready?"

"Give me a minute," I murmured, looking forward to the opportunity to kiss him the way I needed to.

From the glimmer in his eyes, I suspected he knew exactly what I was thinking.

Lynn and Cindy both pushed to their feet and came along to the ladies' room.

As we made our way through the restaurant, I looked for Arnoldo but didn't see him. That didn't surprise me, considering his commitments with the Food Network and other appearances. As much as I wanted to try to repair that relationship, I knew time would tell. Eventually, Arnoldo would see how much I loved my husband, that protecting him and being everything to him was the center of my life.

Gideon and I challenged each other. We pushed each other to change and grow. Sometimes, we hurt each other to accomplish something or make a point, which worried Dr. Petersen but somehow was working for us. We could forgive each other for anything except betrayal.

It was inevitable that others, especially those close to us, would look at us from the outside and wonder how and why it worked, and whether it should. They couldn't understand—and I didn't blame them because I was only just starting to really grasp it myself—that we pushed ourselves harder than we ever pushed each other. Because we wanted to be the best possible versions of ourselves, to be strong enough to be what the other needed.

I used the restroom, then washed my hands, taking a moment to look in the mirror when I was done and fluff my hair. I wasn't sure how Mario had done it, but he'd given me a cut that gained more body the more I touched it.

I caught Cindy's smile in the mirror and felt a little

self-conscious. Then she pulled out a tube of bright red lipstick and I relaxed.

"Eva. I almost didn't recognize you. I love what you've done with your hair."

Through the mirror, I looked for the person speaking to me. For a split second, I thought it was Corinne and my heart rate kicked up. Then I homed in on the face.

"Hello." Turning, I faced Ryan Landon's wife. When I'd first met Angela, she had worn her hair in an artful chignon, which disguised the length of her hair. With it down, the long black strands hung in a straight curtain that reached the middle of her back. She was tall and slender, her eyes a muted blue-gray. Her face was longer than Corinne's and her features a bit less perfect, but she was still a knockout.

Her gaze assessed me so casually from head to toe I couldn't swear that was what she had done. Nice trick. I hadn't mastered it. It dawned on me that I would be constantly scrutinized by more than just the media as I took my place in the city's new elite. I wasn't ready. My mother's debutante training and rules weren't going to help me, that was for damn sure.

Angela smiled and took the sink next to me. "It's good to see you."

"You, too." Now that I was armed with the knowledge of Landon's vendetta against Gideon, I was on alert. But I wasn't trying to land her husband's account anymore. We were equals. Well, almost. My husband was younger, richer, and hotter. And she knew it.

Cindy and Lynn finished up and started moving toward the exit. I fell into step with them.

"I was wondering—" Angela began.

I paused and looked at her inquisitively. Giving us privacy, the other gals left.

"—if you'll be attending the Grey Isles show this week? Your close friend—the one who's living with you—he's the face of their latest campaign, isn't he?"

It was hard, but I kept my face straight. Why ask me that? What was she getting at? I couldn't tell because her face was clear and innocent, with no sign of guile. Maybe I was looking for a hidden objective that wasn't there. Or I just didn't have the skill set I needed to play her game as well as she did.

Because she was obviously paying attention to me. Not just my relationship with Gideon, but all my relationships. She was following the gossip. Why?

"I don't have plans to attend any of the Fashion Week shows," I replied carefully.

Her smile faded but her eyes lit up, putting me further on edge. "That's a shame. I thought we might go together."

I still couldn't get a read on her, which was driving me a little nuts. She'd seemed nice enough when I met her the first time, but then she had been quiet, letting her husband and the rest of the LanCorp team do all the talking. Would she say outright that her husband had a hatred for mine? Neither she nor Landon had given me any clue there was animosity with Gideon. But then again, it wasn't something that would come up during a request-for-proposal meeting.

Or maybe she didn't know . . . ? Maybe Landon's drive for vengeance was something he kept to himself.

"Not this time," I said. I deliberately kept the door open because I might be able to use it. She could be as clueless and innocuous as she seemed or she could be more cunning. Either way, I wouldn't be making friends with anyone whose husband wished Gideon harm, but *Keep your enemies closer* was an adage for a reason.

She dried her hands quickly and walked with me the rest of the way to the exit. "Maybe some other time."

After the relative quiet of the bathroom, the restaurant was boisterous and noisy, filled with the sounds of voices and clinking silverware atop background music.

We'd just stepped out of the hallway into the main dining room when Ryan Landon climbed out of his booth and stood in front of us. There really wasn't a bad seat in the house, but Landon's wasn't great. Had Gideon known he would be dining at Tableau One? I wouldn't be surprised. After all, my husband had once tracked me down via a credit card I used at one of his nightclubs.

Landon was tall, though not as tall as Gideon. Six feet, maybe, with wavy brown hair and eyes the color of amber. He was alpha-fit and attractive, with an easy smile and quick laugh. I'd found him charming when I met him and attentive to his wife.

"Eva," he said in greeting, his gaze briefly sliding past me to where his wife stood at my back. "What a pleasant surprise."

"Hello, Ryan." I wished I could've caught the look that passed between them. If they were colluding against me, I really needed to know.

"I was just talking about you earlier today. Heard that you've left Waters Field and Leaman."

The warning tingles that hit me in the bathroom intensified. I wasn't prepared to play these dangerous social games.

Gideon had the skill to take on anyone—hell, he ruled the playing field—but I didn't. It took a lot of effort not to look over and see if he was watching us.

On new ground, I winged it. "I miss it already, but then Gideon and I are attached to Mark."

"Yes, I've heard great things about him."

"He really knows his stuff. It was while Mark was working on the Kingsman Vodka campaign that I met Gideon."

Landon's brows shot up. "I wouldn't have guessed that."

I smiled. "You're in great hands. Mark is the best. I'd be more sad about leaving if I didn't know that we'll be working with him again."

He visibly regrouped. "Well . . . We've decided to let LanCorp's in-house team run with it. They really felt like they could knock it out of the park and since that's what I hired them to do, I figured I better let them do it."

"Ah. I look forward to seeing what they come up with." I took a step away. "It was great seeing you both again. Enjoy your lunch."

They wished me good-bye and I turned toward my table, noting that Gideon was deep in conversation with the board members. I thought he wasn't aware of me approaching, but he stood just before I reached the table without even looking.

We said farewell and left the restaurant, with Gideon's hand at the small of my back. I loved when he touched me there, the pressure steady and guiding. Possessive.

Angus waited at the curb with the Bentley. So did the paparazzi, who took the opportunity to get plenty of shots of us. It was a relief to settle in the backseat and blend into traffic.

"Eva."

The rough timbre of Gideon's voice sent goose bumps racing across my skin. I glanced at him, saw the fire in his eyes. Then his hands were cupping my face and his lips were slanting across mine. I gasped, startled by his sudden hunger. His tongue stroked deep into my mouth, stirring the need for him that always simmered in my blood.

"You're beautiful," he said, his hands pushing into my hair. "You're always changing. I never know who I'm going to have from one day to the next."

I laughed, leaning into him and kissing him back with everything I had. I adored the feel of his mouth, the sensual lines softened from their usual sternness when he surrendered to me, making him even more gorgeous. "Gotta keep you on your toes, ace."

Gideon pulled me into his lap, his hands sliding all over me. "I want you."

"I should hope so," I whispered, tracing his bottom lip with the tip of my tongue. "You're stuck with me for life."

"Not long enough." Tilting his head, he took my mouth again, his hand at my nape holding me still as he licked strong and quick. Like fucking. I felt the brush of his tongue everywhere.

I squirmed, achingly aware of Angus. "Gideon."

"Let's go to the penthouse," he breathed, as tempting as the devil. His cock was hard against my buttocks, teasing me with the promise of sex and sin and pleasure too great to bear.

"You have a meeting," I panted.

"Fuck the meeting."

I bit back another laugh and hugged him, pressing my nose in the crook of his neck to breathe him in. He smelled amazing, as he always did. Gideon didn't wear cologne. There was just the clean, primal smell of his skin and faint traces of the body wash he preferred.

"I love the way you smell," I told him softly, nuzzling against him. He was so warm, his body so hot and hard, pulsing with life and energy and power. "There's something about it. It touches something inside me. It's one of the things that tells me you're mine."

He growled. "I'm so fucking hard," he said, his lips to my ear. He nipped my lobe, punishing me for his lust with a small bite of pain.

"I'm so fucking wet," I whispered back. "You made me so happy today."

His chest expanded on an unsteady breath, his hands running up and down my back. "Good."

I pulled back, watching as he steadied himself. He so rarely lost control. It was thrilling I could do that to him. Even more thrilling to know he'd been riding that edge since I first showed up and he hadn't shown any outward clue to the others. His restraint was a major turn-on for me.

My fingertips brushed over his striking face. "Thank you. It's not enough for what you gave me today, but thank you."

His eyes closed. He leaned his forehead against mine. "You're welcome."

"I'm glad you like my hair."

"I like when you feel confident and sexy."

I rubbed my nose against his, my love for him filling me until there was no room for anything else. "What if I need purple hair to feel that way?"

His mouth curved. "Then I'll be fucking a purple-haired wife." His hand covered my heart—and took the opportunity to squeeze my breast. "As long as the inside remains the same, the rest is just wrapping."

I thought about telling him he was straying perilously close to being romantic but decided to keep that to myself.

"Did you see the Landons?" I asked instead.

Gideon pulled back. "They talked to you."

My eyes narrowed. "You knew they'd be there, didn't you?"

"It wasn't a surprise."

"You're so good at being cagey," I complained. "All you guys are. I couldn't figure out if Angela Landon was yanking my chain when she asked to attend the Grey Isles Fashion Week show with me or if she was serious."

"Maybe a little of both. What did you say?"

"That I'm not going." I kissed him, then squirmed back onto my own seat. He resisted, but let me go. "Corinne would've known how to manage her." I sighed. "Probably Magdalene, too. Certainly my mom."

"You did fine. What about Landon?"

My lips pursed. "How tightly do you have Mark locked in?"

He gave me a quizzical look. "What did you do?"

"I mentioned we have a strong connection with Mark, since you and I met while you were working with him. I said we look forward to working with him in the future."

"You want to see if Landon will offer Mark a job."

"I'm curious to see how far Landon will go, yes. I'm not worried about Mark. He's loyal and while he doesn't know the particulars, he knows LanCorp is part of the reason I quit. Plus, he's got an in with the head honcho at Cross Industries. He'd just be a drone at LanCorp. He's not stupid."

Gideon settled back in his seat. If I didn't know him so well, I might have thought he was just getting comfortable. "And you want to see if I was straight with you about Landon's motives."

"No." I set my hand on his thigh and felt the tension there. Both of his parents had let him down. I knew there was a part of Gideon that invariably expected everyone else to do the same. "I believe you. I believed you when you told me. Your word is all the proof I'll ever need."

He looked at me for a long minute, then squeezed my hand. Hard. "Thank you."

"But maybe you felt the need to prove it to me?" I asked gently. "You find out Landon's got a reservation. You want to introduce me to the Crossroads board. Meeting at Tableau One accomplishes two things if I run into Landon while I'm there. Although there was a lot left to faith for that to happen."

"Not if he's seated by the bathrooms."

"Maybe I wouldn't have gone to the bathroom."

Gideon shot me a look.

"It wasn't a foregone conclusion," I argued.

"You're a woman," he countered, as if that answered everything.

My eyes narrowed. "Sometimes I just want to smack you."

"I can't help being right."

"You're deflecting."

His lips tightened for a moment. "You left me because of him. I needed you to see him again after that."

"That's not entirely accurate, but okay. I see what you were after." A little frustrated, I pushed my new bangs out of my face. "I still couldn't get a sense of them, though. He's a little easier to read than his wife, but they both play sincere very well. And they're a team."

"You and I are a team."

"We're getting there. I need to learn how to hold up my end better."

"I have no complaints."

I smiled. "I didn't fuck up, which isn't the same as doing a good job."

His fingers brushed my cheek. "I wouldn't care if you fucked it up, although I'm sure your definition of what that would be is very different from mine. I wouldn't care if you have green hair or purple hair or whatever color you choose, although I'll say I like it blond. *You're* what I want."

Turning my head, I kissed his palm. "Angela looks like Corinne."

He huffed out a surprised laugh. "No, she does not."

"Oh my God, she totally does! I mean, not like twins or anything. But the hair and the body type."

Gideon shook his head. "No."

"Do you think Landon went for someone who looks like your ideal woman?"

"I think your imagination is running away with you." He put his fingers over my lips when I would've said more. "And if not, he got it wrong, so the point is moot."

I wrinkled my nose at him. My clutch vibrated next to my thigh and I reached for it, pulling my phone out.

There was a text from Raúl. *She's at work.*

I glanced at Gideon and found him watching me.

"I asked Raúl to track down Anne today," I told him.

He muttered something under his breath. "You're damned stubborn," he bit out.

"As you pointed out, I feel confident and sexy." I blew him a kiss. "It's a good day to say hi."

His eyes lifted to the rearview mirror. Angus met his gaze and something passed between them. Then my husband turned his brilliantly blue gaze back to me. "You'll do whatever Angus says. If he doesn't think it's a good idea when the time comes, you back off. Understood?"

It took me a beat to reply, because I'd expected more push-back. "Okay."

"And you'll come to the penthouse tonight for dinner."

"When did this become a negotiation?"

He just looked at me, implacable and unwavering.

"I told Cary I'd take him out to dinner, ace. He's been making calls for me today while I've been with you. You're welcome to come along."

"No, thanks. Come over afterward."

"Will you behave?"

His eyes sparkled with mischief. "Only if you do."

I figured if he could have a sense of humor about it, we were making progress. "Deal."

We pulled up in front of the Crossfire and Gideon straightened, preparing to get out. As Angus rounded the car to open the door, I leaned forward and offered my mouth. Cupping my face in both hands, Gideon kissed me, his lips firm and possessive. Unlike the melt-my-panties kiss he'd given me when we left Tableau One, this one was sweeter. And thorough.

I was breathless when he pulled away.

He studied me a moment, then gave a satisfied nod. "Call my cell as soon as you're done."

"What if you're—"

"Call me."

"All right."

Gideon slid out of the back of the Bentley and strode into the Crossfire.

I watched him until I couldn't see him anymore, remembering the first day we met. I'd been inside the lobby then and he'd come back for me. I kept that in mind, knowing it was senseless to feel bereft now, but it was never easy watching him walk away. That was one of my many flaws and something I would have to get over.

I miss you already, I texted to him.

His reply was quick. *I'm glad, angel mine.*

I was laughing as Angus slid in behind the wheel. He looked at me through the rearview mirror. "Where to?"

"Wherever Anne Lucas works."

"She may be working for hours yet."

"I figured. I've got a few things I can handle while I wait. If I run out of things to do, we'll try again some other time."

"Got it." He started the Bentley and took off.

I called Cary.

"Hey," he answered. "How was lunch?"

"It was good." I caught him up.

"Eventful," he said when I finished. "Can't say I get the whole Landon thing, but then I don't understand much of what goes on with your old man. Is there anyone not pissed off at him?"

"Me."

"Right, but you're not banging him."

"Cary, I'm going to kill you, I swear."

His low chuckle rippled over the line. "I got in touch with Blaire. He said he can meet you at the penthouse tomorrow if you like. Just text him a window of time and he'll see what he can do."

"Sweet. How about Kristin?"

"Getting to that, baby girl. She's in the office all day today, so you can call her anytime. Or drop her an e-mail, if that's easier. She's champing at the bit to talk to you."

"I'll call her. You figure out where we're going to dinner yet?"

"I feel like Asian. Chinese, Japanese, Thai . . . something like that."

"Well, all right, then. Asian it is." I leaned my head back against the seat. "Thanks, Cary."

"Happy to help. When are you coming home?"

"Not sure yet. I've got one more thing to do, then I'll head back."

"I'll see you then."

I killed the call as Angus slid into a spot by the curb.

"That's her office across the street," he explained, directing my attention to the brick-faced building on my side. It had several stories and a small, neat lobby visible through glass doors.

I checked it out briefly, imagining her inside with a patient, someone who was baring their most personal secrets without knowing who they were really talking to. That was the way it worked. The mental health professional we trusted knew everything about us, while we only knew what we could discern from photos on desks and degrees on walls.

Scrolling through my contacts, I found Kristin's number and called her office. Her assistant put me through straightaway.

"Hi, Eva. I had you on my list to call, but your friend beat me to it. I've been trying to reach you for a few days now, actually."

"I know. I'm sorry about that."

"No problem. I saw the pictures of you and Cross at the beach. I don't blame you for not calling back. We do need to get together, though, and nail down some details."

"September twenty-second is the date."

There was a pause. "Okay. Wow."

I winced, knowing I was asking a lot on incredibly short notice. And that it was going to cost a pretty penny to get it done in time. "I've decided my mom's right about the white, cream, and gold palette, so let's run with that. I'd like small accents of red. For example, I'll have a neutral bouquet, but my jewelry will be rubies."

"Ooh. Let me think. Maybe red damask skirts beneath white tablecloths . . . ? Or Murano glass chargers under crystal plates . . . I'll pull together some options." She blew out her breath. "I really have to see the location."

"I can arrange for a flight down. When can you go?"

"As soon as possible," Kristen said briskly. "I'm tied up tomorrow evening, but the morning would work."

"I'll work it out and send you the details."

"I'll keep an eye out for it. Eva . . . do you have your dress?"

"Uh . . . no."

She laughed. When she spoke again, the tension I'd heard before was gone. "I completely understand wanting to hurry things along with a man like yours, but more time would help make sure everything runs smoothly and you have your perfect day."

"It'll be perfect no matter what might go wrong." I rubbed

the back of my ring with my thumb, taking comfort from its presence on my hand. "It's Gideon's birthday."

"Whew. Okay, then. We'll make it happen."

My mouth curved. "Thank you. Talk to you soon."

I hung up and looked at the building across the street. Next door was a small café. I'd walk over and get a latte after I contacted the designer.

I sent Gideon a text. *Who should I talk to about flying the wedding planner down to the Outer Banks house tomorrow AM?*

It felt a little weird to ask the question. Who would've thought I'd ever have private jets at my disposal? I wasn't sure I'd ever be blasé about using them.

I waited a minute for a reply. When it didn't come, I called Blaire Ash.

"Hi, Blaire," I said, when he answered. "It's Eva Tramell, Gideon Cross's fiancée."

"Eva. Of course I know who you are." His voice was warm and friendly. "It's good to hear from you."

"I'd like to go over some of the design details with you. Cary said you can meet tomorrow?"

"Sure. What time works for you?"

Thinking of the trip to the Outer Banks with Kristin, I answered, "Would evening work? Say six-ish?"

Gideon would be with Dr. Petersen until at least seven o'clock. Then he'd have to commute home. That gave me enough time to switch some things up with our design plans.

"That works for me," Blair agreed. "I'll meet you at the penthouse?"

"Yes, I'll see you there. Thanks. Bye."

The second I ended the call, my phone buzzed. Looking

at the screen, I saw Gideon's reply: *Scott's making the arrangements.*

I chewed my lower lip, feeling bad for not going through Scott first. *I'll ask him next time. Thank you!* ☺

I took a deep breath, feeling like I should reach out to Gideon's mother, Elizabeth.

In the front seat, Angus's phone pinged. He lifted it, then looked back at me. "She's on her way down in the elevator."

"Oh!" Surprise turned to bafflement. How did he know that? I glanced at the building again. Did Gideon own that one, too? Like he owned the building her husband worked in?

"Here, lass." Angus reached into the backseat and offered a small black disk the size of a quarter and three times as thick. "It's sticky on one side. Tuck that into the strap of your dress."

I shoved my phone in my purse and took the disk, staring at it. "What is this? A microphone?"

"It's either that or I come with you." He gave me an apologetic smile. "It's not you that's the worry, it's her."

Since I had nothing to hide, I stuck the mic inside my bra and hopped out of the back when Angus opened the door. He grabbed my arm securely, then hurried me across the street.

He winked at me before retreating to the café.

I was suddenly standing alone on the sidewalk, struck by a wicked case of nerves. They were gone a second later when Anne pushed out of the lobby. Dressed in a leopard-print wrap dress and black Louboutins, she looked fierce and vibrant with her spiky red hair.

Tucking my clutch under my arm, I started walking toward her.

"What are the chances?" I asked, as I got close to her.

She glanced at me, her hand raised to hail a cab. For a moment, there was blankness on her foxlike face, and then recognition hit her. Her shock was worth the price of admission. Her arm fell to her side.

I gave her a once-over. "You should ditch the wig you've been wearing around Cary. The short hair suits you better."

Anne recovered quickly. "Eva. Don't you look pretty? Gideon is polishing you up nicely."

"Yeah, he polishes me a lot. Every chance he gets." That got her attention. "Can't get enough, actually. He's got nothing left for you, so I suggest you find someone else to be crazy over."

Her face hardened. I realized I'd never seen true hatred before. Even in the heat of the New York summer, I felt a chill.

"You're so clueless"—she stepped closer—"when he's probably fucking someone else at this very moment. That's who he is and what he does."

"You have no idea who he is." I hated having to tilt my head back to look up at her. "I don't have any worries about him. You, however, should be worried about me. Because if you come near him or Cary again, you'll be dealing with me. It won't be pleasant."

I turned away from her. I'd done what I came to do.

"He's a monster," she called out. "Did he tell you he's been in therapy since he was a child?"

That stopped me. I rounded on her.

She grinned. "He's been broken from birth. He's sick and twisted in ways he hasn't shown you yet. He's thinking he can hide it from you, his pretty little girl who creates just the right fairy tale. Beauty and the beast for the masses. A clever cover-up, but it won't hold. He can't suppress his true nature for long."

My God . . . Did she know about Hugh?

How could she know that Gideon was a victim of her brother's perversions and have sex with him anyway? It made me so sick to think of it, bile rose in my throat.

Her laugh slid over me like shards of glass. "Gideon is vicious and cruel at his core. He'll break you before he's done with you. If he doesn't kill you first."

My back straightened, my hands fisting at my sides. I was so angry I was shaking with it, fighting the urge to punch her in her smug, nasty face.

"Who do you think monsters marry, you stupid bitch?" I walked back to her. "Pretty little breakable girls? Or other monsters?"

I pushed up into her face. "You got the fairy tale right. But Gideon's the beauty. *I'm* the beast."

6

"YOU THINK GIDEON'S SCARY? Wait 'til you get a load of me."

I sat still as stone for a long minute, Eva's voice echoing in my ears as the recording ended. My gaze lifted from my desk to Angus's face. "Jesus."

We had looked for any case files Hugh might've kept about me. None were found and we assumed he hadn't kept records. It made sense. Why document your crimes?

"I'll look again," Angus said quietly. "Her homes and office. Her husband's office. Everywhere. I'll find them."

I nodded, pushing back from my desk. I sucked in a deep breath and fought off a wave of nausea. There was nothing I could do but wait.

I walked to the nearest window and looked at the building that housed LanCorp's offices.

"Eva handled her well," he said behind me. "She put the fear of God in Anne. I saw it on her face."

I had eschewed viewing the available security video footage in favor of listening to the audio of their meeting, but it was enough. I knew my wife, her voice and inflections. Knew her temper. And I knew that nothing roused it as swiftly or ferociously as when she was leaping to my defense.

Over the short time we'd been together, Eva had managed direct confrontations with Corinne at her home, my mother on multiple occasions, Terrence Lucas at his office, and now his wife at hers. I knew my wife felt she had to, which was why I'd forced myself to step back and let her do it.

I didn't need defending. Could take care of myself just fine on my own, as I always had. But it felt good to know I wasn't on my own any longer. Better still to know she could look crazy in the face and frighten it.

"She's a tigress." I faced him. "I've got a few badges of honor from her scratches myself."

The hard, tense line of Angus's shoulders relaxed slightly. "She'll stand by you."

"If my past goes public? Yes, she will."

As I said the words, I realized how true they were. There had been times in our relationship when I hadn't been certain I could hold on to Eva. I loved my wife and had no doubts she loved me as deeply, but as perfect as she was for me, she had her flaws. She doubted herself too often. She believed, at times, that she wasn't strong enough to face certain situations. And when she felt her independence and equanimity threatened, she ran away to protect herself.

My gaze went to the picture of her on my desk. Things had changed and only recently. She'd pushed me to the edge, cutting me off from the one thing I could not live without—her. I'd tumbled off that edge reluctantly, forced to do so to get her back. The result: She no longer looked at our marriage as her and me but *us*. My initial resentment was gone. No matter what, I would do it again to keep her, but now, I would do it without the push.

"She loves that I can take care of her, keep her safe," I said, mostly to myself. "But if I lost everything, she'd still be here. It's *me* she wants, as fucked up as I am."

The money . . . the public image . . . They weren't important to her.

"You're not fucked up, lad. Too pretty for your own good, to be certain." Angus's mouth twisted wryly. "And ye've made some dubious choices when it comes to the lasses, but who hasn't? Hard to say nay when you're randy and they're lifting their skirts."

Amused by his blunt comments, I pushed thoughts of Anne Lucas aside. Worrying would get me nowhere. Angus would do what he was so very good at. I would focus on my wife and our life as it now was.

"Where is Eva now?" I asked him.

"Raúl is driving her to Parker Smith's studio in Brooklyn."

I nodded, understanding that Eva needed to work off some steam. "Thank you, Angus."

He left and I returned to my desk to get my day back on track. I'd shuffled a dozen things to fit in the Crossroads lunch with Eva and now I had to catch up.

My smartphone buzzed, rattling atop the smoked glass of my desktop. I glanced at it, hoping to see Eva's face on the screen and seeing my sister, Ireland's, instead. I felt a familiar momentary twinge of discomfort, something mildly akin to panic, just before I answered the call.

I couldn't see how being in my teenage sister's life bene-fited her at all, but Eva felt it was important for some reason and so I made the effort for her.

"Ireland. To what do I owe the pleasure?"

"Gideon." She hiccupped violently, her voice clogged with tears.

I immediately tensed, the first surge of fury bristling along my spine. "What's wrong?"

"I c-came home from school and Dad was waiting for me. They're getting a divorce."

I circled my desk and sank into my chair. The anger drained away.

Before I could say anything, she rushed on.

"I don't understand!" She wept. "A couple weeks ago everything was fine. Then they started arguing all the time and Dad moved into a hotel. Something happened but nei-ther of them will tell me what it is! Mom won't stop crying. Dad doesn't, but his eyes are always red when I see him."

My stomach knotted up all over again. My breath came fast and quick.

Chris knew. About Hugh and me. About Terrence Lucas's lies, covering up his brother-in-law's crime. About my mother's refusal to believe me, to fight for me, to save me.

"Ireland . . ."

"Do you think he's having an affair? He's the one insti-gating all of this. Mom says he's confused. She says he'll come around, but I don't think so. He acts like his mind is totally made up. Can you talk to him?"

I gripped the phone too tightly. "And say what?"

Hello, Chris. Sorry I was raped and your wife can't handle it.

Bummer about the divorce. No chance you could forgive her and live happily ever after?

Just thinking about Chris going on with his life, with his wife, as if nothing had happened filled me with rage. Someone knew. Someone cared. Someone couldn't live with it any more than I. I wouldn't change that even if I could.

Something small and cold inside me enjoyed the reckoning. Finally.

"There has to be something, Gideon! People don't go from being madly in love to filing for divorce in less than a month!"

God. I rubbed at the back of my neck, where a vicious headache clawed at me. "Maybe counseling."

A harsh, humorless laugh burned in my throat, silenced. A therapist had started all of this. How fucking ironic for me to suggest seeing another one to figure it out.

Ireland sniffled. "Mom said Dad suggested it, but she won't go."

The mirthless snicker escaped me then. What would Dr. Petersen say if he could see into that mind of hers? Would he pity her? Feel disgust? Anger? Maybe he wouldn't feel anything at all. I was no different from any other molested child and she was no different from any other weak, self-absorbed woman.

"I'm sorry, Ireland." Sorrier than I could ever tell her. How would she feel about me if she knew this was all my fault? Maybe she would hate me, too, like our brother Christopher.

The thought tightened my chest like a vise.

Christopher couldn't stand me, but he loved Ireland and

was invested in the relationship between their parents. I was the outsider. Always had been. "Have you talked to Christopher?"

"He's as torn up as Mom is. I mean, I'm a mess, but the two of them . . . I've never seen them so upset."

I pushed to my feet again, too restless to sit. *What should I do, Eva? What could I say? Why aren't you here when I need you?*

"Your father isn't having an affair," I said, offering her what comfort I could. "He's not the type."

"Then why did he file for divorce?"

I exhaled roughly. "Why does anyone quit a marriage? It's not working."

"After all these years, he decides he's not happy and that's it? He quits?"

"He suggested therapy and she said no."

"So it's her fault he's suddenly got a problem with her?"

The voice was Ireland's, but the words were my mother's. "If you're trying to find someone to blame, I won't help with that."

"You don't care if they stay together. You probably think it's stupid I'm so upset at my age."

"That's not true. You have every right to be upset."

I glanced at the door to my office when Scott appeared on the other side of it, nodding to acknowledge him when he tapped the face of his watch. He went back to his desk.

"Then help them fix it, Gideon!"

"Jesus. I don't know why you think I can do anything."

She started crying again.

I cursed silently, hating to hear her in so much pain, knowing I'd caused some of it. "Sweetheart . . ."

"Can you at least try to talk some sense into them?"

My eyes closed. I was the goddamned problem, which made it impossible for me to be part of the solution. But I couldn't say that. "I'll call them."

"Thank you." She sniffled again. "I love you."

A small sound escaped me, the blow of her words sending me reeling. She hung up before I could find my voice, leaving me with the sense of an opportunity lost.

I set my phone back down on my desk and fought the urge to throw it across the room.

Scott opened the door and poked his head in. "Everyone's ready for you in the conference room."

"I'm coming."

"Also, Mr. Vidal would like you to call him when you can."

I gave a curt nod but growled inwardly at the sound of my stepfather's name. "I'll get back to him."

It was nearing nine in the evening when Raúl texted me to let me know Eva was on her way up to the penthouse. I left my home office and went to meet her in the foyer, my brows arching in surprise when she stepped out holding a big box in both hands. Raúl stood behind her carrying a duffel bag.

She grinned at me as I took the box from her. "Brought some stuff to invade your space."

"Invade away," I told her, captivated by the bright, mischievous light in her gray eyes.

Raúl deposited the duffel on the living room floor, then slipped away quietly, leaving us alone. I followed Eva with my gaze, taking in the dark jeans that hugged every curve and the loose silk blouse she'd tucked into them. She was wearing flats, which left her nearly a foot shorter than I was in my bare feet. Her hair fell around her shoulders, framing her face, which was scrubbed free of makeup.

She tossed her purse onto the wingback chair nearest the front door. As she kicked off her shoes by the coffee table, she looked at me, her gaze sliding over my bare chest and black silk pajama bottoms. "You said you were going to behave, ace."

"Well, considering I haven't even kissed you yet, I think I'm being very well behaved." I walked to the dining room table and set the box down, looking inside it to see a collection of framed photos swathed in bubble wrap. "How was dinner?"

"Tasty. I wish Tatiana weren't pregnant, but I think it's making Cary reevaluate and grow up a little bit. That's a good thing."

I knew better than to offer my opinion on that, so I just gave a nod. "Should I open a bottle of wine?"

Her smile lit up the room. "That would be great."

When I returned to the living room a few moments later, I found the fireplace mantel decorated with a collection of photographs. The montage I'd given her to keep at work was there, showcasing images of us together. There were also pictures of Cary, Monica, Stanton, Victor, and Ireland.

And a framed image of my father and me on the shore long ago, one that I'd shared with her when we signed the purchase contract on the beach house in the Outer Banks.

I sipped from my glass, taking in the change. There were no other personal items in the main living space, so the al-

teration was . . . profound. She'd also chosen brilliantly colored mosaic glass frames, which sparkled and drew the eye.

"Are your bachelor self-preservation warnings going off
yet?" Eva teased, taking the glass I held out to her.

Amused, I glanced at her. "It's too late to scare me off."

"You sure about that? I'm just getting started."

"It's about time."

"Okay, then." She shrugged, then took a drink of the
pinot noir I'd selected. "I was willing to pacify you with a
blowjob, if you started freaking out."

My dick thickened and lengthened. "Now that you mention it . . . I am feeling a little cold sweat—"

A furry ball rolled out from beneath the coffee table,
jolting me so hard I nearly spilled red wine onto the Aubus-
son rug beneath my feet. "What the hell is that?"

The ball shook itself out and became a puppy not much
bigger in size than my shoes. It stumbled toward me on
shaky legs. Mostly black and tan with a white belly, it had
huge ears that flopped around a sweet face alight with joy
and excitement.

"He's yours," my wife said, with laughter in her voice. "Isn't
he adorable?"

Speechless, I watched as the tiny dog made it to my feet
and began licking my toes.

"Aww, he likes you." She set her glass onto the coffee
table and sank down on her knees, reaching out to rub the
puppy's silky head.

Confused, I looked around and noticed what I hadn't
before. The duffel bag Raúl had carried in had ventilation
mesh on the top and sides.

"Oh my God, you should see your face!" Eva laughed and

picked up the dog, rising to her feet. She took my glass and shoved the puppy at me instead.

I caught the squirming bundle of fur because I had no choice, arching my head back when it started licking madly at my face. "I can't have a puppy."

"Sure you can."

"I don't want a puppy."

"Sure you do."

"Eva . . . No."

She took my wine to the sofa and sat, curling her legs beneath her. "Now the penthouse won't feel so empty until I move in."

I stared at her. "I don't need a dog. I need my wife."

"Now you have both." She drank from my glass and licked her lips. "What will you name him?"

"I can't have a puppy," I repeated.

Eva looked at me serenely. "He's an anniversary gift from your wife, you have to keep him."

"Anniversary?"

"We've been married a month." She leaned back into the sofa and gave me the fuck-me look. "I was thinking we could go to the beach house and celebrate."

I readjusted my hold on the wriggling dog. "Celebrate how?"

"All access."

I was hard instantly, something she didn't fail to notice.

Her gaze darkened as it caressed my erection where it tented my pants. "I'm dying, Gideon," she breathed, her lips and cheeks flushing pink. "I wanted to wait, but I can't. I need you. And it's our anniversary. If we can't make love then and have it be just you, me, and what we have—with no bullshit—then we can't make love ever and I don't believe that's true."

I stared at her.

Her lips curved wryly. "If that makes any sense at all."

The puppy licked my jaw frantically and I hardly noticed, my attention focused on my wife. She just kept surprising me, in all the best ways. "Lucky."

Her head tilted to the side. "What?"

"That's his name. Lucky."

Eva laughed. "You're a fiend, ace."

❧

By the time Eva went home, I had new dog crates in my bedroom and home office, and fancy water and feed bowls in my kitchen. Puppy food in an airtight plastic storage container sat in my pantry, and plush dog beds took up space in every room in the house. There was even a patch of fake grass, which supposedly Lucky would urinate on—when he wasn't relieving himself on my priceless rugs, as he'd done not long ago.

All the items, including treats, toys, and enzymatic sprays for accidents, had been left waiting in the foyer outside the elevator, telling me that my wife had enlisted Raúl and Angus in her plan to foist a pet on me.

I stared at the puppy, who sat at my feet, looking up at me with soft, dark eyes filled with something akin to adoration. "What the hell am I supposed to do with a dog?"

Lucky's tail wagged so hard, his back end shifted from side to side along with it.

When I'd asked Eva the same question, she'd laid out her

plan: Lucky would ride with me to work, and then Angus would drop him off at doggy daycare—who knew there was such a thing?—and pick him up in time to ride home with me.

The real answer was written in the note she'd left on my pillow.

My dearest Dark and Dangerous,

Dogs are excellent judges of character. I'm certain the adorable beagle you now own will worship you nearly as much as I do, because he'll see what I see in you: fierce protectiveness, thoughtfulness, and loyalty. You're an alpha through and through, so he'll obey you when I don't. (I'm sure you'll appreciate that!) In time, you'll get used to being loved unconditionally by him and me and everyone else in your life.

Yours always and forever,

Mrs. X

Rising up onto his back legs, Lucky pawed at my shin, whining softly.

"Needy little thing, aren't you?" I picked him up and tolerated the inevitable face licking. He smelled faintly of Eva's perfume, so I pressed my nose into him.

Owning a pet had never been on my wish list. Then again, neither was having a wife and that was the best thing to ever happen to me.

Holding Lucky away from me, I eyed him consideringly. Eva had put a red leather collar on him with an engraved brass plate. *Happy Anniversary.* Next to that was the date of our wedding, so I couldn't give him away.

"We're stuck with each other," I told him, which made

him bark and wiggle harder. "You may regret that more than me."

⧽⧼

Sitting alone in my bedroom, I can hear Mom yelling. Dad pleads with her, then shouts back. They turned the television on before they slammed their bedroom door shut, but it's not loud enough to cover their fighting.

Lately, they fight all the time.

I pick up the remote to my favorite radio-controlled car and drive it into the wall, over and over. It doesn't help.

Mom and Dad love each other. They look at each other for a long time, smiling, like they forget anyone else is around. They touch each other a lot. Holding hands. Kissing. They kiss a lot. It's gross, but it's better than the screaming and crying they've been doing the last couple of weeks. Even Dad, who's always smiling and laughing, has been sad. His eyes are red all the time and he hasn't shaved the hair off his face in days.

I'm scared they're going to split up, like my friend Kevin's parents did.

The sun goes down slowly, but the fighting doesn't stop. Mom's voice is hoarse now and scratchy from tears. Glass breaks. Something heavy hits the wall and makes me jump. It's been a long time since lunch and my stomach is growling, but I'm not hungry. I really feel like throwing up.

The only light in my room comes from the television, which is showing some boring movie I don't like. I hear my parents' bedroom door open, then shut. A few minutes later, the front door opens and shuts, too. Our apartment goes all quiet in a way that makes me feel sick again.

When my bedroom door finally opens, Mom stands there like a shadow with light shining all around her. She asks me why I'm sitting in the dark, but I don't answer her. I'm mad at her for being so mean to Dad. He never starts the fights, it's always her. About something she saw on television or read in the paper or heard from her friends. They're all talking bad about Dad, saying things I know aren't true.

My dad isn't a liar or a thief. Mom should know that. She shouldn't listen to other people who don't know him like we do.

"Gideon."

Mom flips the lights on and I jerk in surprise. She's older. She smells like stale milk and baby powder.

My room is different. My toys are gone. The carpet beneath me is now a rug over stone floors. My hands are bigger.

I stand and I'm the same height as her.

"What?" I snap, crossing my arms.

"You have to stop this." She swipes at the tears streaming from her eyes. "You can't keep acting like this."

"Get out." The sickness in my gut spreads, dampening my palms until I clench them into fists.

"These lies have to stop! We have a new life now, a good life. Chris is a good man."

"This doesn't have anything to do with Chris," I bite out, wanting to hit something. I never should have said anything. I don't know why I thought anyone would believe me.

"You can't—"

I jerked upright, panting, the sheet in my hands tearing violently. It took a moment for the pounding of my blood to subside as I tuned in to the incessant barking that woke me.

Scrubbing at my face, I cursed, then jumped as Lucky scrambled up the hanging comforter, pulling himself onto the bed. He leaped, tackling me in the chest.

"For fuck's sake, calm down!"

He whined and curled into my lap, making me feel like a dick.

I caught him up, holding him against my sweaty chest. "Sorry," I muttered, stroking his head.

Closing my eyes, I pushed back and leaned against the headboard, willing my pulse to slow. It took several minutes to get my bearings, and about that long to realize that petting Lucky was calming me down.

I laughed to myself, then reached for my phone on the nightstand. The time, a little after two in the morning, gave me pause. So did the need to be strong, to handle my own crap.

But a lot had happened since I first called Eva to talk about a nightmare. Good things.

"Hey," Eva answered, sounding groggy and sexy. "You okay?"

"Better now that I'm hearing your voice."

"You having puppy troubles? Or a nightmare? Maybe you're feeling frisky?"

Calm settled over me. I'd been braced for a push. Seemed she was going to ease me into it, instead. Yet another reason for me to try harder to give her what she wanted, regardless of my first instincts about it. Because when Eva was happy, I was happy. "Maybe all of the above."

"Okay." Sheets rustled. "Take it from the top, ace."

"If I latch the crate door, Lucky bitches about it and I can't sleep."

She laughed. "You're a softie. He's got your number. Did you put him in your office?"

"No. He barks in there and I still can't sleep. I ended up just closing the crate door without locking it and he settled down."

"He's not going to learn to control his bladder if you don't crate-train him."

I looked down at the beagle curled up and sleeping in my lap. "He woke me from a nightmare. I think he did it on purpose."

She was quiet a minute. "Tell me about it."

I did and she listened. "He'd been trying to jump up to the bed earlier and couldn't make it," I finished. "He's too little and the bed's too high. But he hauled his ass up here to wake me."

Her exhale drifted across the line. "Guess he can't sleep when you're making noise, either."

It took me a second, then I laughed. The lingering distress from the dream dissipated like smoke in a breeze. "I feel the sudden urge to take you over my knee and spank you, angel."

Amusement warmed her voice. "Try it, babe. See what happens."

I knew what would happen. She was the one who couldn't see it. Yet.

"Going back to your dream . . ." she murmured, "I know I've said it before, but I'll say it again. I really think you need to bring Hugh up to your mother again. I know it'll be painful, but I think it has to be done."

"It won't change anything."

"You don't know that for sure."

"I do." I shifted and Lucky gave a protesting grunt. "I didn't get around to telling you earlier. Chris filed for divorce."

"What? When?"

"I'm not sure. I just heard about it today from Ireland. I talked to Chris after work, but he just went over their pre-nup and let me know that he wanted to make some added concessions. We didn't discuss his reasons for wanting to end the marriage."

"Do you think it's because he found out about Hugh?"

I sighed, grateful I could talk to her about it. "I think it's too much of a coincidence to be totally unrelated."

"Wow." She cleared her throat. "I think I really love your stepfather."

I couldn't say how I felt about Chris. I didn't know. "When I think about my mother being upset about this . . . I can picture it, Eva. I've seen it before."

"I know you have."

"I hate it. I hated her like that. It hurt me to see her that way."

"You love her. That's okay."

And I loved Eva. For her lack of judgment. Her unquali-fied devotion. It gave me the courage to say, "I'm also glad. What kind of asshole feels good that his mother is hurting?"

There was a long pause. "She hurt you. She's *still* hurt-ing you. It's a natural animal instinct to want to see her wounded, too. But I think what you're glad about is having a . . . champion. Someone who's telling her it really did hap-pen to you and it's not okay."

My eyes closed. If I had a champion, it was my wife.

"Do you want me to come back over?" she asked.

I almost said no. My routine after a nightmare was a long shower, followed by losing myself in work. It was what I knew, how I dealt with it. But soon she'd be living with me, sharing my life in a way I needed but wasn't wholly prepared for. I had to start making adjustments for that.

More than the logistics, though, was that I wanted her right then. Wanted to see her, smell her, feel her close.

"I'll come get you," I told her. "I'll take a quick shower and text you before I head out."

"Okay. I'll be ready. I love you, Gideon."

I took a deep breath, let the words flow through me. "I love you, too, angel."

~~~

I woke again with the sun, feeling rested despite the hours I'd spent awake. Stretching, I felt something warm and furry shift against my arm, then the lash of a friendly tongue against my biceps.

Opening one eye, I glanced at Lucky. "Can't you keep that thing in your mouth?"

Eva rolled onto her back and smiled, her eyes still closed. "Can't blame him. You're extremely, lickably delicious."

"Bring *your* tongue over here, then."

Her head turned my way and her eyes opened. Her hair was mussed and her cheeks pink.

I grabbed Lucky and tucked him against my stomach as I rolled to my side. Propping my head on one hand, I took in the sight of my sleepy wife, feeling a rare contentment just from starting the day with her in my bed.

Fact was, I shouldn't have risked it. Eva hadn't seen the state of my sheets, since I changed them before leaving to get her, but they were only a small sample of the damage I could cause when sleeping. Neither Lucky nor my wife was safe near me while I was sleeping. It was only because I never had multiple nightmares in one night that I'd taken the chance.

And because I missed Eva fiercely. She wasn't alone in her craving.

"I'm glad you called me," she murmured.

Reaching over, I brushed my fingertips down her cheek. "Didn't turn out so badly."

She moved slightly and kissed my hand.

Eva saw the worst there was in me and loved me more each time she did. I'd stopped questioning it. I just had to deserve her and I would. I had a lifetime to work on it.

"You're not planning any more ambushes on enemies today, are you?" I asked.

"No." She stretched, drawing my eye to where her full tits strained against the ribbed cotton of her tank top. "But I'm ready if someone decides to ambush me."

I dropped Lucky to the floor and snatched Eva close, rolling on top of her. Her legs widened instinctively and I settled between them, circling my hips to rock my cock against her cunt.

She gasped and grabbed my shoulders, her eyes wide. "I wasn't talking about you, ace."

"I'm not someone?" I buried my face in the warmth of her neck, nuzzling her. She smelled heavenly, soft and sweet. Totally sexy. Hard, I rubbed against her, feeling the heat of her through her underwear and the silk of my pants. She softened for me, melted in the way that turned me on ferociously.

"No," she whispered, her eyes darkening. She reached down and grabbed my ass, digging her nails in, urging me on. "You're The One. The only one for me."

As luxurious and feminine as Eva was, she'd grown stronger through Krav Maga. That turned me on, too. My head lowered, my mouth brushing over hers. My heart pounded, struggling to accept what she meant to me. The way she made me feel was so fresh and new, yet would never get old.

Maybe that was why I'd gone through everything I had, so I would be able to appreciate her when I found her. I would never take her for granted.

A tongue that wasn't my wife's licked my side, tickling me. I jerked, cursing, and Eva laughed.

I glared over my shoulder at the little offender, who hopped with excitement, tail wagging madly. "Listen, Lucky. You're not living up to your name."

Eva giggled. "He's helping you live up to your promise to behave."

I turned my glare back to the wife whose nails were still firmly dug into my ass. "Which had the caveat that you behave as well."

Pulling her hands away, Eva held them up by her head, waggling her fingers. But her gaze was hot and her lips parted with rapid breaths. She shivered beneath me, even while her skin felt feverish. Her desire for me soothed my own raging need. And her commitment to waiting, now that I knew the reason for it, gave me the strength to move away.

It was physically painful to separate from her. Her low

moan of anguish echoed inside me, reflecting my own. I flopped onto my back and was immediately subjected to a tongue bath, Lucky-style.

"He really loves you." Eva rolled onto her side and reached out to scratch behind his ears. That had the welcome effect of luring him over to her. Her squeal of laughter as Lucky proceeded to slather her face made me smile despite my aching dick.

I could complain about the damn dog, lack of sex and sleep, and more. But really, my life was as close to perfect as I could want.

~·~

Once I got to work, I powered through my morning.

The release of the new GenTen gaming console was imminent and while speculation was rampant, we had managed to keep the virtual reality component a secret. VR was in development everywhere, but Cross Industries was years ahead of the competition. I knew decisively that LanCorp's PhazeOne system was simply an overhaul, with advanced optics and increased speed. It could compete with the previous-generation GenTen, but that was all.

Shortly before lunch, I took the time to call my mother.

"Gideon." She sighed tremulously. "I suppose you heard?"

"Yes. I'm sorry." I could tell she was hurting. "If you need anything, please let me know."

"Chris is the one who suddenly isn't happy in our marriage," she said bitterly. "And it's all my fault, of course."

I softened my tone, but spoke firmly. "Not to be insensitive, but the details don't concern me. How are you?"

"Talk to him." The plea was heartfelt. Her voice cracked. "Tell him he's made a mistake."

I debated how to answer. The assistance I offered was fiduciary, not personal. There was nothing personal left in my relationship with my mother. Still, I found myself saying, "You won't want my advice, but I'll offer it anyway. You might want to consider therapy."

There was a pause. "I can't believe *you*, of all people, would suggest that."

"Preaching what I practice." My gaze slid to the photo of my wife, as it so often did during my day. "Eva suggested couples counseling shortly after we began dating. She wanted something more out of our relationship. I wanted her, so I agreed. Initially, I was just going through the motions, but now I can say it's been really worthwhile."

"She started all of this," she hissed. "You're such a smart man, Gideon, but you can't see what she's doing."

"And this is where I say good-bye, Mother," I replied before she got me riled. "Call if you need anything."

I hung up, then spun in my chair, making a slow revolution all the way around. The disappointment and anger that always accompanied interactions with my mother was there, simmering, but I was more aware of it than usual. Maybe because I'd so recently dreamed of her, reliving the moment when I had realized she would never come around, was *deliberately* choosing to turn a blind eye for reasons I would never comprehend.

For years, I made excuses for her. I manufactured dozens of reasons for her refusal to protect me to give myself some comfort. Until I realized she was doing the same thing in reverse, making up stories about why I'd lie about being abused so she could live with her decision to pretend it never happened. So I stopped.

She had failed me as a mother but preferred to believe I'd failed her as a son.

And so it went.

When I faced my desk again, I picked up the phone and called my brother.

"What do you want?" he answered.

I could picture the scowl on his face. A face very unlike mine. Of my mother's three children, only Christopher resembled his father more than he did our mom.

His acrimony had the predictable effect of making me want to bait him. "The pleasure of hearing your voice. What else?"

"Cut the shit, Gideon. Did you call to gloat? Your fondest wish has finally come true."

Leaning back in my chair, I looked up at the ceiling. "I'd tell you I'm very sorry your parents are divorcing, but you wouldn't believe me, so I won't bother. Instead, I'll say that I'm here for you, if you need me."

"Go to hell." He hung up.

I pulled the receiver away from my ear and held it aloft a moment. Contrary to Christopher's belief, I hadn't always disliked him. There had been a time when I welcomed him in my life. For a short time, I'd had a comrade. A brother. The animosity I felt now, he'd earned. But no matter, I would take care of him and see that he didn't stumble too badly, whether he liked it or not.

Returning the handset to its cradle, I got back to work.

After all, I couldn't have anything pressing over the weekend. I planned to be completely incommunicado while with my wife.

～◎〇◇～

I studied Dr. Petersen, who sat completely at ease across from me. He wore dark, loose jeans with a tucked-in white shirt, as comfortable as I'd ever seen him. I wondered if that was a deliberate decision in an effort to seem as innocuous as possible. He knew my history with therapists now, understood why I would always find them threatening to some degree.

"How did your weekend in Westport go?" he asked.

"Did she call you?" In the past, when Eva wanted to make sure I discussed something in therapy, she would bring it up to Dr. Petersen in advance. I grumbled about it and often didn't appreciate it, but her motivation was her love for me and I couldn't bitch about that.

"No." He smiled, and it was gentle, almost fond. "I saw the photographs of you and Eva."

That surprised me. "I wouldn't have taken you for the type to follow the tabloids."

"My wife does. She showed me the pictures because she found them very romantic. I have to agree with her. You both looked very happy."

"We are."

"How do you get along with Eva's family?"

I settled back, draping my arm over the armrest. "I've known Richard Stanton for many years and Monica for the last few."

"Casual and business acquaintances are very different from in-laws."

His perceptiveness rankled. Still, I was honest. "It was . . . awkward. Unnecessarily so, but I dealt with it."

Dr. Petersen's smile widened. "How did you deal with it?"

"I focused on Eva."

"So you maintained distance from the others?"

"No more than usual."

He scribbled notes into his tablet. "Anything else happen since I saw you on Thursday?"

My mouth twisted wryly. "She bought me a dog. A puppy."

He looked up at me. "Congratulations."

I shrugged. "Eva's tickled by the whole thing."

"Is it her dog, then?"

"No. She got all the gear and dropped him in my lap."

"That's quite a commitment."

"He'll be fine. Animals are good at self-sufficiency." Because he waited with expectant patience, I moved on. "My stepfather filed for divorce."

Dr. Petersen's head tilted a little as he studied me. "We've gone from in-laws, to a new dog, to the dissolution of your parents' marriage in the space of a few minutes. That's a tremendous amount of change for someone who strives for structure."

That was stating the obvious, so I didn't add anything.

"You seem remarkably composed, Gideon. Because things are going well with Eva?"

"Exceptionally well." I knew the contrast to last week's therapy session was striking. I'd been wild with panic over the separation from Eva, terrified and frantic that I might lose her. I could recall the feelings with anguished clarity, but I had difficulty accepting how quickly I had . . . unraveled. I didn't recognize that desperate man, couldn't reconcile him with what I knew about myself.

He nodded slowly. "Of the three things you mentioned, how would you rank them from most important to least important?"

"That would depend on your definition of importance."

"Fair enough. Which would you say impacts you most?"

"The dog."

"Does he or she have a name?"

I held back a smile. "His name is Lucky."

He noted that, for whatever reason. "Would you buy Eva a pet?"

The question took me aback. I answered without really thinking about it. "No."

"Why not?"

I considered that a minute. "As you pointed out, it's a commitment."

"Are you resentful that she made you take on that commitment?"

"No."

"Do you have any pictures of Lucky?"

I frowned. "No. Where are you going with this?"

"I'm not sure." He set his tablet aside and held my gaze. "Bear with me a minute."

"Okay."

"Taking on a pet is a big responsibility, similar to adopting a child. They're dependent on you for food and shelter, for companionship and love. Dogs more so than cats or other animals."

"So I've been told," I said dryly.

"You have the family you were born into and the family you've married into, but you keep yourself separate from both. Their activities and overtures don't impact you in a meaningful way because you don't allow them to. They're disruptive to the order of your life, so you keep them at a comfortable distance."

"I don't see anything wrong with that. I'm certainly not the only person to say family is who you choose."

"Who have you chosen, aside from Eva?"

"It . . . wasn't a choice."

I pictured her in my mind the way she'd been when I first saw her. She had been dressed to work out, her face naturally bare, her amazing body hugged by form-fitting fitness gear. Just like thousands of other women on the island of Manhattan, but she'd struck me like lightning without even knowing I was there.

"My concern is that she's become a coping mechanism for you," Dr. Petersen said. "You've found someone who loves you and believes you, who supports you and gives you strength. In many ways, you feel like she's the only one who will ever truly understand you."

"She's in a unique position to do so."

"Not that unique," he said kindly. "I've read the transcripts of some of your speeches. You're aware of the statistics."

Yes, I knew that one in every four women I met had been exposed to sexual abuse. That didn't change the fact that none of them had evoked the feelings of affinity that Eva did. "If there's a point, Doctor, I'd like you to get to it."

"I want you to be mindful of a potential tendency to seclude yourself with Eva, to the exclusion of everyone else. I asked if you would gift her with a pet, because I can't see you doing so. That would shift her focus and affection away from you, even if only slightly, while your focus and affection is centered entirely on her."

I drummed my fingertips on the arm of the sofa. "That's not unusual for newlyweds."

"It's unusual for you." He leaned forward. "Did Eva say why she gave Lucky to you?"

I hesitated, preferring to keep something so intimate to myself. "She wants me to have more unconditional love."

He smiled. "And I'm certain it will give her great pleasure to see you reciprocating that. She's pushed very hard for you to open up to her and to me. Now that you're taking those steps, she'll want you to open up to others. The bigger her intimate circle is, the happier she is. She wants to pull you into that, not have you pull her out of it."

My lungs expanded on a long, deep breath. He was right, much as I hated to admit it.

Dr. Petersen sat back again and resumed scrawling on the screen of his tablet, giving me time to absorb what he said.

I asked him something that had been on my mind. "When I told you about Hugh . . ."

He gave me his full attention. "Yes?"

"You didn't seem surprised."

"And you want to know why." His gaze was kind. "There were certain markers. I could say I deduced it, but that wouldn't be entirely true."

I felt my phone buzz in my pocket but ignored it, despite knowing that only a handful of people were programmed to bypass the do-not-disturb setting I used during my meetings with Dr. Petersen.

"I saw Eva shortly after she moved to New York," he went

on. "She asked me if it was possible for two abuse survivors to have a meaningful relationship. It was only a few days later when you contacted me and asked if I'd be open to seeing you, in addition to seeing you and Eva as a couple."

My pulse quickened. "I hadn't told her then. I didn't until we'd been coming to you for a while."

But I'd had nightmares, the really bad ones that had been coming less frequently of late.

My phone buzzed again and I pulled it out. "Excuse me."

It was Angus. *I'm outside the office door*, he'd texted first. This time, *It's urgent.*

My spine stiffened. Angus wouldn't disturb me without a very good reason. I stood. "I'll have to cut this short," I told Dr. Petersen.

He set aside his tablet and rose to his feet. "Is everything all right?"

"If not, I'm sure you'll hear about it on Thursday." I shook his hand quickly and left the office, passing through the empty reception area before stepping out to the hallway.

Angus stood there, looking grim. He wasted no time. "The police are at the penthouse with Eva."

My blood turned to ice. I strode to the elevator with Angus falling into step beside me. "Why?"

"Anne Lucas filed charges of harassment."

7

My hand shook as I poured freshly brewed coffee into three mugs. I couldn't tell if that was because I was so pissed off or because I was afraid. Certainly, I was both. Being a cop's daughter, I understood the unwritten rules followed by those who worked behind the blue wall of law enforcement. And after everything Gideon and I had been through regarding Nathan's death, I was doubly on my guard now.

But it wasn't Detectives Graves and Michna of the homicide division who wanted to speak to me. I couldn't decide if that made me more or less anxious. They were the devil I knew, so to speak. And while I wouldn't go so far as to call Shelley Graves an ally, she'd dropped the case when she still had questions without answers.

This time around, it was Officers Peña and Williams who had shown up on our doorstep.

And it was Anne Lucas who sent them my way. That fucking bitch.

I'd had to cut my appointment with Blaire Ash short, knowing it was unavoidable that the designer would pass the officers in the lobby when he exited the private elevator. I didn't have time to worry about what he'd make of that. Instead, I took the brief time alone to call Raúl and tell him to find Arash Madani. I wanted to call Gideon, but he was with Dr. Petersen and I considered that more important. I could handle the police. I knew the basics: Have an attorney present and be succinct. Don't elaborate or offer information not asked for.

Setting the three mugs of coffee on a serving tray, I searched for something to pour the half-and-half into.

"You don't have to go to any trouble, Ms. Tramell," Officer Peña said as he and his partner entered the kitchen with their hats tucked under their arms.

Peña had a baby face that made him look younger than he probably was, which I guessed was close to my age. Williams was a petite, curvy black woman, with sharp cop eyes that told me she'd seen things I would never want to.

I'd asked them to wait in the living room and they had followed me instead. That made me feel hunted, which I'm sure was part of their intention.

"It's no trouble." I gave up trying to be classy about the half-and-half and just set the carton on the island. "And I'm waiting for my attorney to arrive, so there's really not much else for me to do in the meantime."

Officer Williams eyed me coolly, as if she were wondering why I felt the need for counsel.

I didn't have to justify myself but knew it wouldn't hurt to let them know why I was cautious. "My dad's on the job in California. He'd chew me out if I didn't follow his advice."

I grabbed the box of sugar I'd dug out of the pantry and set it on the tray before moving it all over to the island.

"Where in California?" Peña asked, grabbing a mug and taking his coffee black.

"Oceanside."

"San Diego area, right? Nice."

"It is, yes."

Williams took her coffee with a splash of half-and-half and a whole lot of sugar, which she poured straight from the box. "Is Mr. Cross here?"

"He's in a meeting."

She kept her gaze on me as she lifted her mug to her lips. "Who was the guy leaving when we came up?"

The deliberate casualness of her tone made me glad I'd sent word to Arash. I didn't believe for a minute that the question was just small talk. "Blaire Ash. He's the interior designer working on some renovations we're doing."

"You live here?" Peña asked. "We stopped by an apartment on the Upper West Side we heard was yours."

"I'm in the process of moving in."

He leaned into the island and looked around. "Nice place."

"I think so, too."

Williams caught my eye. "Have you been dating Gideon Cross long?"

"She's married to me, actually," Gideon said, appearing in the doorway.

Peña straightened, swallowing quickly. Williams set her mug down with enough force to spill some coffee.

Gideon's gaze swept over all of us, then locked with mine. He looked perfect, his suit pristine, his tie immaculately knotted, his dark hair framing that savagely beautiful face. There was the faintest shadow of stubble around his sensual mouth. That, and the sexy length of his hair, lent a dangerous edge to his otherwise civilized appearance.

Not even the two cops standing between us could diminish the surge of hunger that flooded me at the sight of him.

I watched as he came toward me, shrugging out of his suit jacket as if it were the most natural thing to have two of New York's finest there to question me. He tossed it over the back of a bar stool at the island and moved beside me, taking my coffee out of my hands and pressing a kiss to my temple.

"Gideon Cross," he said, extending his hand to both officers. "And this is our counsel, Arash Madani."

It was then I noticed that Arash had entered the kitchen behind my husband. The officers, as focused on Gideon as I was, didn't seem to have noticed him either.

Supremely confident, with dark good looks and easy charm, Arash swept into the room and took over, introducing himself with a wide smile. The disparity between him and Gideon was striking. Both men were elegant, handsome, and poised. Both were courteous. But Arash was accessible, relatable. Gideon was imposing and remote.

I looked up at my husband, watching as he drank from my mug. "Would you like some black coffee instead?"

His hand swept down my back, his eyes on the officers and Arash. "I'd love some."

"It's good that you're here, Mr. Cross," Peña said. "Dr. Lucas also filed a complaint against you."

❧

"Well, that was fun," Arash said an hour later, after showing the officers out to the elevator.

Gideon shot him a look as he deftly opened a bottle of malbec. "If that's your idea of entertainment, you need to get out more."

"I was planning on doing that tonight—with a very hot blonde, I might add—until I got your call." Arash pulled out one of the island bar stools and sat.

I scooped up all the mugs and moved them to the sink. "Thank you, Arash."

"You're most welcome."

"I bet you don't step into courtrooms all that often, but I want to be there the next time you do. You're awesome."

He grinned. "I'll be sure to let you know."

"Don't thank him for doing his job," Gideon muttered. He poured the dark red wine into three glasses.

"I'm thanking him for doing his job *well*," I countered, still impressed by the way Arash worked. The attorney was charismatic and disarming, as well as humble when it served his purposes. He put everyone at ease, then let them do the talking while he figured out his best angle of attack.

Gideon scowled at me. "What the hell do you think I'm paying him so much to do? Fuck up?"

"Dial it back, ace," I said calmly. "Don't let that bitch get to you. And don't take that tone with me. Or your friend."

Arash winked at me. "I think he's jealous you like me so much."

"Ha!" Then I saw the way Gideon glared at Arash and my brows went up. "Seriously?"

"Get back on topic. How are you fixing this?" my husband

challenged, looking daggers at his friend over the rim of his wineglass.

"Fixing your fuck-up?" Arash asked, his brown eyes bright with silent laughter. "You both provided Anne Lucas the ammunition for this by going to her place of employment on two separate occasions. You're damned lucky she embellished her story with a little assault accusation against Eva. If she'd just stuck with the truth, she'd have you both by the throats."

I went to the fridge and started pulling out items to throw together for dinner. I'd been kicking myself for being stupid all evening. It would never have occurred to me to think she might voluntarily reveal her sordid extramarital affair with Gideon. She was supposed to be an upstanding member of the mental health community and her husband was a well-regarded pediatrician.

I'd underestimated her. And I hadn't listened to Gideon when he had warned me she was dangerous. The result was that she had a legitimate complaint that first Gideon had barged into her office during a therapy session, and then I'd ambushed her at work again two weeks later.

Arash accepted the glass Gideon slid briskly over to him. "The district attorney may or may not decide to go after her for falsely reporting an incident, but she damaged her credibility by accusing Eva of putting hands on her when security footage proves otherwise. Very fortunate, you having that, by the way."

Learning that Gideon did indeed own the building Anne Lucas worked in hadn't surprised me too much. My husband needed control, and having that sort of hold over the businesses of both the Lucases was just like him.

"It shouldn't have to be said," Arash went on, "but when confronted by crazy, Do Not Engage."

Gideon arched his brow at me. It chafed, but he was right. He'd told me so.

The attorney shot warning glances at both of us. "I'll work on getting her erroneous assault complaint dismissed and see if I can leverage it to our advantage by filing a counterclaim of harassment. I'll also try for protection orders for both of you and Cary Taylor, but regardless, you all need to stay far, far away from her."

"Absolutely," I assured him, taking the opportunity to palm my husband's fine, taut ass as I passed behind him.

He shot me a wry glance over his shoulder. I blew him a kiss.

It tickled me that he would feel even the slightest bit of jealousy. The most impressive thing about Arash was that he held his own next to Gideon; he certainly couldn't surpass him. While I'd seen that Arash could be every bit as threatening as my husband, it wasn't his default setting.

Gideon was always dangerous. No one ever mistook him for anything else. I was intensely attracted to that about him, understood that I would never tame him. And God, was he gorgeous. He knew it, too. Knew how dazzled I was by him.

But the green-eyed monster could still get the better of him.

"You'll stay for dinner?" I asked Arash. "No idea what I'm making yet, but we ruined your plans and I feel bad about that."

"It's still early." Gideon took a deep swallow of his wine. "He can make other plans."

"I'd love to stay for dinner," Arash said, grinning wickedly.

I couldn't resist copping another feel, so I reached around my husband to get my wine and caressed his thigh while I was at it. I brushed my breasts across his back as I withdrew my hand.

Lightning quick, Gideon's hand caught my wrist. He squeezed and a shiver of arousal slid through me.

Those blue eyes turned on me. "You want to misbehave?" he asked silkily.

I was instantly desperate for him. Because he looked so cool and savagely civilized, completely contained while he basically asked if I wanted to fuck.

He had no idea how much.

I heard a faint buzz. Still holding me captive by the wrist, Gideon looked across the island at Arash. "Pass my phone over."

Arash looked at me and shook his head, even as he turned to dig Gideon's phone out of the suit jacket on the bar stool. "How you put up with him, I will never know."

"He's great in bed," I quipped, "and he's not surly there, so . . ."

Gideon yanked me into his side and bit my earlobe. My nipples tightened into hard points. He growled almost inaudibly against my neck, though I doubted he cared if Arash heard.

Breathless, I pulled away and tried to focus on cooking. I hadn't taken over Gideon's kitchen before, hadn't a clue where anything was or what he had stocked, aside from what I'd glimpsed while getting coffee ready for the police. I found an onion, and located a knife and cutting board. Grateful as I was for the distraction, I had to do something else besides getting us both revved up.

"Right," Gideon said into the phone with a sigh. "I'm coming."

I looked up. "Do you have to go somewhere?"

"No. Angus is bringing Lucky up."

I grinned.

"Who's Lucky?" Arash asked.

"Gideon's dog."

The lawyer looked suitably shocked. "You have a dog?"

"I do now," Gideon said ruefully, leaving the kitchen.

When he returned a moment later with a squirming Lucky happily licking his jaw, I melted. There he stood, in his vest and shirtsleeves, a titan of industry, a global powerhouse, and he was being overwhelmed by the cutest puppy ever.

Picking up his phone, I unlocked it and snapped a picture. That was going into a frame, ASAP.

While I was at it, I texted Cary. *Hey, it's Eva. Want to come over to the penthouse for dinner?*

I waited a beat for him to reply, then set Gideon's phone down and went back to chopping.

❧

"I should've listened to you about Anne," I told Gideon as we returned to the living room after saying good-bye to Arash. "I'm sorry."

His hand at my lower back slid over farther, cupping my waist. "Don't be."

"It's got to be frustrating for you to deal with my stubbornness."

"You're great in bed, and you're not stubborn there, so . . ."

I laughed as he tossed my words back at me. I was happy. Spending the evening with him and Arash, watching how relaxed and easy he was with his friend, being able to move around the penthouse as if it were my home . . .

"I feel married," I murmured, realizing that I hadn't truly felt that way before. We had the rings and the vows, but those were the trappings of marriage, not the reality of it.

"You should," he replied, with a familiar note of arrogance, "since you are and will be for the rest of your life."

I looked at him as we settled on the sofa. "Do you?"

His gaze went to the playpen by the fireplace where Lucky slept. "Are you asking if I feel domesticated?"

"That will never happen," I said dryly.

Gideon looked at me, searching. "Do you want me to be?"

I ran my hand down his thigh, because I couldn't help myself. "No."

"Tonight . . . You liked having Arash here."

I shot him a look. "You're not jealous of your lawyer, are you? That would be ridiculous."

"I don't like it, either." He scowled. "But that's not what I meant. You like having people over."

"Yes." I frowned. "Don't you?"

He looked away, his lips pursed. "It's fine."

I stilled. Gideon's home was his sanctuary. Before me, he'd never brought any women here. I'd assumed he had entertained his guy friends, but maybe not . . . ? Maybe the penthouse was where he retreated from everyone.

I reached for his hand. "I'm sorry, Gideon. I should've asked you first. I didn't think about it and I should have. It's your home—"

"*Our* home," he corrected, focusing back on me. "What

are you apologizing for? You have every right to do whatever you like here. You don't have to ask me for permission for anything."

"And you shouldn't feel invaded in your own home."

"*Our* home," he snapped. "You need to grasp that concept, Eva. Quickly."

I jerked back from his sudden flare of temper. "You're mad."

He stood and rounded the coffee table, his body vibrating with tension. "You went from feeling married to acting like you're a guest in my house."

"*Our* house," I corrected. "Which means we share it and you have the right to say you'd rather we didn't entertain here."

Gideon shoved a hand through his hair, a sure sign of his increasing agitation. "I don't give a shit about that."

"You're certainly acting like you do," I said evenly.

"For fuck's sake." He faced me, his hands on his lean hips. "Arash is my friend. Why would I care if you cook him dinner?"

Were we circling back to jealousy? "I cooked dinner for *you*, and invited him to join us."

"Fine. Whatever."

"It doesn't seem fine, 'cuz you're pissed."

"I'm not."

"Well, I'm confused and that's starting to make *me* pissed."

His jaw tightened. He turned away, walking to the fireplace and looking at the family photos I'd placed on the mantel.

I suddenly regretted doing that. I would be the first to

admit that I pushed him into change faster than I should, but I understood the need for a haven, a quiet place to let your guard down. I wanted to be that for him, wanted our home to be that for him. If I made it a place he wanted to avoid—if he ever found it easier to avoid *me*—then I would effectively be jeopardizing the very marriage I valued more than anything.

"Gideon. Please talk to me." Maybe I'd made that difficult, too. "If I've crossed a line, you have to tell me."

He faced me again, frowning. "What the hell are you talking about?"

"I don't know. I don't understand why you're upset with me. Help me understand."

Gideon heaved a sigh of frustration, then focused on me with the laserlike precision that had exposed every secret I'd had. "If there weren't anyone else on earth, just you and me, I'd be okay with that. But that wouldn't be enough for you."

I sat back, startled. His mind was a labyrinth I would never map. "You would be okay with just me and no one else—indefinitely? No competitors to squash? No global domination to plan?" I snorted. "You'd be bored out of your mind."

"Is that what you think?"

"That's what I know."

"What about you?" he challenged. "How would you manage with no friends to invite over and no one else's life to meddle in?"

My gaze narrowed. "I don't meddle."

He gave me a patient look. "Would I be enough for you, if there were no one else?"

"There is no one else."

"Eva. Answer the question."

I had no idea where he was coming from, but that only made it easier for me to answer him. "You fascinate the fuck out of me, you know that? You're never boring. A lifetime alone with you wouldn't be long enough to figure you out."

"Could you be happy?"

"Having you all to myself? That would be heaven." My mouth curved. "I have a Tarzan fantasy. You Tarzan, me Jane."

The tension in his shoulders visibly eased and a faint smile touched his mouth. "We've been married a month. Why am I just now hearing about this?"

"I figured I'd give it a few months before I whipped out the freaky."

Gideon flashed me a rare, wide smile and fried my brain in the process. "How does the fantasy go?"

"Oh, you know." I waved one hand carelessly. "Tree house, loincloth. Weather hot enough to put a sheen of sweat on you, but not too hot. You'd be seething with the need to fuck but have no experience doing it. I'd have to show you how."

He stared at me. "You have a sexual fantasy in which I'm a *virgin*?"

It took a lot of effort not to laugh at his incredulity. "In every way," I said, with utmost seriousness. "You've never seen breasts or a woman's pussy before mine. I have to show you how to touch me, what I like. You catch on quick, but then I've got a wild man on my hands. You can't get enough."

"That's reality." He headed toward the kitchen. "I have something for you."

"A loincloth?"

He answered over his shoulder. "How about what goes in it?"

My mouth curved. I half expected him to come back out with wine. I straightened when I saw that he had something small and bright red in his hand, a color and shape I recognized as Cartier. "A present?"

Gideon crossed the distance between us with his confident, sexy stride.

Excited, I rose onto my knees. "Gimme, gimme."

He shook his head, holding his hand aloft as he sat. "You can't have what I haven't given you yet."

I sank back down, putting my hands on my thighs.

"In answer to your questions . . ." He brushed his fingertips across my cheek. "Yes, I feel married."

My pulse fluttered.

"Coming home to you," he murmured, his gaze on my mouth, "watching you whip up dinner in our kitchen. Even having damned Arash here. That's what I want. You. This life we're building."

"Gideon . . ." My throat burned.

He looked down at the red suede pouch in his hand. He flipped open the button that kept it closed and poured two platinum crescents into the palm of his hand.

"Wow." My hand went to my throat.

He caught my left wrist and pulled it gently into his lap, sliding one half of the bracelet beneath it. The other half he held up to me, so I could see that he'd inscribed something inside.

ALWAYS MINE. FOREVER YOURS. —GIDEON

"Oh, boy," I breathed, watching as my husband fit the top half of the bracelet to the bottom. "This is sooo getting you laid."

His soft laugh made me fall deeper in love with him.

The bracelet had a screw motif that circled the entire band, with two actual screws on the sides that he secured with a small screwdriver.

"This," he held up the screwdriver, "is mine."

I watched him tuck it into his pocket, understanding that I wouldn't be able to get the bracelet off without him. Not that I'd want to. I already treasured it—and the proof of his romantic soul.

"And this"—I straddled his hips, draping my arms over his shoulders—"is mine."

His hands gripped my waist, his head tipping back to expose his throat to my questing lips. It wasn't surrender. It was indulgence, and that was just fine with me.

"Take me to bed," I whispered, my tongue rimming the shell of his ear.

I felt his muscles bunch, then flex effortlessly as he stood while holding me as if I weighed nothing at all. I gave a throaty purr of appreciation and he swatted my ass, hitching me higher before carrying me out of the living room.

I was panting, my heart racing. My hands were everywhere, sliding through his hair and over his shoulders, unknotting his tie. I wanted to get to his skin, to feel him flesh to flesh. My lips roved over his face, kissing everywhere I could reach.

His stride was purposeful, but leisurely. His breathing even and steady. He kicked the door closed with a graceful, easy push.

ONE WITH YOU • 193

Oh God, it drove me insane when he was that controlled.

He tried to set me down on the bed, but I held on.

"I can't take your clothes off if you don't let me go." Only the hoarseness of his voice betrayed his need.

I released him, tackling the buttons of his vest before he straightened. "Take *your* clothes off."

He swatted my fingers away so he could take over. I stared, my breath held, as he started to strip.

The sight of his hands, tanned by the sun, glittering with the rings I'd given him, deftly unknotting his tie . . . How could that be so erotic?

The whisper of the silk as he tugged it off. The careless way he let it fall to the floor. The heat of his eyes as he watched me watching him.

It was the worst sort of denial, extreme self-torture, and I forced myself to bear it. Wanting to touch him but restraining myself. Waiting for him while coveting him. I'd tortured us both by making us wait, so it was the least I deserved.

I'd *missed* him. Missed having him like this.

The collar of his shirt parted as he slid the buttons from their holes, exposing the strong column of his throat, then a glimpse of his chest. He stopped at the button below his pecs, teasing me, switching to his cuff links.

He removed them slowly, one at a time, setting them carefully and deliberately on the nightstand.

A soft whimper escaped me. Desperation was a wild thing inside me, sliding through my veins, the most potent aphrodisiac.

Gideon shrugged out of his shirt and vest, his shoulders bunching, then relaxing.

He was perfect. Every inch of him. Every hard slab of

honed muscle visible beneath the rough silk of his skin. Nothing brutish in any way. Not too much of anything.

Except his cock. Jesus.

My thighs squeezed together as he toed out of his oxfords and pushed his slacks and boxer briefs down his long, strong legs. My sex ached and swelled, the blood rushing to my core, my slit slick with wanting.

The rigid lacing of his abs flexed as he straightened. The muscles veed at his hips and pointed to the thick, long penis that curved upward between his thighs.

"Oh God. Gideon."

Pre-ejaculate slicked the wide head. His testicles hung heavily, balancing the weight of his thickly veined cock. He was magnificent, beautiful in the most primal way, savagely masculine. The sight of him stirred everything feminine inside me.

I licked my lips, my mouth flooded with moisture. I wanted to taste him, to hear his pleasure when I wasn't lost to my own, to feel him quake and shiver when I took him over the edge.

Gideon fisted his erection, stroking it hard from root to tip, pumping a thick pearl of moisture up to bead the tip.

"It's yours, angel," he said roughly. "Take it."

I scrambled off the bed and started to sink to my knees.

He caught me by the elbow, his mouth a taut line. "Naked."

It was hard to straighten my legs, my knees weak with desire. Harder still to resist yanking off my clothes in a rush. I was shaking as I untied my sleeveless wrap top, trying to pull open the loosened halves with some semblance of a striptease.

His hissed intake of air when I exposed the lace of my bra

betrayed his fraying control. My breasts were heavy and tender, the nipples hard and tight.

Gideon took a step toward me, his hands sliding beneath the shoulder straps and pulling them down until I fell into his waiting palms. My eyes closed on a low moan as he squeezed gently, hefting the weight of my breasts before stroking over my nipples with the pads of his thumbs.

"Should've kept you dressed," he said tightly. But his touch said something else. That I was beautiful. Sexy. That I was all he could see.

He pulled away and I cried out, missing his hands.

His eyes were so dark they seemed black. "Offer them to me."

I shifted on my feet, my sex throbbing. Shrugging, I let my shirt drop, then reached behind me to unclasp my bra. It slid down my arms, freeing me to cup my breasts and lift them up to him.

Bending his head with frustrating patience, Gideon ran the tip of his tongue over my nipple in a slow, unhurried lick. I wanted to scream . . . hit him . . . something. *Anything* to break that maddening restraint.

"Please," I begged, shameless. "Gideon, please . . ."

He sucked, *hard*. Drawing on me with deep rapid pulls, his tongue furiously lashing the sensitive tip. I could smell the animal lust on him, pheromones and testosterone, the scent of a ferociously aroused virile male. It called to me, demanding and possessive. I felt the pull of it, of him. Felt the melting inside me, the surrender.

I swayed and he caught me, tipping me back over his arms and moving to my other breast. His cheeks hollowed with the force of his sucking, my core clenching in rhythm.

My spine ached with the strain of the pose I had to hold for him to take his pleasure, and that turned me on to the point of madness.

I'd fought for him. He had killed for me. There was a bond between us, primitive and ancient, that transcended definition. He could take me, use me. I was his. I'd made him wait and he'd *allowed* me to for reasons I wasn't sure I knew. But he was reminding me now that I could walk far and try to keep my distance at times, but his hand would always hold the chains that bound us together. And he would pull me back when it suited him, because I belonged to him.

Always mine.

"Don't wait." My hands went into his hair. "Fuck me. I need your cock inside me—"

He spun me and bent me over the bed, pinning me down with a hand between my shoulder blades, reaching for the back zipper of my capris. He yanked on the pull, ripping it open and rending the cotton.

"Are you with me?" he growled, shoving his hand into the opening to cup the cheek of my buttock.

"Yes! God, yes . . ." And he knew it, but he asked. Always making sure to remind me that I had the control, that I gave him permission.

He destroyed my pants getting them down to my knees, using just one hand while the other fisted my hair. He was rough, impatient. He gripped the band of my thong and tugged, the material digging into my skin before breaking with a snap.

He pushed his hand between my bound legs, cupping my sex. My back arched, my body trembling.

"Christ, you're wet." He pushed a finger inside me. Pulled out. Pushed in with two. "I'm so fucking hard for you."

The tender tissues grasped at his plunging fingers. He withdrew, circling my clit, rubbing it. I pressed into his fingertips, seeking the pressure I needed, soft pleading sounds pouring from my throat.

"Don't come until I'm inside you," he growled. He grabbed my hips with both hands, pulling me back as he notched the broad head of his cock into my slit.

He paused a moment, breathing hard and loud. Then he shoved inside me. I screamed into the mattress, stretched wide and too full, writhing to accommodate him.

He held me aloft, my feet leaving the floor. He rolled his hips and claimed that last little space inside me, his penis tunneling deep. I squeezed every inch of him, pulsing around him in frantic pleasure.

"Okay?" he bit out, his fingers kneading restlessly into my flesh.

I pushed back with my arms, so close to coming it hurt. "More."

Through the roaring of blood in my ears I heard him groan my name. His cock swelled and lengthened, jerking as he orgasmed in hard spurts. It felt endless and maybe it was, because he started fucking through his climax, pumping me full of hot, creamy semen. The feel of him coming sparked my orgasm. It rushed over me in powerful spasms, racking my body with violent shudders.

My nails clawed at the comforter, trying to find purchase as Gideon pounded his cock into me, lost in a hot furious rut. The slickness of his semen wet the lips of my sex, then rolled down my legs. He groaned and thrust deep, rolling his hips, screwing into me. He shuddered, coming again, only moments after his first.

Folding over me, Gideon kissed my shoulder, his breath gusting hot and fast over the sweat-slick curve of my back. His chest heaved against my spine, his bruising grip on my hips easing. His hands began to stroke, to soothe. His fingers found my clit and massaged, stirring me, rubbing me into another trembling climax.

His lips moved against my skin. *Angel . . .* Over and over he said the word. Brokenly. Desperately. Breathlessly.

Forever yours.

While deep inside me, he remained hard and ready.

❧

I was lying on the bed, tucked against Gideon's side. My pants were gone and he was nude, his magnificent body still damp with sweat.

My husband lay sprawled on his back, one thickly muscled arm arched over his head, while the other curled beneath and around me, his fingers running absently up and down the length of my torso.

We lay naked atop the sheets, his legs spread, his cock semierect and curving up to his navel. It glistened in the light of the bedside lamps, wet from me and him. His breathing was just beginning to slow, his heartbeat calming beneath my ear. He smelled delicious, like sin and sex and Gideon.

"I don't remember how we got on the bed," I murmured, my voice throaty and near hoarse.

Gideon's chest rumbled with a laugh. Turning his head, he pressed his lips to my forehead.

I curled tighter into him, my arm draping across his waist and holding on tight.

"You good?" he asked softly.

Tipping my head back, I looked at him. He was flushed and sweaty, his hair clinging to his temples and neck. His body was a well-oiled machine, used to the strenuous mixed martial arts he used to condition it. He wasn't wiped from fucking; he could do that all night, tirelessly. It was the effort of holding back as long as he could, reining himself in until I was as wild for him as he was for me.

"You fucked my brains out." I smiled, feeling drugged. "My toes and fingers are tingling."

"I was rough." He touched my hip. "I bruised you."

"Umm . . ." My eyes closed. "I know."

I felt him shift, rising, blocking out the light.

"You like that," he murmured.

I looked up at him leaning over me. I touched his face, tracing his brow and his jaw with my fingertips. "I love your control. It turns me on."

He caught my fingers in his teeth, then released them. "I know."

"But when you lose it . . ." I sighed, remembering. "It drives me crazy to know I can do that to you, that you want me that much."

His head dropped, his forehead touching mine. He tugged me closer, making me feel how hard he was again. "More than anything."

"And you trust me." In my arms, he let every guard down.

The ferocity of his need didn't hide his vulnerability; it revealed it.

"More than anyone." He slid over me, covering my body from ankle to shoulder, effortlessly supporting his weight so he didn't crush me. The sensual pressure made me hot for him all over again.

Tilting his head, Gideon brushed his lips over mine. "Crossfire," he murmured.

Crossfire was my safeword, what I said to him when I was overwhelmed and needed him to stop whatever he was doing. When he said the word to me, he was overwhelmed, too, but he didn't want me to stop. For Gideon, *Crossfire* conveyed a connection deeper than love.

My mouth curved. "I love you, too."

❧

Wrapping myself around a pillow, I looked toward the closet and listened to the sound of Gideon singing. I smiled ruefully. He was showered and dressing, and obviously feeling energetic despite beginning the morning by screwing me into an orgasm that left me seeing stars.

It took me a moment to recognize the song. When I did, I felt butterflies. "At Last." Whether it was the Etta James or Beyoncé version he was hearing in his mind didn't matter. What *I* heard was his voice, rich and nuanced, singing about seeing blue skies and smiles that cast a spell on him.

He stepped out knotting a charcoal tie, his vest unbuttoned and his jacket slug over his arm. Lucky scurried out after him, never far behind. After being freed from the playpen that morning, the puppy had become his shadow.

Gideon's gaze landed on me. He flashed me a heart-breaker of a smile. "And here we are," he crooned.

"Here I am, anyway. Leveled by hours of sex. I don't think I can stand and you're"—I gestured at him—"you. It's not fair. I'm not doing something right."

Gideon sat on the edge of the rumpled bed, looking impeccable. Bending over, he kissed me. "Remind me . . . How many times did I come last night?"

I shot him a look. "Not enough, apparently, since you were ready to go again when the sun came up."

"Which proves the point that you're doing something *very* right." He brushed the hair off my cheek. "I'm tempted to stay home, but I've got to clear the decks so we can disappear for a month. As you can see, I'm extremely motivated."

"You were serious about that?"

"You thought I wasn't?" Brushing the sheet aside, he cupped my breast.

I caught his hand before he aroused me again. "A monthlong honeymoon. I'll wear you out at least once. I'm determined."

"Will you?" His eyes sparkled with laughter. "Only once?"

"You're asking for it, ace. By the time I'm done, you'll beg me to leave you alone."

"That will never happen, angel. Not in a million years."

His confidence challenged me.

I tugged the sheet back up again. "We'll just see about that."

8

As ANGUS WALKED into my office, I looked up from the e-mail I was reading. He held his hat in his hands and came to a stop in front of my desk.

"I went through Terrence Lucas's office last night," he said. "I didnae find anything."

I hadn't expected him to, so wasn't surprised. "It's possible Hugh told Anne what he knows and there are no records to be found."

He nodded grimly. "While I was at it, I deleted all traces of Eva's appointment on both their onsite hard drives and backups. I also wiped the video footage of you and Eva being there. I checked and he never asked security for a copy, so you should be fine if he takes his wife's cue and files any complaints of his own."

That was Angus, always taking all possibilities into consideration.

"Wouldn't the police find that interesting?" I sat back. "The Lucases have as much to lose as I do."

"They're culpable, lad. You're not."

"It's never that simple."

"You have everything you've wanted and deserve. They cannae take anything from you."

Except my self-respect and the respect of my friends and colleagues. I'd worked so hard to regain both in the aftermath of my father's very public disgrace. Those who wanted to find weaknesses in me would be satisfied. That didn't alarm me as much as it once would have.

Angus was right. I'd made my fortune and I had Eva.

If securing her peace of mind meant retreating from public scrutiny, I could do it. It was something I'd taken into consideration when Nathan Barker was still a threat. Eva had been willing to hide our relationship from the world to spare me from any possible scandal stemming from her past. It was a sacrifice I hadn't been willing to make. Hiding. Sneaking moments together. Pretending for others that we weren't falling deeply and irrevocably in love.

It was different now. She'd become as necessary as air. Protecting her happiness was more crucial than ever. I knew what it felt like to be judged for the sins of someone else and I would never put my wife through that. Contrary to her belief, I could live without having my hand in everything Cross Industries was involved in.

I wouldn't spend my days in a damned loincloth role-playing Tarzan, but there was a comfortable medium between the two extremes.

204 • SYLVIA DAY

"You warned me about Anne." I shook my head. "I should've listened to you."

He shrugged that off. "What's done is done. Anne Lucas is a grown woman. She's old enough to take responsibility for her decisions."

What are you doing, lad? he'd asked, as Anne slid into the back of the Bentley that first night. In the weeks that followed, he made his disapproval more and more clear until one day, he raised his voice to me. Disgusted with myself for punishing a woman who'd done nothing to me, I'd taken it out on him, telling him to remember his place.

The brief look of pain he'd quickly hidden would haunt me to my grave.

"I'm sorry," I said, holding his gaze. "For how I handled it."

A small smile crinkled the lines on his face. "The apology isn't necessary, but I accept it."

"Thank you."

Scott's voice came through the speaker. "The PosIT team is here. I also have Arnoldo Ricci on the line for you. He says it won't take long."

I looked at Angus to see if he had anything further for me. He tapped his brow in a casual salute and left.

Speaking to Scott, I said, "Put him through."

I waited for the red light to flash, then opened the line on speaker. "Where are you now?"

"Hello to you, too, my friend," Arnoldo greeted, his voice accented with the notes of Italy. "I hear I missed you and Eva at the restaurant this week."

"We had an excellent lunch."

"Ah, it is the only kind we serve. We are not so bad with dinner, either."

I rocked back in my chair. "You're in New York?"

"Yes, and planning your bachelor party, which is why I'm calling. If you have plans this weekend, cancel them."

"Eva and I will be out of town."

"*She* will be out of town. In fact, out of the country, from what I understand from Shawna. And you will be out of town, too. The rest of the guys are in agreement with me. We are going to force you to leave New York for a change."

I was so taken aback by the first part of what Arnoldo said that I hardly heard the last. "Eva isn't leaving the country."

"You'll have to take that up with her and her friends," he said smoothly. "As for us, we are going to Rio."

I found myself standing. Damn it. Eva wasn't in the Crossfire. I couldn't just take an elevator and find her.

"I'm going to ask Scott to arrange the flight," he continued. "We'll leave Friday evening and plan to return Monday in time for you to go to work, if you are ambitious enough."

"Where is Eva going?"

"I have no idea. Shawna wouldn't say, because it's not for you to know. She told me only that they would be gone for the weekend and I should plan on keeping you occupied, because Cary doesn't want you to interfere."

"That's not his decision to make," I snapped.

He paused. "Being angry at me won't help you, Gideon. And if you don't trust her, my friend, you shouldn't be marrying her."

My grip on the phone tightened. "Arnoldo, you're the closest friend I have. But that'll change if you don't get your head out of your ass when it comes to Eva."

"You mistake me," he corrected hurriedly. "If you cage

her for your own security, you will lose her. What is considered romantic in a boyfriend can be stifling in a husband."

Realizing he was offering advice, I started counting to ten. I made it to seven. "I can't believe this."

"Don't get me wrong. Arash assures me she is the best thing to ever happen to you. He says he has never seen you happier and that she adores you."

"I've said the same."

Arnoldo exhaled audibly. "Men in love do not make the best witnesses."

Amusement replaced irritation. "Why are you and Arash discussing my personal life?"

"It is what friends do."

"*Girl*friends. You're grown men. You should have something better to do with your time." I rapped my knuckles on the desktop. "And you want me to spend a weekend in Brazil with a bunch of guy gossips?"

"Listen." His tone was annoyingly calm. "Manhattan is out. I love the city, too, but I think we've exhausted its charms. Especially for such an occasion."

Chagrined, I looked out the windows at the city I loved. Only Eva knew about the hotel room I'd kept perpetually reserved—my "fuck pad," as she'd called it. Until her, it was the only place where I took women for sex. It was safe. Impersonal. There was nothing to learn about me there but how I looked nude and how I liked to fuck.

Leaving New York meant I wouldn't get laid, so of course I'd always insisted the guys keep our prowling close to home.

"All right. I won't argue." I was going to discuss it with Eva—and Cary—but that wasn't Arnoldo's concern.

"Excellent. I will let you get back to work. We can catch up this weekend."

We ended the call. I looked over at Scott through the glass wall and lifted one finger, telling him I needed an additional minute of time. Picking up my smartphone, I called Eva.

"Hey, ace," she answered, sounding flirty and happy.

I absorbed that, along with the punch of pleasure and heat that moved through me. Her voice, always throaty, was huskier than it had been lately. I was reminded of the long night, the sounds she made when aroused, her cries for me when she came.

It was a new goal of mine to keep her sounding like that eternally, to keep her skin flushed and her lips swollen, her stride slow and sultry because she could still feel me inside her. Wherever she went, it should be obvious that I fucked her often and thoroughly. It felt obvious on me. I was loose-limbed and relaxed, a bit weak in the knees—although I'd never admit it.

"Have our plans for the weekend changed?" I asked.

"I might increase my vitamins," she teased, "but otherwise, no. I'm really looking forward to it."

The purr in her voice aroused me. "I've been told our friends plan to keep us apart this weekend for our respective bachelor and bachelorette parties."

"Oh." There was a pause. "I was kinda hoping everyone forgot about that."

My mouth curved in a smile I wished she could see. "We could run away where they can't find us."

"I wish." She sighed. "I think these things are more for

them than us. It's their last chance to have us all to themselves in the way they're used to."

"Those days were over when I met you." But I knew they weren't yet over for Eva. She'd hung on to her independence, maintaining her friendships as she always had.

"It's an odd sort of ritual, isn't it?" she mused. "Two people commit to each other for life and their friends take them out, get them drunk, and encourage them to be bad one last time."

All the sexy playfulness she'd had when the conversation started was gone. My wife was an intensely jealous woman. I knew that, accepted it, just as she accepted my possessiveness. "We'll discuss this more tonight."

"Yay," she said, sounding anything but happy about it.

There was some consolation in that. I preferred to picture her suffering through a weekend without me rather than having the time of her life.

"I love you, Eva."

Her breath caught. "I love you, too."

Ending the call, I turned to retrieve my jacket from the coatrack, then changed my mind. I retraced my steps to my desk and called Cary.

"What's up?" he answered.

"Where are you planning on taking my wife this weekend?"

He answered so quickly, I knew he'd been braced to hear from me. "You don't need to know."

"The hell I don't."

"I'm not going to have you controlling her," Cary said tightly, "with guards cockblocking any dude that comes near her, like you did in Vegas. She's a big girl. She can handle herself and she deserves to have fun."

So that was what this was about. "There were extenuating circumstances then, Cary."

"Really?" Sarcasm was heavy in his tone. "Like what?"

"Nathan Barker was still breathing and you'd just had a goddamned orgy in your living room. I couldn't trust her safety to you."

There was a pause. When he spoke again, his voice was markedly less heated. "Clancy's covering security. She'll be fine."

I took a deep breath. Clancy and I were wary of each other, since he knew what I'd done to remove Nathan as a threat to Eva's life. Regardless, we both wanted the same thing—for Eva to be happy and safe. I trusted him with her, knew him to be very good at his job running Stanton and Monica's security.

I would talk to Clancy personally, put him in contact with Angus. Contingencies had to be planned for and communication aligned. If she needed me, I had to be able to get to her as swiftly as possible.

My gut tightened at the thought. "Eva needs her friends and I want her to enjoy herself."

"Great," he said airily. "We agree."

"I won't interfere, Cary, but keep in mind that no one's as invested in keeping her safe as I am. She's only part of your life. She *is* my life. Don't be too stubborn to reach out to me if you need me. Is that clear?"

"Yeah. I get it."

"If it helps you feel better, I'll be in Brazil."

He was quiet a minute. "I haven't nailed down where we're going yet, but I'm leaning toward Ibiza."

I cursed silently. It would take half a day to get to her from Rio.

I wanted to argue—I would certainly be making some alternate suggestions for locales in South America—but I held my tongue for the moment, too aware of Dr. Petersen's comments about Eva's need for a wide social circle. Instead, I said, "Let me know what you decide."

"Okay."

Ending the call, I grabbed my jacket and slipped it on.

I was sure Eva and Dr. Petersen would disagree, but friends and family could be more of a pain in the ass than anything.

The rest of the afternoon passed as scheduled and planned. It was nearing five o'clock when Arash strolled in and settled comfortably on the nearest sofa, spreading his arms wide across the back.

I wrapped up my call with one of our distribution centers in Montreal and stood, stretching my legs. I was due for a session with my trainer, but he was going to kick my ass. I was sure Eva would be delighted to know she'd sapped my stamina.

Not that it would prevent me from having her again when the day was done.

"There'd better be a good reason why you're making yourself at home," I told Arash dryly, rounding my desk.

He flashed a cocky grin. "Deanna Johnson."

My stride slowed, the name taking me by surprise. "What about her?"

Arash whistled. "You *do* know her."

"She's a freelance journalist." I walked to the bar and pulled two chilled bottles of water out of the refrigerator. Deanna was also a woman I'd fucked, which turned out to be a colossal mistake in more ways than one.

"Okay. The hot blonde I bailed on last night?"

I shot him an impatient look. "Get on with it."

"She works in the legal department of the publishing house that acquired the rights to Corinne's book. She told me the ghostwriter is Deanna Johnson."

I exhaled roughly, my hands squeezing the bottles so hard they leaked under the strain. "Damn it."

My wife had warned me about Deanna and I hadn't listened.

"Let me take a wild guess," Arash drawled. "You know Ms. Johnson in the biblical sense."

I turned and faced him, moving back to where he sat. I tossed a bottle at him, sending sprinkles of water arcing between us. Opening my own, I drank deeply.

Eva was right: We needed to be a better, more cohesive team. She and I were going to have to learn to trust—and take—each other's advice implicitly.

My friend set his elbows on his knees, holding his water in both hands. "Now I see why you were in such a rush to get a ring on Eva. Seal the deal before she runs away screaming."

Arash was joking, but I could see the concern on his face. It echoed my own. Really, how much could my wife take?

I pulled the bottle away from my lips. "Well, that's a nice bit of news to wrap up the day," I muttered.

"What is?"

Arash and I both turned our heads to discover Eva bouncing through the open door of my office with only her smartphone in her hands. She was dressed in the same workout gear she'd been wearing the day I first saw her. Her ponytail was lighter nowadays and shorter, her body leaner and more defined. But she would always be that girl who took my breath away.

"Eva." Arash stood quickly.

"Hey." She flashed him a smile as she came toward me, rising onto her tiptoes to press a kiss to my mouth. "Hi, ace."

As she lowered back down, she frowned. "What's wrong? Is it a bad time?"

I slid an arm around her waist, pulling her close. I loved the feel of her body against mine; it soothed the anxiousness I felt whenever we were apart. "Never, angel. You come to me whenever you want."

Her eyes sparkled. "Megumi and I are going to hit the gym together, but I'm early, so figured I'd drop in on you. Grab a glimpse of your hotness to motivate me."

I dropped a kiss on her forehead. "Don't wear yourself out," I murmured. "That's my job."

There was a frown between her brows as I straightened. "Seriously. What's the matter?"

Arash cleared his throat and gestured toward the door. "I'll head back to my office."

I answered her question before he left. "Deanna is ghostwriting Corinne's book."

Eva stiffened. "Is that so?"

"She knows about Deanna?" Arash looked at us both with wide eyes.

My wife pinned him with her gaze. "Do *you* know Deanna?"

He held up both hands. "Never met her. Never even heard of her before today."

Stepping out of my embrace, Eva shot me a look. "I told you."

"I know."

"Told him what?" Arash asked, shoving his hands in his pockets.

She took my water bottle and dropped into a club chair. "That she couldn't be trusted. She's butthurt because he got her naked, then blew her off. Not that I blame her. I'd be totally humiliated if I showed the goods but couldn't make the sale."

Arash sat back down on the sofa. "You have performance problems, Cross?"

"You have your eye on unemployment, Madani?" I took the other chair.

"She'd already played hide-the-salami with Gideon once," Eva went on. "And she *really* liked the salami. Can't blame her there, either. I told you what a great lay he is."

Arash glanced at me, highly amused. "You did, yes."

"Blows the top of your head right off. Your toes curl and—"

"For fuck's sake, Eva," I muttered.

She looked at me innocently. "Just trying to give some context, baby. And give credit where it's due. Anyway, poor Deanna is torn between hating his guts and wanting to bang him like a drum. Since she can't do the latter, she's stuck with the former."

I looked at her. "Are you done?"

My wife blew me a kiss, then took a big swallow of water.

Arash sat back. "Props for laying that all out for her," he said to me. "You're a saint, Eva, for putting up with him and the trail of scorned women in his wake."

"What can I say?" Her lips pursed. "How'd you guys find out?"

"I've got an inside connection at the publishing house."

"Oh. I thought maybe Deanna said something."

"She won't. They don't want it known that Corinne isn't writing the book, so they've got a confidentiality clause. They're negotiating the contract now."

Eva sat forward, her fingers picking at the label on the bottle. Her phone buzzed on the chair by her thigh and she picked it up to read the text. "Off I go. Megumi's ready."

She stood. Arash and I stood with her. She was in my arms a moment later, tilting her head back for a kiss. I gave it to her, nuzzling my nose against hers before she retreated.

"You're so lucky I came along." She handed me back the water. "Think of how much more trouble you would've gotten into if you'd stayed single any longer."

"You're trouble enough for a lifetime."

She said good-bye to Arash, then headed out. I watched her leave, hating to see her go. She waved to Scott as she passed him, then disappeared.

"She got any sisters?" Arash asked, as we both sat down again.

"No, she's one of a kind."

"Hey, wait," Eva called out as she ran back in.

Arash and I both jumped to our feet.

She rejoined us. "If they're negotiating, nothing's been signed, right?"

"Right," Arash answered.

She looked at me. "You can get her not to sign."

My brows rose. "How am I supposed to do that?"

"Offer her a job."

I stared at her, then said, "No."

"Don't say no."

"No," I repeated.

My wife looked at Arash. "Your employee agreements include things like nondisclosure, nondisparagement, non-competes, et cetera, right?"

Arash considered that a minute. "I see where you're going, and yes, they do. But there are limitations as to what those clauses cover and how they can be enforced."

"Better than nothing, though, maybe? Keep your enemies close and all that." Her gaze turned to me expectantly.

"Don't look at me like that, Eva."

"Okay. It's just an idea. I have to go." She waved and hurried back out.

The lack of a kiss or good-bye rubbed me the wrong way. Seeing her leave again . . . I hated it more the second time.

She'd made me wait to have sex with her. She'd just casually suggested I seduce another woman.

The Eva I knew and loved would never have done either of those things.

"You don't want that book published," I called after her.

Eva stopped at the door and turned. She looked at me, her head tilting slightly. "No, I don't."

That examining look of hers got my back up. She saw right through me, saw the roiling inside me. "You know she'd expect me to offer her more than just a job."

"You'd have to entice her," she agreed, retracing her steps.

"You're a juicy carrot, Cross. And you know how to dangle out of reach without even trying. She just needs to sign on the dotted line. Afterward, you can transfer her to Siberia as long as you give her work that fits the job description."

Something in her voice set me on edge—that and the way she looked at me like a lion tamer circling the lion, cautious and watchful but very much in control.

Provoked, I baited her. "You're whoring me out to get what you want."

"Jesus, Cross," Arash muttered. "Don't be an ass."

Eva's gaze narrowed, the clear gray of her eyes turning stormy. "Bullshit. You'd have to lead her on, not fuck her. I want that book published as much as you want to hear 'Golden Girl' on repeat, but you're living with the damn song and I can live with the damn book."

"Then why bring up hiring her?" I countered, taking a step toward her. "I don't want that fucking woman within a mile of me, let alone working for me."

"Fine. It was just a suggestion. I could tell you were upset about it when I got here and I don't like you upset—"

"For Christ's sake, I don't get *upset*!"

"Right," she drawled. "Of course not. You like *bad-tempered* better? *Sullen? Moody?* Are those more masculine for you, ace?"

"I should take you over my knee."

"Try it and I'll split your sexy lip," she snapped back, her quick temper ignited. "You think I like the idea of you getting that bitch hot and bothered? Just imagining you flirting with her, giving her the idea you'd like to screw her, makes me want to break stuff—including her face."

"Good." I'd gotten what I needed. Eva couldn't hide her

jealousy when she was angry. She was seething with it, vibrating with fury. I, however, was appeased.

"And maybe Deanna dropping out won't change anything," she continued, still spitting mad. "The publisher could hire someone else to ghostwrite the fucking book. Hopefully someone unbiased, but hey, you've got ex-lovers crawling out of the woodwork, so they might get lucky again."

"That's enough, Eva."

"I wouldn't whore you out just to stop that book from being published. You're the fuck of the century. I could get a few grand an hour for you, at least."

"Goddamn it!" I lunged for her and she hopped out of the way.

"Whoa!" Arash interjected, jumping between us. "As your attorney, I have to point out that pissing off your wife could cost you millions."

"He likes pissing women off," she goaded, darting back and forth behind Arash to elude me. "It turns him on."

"Get out of the way, Madani," I growled.

"He's all yours, Arash," she tossed out, then made a break for it.

I gave chase. I caught her as she passed through the doors, grabbing her around the waist and hauling her off her feet. She struggled, growling.

I sank my teeth into her shoulder and she squealed, drawing a dozen pairs of eyes our way. Including Megumi's as she rounded the corner at just the right moment.

"Kiss me good-bye," I demanded.

"You don't want my mouth anywhere near you right now!"

Tossing her up, I spun her in midair and brought her down facing me, catching her mouth in a hard kiss. It was sloppy, graceless. Our noses bumped. But the feel of her mouth under mine, her warm skin beneath my hands, was just what I needed.

She nipped my bottom lip with her teeth. She could've hurt me, drawn blood. Instead the bite was a gentle scold, as was the tug of my hair in her fists.

"You're crazy," she complained. "What the hell is the matter with you?"

"Don't leave without kissing me good-bye."

"Are you for real?" She glared at me. "I did kiss you."

"The first time. Not the second or third."

"Well, fuck me sideways," she breathed. Tightening her grip on my neck, she pulled herself up and wrapped her legs around my waist. "Why didn't you just ask?"

"I won't beg."

"You never do." She touched my face. "You give orders. Don't stop now."

"The stuff you get away with when you're the boss," Megumi said to Scott, who sat at his desk with his gaze studiously fixed on his monitor.

Scott wisely said nothing.

Arash, however, wasn't as circumspect. "Temporary insanity caused by prewedding jitters, right, Scott?" He came up beside me. "Diminished capacity. An epic brain fart of some kind."

I shot him a warning look. "Shut up."

"Be nice." Eva kissed me lightly. "We're going to talk about this later."

"Your place or ours?"

She smiled, her temper gone. "Ours."

Her legs unwound and I set her down.

I could let her go now. I still didn't like it, but the knot in my stomach had eased. Eva was no worse for wear. Her temper always hit like a sudden storm and dissipated as swiftly, washing the slate clean.

"Hello, Megumi." I extended my hand.

She took it, showing off glittering nude nails. Megumi was an attractive woman, with jaw-length black hair and almond-shaped eyes.

Eva's friend and former co-worker looked stronger than she had the last time I'd seen her, which pleased me, because I knew how much my wife worried about her. I knew her only in passing prior to the sexual assault that had recently changed her life. I regretted that. The woman who stood before me now had a wounded look in her dark brown eyes and an air of bravado that betrayed vulnerability.

Experience had taught me she had a long road ahead of her. And she would never again be the person she'd been before.

I glanced at Eva. My wife had come so far, from both the girl she'd been long ago and the young woman I had first met. She was stronger now, too. I was happy to see that and wouldn't change it for anything.

I could only pray that strength wouldn't eventually take her away from me.

I left James Cho's studio exactly the way I expected—with my ass handed to me. Still, I'd managed to redeem myself at the end, taking the former champion fighter down in our last sparring match.

Angus was waiting for me outside, standing beside the Bentley. He opened the door and took my duffel bag but didn't smile. On the backseat, Lucky barked in his carrier, his excited face peering from behind the bars.

Pausing before sliding into the back, I held Angus's gaze.

"I have some information," he said grimly.

Considering the search for Hugh's files, I'd been braced for bad news. "We'll talk when we get to the penthouse."

"Your office would be better."

"All right." I slid into the back, frowning. Either location was private. I'd suggested home so that Eva could be with me, supporting me, when he relayed whatever information he had. Angus's preference for the office could only mean he didn't want Eva nearby.

What would he have to tell me that was best kept from my wife?

Lucky pawed at the carrier door, whining softly. Absently, I opened it and he tumbled out, climbing into my lap and rearing up to lick my jaw.

"Okay, okay." I held him so he wouldn't fall in his frenzy, tilting my head back to avoid getting licked on the mouth. "It's nice to see you, too."

Rubbing his warm, soft body with one hand, I looked out at the city as we drove through it. New York was an entirely different landscape at night, a fusion of dark alleys and twinkling high-rises, garish neon storefronts and intimate sidewalk dining.

With nearly two million people living on an island of less than twenty-three square miles, privacy was both rare and imagined. Apartment windows faced each other, with scarcely any distance between them. Often those windows remained uncovered, exposing private lives to anyone who chose to look. Telescopes were a popular item.

It was a New Yorker's way to live within a bubble, minding their own business with the expectation that others would do the same. The other option was to feel claustrophobic, the antithesis of the spirit of freedom that was the foundation of the Empire State.

We reached the Crossfire and I exited the Bentley with Lucky. Angus followed me through the revolving doors and we crossed the lobby in silence. The security guards stood as I approached, greeting me briskly by name, while darting glances at the tiny puppy tucked under my arm. I smiled inwardly as I caught my reflection. Dressed in sweats and a T-shirt with shower-damp hair, I doubted any person not in the know would believe I owned the building.

The elevator shot us up quickly and we were walking through the Cross Industries headquarters within moments of our arrival. Most offices and cubicles were dark and empty, but some ambitious employees were still getting things done—or didn't have a reason to go home. I could relate. It wasn't long ago that I'd spent more time at work than the penthouse.

Entering my office, I turned the lights on and activated the opacity of the glass wall. Then I went to the seating area, settling on the couch and dropping Lucky on the cushion beside me. It was at that time I noticed Angus carried a worn leather binder.

He pulled a club chair close to the coffee table and sat. His gaze held mine.

My throat closed as another possibility came to mind. Angus seemed too somber, the meeting too formal.

"You're not retiring," I preempted him, the words thick in my mouth. "I won't let you."

He stared at me a moment, and then his face softened. "Ah, laddie. Ye'll be stuck with me for a while yet."

Relief hit me so hard, I sagged back into the sofa, my heart pounding. Lucky, always ready to play, jumped on my chest.

"Down," I ordered, which only made him more excitable. I pinned him in place with one hand and gave a brisk nod to Angus to get started.

"You'll remember the dossier we compiled when you met Eva," he began.

Focused by the sound of my wife's name, I straightened. "Of course."

The memory of the day I met Eva came rushing back. I'd been seated in the limo at the curb, seconds from pulling away from the Crossfire. She had been entering the building. I watched her, felt the pull of her. Unable to resist, I told Angus to wait and I went back in to find her, chasing after a woman—something I'd never done.

She'd dropped her name badge when she saw me and I retrieved it for her, noting her name and the company she worked for. By the end of the night, I'd had a thin folder on my home office desk containing a quick background check— again, something I'd never done for a mere sexual interest. Somehow, on a level I hadn't yet recognized, I knew she was mine. Knew that however I deluded myself, she was going to be important to me.

In the days that followed, the dossier grew, encompassing Eva's parents and Cary, then Eva's paternal and maternal grandparents.

"We've kept a lawyer on retainer in Austin," Angus went on, "to send us any reports of unusual activity with Harrison and Leah Tramell."

Monica's parents. Their estrangement from their daughter and granddaughter was just fine with me. Less family to deal with. But I also understood that while they might not have had any interest in Eva as an illegitimate grandchild, their minds might change when Eva publicly became my wife. "What have they done?"

"They died," he said bluntly, unzipping the binder. "Nearly a month ago."

That gave me pause. "Eva doesn't know. We were just talking over the weekend about wedding invitations and they came up. I assume Monica doesn't keep tabs on them."

"She wrote the obituary that appeared in the local paper." Angus withdrew a photocopy and set it on the table.

Picking it up, I scanned through it quickly. The Tramells had died together, in a boating accident during a summer vacation. The accompanying photo was decades old, with clothing and hair dating it to sometime in the seventies. They were an attractive couple, well dressed and expensively accessorized. What didn't fit was the hair—even in a black-and-white newspaper printing I could see they were both dark-haired.

I read the closing sentence. *Harrison and Leah are survived by their daughter, Monica, and two grandchildren.* Looking up at Angus, I repeated aloud, "*Two* grandchildren? Eva has a sibling?"

Lucky wriggled out of my lax grip and jumped to the floor.

Angus took a deep breath. "That mention and the photo made me take a deeper look."

He pulled out a picture and set it down.

I glanced at it. "Who is that?"

"That's Monica Tramell—now Monica Dieck."

My blood turned cold. The woman in the photo was a brunette, like her parents. And she looked nothing like the Monica I knew or my wife. "I don't understand."

"I haven't yet figured out what Eva's mother's actual name is, but the real Monica Tramell had a brother named Jackson who was briefly married to Lauren Kittrie."

"Lauren." Eva's middle name. "What do we know about her?"

"For now, nothing, but that'll change. We're looking."

I raked my hand through my hair. "Is it possible we've confused the Tramells and looked at the wrong family?"

"No, lad."

Standing, I went to the bar. I took two tumblers off the shelf and poured two fingers of Ardbeg Uigeadail single malt into each. "Stanton would've checked out Monica— Eva's mother—thoroughly before he married her."

"You didn't find out about Eva's past until she told you," he pointed out.

He was right. The records of Eva's abuse, her miscarriage, the court transcripts, the settlement . . . they'd all been meticulously buried. When I'd tasked Arash with drafting the prenuptial agreement, we had verified her financial assets and debts, but that was all. I loved her. I wanted her. Discrediting her in any way had never been considered.

Stanton loved his wife as well. Her personal fortune, accumulated after two financially advantageous divorces, would have addressed the most pressing concern. As for the rest, I expect he and I had acted similarly. Why search for trouble when all indications were that there was none? Love was willfully blind and made fools of men.

I rounded the bar and nearly tripped over Lucky as he bounded in front of me. "Benjamin Clancy is damned good. He wouldn't have missed this."

"We missed it." He took the glass I handed him. "If the Tramells hadn't passed away, we still wouldn't know. The background check was clean."

"How can it be clean, for fuck's sake?" I knocked back the whiskey in one swallow.

"Eva's mother used Monica's name, birthdate, and family history, but she never opened a line of credit, which is how most identity theft is discovered. The bank account she's using was established twenty-five years ago and is a business account with a separate tax ID."

She would've had to provide a personal SSN, as well, when she opened it, but the world was a very different place before the Internet.

The enormity of the fraud was difficult for me to grasp. If Angus was right, Eva's mother had lived more of her life as another woman than she had as herself.

"There's no trail, lad," he reiterated, setting his tumbler down untouched. "No crumbs to follow."

"What about the real Monica Tramell?"

"Her husband manages everything. In that sense, she hardly exists."

I looked down at the puppy who pawed at my shin. "Eva doesn't know about any of this," I said grimly. "She would've told me."

Even as I said it, I had to wonder *how* she would've told me. How would I tell her, if I were in her place? Could she keep such a huge secret, having lived with the lie so long she now believed it was true?

"Aye, Gideon," Angus said, his tone low and conciliatory. He wondered, too. It was his job to do so. "She loves you. Deeper and truer than I've ever seen a lass love a man."

I lowered back onto the sofa, felt the slight weight of Lucky as he scrambled up beside me. "I need to know more. Everything. I can't bring information like this to Eva in bits and pieces."

"You'll have it," he promised.

9

~❧~

"It's . . ." Wincing at the detailed sketch Cary had placed in front of me, I shook my head. "It's pretty, but it's not . . . right. It's not the right one."

Cary heaved out his breath. From where he sat on the floor at my feet, he dropped his head back on the couch to look at me upside down. "You're kidding. I hand you a one-of-a-kind wedding dress designed just for you and you blow it off?"

"I don't want a strapless dress. And this has a high-low hemline—"

"That's a train," he said dryly.

"Then why can I see the shoes? You shouldn't be able to see the shoes."

"It's a five-minute sketch. You can tell him to make the front longer."

Leaning forward, I grabbed the bottle of wine we'd opened earlier and added more to my glass. Journey's greatest hits piped out through the surround sound speakers, the volume on low. The rest of the penthouse was quiet and dark, the living room illuminated by two end table lamps.

"It's too . . . contemporary," I complained. "Too modern."

"Uh, yeah." He lifted his head to look at the drawing again. "That's what makes it cool."

"It's trendy, Cary. When I have kids, they'll look at it and wonder what I was thinking." I took a sip of my wine and ran my fingers through his thick hair. "I want something timeless. Like Grace Kelly or Jackie Kennedy."

"Kids, huh?" He leaned into my touch, like a cat. "If you hurry up, we can push strollers through the park together and plan playdates."

"Ha! Maybe in ten years." That sounded about right to me. Ten years of having Gideon to myself. Time for us to both grow a little more, smooth things out and find our groove.

Things were getting better every day, but we remained a volatile couple with a tempestuous relationship. What we'd argued about earlier in his office? . . . I still didn't know. That was Gideon, though. As sleek, wild, and dangerous as a wolf. Eating out of my hand one minute and snapping at it the next. Which was usually followed by fucking me like a beast, so . . . it worked for me.

"Yeah," Cary said morosely. "It'll take ten years—and immaculate conception—for you to get knocked up if you don't start nailing him again."

"Ugh." I yanked on his hair. "Not that it's any of your business, but I rocked his world last night."

"Did you?" He leered at me over his shoulder. "That's my girl."

I smirked. "Going to rock it again when he gets home."

"I'm jealous. I'm not getting any. Zip. Zero. Zilch. My palm's going to have a permanent indentation from my lonely dick."

Laughing, I leaned back into the sofa. "It's good to take a break for a while. Puts things in perspective."

"You barely made it a week," he scoffed.

"Ten days, actually. Ten horrible, hellacious, horrendous days." I took another drink.

"Right? Sucks. Bad."

"I wouldn't want to go through it again, but I'm glad we were able to take sex out of the equation for a little bit. Made us focus on talking things out and enjoying just hanging out. When we finally let loose, it was . . ." I licked my lips. "Explosive."

"You're making me hard."

I snorted. "What doesn't?"

He shot me an arch glance. "I will not be ashamed of my healthy sex drive."

"Just be proud of yourself for taking some time to figure out where you're going. I'm proud of you."

"Aww, thanks, Mom." He leaned his head on my knee. "You know . . . I could be lying to you."

"Nope. If you were fucking around, you'd want me to know about it, because then I'd kick your ass, which is part of the fun." Not. But it was a way he used me to punish himself.

"What's going to be fun is Ibiza."

"Ibiza?" It took me a second to put it together. "For my bachelorette party?"

"Yep."

Spain. Half a world away. I hadn't been expecting that. "How long is this party supposed to last?"

Cary flashed his million-dollar smile. "The weekend."

"Not that he gets a say, but Gideon's not going to like it."

"I smoothed him out. He's antsy about security, but he's going to be busy himself, in Brazil."

I sat up. "Brazil?"

"You're like a parrot tonight, repeating everything."

I loved Brazil. Loved the music, the weather, the passion of the people. There was a sensuality to the culture of Brazil that was unmatched in the world.

And thinking of Gideon there, with that pack of hot, rich men he called friends, celebrating the last days of a bachelorhood he'd already given up . . .

My best friend twisted to face me. "I know that look. You're getting twitchy just thinking about him surrounded by Brazilian bikinis and the hot-blooded women wearing them."

"Shut up, Cary."

"He's got the right crew to hit it hard, too. Especially that Manuel character. He's a major player."

I remembered watching Manuel Alcoa make a conquest when we'd all gone out together to a karaoke bar. Like Arnoldo, Gideon, and Arash, Manuel didn't even have to try. He just had to pick from the wide selection of women throwing themselves at him.

What would my husband do when his friends paired off with beautiful babes? Sit by himself and nurse a caipirinha? I didn't think so.

Gideon wouldn't cheat. He wouldn't even flirt; it wasn't

his style. He hadn't even flirted with me in the beginning and I was the love of his life. No, he would dominate the room, looking dark and dangerous and untouchable, while an endless tide of gorgeous women frothed around him.

How could he possibly be unaffected by that?

Cary laughed. "You look ready to murder someone."

"You're closest," I warned him.

"You can't kill me. Who else will pack just the right outfits for you to make Gideon as jealous as you are?"

"Sounds like I came home at just the right time."

Cary and I both looked over at the front door and found Gideon coming in with a duffel bag slung over his shoulder and a pet carrier dangling from his hand.

My scowl was chased away by the delight that ran through me at the sight of him. I couldn't say how he did it, but Gideon made even sweats and a T-shirt look insanely hot.

He set his stuff down on the floor.

"What have you got there?" Cary climbed to his feet and walked over to the carrier.

I stood and went to my husband, thrilled with the simple joy of welcoming him home. He met me halfway, his arms coming around me. I pushed my hands up beneath the back of his shirt, caressing the warm, hard muscle. As he bent to kiss me, I tilted my head back. His lips brushed mine, then settled in for a soft, wordless hello.

As he straightened, he licked his lips. "You taste like wine."

"Would you like some?"

"Absolutely."

I headed into the kitchen to grab another glass. Behind

232 • SYLVIA DAY

me, I heard the guys greet each other, and then Gideon introduced Lucky to Cary. Happy barking and Cary's rich laugh
filtered through the air.

I hadn't moved in yet, but it felt like home.

〜◦〜

Cary had been gone an hour before I worked up the nerve to
ask Gideon the burning question on my mind.

We were sitting on the couch. He slouched comfortably,
knees wide, one arm slung over my shoulder, one hand lying
casually on his thigh. I was curled against his side, my legs
pulled up, my head on his shoulder, my fingers toying with
the hem of his T-shirt. Lucky slept in the playpen by the
unlighted fireplace, occasionally whimpering as he dreamed
about whatever it was that dogs dreamed about.

Gideon had been quiet for the last thirty minutes, almost
contemplative, as I discussed the merits of the wedding dress
sketch he'd picked up from the coffee table.

"Anyway," I said, finishing, "I feel like I'll know it when I
see it, but I'm running out of time. I'm trying not to panic
about it. I just don't want to settle."

His hand lifted from my shoulder and cupped the back of
my head. His lips pressed against my forehead. "You could
wear jeans, angel, and be the most beautiful bride ever."

Touched, I snuggled closer. I inhaled deeply, then asked,
"Where in Brazil are you going?"

Gideon's fingers sifted through my hair. "Rio."

"Oh." I could picture him lazing on the white sand shore of
Copacabana, his magnificent sun-bronzed body on display,
the brilliant blue of his eyes shielded behind dark sunglasses.

The lovely women on the beach wouldn't be able to tell if he was watching them or not. That would excite them, make them bold.

At night, he and the guys would take in the nightlife in Ipanema or maybe they'd be true hedonists and head to Lapa. Anywhere they went, stunning, passionate, scantily clad women would follow. It was inevitable.

"I heard Cary say you're jealous," he murmured, nuzzling the crown of my head. There was a smug note of satisfaction in his voice.

"Is that why you picked Brazil? So I'd suffer?"

"Angel." His grip on my hair tightened, gently urging my head back to look at him. "I had nothing to do with the selection of the destination." His lips tilted up in a sexy smile. "But I'm glad you'll suffer."

"Sadist." I pulled away from him.

Gideon wouldn't let me get far, tugging me back. "After your suggestion about Deanna, I was beginning to think you were getting bored with me."

"That's hysterical."

"Not to me," he said evenly. His gaze searched my face.

Realizing he was at least partly serious, I stopped trying to get away. "I told you I didn't like the idea of you hiring her."

"Not right away you didn't. You recommended I seduce her like you'd tell me to pick up a bottle of wine on the way home from work. At least when I mentioned Rio, you tensed up and sulked about it."

"There's a difference—"

"Between actively seducing a woman I've fucked before and agreeing to a bachelor party I didn't plan? Absolutely.

And it makes no sense why you'd be okay with the first one and have a problem with the second one."

I glared. "Because one is a business transaction in a controlled environment. The other is a last hurrah for sport fucking in the one of the sexiest cities in the world!"

"You know better." His voice was low and smooth, easy. Which meant it was dangerous.

"I'm not worried about you," I stressed. "It's the women who'll want you. And your friends, who'll get drunk and horny and want you to play, too."

His face was impassive, his gaze cool. "And you think I'm not strong enough to handle the peer pressure?"

"I didn't say that. Don't put words in my mouth."

"I'm just trying to clarify your convoluted thinking."

"Look. Let's get back to the Deanna scenario." I wriggled away and stood. Facing the coffee table, I stretched out my hands, directing. "This is how I pictured it before I made the suggestion. You in your office, leaning back against your desk in that way you do that's sexy as hell. Jacket on the coatrack, maybe a scotch on the rocks next to your hand for an informal touch."

I faced the couch. "Deanna's in the chair farthest from you, so she can get the full picture. You give her a slow once-over, say a few double entendres about getting things done together. She gets ideas and seals the deal with a signature on the dotted line. That's it. You never get closer than a few feet from her and you never sit down. The glass wall stays clear, so she won't make a move."

"You imagined all this in a split second?"

"Well"—I tapped my temple—"I have some memories rattling around up here that fueled the fire."

"My memories of seduction in my office don't include anyone else," he said dryly.

"Listen, ace." I sat on the coffee table. "It was a spontaneous thought that came to me because I was worried about you."

Gideon's face softened. "Angels rush in. I get it."

"Do you?" Leaning forward, I put my hands on his knees. "I'm always going to be possessive, Gideon. You're *mine*. I wish I could put a sign on you that says it."

He held up his left hand, showing off his wedding band.

I scoffed. "You know how many women are going to pay attention to that when you're trolling through Rio with your crew?"

"They'll pay attention when I point it out."

"Then one of the guys will let slip that it's a bachelor party and they'll just try harder."

"Trying won't get them anywhere."

My gaze ran over him. "You'll be irresistible in graphite gray dress slacks and a black V-neck shirt—"

"You're remembering that night at the club."

He obviously did, too. His cock thickened and lengthened, tenting his sweatpants obscenely.

I almost moaned as his arousal proved what I'd suspected: He was commando beneath the soft cotton.

"I couldn't stop thinking about you after you left my office," he murmured. "Couldn't get the vision of you out of my mind. Then I called you at work and you taunted me, telling me you were going home to play with your vibrator when my cock was hard and ready for you."

I squirmed, recalling every detail. He had been wearing a V-neck sweater that night in New York, but what I imagined him wearing in Rio made allowances for the tropical climate and the steamy press of bodies in a nightclub.

"In my mind, I saw you on your bed," he went on, reaching between his legs to stroke his erection through his pants. "Your legs spread. Your back arching. Your body naked and shiny with sweat as you pushed a thick plastic cock in and out of your creamy cunt. I was half crazed with the idea of it. I'd never felt lust like that. It felt like I was in heat. The need to fuck was a fever inside me."

"God, Gideon." My sex ached. My breasts felt swollen and tender, the nipples tight and sore.

He watched me, his eyes hooded. "I went out before I arranged to meet you. I was going to find someone who wouldn't say no like you did. I was going to take her to the hotel, spread her out, fuck her until the madness went away. Who she was didn't matter. She was going to be faceless, nameless. I wasn't going to look at her while I was inside her. She was just a stand-in for you."

A low sound of pain left me, the thought of him with someone else in that way too agonizing to bear.

"I got close a couple times." His voice was hoarser now. "Had a drink while I waited for each one to finish flirting and signal they were ready to leave. I figured I backed off the first time because she just wasn't doing it for me. The second time, I knew no one would do it for me. No one but you. I was furious. At you for denying me. At them for being inferior. At me for being too weak to forget you."

"That's how I felt," I confessed. "Every guy I met was wrong. They weren't you."

"It's always going to be that way for me, Eva. Just you. Always."

"I'm not worried about you cheating," I reiterated, standing. I took off my tank top, then my shorts. My nude lace Carine Gilson bra and panties followed. I stripped quickly, methodically. No tease whatsoever.

Gideon lounged, watching, unmoving. Like the sex god he was, waiting to be pleasured.

Then I saw him through someone else's eyes, my husband sitting just like that in a crowded Brazilian club, the silent demand for sex pouring off him in waves of heat and need. It was just who he was, an intensely and insatiably sexual creature. Was there a woman alive able to resist the challenge of him? I hadn't met one yet.

I moved to him. Straddled him. My hands slid over his broad shoulders, feeling the warmth of him through the cotton of his T-shirt. His hands went to my hips, burning my skin. "The women who see you will want to do this," I murmured. "Touch you like this. They'll imagine it."

Looking up at me, Gideon stroked his tongue slowly over his bottom lip. "I'll be imagining you. Just like this."

"That'll only make it worse, because they'll see how bad you want it."

"How badly I want *you*," he corrected, moving his hands to cup my ass and urge me against his erection. The lips of my sex, parted by the spread of my thighs, hugged his cock through the lace. My clit pressed against his hardness and I rolled my hips with a gasp of pleasure.

"I can see them finding the best vantage point," I told him breathlessly, "staring at you with fuck-me eyes. Running their fingers down their cleavage so you appreciate their assets. They shift on their feet, crossing and recrossing their legs because they want this."

I cupped his hard, thick penis and stroked it. He flexed in my palm, vitally alive and eager. His lips parted, the only break in his control.

"Your mind's on me, so you're hard. And if you're sitting like this, with your legs spread, they can see how big your cock is and how ready you are to use it."

Reaching behind me, I circled his wrist with my fingers and pulled his left arm up to drape over the low back of the sofa. "You look like this. Don't move." I moved his other arm to his lap. "You'll have a tumbler in this hand, with two fingers of dark cachaça inside it. You sip it every now and then, licking it off your lips."

I leaned forward and stroked my tongue over the sensual curve. He had a gorgeous, sexy mouth. The lips were full, but firm. They were often stern, giving little clue to his thoughts. He smiled rarely, but when he did, he could flash a boyishly playful grin or a smugly confident challenge. His slow smiles were erotic teases, while his wry half-smiles mocked both himself and others.

"You'll seem distant and remote," I went on. "Lost in your own thoughts. Bored by the frenetic energy and pounding music. The guys ebb and flow around you. Manuel always has a hot beauty on his lap. A different one every time you look. As far as he's concerned, there's more than enough of him to go around."

Gideon smiled. "And he has a fondness for Latinas. He totally approves of my choice in wives."

"Wife," I corrected. "Your first and last."

"My only," he agreed. "Hot-tempered. Hot-blooded. My one and only permanent one-night stand. I know exactly how it will be between us, and then you go and take me by surprise. You eat me alive, every time, and want more."

I cupped his jaw in one hand and kissed him, still stroking his penis in long, leisurely pulls. "Arash stops by with a new drink for you every time he makes his way around the room. He tells you stories about what he's seen while circling and you briefly look amused, which drives the women watching you wild. That little flash of intimacy and warmth only makes them want more."

"And Arnoldo?" he murmured, watching me with hot dark eyes.

"He's detached, like you. He's wounded and wary from his broken heart, but he's accessible. He flirts and smiles, but there's always that sense of something unreachable about him. The women who are too intimidated by you will go for Arnoldo. He'll make them forget you, even while he's forgetting about them altogether."

A ghost of a smile touched his mouth. "While I sit there stewing and brooding with a perpetual hard-on, missing you so badly I can't have any fun at all?"

"That's the way I'm picturing it, ace." I sat back on his rock-hard thighs. "And the women will be envisioning themselves coming up to you and sitting on your lap like I am. They'll want to push their hands up your shirt like this."

I slid my palms beneath the hem of his T-shirt and pressed them against the rigid lacing of his abs. My fingers followed the grooves, tracing every muscle of his eight-pack that I could reach. "They'll fantasize about how hard your body is beneath your clothes, how your pecs will feel when they squeeze them."

My actions accompanied my words, my heartbeat starting to race at the feel of him beneath my hands. Gideon was so cut and strong, a powerful sexual machine. There was a primitive female drive that responded instantly to that. Craved it. He was a male worthy of mating with, an alpha in his prime. Vigorous. Potent. Eminently dangerous and untamable.

He moved and I stopped. "No, stay still," I admonished. "You wouldn't touch them back."

"They wouldn't be near me at all." But he resumed the pose I'd put him in. A sultan of old, being worshipped by an eager harem girl.

I lifted his shirt. I pulled it up and over his head, pinning his shoulders back with the hard stretch of fabric. His head turned, his mouth latching onto my nipple and suckling, easy, gentle tugs of suction on the sensitive point. I whimpered and tried to pull away, too turned on to bear it. His teeth caught the hardened tip, trapping me.

My head bowed, my eyes riveted to the sight of his hollowing cheeks. Inside the heat of his mouth, his tongue lashed my nipple, his lean throat working as he swallowed. My core tightened and trembled, echoing the rhythmic pulls.

Reaching between us, I untied the drawstring of his waistband and pushed the elastic down enough to free him. I held him in both hands, my fingertips tracing the thick pulsing veins coursing along his brutally sexy length. He was wet at the crown, my hands gliding over the slickness of pre-ejaculate.

His mouth released me when I aligned his cock with the opening to my sex. "Take it slow, angel," he ordered gruffly. "Work it in. I'll be in you all night and I don't want you sore."

Goose bumps swept over my skin. "They wouldn't imagine taking you slow," I argued.

Gideon reached up with both hands, pushing the hair

back from my face. "You're not thinking of other women now, angel. It's *you* you're picturing."

With a start, I realized he was right. The woman mounting him wasn't one of the leggy brunettes I'd visualized eye-fucking him. That was me. I was the one stroking his cock adoringly. I was the one positioning him, lowering onto him, taking a moment to rub the wide head of his penis back and forth between the lips of my sex.

My husband groaned at the feel of me, his hips lifting slightly, pushing demandingly into the entrance of my body. He grabbed my hips, pulled me down, spreading my sex open with the flared tip of his cock.

"Oh, Gideon." My eyelids grew heavy as I sank onto him, taking a thick inch inside me.

He lifted me slightly, until just the crown was in me, then lowered me again, making me take more. The tendons in his neck stood out in stark relief. "You don't want me wearing a sign. You want me wearing *you*, your tight, little cunt squeezing my cock. You imagine yourself topping me, as I just sit back and let you have it."

He stretched his arms out along the back of the sofa, displaying that magnificently male torso. "Or do you want me to participate?"

Wetting my dry lips, I shook my head. "No."

I pushed up, then slid back down. Over and over. Working him deeper each time, until my buttocks sat atop his thighs. He was thick and long. I whimpered softly as he throbbed inside me.

And I didn't have all of him yet.

Tilting my head, I kissed him, savoring the slow slide of his tongue against mine.

"They're watching you, aren't they?" he purred.

"Watching *you*. When I lift, they can catch a glimpse of you, see how large your cock really is. They want it, ache for it, but it's mine. You're the one watching me. You can't take your eyes off me. For you, there's no one else in the room."

"But I still don't touch you, do I?" His mouth curved wickedly when I shook my head. "I sip the cachaça casually, as if I don't have the sexiest woman alive riding my dick in full view of everyone. I'm not bored anymore, but then, I never was. I was waiting. For you. Knowing you were there because of the hum in my blood."

With my hands on his shoulders, I fucked him with cadenced pumps of my hips. He was delicious. The feel of his cock moving inside me. The low, dangerous rumble in his chest that betrayed how aroused he was. The sheen of sweat on his chest. The way his abs clenched when I dropped down and his cock pushed deep. I couldn't get enough.

And the way he joined my game . . . how well he knew me . . . how much he loved me . . .

Gideon lost himself in sex with me, but he was always aware, his focus on me before his orgasm. He'd recognized my fantasy of exhibitionist sex before I had, and he indulged it. Always keeping me safe, never truly risking exposure but teasing me with the possibility of it. I would never share him that way, I was too possessive. And he would never share even a glimpse of me because he was too protective.

But we teased and we played. For two people for whom sex had been introduced with pain and shame, that we could find such joy and love in the act was wondrous.

"I'm so hard inside you," he growled, flexing in my sex

the way he had in my hand. "The music is loud, so no one hears the sounds I make, but you can feel them. You know you're driving me crazy. The fact that I don't show it turns you on as much as being watched."

"Your control," I gasped, speeding up the tempo.

"Because I'm topping from the bottom," he said darkly. "You pretend to be in charge, but that's not what you want. I know your secrets, Eva. I'll know them all. There's nothing you can hide from me."

He put the pad of his thumb to his lips and ran his tongue across it in a slow, sensual lick, his eyes never leaving my face. Reaching between us, he rubbed my clit in hard, quick circles and I came with a cry, my sex milking his cock in ecstatic ripples.

He exploded into action, catching me close and rising, bearing me down to the couch on my back as he pushed off the floor with his feet, driving that final thick inch of cock inside me. Then he was fucking me with a violent, primal hunger, powering through the ripples of my climax in the race for his own.

Throwing his head back, he gasped my name and jerked inside me. He spurted hotly, groaning, his hips still thrusting as if he couldn't stop.

Blinking, I came to, slowly aware of moonlight on the ceiling. A pillow cushioned my head and the warmth of a comforter blanketed my nude body.

I turned my head to look for Gideon, but the space beside

me was empty, the covers disturbed but folded up neatly. I sat up and looked at the clock. It was almost three in the morning.

Sitting up, I looked toward the bathroom, then the hallway. Faint light filtered in through the crack of the partially closed door. I climbed out of bed and went to it, unhooking the robe that hung on the back. I slid into the peacock blue silk as I left the room, cinching the belt while I walked to Gideon's home office.

It was the light from that room that lit the hallway and I squinted as I entered, my eyes unaccustomed to the brightness. I took in the scene with a swift glance: the puppy asleep on the dog bed and the pensive man sitting at his desk. His gaze was on the collage of photos of me that graced his wall, his arms balanced on the armrests of his chair, a tumbler of amber liquid held between his hands.

He looked at me.

"What's wrong?" I asked, padding across the room in my bare feet. "You're not avoiding the bed, are you?"

"No. I should," he qualified, "but no. I couldn't sleep."

"Want me to wear you out?" I offered a smile, which probably looked silly considering I had one eye closed against the glare.

My husband set his drink down and patted his lap. "Come here."

I went to him, curling up against him with my arms around his neck. I pressed my lips to his jaw. "Something's bugging you."

And it had been bothering him all night, whatever it was.

Nuzzling the tip of his nose against the curve of my ear, he whispered, "Is there anything you haven't told me?"

I frowned and pulled back, searching his face. "Like what?"

"Like anything." His chest expanded on a deep breath. "Do you have any secrets left?"

I absorbed that, feeling an odd twisting in my stomach. "Your birthday present. But I'm not telling you what it is."

A tiny smile softened his mouth.

"And you," I murmur, charmed by that smile. "All the pieces of you that only I know. You are a secret I will keep until I breathe my last breath."

His head bowed, his hair briefly shielding his face. "Angel."

"Has something happened, Gideon?"

It took him a long moment to reply. He looked at me. "Would you tell me if someone you knew, someone close to you, was doing something illegal?"

The twisting in my gut turned into a knot. "What have you heard? Is some gossip blog spreading lies?"

He grew tense. "Answer the question, Eva."

"No one's doing anything illegal!"

"That's not what I asked," he said patiently but firmly.

I recalled the question. "Yes, I'd tell you. Of course. I tell you everything."

He relaxed. His hand reached up and touched my face. "You can trust me with anything, angel. It doesn't matter what it is."

"I do." I caught his wrist. "I don't understand why you're talking like this."

"I don't want any secrets between us."

I shot him a look. "You're the one who's been guiltiest about that. You never used to tell me anything."

"I'm working on that."

"I know you are. That's why things are really good between us right now."

The soft smile came back. "They are, aren't they?"

"Totally." I kissed his smiling mouth. "No more running, no more hiding."

Adjusting his hold on me, Gideon stood, lifting me with him.

"What are we doing?" I queried, burrowing into his warm body.

He headed back to the bedroom. "You're going to wear me out."

"Yay."

༚༝

The next morning passed like the morning before, with Gideon up at the usual time while I lazed naked in the bed like a sloth.

As he knotted his tie in the closet, he glanced away from the mirror to look at me. "What are your plans for the day?"

Yawning, I hugged my pillow closer. "I'm going back to sleep when you leave. Just for an hour. Blaire Ash is stopping by at ten."

"Is he?" He looked back at the mirror. "Why?"

"I'm changing things around. We're going to turn the guest bedroom into a home office with a Murphy bed. That way, we still have room for guests and I have a place to work."

Gideon smoothed his tie, then started buttoning his vest, stepping out into the bedroom. "We didn't discuss that."

"True." I deliberately moved my leg so that the sheet slid off it. "I didn't want you to argue about it."

We'd originally agreed to turn the guest room into my room and connect it to the master bath to form a his-and-hers master suite. The layout would address Gideon's parasomnia but also meant we'd have to sleep in separate rooms.

"We shouldn't be sharing a bed," he said quietly.

"I disagree." Before he could press the point, I went on. "I tried to make the best of it, Gideon, but I'm not happy with the idea of being apart like that."

He stood there silently, shoving his hands into the pockets of his slacks. "It's not fair to make me choose between your happiness and your safety."

"I know. But I'm not making you choose, I already decided. I'm aware that's not fair, either, but the call had to be made and I made it." I sat up and shoved the pillow behind me, scooting back so I could lean against the headboard.

"We made the call together. Then you apparently changed your mind without discussing it further. And flashing your tits at me—as stunning as they are—isn't going to distract me."

I narrowed my eyes at him. "If I wanted to distract you, I wouldn't have brought the subject up in the first place."

"Cancel the consult, Eva," he said tightly. "We need to talk about this first."

"The consult already happened. We had to cut it short because the cops came over, but Blaire's already working on new designs. He's bringing me some ideas today."

Gideon's hands came out of his pockets and his arms crossed. "So your happiness comes first and to hell with mine?"

"You're not happy sharing a bed with me?"

A muscle in his jaw ticced. "Don't jerk me around. You're not taking into consideration what it would do to me if I hurt you."

Abruptly my frustration turned to shame. "Gideon—"

"And you're not thinking about what it would do to *us*," he bit out. "I'll let you experiment with a lot of things, Eva, but nothing that's going to damage our relationship. If you want to fall asleep next to me, I'll be there. If you want to wake up with me beside you, I can do that, too. But the hours in between when we're both unconscious are too dangerous to gamble with on a fucking whim."

I swallowed past a lump in my throat. I wanted to explain further, to tell him that I worried about the distance separate bedrooms would create. Not just physically but emotionally.

It hurt me to have him make love to me, then leave my bed. It took something beautiful and magical and turned it into something else. And if he stayed until I slept, then woke before me to return, he would suffer from lack of sleep. As tireless as he so often seemed, he was still human. He worked hard, worked out harder, and had to deal with tons of stress day after day. Being short on sleep couldn't become routine.

But his fears for my safety weren't going to be dismissed in a single conversation. We would have to go step-by-step.

"Okay," I conceded. "Let's agree to this: Blaire will drop off his concepts and we'll look them over together later. In the meantime, we'll agree not to knock down any walls in the guest room. I think that's going too far, Gideon."

"You didn't think so before."

"It's a stopgap that may become permanent and we don't

want that. I mean, you don't want that, do you? You want to work on sleeping together, right?"

He unfolded his arms and rounded the bed, taking a seat on the edge. Taking my hand in his, he lifted it to his lips. "Yes, I want that. It kills me that I can't give you something so basic in our marriage. And knowing you're unhappy about it . . . I'm sorry, angel. I can't tell you how much."

Leaning forward, I cupped his cheek. "We'll work on it. I should've started by talking it out. Guess I pulled a Gideon on you—act first, explain later."

His mouth twisted ruefully. "Touché." He gave me a quick, hard kiss. "Watch out for Blaire. He wants you."

I sat back. "He finds me attractive," I corrected. "And he's a natural-born flirt."

Gideon's eyes took on a dangerous gleam. "Has he been hitting on you?"

"Nothing unprofessional. If he crossed a line I'd fire him myself, but I think he probably finesses all his female clients. I bet it's good for business." I smiled. "He cooled his jets when I told him I was getting used to your stamina and didn't feel like I needed a separate bed for sleep anymore."

His brows shot up. "You didn't."

"I totally did. I can sleep when I'm dead, I told him. In the meantime, if my husband wants to hit it with me a half-dozen times every night and he's as skilled as he is at doing it, who am I to complain?"

The first time we'd consulted with Blaire, I hadn't considered what the designer would think about Gideon marrying a woman he didn't intend to sleep with. When Blaire's subtle flirtation registered, I realized why he might think

I'd be receptive—and understood how awkward the whole situation was for my husband. Yet Gideon had never complained about how it might look to an outsider. His concern was for me, not his reputation as a world-class player.

I'd enjoyed setting Blaire straight.

I fluffed my messy hair. "I'm a blonde with big tits. Throw a giggle in there and I can usually get away with saying anything."

"Christ." Gideon feigned a long-suffering sigh but was clearly amused. "Is it a compulsion of yours to share the details of our sex life with everyone?"

"No." I winked. "But it's certainly fun."

❧

I didn't go to sleep after Gideon left for work. Instead, I picked up the phone and called my trainer, Parker Smith. Since it was early, he wasn't working yet and picked up.

"Hey, Parker. It's Eva Tramell. How are you?"

"I'm good. You coming in today? You're slacking lately."

I wrinkled my nose. "I know. And yes, I'm coming in. That's why I'm calling. I want to work on something with you."

"Yeah? What's on your mind?"

"We've gone over situational awareness and what to do if you're cornered, how to get away. But what if I'm completely taken off guard, like when I'm sleeping?"

He absorbed that. "A hard knee shot in the balls will lay any man out. Gives you the opening you need."

I'd done that before to Gideon, to snap him out of a vicious nightmare. I would do it again, if it came to that, but I'd prefer to break his hold and get away without hurting him. He was already hurting so much in his dreams. I didn't want him to wake up to pain, too.

"But what if . . . How would you knee someone when they're lying on top of you?"

"We can work it out. Choreograph some different scenarios." He paused. "Everything all right?"

"Everything's great," I assured him, and then I lied. "It just came up on a TV show I was watching last night and I realized that no matter how prepared you are, you can't be situationally aware when you're sleeping."

"No problem. I'll be at the warehouse in a couple hours and stay until closing."

"Okay. Thanks."

I ended the call, then headed into the shower. When I came back out, there were two missed calls from Cary. I dialed him back.

"Hey, what's up?"

"I've been thinking. You said something about a classic dress, right?"

I sighed. It made me cringe every time I thought about it. Because no matter how much I wanted to believe the perfect dress would fall out of the sky before the big day, it was more realistic to accept that I was going to have to settle.

Still, I had to love Cary for staying on me about it. He knew me as well as I knew myself.

"What about one of Monica's bridal gowns?" he suggested. "Something old and all that. You two have the same build. It wouldn't take much alteration."

"Ugh. Really? No, Cary. If she'd married my dad in it, maybe. But I can't wear something she wore to marry a stepdad. That's just weird."

He laughed. "Yeah, you're right. She has great taste, though."

I ran my fingers through my damp hair. "I don't think she keeps her wedding dresses, anyway. Not a great souvenir to have hanging around your new husband's house."

"Okay, so it's a stupid idea. We can hunt for something vintage. A pal of mine knows every couture and designer consignment shop in Manhattan."

The thought had merit. "Cool. That's a good idea."

"Sometimes, I'm brilliant. I'm tied up with Grey Isles today, but tonight works."

"I have couples counseling tonight."

"Oh, right. Have fun with that. Tomorrow? Maybe we'll pick up a few things for Ibiza, too."

The reminder of the weekend's plans made me feel pressed for time. I couldn't help being anxious about it, even knowing how much fun it would be to spend time with my friends. "Tomorrow's good. I'll come to the apartment."

"Sweet. We'll pack, too."

We hung up and I held my phone in my hand for a long time, feeling a sense of grief. For the first time since we'd moved to New York, it felt like Cary and I were living in two separate places. I was settling into being home with Gideon, while Cary's home was still very much the apartment.

My calendar app beeped a reminder that Blaire would be showing up in thirty minutes. Cursing to myself, I dropped my phone on the bed and hurried to get ready.

❧

"How are you both doing?" Dr. Petersen asked, as we all three took our seats.

Gideon and I sat on the couch, as usual, while Dr. Petersen settled into his armchair and picked up his tablet.

"We're better than ever," I answered.

My husband said nothing, but he reached over and took my hand, pulling it over to rest on his thigh.

"I received an invitation to your reception." Dr. Petersen smiled. "My wife and I are very much looking forward to it."

I hadn't been able to convince my mom to include even the tiniest bit of red on the invites, but I thought they were pretty all the same. We'd agreed on a vellum invitation, tucked into a sheer pocket, with an exterior white envelope for mailing and privacy. It gave me butterflies thinking of them being received. We were another step closer to putting the façade of an engagement behind us.

"Me, too." I leaned my shoulder against Gideon's and he put his arm around me.

"The last time we met," Dr. Petersen said, "you'd just quit your job, Eva. How has that been?"

"Easier than I thought. I've been busy, though, so that helps."

"Helps with what?"

I considered my answer. "From feeling aimless. I'm busier now. And I'm working on things that actually make a difference in my life."

"Such as?"

"The wedding, of course. And moving into the penthouse, which I'm doing in baby steps. And planning some renovations, which I'd like to talk about."

"Of course." He studied me. "Let's talk about those baby steps first. Is there any significance to that?"

"Well, just that I'm not doing it all at once. It's ongoing."

"Do you view it as a way to ease into the commitment? Previously, you've acted very decisively. Eloping. Separating. Quitting your job."

That made me think. "It's a transition that affects Gideon and Cary as much as it does me."

"As far as I'm concerned," Gideon interjected, "the sooner she's moved in, the better."

"I'm just being careful." I shrugged.

Dr. Petersen scrawled across his tablet screen, taking notes. "Is Cary having difficulty adjusting?"

"I don't know," I admitted. "He's not acting like he is. But I worry. He falls into bad habits without support."

"Do you have any thoughts about that, Gideon?"

He kept his tone neutral. "I knew what I was getting into when I married her."

"Always a good thing." Dr. Petersen smiled. "But that doesn't tell me much."

Gideon's hand lifted from my shoulder and went to my hair, playing with it. "As a married man yourself, Doctor, you know there are concessions a husband makes to keep the peace. Cary is one of mine."

That hurt me to hear, but I understood Cary had started out with a clean slate with Gideon. Then he'd made several wrong moves—like having group sex in our living room one night—that put marks against him.

Dr. Petersen looked at me. "So you're attempting to balance the needs of both your husband and your best friend. Is that stressful?"

"It's not fun," I hedged, "but it's not really balancing, either. My marriage—and Gideon—comes first."

I could tell Gideon liked hearing that when his hand fisted gently—possessively—in my hair.

"But," I continued, "I don't want to overwhelm Gideon and I don't want Cary to feel abandoned. Moving a small bag of stuff over every day makes the change gradual."

Once the thought was out, I had to admit how maternal that sounded. Still, I couldn't help wanting to protect those in my life who needed it, especially from pain my own actions might cause.

"You've mentioned everyone but you," he pointed out. "How do you feel?"

"The penthouse is starting to feel like home. The only thing I'm struggling with is our sleeping arrangements. We've been sharing a bed, but Gideon wants us to sleep separately and I don't."

"Because of the nightmares?" Dr. Petersen asked, his gaze on Gideon.

"Yes," he answered.

"Have you had any lately?"

My husband nodded. "Not the really bad ones."

"What constitutes a really bad nightmare? One that you act out physically?"

Gideon's chest expanded on a deep breath. "Yes."

The doctor looked at me again. "You understand the risk, Eva, but you still want to share a bed with Gideon."

"Yes, of course." My heartbeat quickened at the memories. Gideon had pinned me down viciously, ugly words of pain and fury spilling out in terrible threats of violence.

In the grip of a nightmare, Gideon didn't see me, he saw Hugh—a man he wanted to tear apart with his bare hands.

"Many happily married couples sleep separately," Dr. Petersen pointed out. "The reasons are varied—the husband snores, the wife steals the covers, et cetera—but they find that sleeping apart is more conducive to marital harmony than sleeping together."

I straightened away from Gideon, needing them both to understand. "I *like* sleeping next to him. Sometimes, I wake up in the middle of the night and I watch him sleep. Sometimes, I wake up and I don't even open my eyes, I just listen to him breathing. I can smell him, feel his warmth. I sleep better when he's beside me. And I know he sleeps better, too."

"Angel." Gideon's hand stroked my back.

Looking over my shoulder, I caught his gaze. His face was impassive. Gorgeous. His eyes, however, were dark blue pools of pain. I reached for his hand. "I know it hurts you. I'm sorry. I just need us to work toward having that. I don't want us to ever give up on it."

"What you describe," Dr. Petersen said gently, "is intimacy, Eva. And it's one of the true joys of marriage. It's understandable that you crave it. Everyone does to some extent. For you and Gideon, however, it probably seems particularly important."

"It does to me," I agreed.

"Are you implying it's different for me?" Gideon said tightly.

"No." I twisted to face him. "Please don't get defensive. This isn't your fault. I'm not blaming you."

"Do you know how shitty this makes me feel?" he accused.

"I wish you wouldn't take it personally, Gideon. It's—"

"My wife wants to watch me sleep and I can't even give her that," he snapped. "What is that, if not fucking personal?"

"Okay, let's discuss," Dr. Petersen said quickly, drawing our attention to him. "The root of this conversation is a craving for intimate familiarity. Human beings, by nature, desire intimacy, but childhood sexual abuse survivors can find this need especially acute."

Gideon was still tense, but he was listening attentively.

"In many cases," the doctor continued, "the abuser works hard to isolate the victim to help conceal their crime and make the victim dependent. The victims themselves very often withdraw from friends and family. Everyone else's lives seem so ordinary and the troubles of others so insignificant next to the terrible secret they feel forced to hide."

I slid back into place against Gideon's side, pulling my knees up to hug him with the whole of my body. His arm came tight around me once more, his other hand reaching for mine.

Dr. Petersen's face softened as he watched us. "That deep loneliness was alleviated when you both opened up to each other, but being starved of true intimacy for so long leaves a mark. I urge you to consider alternative ways to achieve the closeness you crave, Eva. Create signals and rituals that are unique to your relationship, that don't threaten either one of you and bring you both a sense of connection."

Sighing, I nodded.

"We'll work on it," he said. "And your nightmares, Gideon, are likely to continue to lessen in quantity and severity as we do. But this is just the beginning. We've taken some first steps in a long journey."

Tilting my head back, I looked up at Gideon. "A life-time," I vowed.

Gideon touched my cheek with gentle fingers. He didn't say the words, but I saw them in his gaze, felt them in his caress.

We had love. The rest would come.

10

"I've been communicating with Benjamin Clancy," Raúl said, leaning forward with his elbows on his knees. "You and Mrs. Cross will be heading toward the airport at the same time, so you can travel together, if you like."

"Of course." I needed that time with Eva before we went our separate ways. The hours in the workday were too long to be away from her. A weekend was going to be torture. "I'll call her and let her know we'll be picking her up. We'll need the limo."

A professional to the core, Raúl showed no reaction. It would make more sense to use the limo for Eva's friends, instead of us, but neither the Bentley nor the Benz offered the privacy I required.

Sitting on the couch in my office, I faced both Angus and Raúl, who'd settled into the two club chairs. We'd decided that Angus should stay behind while Raúl headed the security team accompanying me to Brazil.

Angus would be heading to Austin to dig into the background of Lauren Kittrie.

Raúl nodded his understanding. "We'll make separate transportation arrangements for her friends and yours."

"How is Eva getting to Ibiza?"

"Private jet," he replied, "chartered by Richard Stanton. I suggested they stay at the Hotel Vientos Cruzados Ibiza and Clancy agreed. It took some doing, as the resort is fully booked for the summer season, but the property manager was able to make it happen. They've stepped up security in anticipation of Mrs. Cross's arrival."

"Good." Having Eva stay in a Cross Industries resort gave me added peace of mind. We had two well-known nightclubs in Ibiza as well, one in Ibiza Town and one in Sant Antoni. I knew without asking that both had been pointed out to Clancy in advance. I expected he'd use the information. He was a smart man and would appreciate the added support provided by their security and staff.

"As we discussed previously," he went on, "we'll have our own team in place at the airport, and they'll follow Mrs. Cross over the weekend. They've been instructed to stay in plainclothes and blend in, providing backup for Clancy's team and interceding only when absolutely necessary."

I nodded. Clancy was good, but he had both Monica and Eva under his watch, and they considered Cary family, so Clancy would be watching him closely, too. His focus would be divided three ways, with Monica taking precedence as the wife of his employer. Eva wasn't the priority for anyone else that she was for me. I wanted dedicated eyes on her every moment she was out of the hotel.

Thank God this weekend was a once-in-a-lifetime event.

Raúl stood. "I'll touch base with Clancy to discuss the protocol for getting to the airport."

"Thanks, Raúl."

With a nod, he left.

Angus rose to his feet. "I'll be hieing off to take Lucky to your sister. She's texting me every hour to see if I've left yet."

That almost made me smile. Ireland had been excited when I asked if she would watch the dog for me. I figured Lucky would like that better than boarding, and Ireland could use a distraction from our mother's depression over the divorce.

Angus paused on the way to the door. "Have fun, lad. It'll do you good."

I snorted. "Call me if you find anything."

"Of course." He departed, too, leaving me alone to finish up the workweek.

I noted the time on my phone before I speed-dialed my wife.

"Hi, ace," she answered, her voice light and bright. "Can't stop thinking about me, can you?"

"Tell me you were thinking about me."

"Always."

I remembered her as she'd been last night, lying prone on the bed with her heels kicked up behind her. She had watched me pack with her chin propped on her hands, commenting occasionally on my choices. She'd noted that I didn't pack either the graphite gray slacks she fantasized about or a black V-neck T-shirt. The deliberate omission was the one thing that made her smile. Otherwise, she had been mostly quiet and moody.

262 • SYLVIA DAY

"You and I are going to ride to the airport together," I told her. "Alone."

"Oh." She let that sink in. "That'll be nice."

"I'm shooting for more than nice."

"Ohhh . . ." Her voice lowered, took on the soft huskiness that told me her thoughts had turned to sex. "Got a little transportation fetish yourself?"

Warm amusement slid through me, helping to ease the stress brought on by thinking of the days ahead. Eva would let me have her anywhere, but she frequently seduced me while we were en route to somewhere. Having previously been restricted to having sex only in the hotel, she'd rocked my world by inciting me to make love to her in cars and planes, as well as my home and various places of business.

I would never say no to her. I wasn't capable of it. When she wanted me, I was ready and more than willing.

"I have an Eva fetish," I murmured, turning around something she'd once said to me.

"Good." She took a breath. "Is the weekend over yet?"

I heard Cary say something I couldn't quite make out. "Soon, angel. I'll let you go."

"Don't ever let me go, Gideon." There was a fervency to her words that moved me, betraying how unsettled she was by the weekend ahead. After the separation she'd enforced, it was good to know she wasn't looking forward to another, even under much happier circumstances.

"I'll let you get back to it," I corrected. "So you can be ready when Raúl comes for you."

"Never mind him. I'll be ready to come for you," she purred back, leaving me hard and aching as I ended the call.

᷉

Arash entered my office shortly after four, sauntering in with his hands in his pockets and humming a tune. He grinned as he sank into one of the chairs in front of my desk. "You ready for the weekend?"

"As ready as I'm going to be." I sat back and drummed my fingers on the armrests of my chair.

"You'll be happy to hear that Anne Lucas's assault complaint is going away."

I'd expected as much, but it was still good to have confirmation. "As it should."

"I haven't heard if she'll be charged with falsely reporting an incident. In the meantime, if she attempts contact with you, Eva, or Cary in any way, I need to know immediately."

I nodded absently. "Of course."

He studied me. "Where's your head at right now?"

My mouth twisted wryly. "I just got off the phone with one of the Vidal Records board members. Christopher is continuing to work on acquiring the capital for a buyout."

Arash's brows shot up. "If he pulls it together, would you consider getting out?"

"If I only had him to worry about, I would." Whether Ireland chose to join the family business in the future was still to be seen, but regardless, she had a stake in the success of the company, and Christopher made poor decisions. All of my offers to support him and offer guidance had been rejected. He often refused to listen to Chris as well, apparently assuming his father's wisdom came in some part from me.

"What does the board think?"

"It's viewed as a family feud and they want me to find a quick, painless resolution."

"Is that possible? You've never gotten along with your brother."

I shook my head. "It's a nonstarter."

I knew Arash couldn't understand. He had a brother and sister of his own, and his family was extremely tight-knit.

He sighed. "Sorry, man. That's tough."

In an ideal world, Christopher would be attending my bachelor party weekend. We'd be close. He would be the best man at my wedding . . .

. . . which was a position I hadn't yet asked anyone to fill. Arnoldo had taken the reins with the weekend planning, but I didn't know if he had done so because he assumed he'd be standing beside me at the wedding. Maybe he just had more initiative than the other guys.

Only a few short weeks ago it would have been a no-brainer to have Arnoldo stand with me. Part of me hoped that he still would.

Arash was also a good choice. Unlike Arnoldo, I saw Arash nearly every day. And as my attorney, he knew things about me—and Eva—that no one else did. I could trust him with anything, even without the protection of attorney/client privilege.

But Arnoldo was direct with me in a way no one else was, aside from my wife. I'd long thought that Arnoldo's blunt, incisive advice had kept me from becoming too cynical and jaded.

This weekend should make the choice between the two men clear.

⤬

It felt . . . wrong to stand outside Eva's apartment door and wait for her. As I leaned against the wall opposite the doorway, I considered how swiftly things had turned a corner and how violently opposed I was to having them ever go back. I hadn't known it could be like this between us. Open, nothing to hide, so deeply in love.

There had been glimpses of this life before. Some of the nights we'd spent together in the apartment next door. The weekends we'd sneaked away to be alone together. But those times had existed in a vacuum. Now, we lived those moments openly. It would be even better when the world knew we were married and she lived completely in the penthouse with me.

The door opened and Eva stepped out, looking cool and sexy in a sleeveless red wrap dress and heeled sandals. She had sunglasses perched atop her head and was wheeling a suitcase out beside her. The next time she packed, it would be for our honeymoon. We'd leave together, like we were doing now, but we would stay together from that moment forward.

"Here," I said, straightening to take the suitcase from her.

She tackled me as I reached for it, her body soft and warm against mine. She pulled my head down and kissed me, a quick, sweet kiss. "You should've come in."

"You and me with a bed nearby?" I caught her around the waist and steered her toward the elevator. "I would've taken advantage, if I didn't think Cary would bang on the door and bitch about missing your flight."

Eva separated from me as we descended to the lobby,

reaching behind her to grab the handrail and showing off her sexy legs. It was a full-body flirt, with her eyes playing the game, too. They sparkled at me as she licked her bottom lip. "You look super sexy."

I glanced down at the white V-neck T-shirt and khakis I'd changed into before leaving work.

"You usually wear dark colors," she pointed out.

"Too hot for that where we're going."

"*You're* too hot." She lifted one foot off the elevator floor and slowly rubbed her thighs together.

Amused and feeling the slow heat of building arousal, I settled back and enjoyed the show.

Once we'd reached the lobby, I gestured her out in front of me, catching up to her in two strides so I could place my hand at the small of her back.

She tossed me a smile over her shoulder. "There's going to be traffic."

"Damn." Traffic—and the time it would add to the commute—was what I was counting on.

"You sound sooo disappointed," she teased, before smiling at the doorman, who opened the door for her.

Raúl waited outside by the limo. In moments, we were on our way, merging into the sea of cars battling their way across Manhattan.

Eva took the bench seat that spanned the length of the vehicle, while I settled on the seat in the back. "Want a drink?" she asked, looking at the bar across from her.

"Do you?"

"I'm not sure." Her lips pursed. "I wanted one earlier."

I waited for her to make up her mind, my gaze sliding

over her. She was my joy, the light in my world. I would do anything to keep her carefree and content for the rest of her life. It weighed on me to think I might have to hurt her. She'd been through so much already.

If we found out that Monica was not who Eva thought she was at all, how would I break that news? My wife had been crushed when she realized her mother was tracking her via her mobile phone, her watch, and a compact mirror in her purse. A false identity was a much worse betrayal.

And what did that fake identity hide?

"I can't find a dress," she said abruptly, her lush mouth turned down in a frown.

It took me a beat to snap out of my thoughts and register what she was saying. "For the wedding?"

She nodded, looking so despondent I wanted to pull her close and press kisses all over her beautiful face.

"Want me to help, angel?"

"You can't. The groom isn't supposed to see the wedding dress before the big day." Her eyes widened with shock and horror. "You saw the dress I wore when we got married the first time!"

I had. I'd picked it out. "It was only a dress when I saw it," I soothed. "It wasn't a wedding dress until you wore it."

"Oh." The smile came back. She peeled off her sandals and joined me, lying down with her head in my lap, her hair a silvery gold fan across my thighs.

Running my fingers through the thick silk strands, I took a deep breath, relishing the smell of her perfume.

"What are you going to wear?" she asked, her eyes closing.

"Are you picturing something in particular?"

Her mouth curved. Her answer came out slow and dreamy. "A tux. You're always gorgeous. But in a tuxedo, you're something else."

I brushed my fingertips over her lips. There had been times when I hated my face, hated that my looks attracted intense sexual interest at a time when being lusted after made my skin crawl. Eventually, I got used to the attention, but not until Eva did I begin to value who I was for my own sake.

She took so much pleasure in looking at me. Clothed. Unclothed. In the shower. Wrapped in a towel. On top of her. Underneath her. About the only time her eyes weren't on me was when she was asleep. Which was when I often took the most pleasure in looking at her, lusciously naked, wearing nothing but the jewelry I'd given her.

"A tux it is, then."

Her eyes opened, revealing the soft gray I adored. "But it's a beach wedding."

"I'll make it work."

"Yes, I bet you can."

Turning her head, she nuzzled her nose against my cock. The heat of her breath drifted through the khakis to my sensitive skin. I hardened for her.

I played with her hair. "What do you want, angel?"

"This." She ran her fingers along the length of my erection.

"How do you want it?"

Her tongue darted out to wet her lips. "In my mouth," she breathed, already freeing the button of my waistband.

My eyes closed for a moment on a deep inhalation. The sound of my zipper lowering, the release of pressure as she carefully freed my cock . . .

I steeled myself for the wet heat of her mouth, but it was pointless. I jerked hard when she pulled me in with easy suction, hunger and need tingling down my spine. I knew her moods and how they translated to sex. She planned to take her time, to enjoy me and drive me out of my mind.

"Eva." I groaned as she stroked me with gentle fingers, her mouth working softly. She tongued the head of my dick with slow, savoring licks.

Opening my eyes, I looked down at her. The sight of her, so perfectly presentable, her focus entirely on the feel of my cock in her mouth was both searingly erotic and achingly tender.

"God, that's good," I said hoarsely, cupping the back of her head in one hand. "Take it deeper . . . yes, like that . . ."

My head fell back as my thighs tensed, straining with the need to thrust. I fought the urge, letting her take what she wanted.

"I won't finish like this," I warned her, knowing that was her goal.

She hummed a protest and fisted me, pumping my cock in her soft, firm grip. Challenging me to resist her.

"I'll be riding your perfect cunt, Eva. My cum is going to be deep inside you while you spend the weekend away from me."

My eyes closed as I imagined her in Ibiza, a city famous for its wild nightlife, dancing with her friends in a crush of bodies. Men would covet her, dream of fucking her. All the while she'd be marked by me in the most primitive way possible. Possessed, even though I wasn't there.

I felt her moan vibrate along the length of my dick.

She pulled back, her lips already red and plump. "That's not fair," she pouted.

I caught her wrist and lifted her hand to my chest, pressing it against my pounding heart. "You'll be right here, angel. Always."

～❧～

"*Mano*, you can't be working right now," Manuel complained, dropping into the lounger beside me. "You're missing the view."

I glanced up from my phone, the ocean breeze rifling through my hair. We'd remained in Barra today, directly across Avenida Lúcio Costa from the hotel we were staying in. Recreio Beach was more laid-back than Copacabana, less touristy and crowded. All along the shore, women in bikinis frolicked in the surf, breasts bouncing as they jumped waves, nearly-bare asses glistening with tanning oil. On the white sand in front of them, Arash and Arnoldo continued tossing a Frisbee back and forth. I'd bowed out when I felt my phone buzz in the pocket of my board shorts.

I looked at Manuel, finding him flushed and glistening with sweat. He'd disappeared about an hour ago and it was obvious why, even without knowing him as well as I did.

"My view is better." I turned my phone to show him the selfie Eva had just sent me. She was lying out on the beach, too, stretched across a lounger not much different from the one I occupied. Her bikini was white, her skin already lightly tanned. A thin chain hooked around her neck, nestled between her plump tits, then wrapped around her trim waist. Sunglasses shielded her eyes and bright red gloss stained the lips she'd puckered in a kiss.

Wish you were here . . . she'd texted.

So did I. I was counting down the several hours remaining until we'd get on the plane home. Saturday had been enjoyable enough, a blur of alcohol and music, but Sunday was a day too long.

Manuel whistled. "Hot damn."

I grinned, as that about summed up my thoughts on my wife's photo.

"Don't you worry that things will change after you say *I do*?" he asked, leaning back with his hands tucked behind his head. "Wives don't look like that. They don't send selfies like that."

I exited out to the home screen and flipped my phone around again.

Manuel's eyes widened at the wedding photo that served as my wallpaper. "No way. When?"

"A month ago."

He shook his head. "I can't see it. Marriage, I mean, not you and Eva. How does it not get old?"

"Being happy never gets old."

"Isn't variety the spice of life or some shit?" he asked, in some sort of half-assed philosophical mood. "Part of the fun in fucking a woman is figuring out what makes her tick and being surprised when she shows you something new. You keep tagging it, doesn't it become routine? Touch her here, lick her there, keep the rhythm she likes to get her off . . . Rinse and repeat."

"When your time comes, you'll figure it out."

He shrugged. "You want kids? Is that why?"

"Eventually. Not any time soon." I couldn't even picture it. Eva would make a wonderful mother; she was a nurturer. But the two of us together as parents? One day, I'd be ready

272 • SYLVIA DAY

for that. One day far away, when I could bear to share her with someone else. "Right now, I just want her."

"Mr. Cross."

I looked up and saw Raúl standing behind me, his mouth a tight line. I instantly stiffened, then sat up, my legs swinging off the side to plant my feet in the sand. "What is it?"

Fear for Eva settled heavily in my gut. She'd just texted me moments before, but . . .

"You'll want to see this," he said grimly, drawing my attention to the tablet he carried.

Standing, I shoved my phone in my pocket and closed the distance between us. I held out my hand. The glare from the sun darkened the screen, so I shifted to cast my shadow over the glass. The photo that came into focus froze the blood in my veins. The headline made my teeth grind.

Gideon Cross's Wild Brazilian Bachelor Party.

"What the fuck is this?" I snapped.

Manuel slapped a hand on my shoulder as he came up beside me. "Looks like a good time, *cabrón*. With two very hot babes."

I looked at Raúl.

"Clancy sent that to me," he explained. "I ran a search and it's gone viral."

Clancy. Fuck. *Eva* . . .

Shoving the tablet at Raúl, I yanked my phone back out. "I want to know who took that picture." Who knew I was in Brazil? Who'd followed me into a club one night, into a private VIP area, and taken pictures?

"Already on it."

Cursing under my breath, I called my wife. Impatience and fury rode me hard as I waited for her to pick up. Her voice mail kicked in and I hung up. Dialed again. Worry crowded in.

The worst fears of her fantasies were captured in living color in that photo. I had to explain, even without knowing how. Sweat beaded my forehead and dampened my palms, but inside, I was chilled.

Her voice mail picked up a second time.

"Goddamn it." Hanging up, I dialed again.

11

"You look like you need a refill," Shawna said, setting down two rebujitos on the small table between our two loungers.

"God." I laughed, slightly tipsy. The mix of dry sherry and sweet soda in the drink had a sneaky punch. And it wasn't exactly wise to chase away a hangover with more alcohol. "I'm going to need to detox after this weekend."

She grinned and stretched back out, her freckled skin still pale and slightly pink after two days in the sun. Her red hair was piled atop her head in a sexy mess, her voice slightly hoarse from laughing so hard the night before. She'd donned a bright aqua blue bikini that drew many appreciative eyes her way. Shawna was a bright spot of color, with a ready smile and bawdy sense of humor.

In that way, she was a lot like her brother, who I knew and loved as the fiancé of my former boss, Mark.

Megumi walked up on my other side, carrying two more

drinks. She looked at the empty lounger where my mom had been. "Where's Monica?"

"She went to cool off in the water." I looked for her but didn't see her. She was hard to miss in her lavender bikini, so I figured she'd wandered off somewhere. "She'll be back."

She'd been with us the whole time, partying alongside us every step of the way. It wasn't her style to drink too much and stay up too late, but she seemed to be having fun. She was certainly causing a stir. Men of all ages flocked around her. There was a kittenish sensuality about my mother that was irresistible. I wished I had that.

"Look at him go," Shawna said, drawing my attention to where Cary played in the surf. "He's a total chick magnet."

"Oh yeah."

The beach was packed, so much so that it was hard to see the sand. Dozens of shoulders and heads bobbed amid the ocean waves, but it was easy to see the cluster around Cary. He was flashing his grin, soaking up the attention like a cat in the sun. With his hair slicked back, the beauty of his gorgeous face was on display, despite the aviator shades he wore to block out the bright sun.

Catching me watching him, he waved. I blew him a kiss, just to stir things up.

"You and Cary never got together?" Shawna asked. "Did you ever want to?"

I shook my head. Cary was stunning now, healthy and leanly muscular, a prime example of the perfect male. But when I'd met him, he had been gaunt and hollow-eyed, always shrouded in hoodies even in the warmth of San Diego summers. He'd kept his arms covered to hide the evidence of his cutting and wore the hood over his closely cropped head.

In group therapy sessions, he'd always sat outside the circle and against a wall, his chair kicked back to balance on the rear legs. He commented rarely, but when he did, his humor was dark and laced with sarcasm, his insight almost always cynical.

I had approached him once, unable to ignore the deep inner pain that radiated from him. *Don't waste my time easing into it*, he'd said smoothly, his beautiful green eyes devoid of any light at all. *You want to ride my dick, just say so. I never say no to a fuck.*

I knew that was true. Dr. Travis had a lot of messed-up patients, many of whom used sex as a salve or form of self-punishment. Cary was available to be used by all of them, and many walked through that open-door invitation frequently.

No, thanks, I'd shot back, disgust triggered by his sexual aggression. *You're too skinny for me. Eat a fucking cheeseburger, dickhead.*

I regretted trying to be nice to him after that. He'd stalked me mercilessly, constantly putting me off with crass sexual come-ons. I'd been prickly at first. When that didn't work, I'd killed him with kindness. Eventually, he'd realized I really wasn't going to sleep with him.

In the meantime, he started putting on weight. He let his hair start growing out. He stopped being the resident fuck, although he was simply more selective. I had noticed how gorgeous he was, but there was no attraction there. He was too much like me and my self-preservation instincts had been on high alert.

"We were friends," I told her. "Then he became like a brother to me."

"I adore him," Megumi said, smoothing suntan lotion over

her legs. "He told me that things are rough with him and Trey right now. I'm sorry to hear that. They're so great together."

I nodded, my gaze going back to my dearest friend. Cary was lifting a woman up by the waist to toss her into the waves. She came up sputtering and laughing, clearly smitten. "It's lame to say that it'll work out if it's meant to, but that's what I'm going with."

I still needed to call Trey. And Gideon's mom, Elizabeth. I wanted to touch base with Ireland, too. And Chris. Since I'd probably be wiped out from jet lag and too much alcohol, I made a mental note to fit in all those calls while I recovered at the penthouse. I had to touch base with my dad, too, since I'd put off our scheduled Saturday call due to the time difference between us.

"I don't want to go home." Megumi stretched out with a sigh, her drink in her hands. "These two days went by too fast. I can't believe we're leaving in a few hours."

I could easily stay another week, if I weren't missing Gideon so much.

"Eva, honey."

My head tilted at the sound of my mom's voice. She'd come up behind me and stood behind my lounger wrapped in her cover-up. "Is it time to go already?"

She shook her head. Then I noticed she was wringing her hands. Never a good sign.

"Can you come back to the hotel with me?" she asked. "I need to talk to you about something."

I saw Clancy standing behind her, his jaw tight and hard. My pulse began to race. Standing, I grabbed the sarong I'd worn down to the beach and tied it around my waist.

"Should we come?" Shawna asked, sitting up.

"Stay here with Cary," my mom replied, offering a reassuring smile.

It amazed me how she did that, acting so cool and unruffled when I knew she was anxious. I was too expressive to hide my reactions, but my mom only showed emotion with her eyes and her hands, often saying that even laughter put lines on a face. Since she was wearing sunglasses, she was effectively camouflaged.

Mutely, I followed her and Clancy back to the hotel. Once we reached the lobby, it seemed like every employee had to greet us with a smile or wave. They all knew who I was. After all, we were staying in one of Gideon's resorts. The name Vientos Cruzados meant Crosswinds.

Gideon had married me at a Crosswinds resort. I hadn't realized they were a global chain.

We stepped into an elevator and Clancy slid a key card into the necessary slot, a security measure that limited access to our floor. Since there were other people in the car with us, I still had to wait for answers.

I felt sick to my stomach, my thoughts bouncing all over the place. Had something happened to Gideon? Or my dad? I realized I'd left my phone on the table by my drink and kicked myself. If I could only send a quick text to Gideon, I'd feel like I was doing something besides driving myself crazy.

After three stops, the elevator car was empty except for us as we continued the climb to our floor.

"What's going on?" I asked, turning to face both my mom and Clancy.

She pulled her shades off with trembling fingers. "There's a scandal brewing," she began. "Mostly online."

Which meant it was out of control. Or about to be. "Mom. Just tell me."

She took a deep breath. "There are some pictures . . ." She glanced at Clancy for help.

"Of what?" I thought I might vomit. Had the pictures my stepbrother Nathan had taken gotten out somehow? Or stills from the sex tape with Brett?

"Photos of Gideon Cross in Brazil went viral this morning," Clancy said. He spoke neutrally, but there was something oddly stiff about his stance. So much tension was unusual for him.

I felt as if I'd been punched in the gut. I didn't say anything more. There was nothing to say until I saw the evidence.

We exited directly into our suite, a massive space with several bedrooms and a large central living area. The maids had opened the doors leading out to the wraparound balcony, and the sheer drapes fluttered in the breeze, escaping the ties meant to contain them. Bright with the color and warmth of Spain, the suite had delighted me the moment we arrived.

I barely registered any of it now.

I walked on shaky legs to the couch and waited for Clancy to key in his code on a tablet and pass it over to me. My mom took the seat beside me, silently offering her support.

Looking down, I sucked in a quick audible breath. My chest felt like it was being crushed in a vise. What I saw freaked me out . . . it was as if someone had crawled inside my head and captured one of the images in my mind.

My gaze locked on Gideon, so dark and gorgeous dressed entirely in black. The fall of his hair partially hid his face, but it was clearly my husband. I hoped it wouldn't be, tried to find something that would betray the man in the photo as a fraud. But I knew Gideon's body as well as I knew my own. Knew how he moved. How he relaxed. How he seduced.

I looked away from that beloved figure in the center of the obscene tableau, unable to bear it.

A U-shaped sectional sofa. Black velvet curtains. A half-dozen bottles of top-shelf liquor on a low table.

A private VIP booth.

A slender brunette reclined on a mound of throw pillows. The low V of her sequined top shoved aside. Gideon's body was partly over hers. His mouth sucked her nipple.

A second leggy brunette. Draped over his back. One thigh hooked over his. Her legs spread. Her mouth a wide O of pleasure. Gideon's arm reached behind him. His hand beneath her short skirt.

It wasn't visible, but his fingers were inside her. I knew it. It was a sharp, jagged knife in my heart.

The image blurred as I blinked the tears away, feeling them run hotly down my face. I scrolled, swiping the picture out of sight. Then I saw my name and scanned the writer's crude speculation as to what I would think about my fiancé's sexcapades as he said farewell to bachelorhood.

I set the tablet on the coffee table, breathing hard. My mother scooted closer and put her arm around me, pulling me into her embrace. The room phone rang loudly, jolting me and abrading my nerves.

"Shh . . ." she whispered, her hand stroking over my hair. "I've got you, honey. I'm right here."

Clancy went to the handset and answered with a brusque

"Yes?" Then his tone took on a chilly bite. "I see you're having a good time."

Gideon.

I looked at Clancy and felt the heat rippling off him. He met my gaze. "Yes, she's here."

I straightened away from my mother and managed to stand. Fighting off a wave of nausea, I went to him and held out my hand for the phone. He gave the cordless handset to me and stepped back.

I swallowed a sob. "Hello."

There was a pause. Gideon's breathing quickened. I'd said one word, but from that, he knew that I knew.

"Angel—"

Abruptly sick, I ran to the bathroom and dropped the phone, barely managing to lift the toilet seat before emptying the contents of my stomach in racking, violent heaves.

My mother ran in and I shook my head at her. "Go away," I gasped, sinking to the floor with my back against the wall.

"Eva—"

"I need a minute, Mom. Just . . . give me a minute."

She stared at me, then nodded, closing the door behind her.

From the phone on the floor, I heard Gideon yelling. I reached for it, wrapping my hand around it and dragging it over. I lifted it to my ear.

"Eva! For God's sake, pick up the phone!"

"Stop shouting," I told him, my head pounding.

"Christ." He took a ragged breath. "You're sick. Damn it. I'm too far away . . ." His voice rose. "Raúl! Where the fuck are you? I want the goddamn jet ready now! Get on the damn phone—"

"No. No, don't—"

"It happened before I met you." He spoke too fast, was breathing too fast. "I don't know when or—What?" Someone spoke in the background. "Cinco de Mayo? For fuck's sake. Why is this coming out now?"

"Gideon—"

"Eva, I swear to you that fucking picture wasn't taken this weekend. I would *never* do that to you. You *know* that. You know what you mean to me—"

"Gideon, calm down." My racing pulse began to slow. He was frantic. Panicked. It broke my heart to hear it. He was so strong, capable of managing and surviving and crushing anything.

I was his weakness, when all I wanted was to be his strength.

"You have to believe me, Eva. I would never do that to us. I would never—"

"I believe you."

"—fuck around—What?"

Closing my eyes, I let my head fall back to rest against the wall. My stomach began to settle. "I believe you."

His shuddered exhale came hard and heavy across the line. "God."

Silence.

I knew how much it meant to him that I believed him utterly. About everything. Anything. He couldn't help but find that nearly impossible to accept, even as he craved my trust more than I think he craved my love. To him, my belief in him *was* my love.

His explanation was simple, some might say too simple,

but knowing him the way I did, it was the one that made the most sense.

"I love you." His voice was soft. Weary. "I love you so much, Eva. When you didn't answer your phone—"

"I love you, too."

"I'm sorry." He made a small noise filled with pain and regret. "So sorry you saw that. It's so fucked up. All of this is fucked up."

"You've seen worse." Gideon had seen me kiss Brett Kline, right in front of him. He'd watched at least some of the sex tape that featured Brett and me. Compared to that, a photo was nothing.

"I hate that you're there and I'm here."

"Me, too." I wanted the solace of his arms around me. More than that, I wanted to comfort him. To show him again that I wasn't going anywhere and he had no reason to fear.

"We're not doing this again."

"No, you're only getting married twice—both times to me. No more bachelor parties for you."

He huffed out a laugh. "That's not what I meant."

"I know."

"Tell Clancy to bring you home now. We're packing up to head to the airport."

I shook my head, even though he couldn't see. "Take tomorrow off."

"Tomorrow . . . ? Yes. You're sick—"

"No, I'm fine. I'm coming to you. In Rio."

"What? No. I don't want to be here. I need to be home to sort this shit out."

"It's out in the wild, Gideon. Nothing you can do will change that." I pulled myself up off the floor. "You can hunt him—or her—down later. I'm not letting this ruin our memories of the weekend."

"It doesn't—"

"If they want pictures of you in Brazil, ace, I'm going to be in them."

He took that in. "All right. I'll be waiting for you."

≈

"Maybe it's Photoshopped," Megumi said.

"Or that guy is a lookalike," Shawna suggested, leaning close to Megumi to look at her tablet. "You can't really see that much of him, Eva."

"No." I shook my head. It was what it was. "That's definitely Gideon."

Cary, who sat beside me in the limo, took my hand in his and linked our fingers. My mom sat on the bench seat directly behind the driver, looking at fabric swatches. Her sleek legs were crossed, her foot tapping restlessly.

Both Megumi and Shawna shot me pitying looks.

Their sympathy chafed my pride. I'd made the mistake of looking at social media. It amazed me how cruel people could be. According to some, I was a woman scorned. Or I was just too stupid not to realize I was marrying a man who would give me his name while giving his body and attention to anyone he chose. I was a gold digger willing to put up with the humiliation for the money. I was a woman who could be a champion for all women . . . if I turned my back on Gideon and found someone else.

"It's an old photo," I reiterated.

In reality, May wasn't all that long ago, but no one needed to know exactly when, aside from the fact that the photo hadn't been taken while he was in a relationship with me.

He'd changed so much since then. For me. For us. And I was no longer the woman he'd met that fateful day in June.

"It's ancient," Shawna said decisively. "Totally."

Megumi nodded but still looked dubious.

"Why would he lie?" I asked flatly. "It wouldn't take much work to find the club in the background. It has to be one of Gideon's, and I bet you it's in Manhattan. He couldn't be in New York and have a passport stamped in Brazil on the same day."

It had taken me a couple of hours to figure that out and I was kind of glad about that. I didn't need proof my husband was telling me the truth. But if we could somehow prove the photo was taken in a specific, identifiable location, it would be nice to set the public record straight.

"Oh, right." Megumi gave me a big smile. "And he's crazy about you, Eva. He wouldn't mess around."

I nodded my agreement, then pushed the subject aside. We would be at the airport soon and I didn't want us to leave each other thinking about stupid gossip instead of the amazing trip we'd had. "Thank you for coming. I had a great time."

I would've loved to take them to Rio, too, but they didn't have the required visas to enter the country. Plus, they both had to work on Monday. So we'd part ways, with the girls heading home with Clancy's security team, while Cary, my mom, and Clancy flew with me to Brazil on a jet Gideon had secured for us.

It was going to be a quick trip. We'd arrive on Monday morning and leave Monday night. What sleep we managed to catch would be on the jet. But by the time I was done, Gideon would leave Brazil with a smile. I didn't want him looking back on the weekend with regret. He had enough bad memories. Moving forward, I wanted him to store up nothing but good ones.

"We should be thanking you." Shawna grinned. "I wouldn't have missed this for the world."

"I'm with Shawna," Megumi said. "This was a trip of a lifetime."

Closing her eyes, Shawna leaned her head back against the seat. "Say hi to Arnoldo for me."

I knew Shawna and Arnoldo had become friends since they had been introduced the night we'd gone to the Six-Ninths concert. I think they felt safe with one another. Shawna was waiting for her boyfriend, Doug, to come home from Sicily, where he was attending an exclusive course for chefs. Arnoldo was nursing a broken heart, but he was a man who loved women and likely appreciated being able to enjoy the companionship of one who expected nothing more.

Cary was dealing with something similar. He missed Trey and wasn't interested in screwing around, which was huge for him. Usually, when he was hurting, he fucked to forget. Instead, he'd spent the weekend sticking close to Megumi, who looked like a deer in headlights when men approached her. Cary had been her shield, keeping things light and fun for both of them.

Gideon wasn't the only one who'd come a long way.

As for me, I was dying to be with my husband. Stress

brought on nightmares for him, so I pulled out my phone and texted him. *Dream of me.*

His response was so perfectly Gideon, it brought a smile to my face. *Fly faster.*

And just that quick, I knew he was back on his game.

"Wow." I stared out the window of the jet as it taxied to a halt at a private airport on the outskirts of Rio. "Now, that's a view."

Standing on the tarmac were Gideon, Arnoldo, Manuel, and Arash. All dressed casually in long shorts and T-shirts. All dark-haired and tall. Beautifully muscular. Tanned.

They were lined up like a row of exotic, outrageously expensive sports cars. Powerful, sexy, dangerously fast.

I had no doubts about my husband's fidelity, but if there had been any, looking at him would've settled them. His friends were loose-limbed and relaxed, their engines cooled by long, hard rides. That they'd enjoyed Rio—and its women— was stamped all over them. Gideon, however, was taut. Watchful. His motor was running, purring with the need to roar from zero to sixty in the space of a pounding heartbeat. No one had given my man a test drive.

I had come to him with the intent to soothe, to strategize, to take a bit of my wounded pride back. Instead, I was going to be the driver who burned his fuel.

Yes, please.

I felt a slight bump as the rolling staircase was positioned against the jet. Clancy exited first. My mom followed. I went after her, pausing at the top of the stairs to snap a picture with my phone. The image of Gideon and his friends was going to give the Internet something else to talk about.

I took the first step down and Gideon moved, his arms unfolding as he closed the distance between us. I couldn't see his eyes, only myself in the reflection of his lenses, but I felt the intensity with which he had me in his sights. It made my knees weak, forcing me to hold on to the handrail for balance.

He shook Clancy's hand. He endured and even managed to reciprocate a brief hug from my mother. But he never took his eyes off me or slowed more than a few seconds.

I'd put on red fuck-me heels for him. Tight, white shorts barely covered my ass and fastened well below my navel. My top was red lace, with thin straps. A red satin ribbon secured the corsetlike back. I had clipped my hair in a messy updo. Gideon made it messier when he caught me up on the last step and shoved his hand into it.

His mouth sealed over mine, as if he hadn't noticed the red gloss I'd slicked on my lips. I was held suspended in his embrace, my feet off the ground, his arm banded tightly around my waist. Wrapping myself around him, I locked my ankles together at the small of his back, pushing up so that his head tilted back and I curved around him, my tongue licking deep into his mouth. The hand he'd had in my hair slid down to cup and support me, his grip kneading my ass in the demanding, possessive way I loved.

"That's fucking hot," Cary said from somewhere behind me.

Manuel gave a piercing whistle.

I couldn't care less what kind of spectacle we made. Gideon's hard body felt delicious and the taste of him was intoxicating. My thoughts scattered. I wanted to ride him, rub up against him. I wanted him naked and sweaty, covered in my scent. On his face, his hands, his cock.

My husband wasn't the only one who wanted to mark his territory.

"Eva Lauren," my mother scolded. "Get ahold of yourself."

The sound of my mom's voice cooled us both off instantly. I unwound my legs from his hips and let him ease me down until I was standing again. I pulled away reluctantly, my hands briefly lifting Gideon's sunglasses so I could look into his eyes. *Fury . . . lust . . .*

I wiped the traces of my lip gloss off his mouth with my fingers. His lips were swollen from the passion of our kiss, the sensual curves softened.

He cupped my face in his hands, his thumbs brushing over my lips. Urging my head back, he kissed the tip of my nose. He was tender now, his ferocious joy at seeing me tempered by having touched me.

"Eva," Arnoldo said, coming up beside me with a small smile on his handsome face. "So good to see you."

I turned to greet him, feeling nervous. I wanted us to be friends. I wanted him to forgive me for hurting Gideon. I wanted—

He kissed me full on the mouth. Stunned, I didn't react.

"Off!" Gideon snapped.

"I am not a dog," Arnoldo shot back. He looked at me with amusement. "He has been pining for you. Now, you can release him from his torment."

My anxiety faded. He was warmer toward me than he'd been recently, more like he'd been when we were first introduced. "It's really good to see you, too, Arnoldo."

Arash came up next. When he lifted both hands to touch my face, Gideon's arm shot out between us.

"Don't even think about it," he warned.

"That's not fair."

I blew him a kiss.

Manuel was sneakier. He came up behind me and lifted me off my feet, smacking his lips against the side of my face. "Good morning, beautiful."

"Hello, Manuel," I said with a laugh. "Having fun yet?"

"Don't you know it." Setting me down, he winked at me.

Gideon seemed to have calmed down somewhat. He shook Cary's hand and asked briefly about Ibiza.

His friends met my mother, who instantly turned on the charm and got the expected results—they seemed captivated.

Gideon took my hand in his. "You have your passport?"

"Yes."

"Good. Let's go." He walked off briskly.

Hurrying to keep up with his stride, I looked back over my shoulder at the group we'd left behind. They were heading in a different direction.

"They've had their weekend with us," he said, in answer to my unspoken question. "Today is ours."

He ushered me through an expedited customs process, then back out to the tarmac where a helicopter waited.

The rotor blades began to revolve as we approached. Raúl abruptly appeared and opened the rear door. Gideon helped me up into the back, climbing in directly behind me. I reached for the safety belt, but he brushed my hands aside, securing me in quickly before settling back. He handed me a headset, then slipped on his own.

"Let's go," he told the pilot.

We were lifting into the air before Gideon had his seat belt on.

I was breathless when we reached the hotel, still awed by the sight of Rio sprawled beneath us, its beaches dotted with high rises and its hills covered in colorfully painted favelas. Cars packed the roads below, the traffic impressively dense even considered against the commutes I experienced in Manhattan. The famous Christ the Redeemer statue glistened on Corcovado Mountain in the distance to my right, as we rounded Sugarloaf and followed the coastline up to Barra da Tijuca.

It would have taken hours by car to get to the hotel from the airport. Instead, the trip took minutes. We were entering Gideon's suite before my jet-lagged brain fully appreciated that I'd been in three countries in as many days.

Vientos Cruzados Barra was as luxurious as all the Crosswinds properties I had seen but with a local flavor that made it unique. Gideon's suite was as large as the one I'd had in Ibiza and his view as impressive.

I paused to admire the beach from the balcony, noting the endless rows of coconut stands and the golden bodies on the beach. Samba music drifted through the air, earthy and sexy and upbeat. I took a picture, then uploaded both it and the one of the guys on the tarmac to my Instagram account. *The view from here . . . #RioDeJaneiro*

I tagged everyone and discovered that Arnoldo had

snapped a picture of Gideon and me kissing passionately at the airport. It was a great photo, sexy and intimate. Arnoldo had a few hundred thousand followers and the photo already had dozens of comments and likes.

Dear friends enjoying #RioDeJaneiro and each other.

Gideon's smartphone rang and he excused himself. I heard him speaking in another room and followed. We hadn't said a word since we left the airport, as if we were saving them for intimate conversation. Or maybe we just didn't need to say anything. Let the world talk and spread lies. We knew what we had. It didn't need to be qualified, justified, or expressed.

I found him in an office, standing in front of a U-shaped desk covered in photos and notes, some of which had spilled onto the floor. The place was a mess, so unlike the rigid order my husband usually maintained. It took a moment to register that the photos were of the inside of a club and that they matched the background I'd seen in the photo of Gideon on Cinco de Mayo.

It was kind of eerie that we'd come to the same idea. It was also kind of awesome.

I turned to leave.

"Eva. Wait."

I glanced at him.

"Tomorrow morning is better," he said to whoever was on the other end of the call. "Text me when it's confirmed."

Gideon hung up and silenced his phone, setting it down by his sunglasses. "I want you to see these."

Shaking my head, I told him, "You don't have to prove anything to me."

He stared at me. Without his shades, I saw the shadows under his eyes.

"You didn't sleep last night." It wasn't a question. I should have known he wouldn't.

"I'm going to fix this."

"Nothing's broken."

"I heard you over the phone," he said tightly.

I leaned into the doorjamb. I knew how he'd felt when I kissed Brett—murderous. They'd fought like beasts. A violent physical confrontation hadn't been an option for me. My body had purged my jealousy the only way it could.

"Do what you have to do," I murmured. "But I don't need anything. I'm good. You and me—*us*—we're good."

Gideon took a deep breath. Let it out. Then he reached up behind him and yanked his shirt over his head. He kicked off his sandals while he unfastened his shorts, letting them drop to the floor. He wore nothing underneath.

I watched him prowl toward me naked, noting the darker tan lines and the rigidness of his cock. He was impossibly hard, his balls already drawn up tight. Every muscle flexed as he moved. His powerful thighs, his washboard abs, his thick biceps.

I didn't move, barely breathed, hardly blinked. It amazed me that I could take him. He was nearly a foot taller and close to a hundred pounds heavier. And strong. So very strong.

When we made love, it turned me on to lie beneath him and feel all of that incredible power focused solely on pleasuring my body and taking pleasure in it.

Gideon reached me and pulled me into his arms. He lowered his head to take my mouth in a lush, deep kiss. Savoring and unhurried. Soft licks and coaxing lips. I didn't realize he'd untied my top until it slipped down my arms. He slid his thumbs beneath the waistband of my shorts, gliding them back and forth across the sensitive skin, until he halted the kiss to crouch and help me step out of my clothes. I whimpered, wanting more.

"Let's leave the heels on," he murmured, straightening to his full height. His eyes were so brilliantly blue they reminded me of the water we'd skinny-dipped in when we married.

I wrapped my arms around his shoulders and he lifted me, carrying me to the bedroom.

◦~◦◦~◦

"And some of those little round cheese puff breads," I told Gideon, who relayed the addition to room service in Portuguese.

Lying prone on the bed facing the open sliding doors to the balcony, I kicked my legs up behind me, still wearing the fuck-me shoes. But nothing else. I rested my chin on my crossed arms. The warm ocean breeze felt good on my skin, cooling the sweat that covered every inch of me. The fan over the bed, with its mahogany blades carved into the shape of palm fronds, swirled lazily above.

I took a deep breath and smelled sex and Gideon.

He hung up and the mattress dipped as he moved toward me, his lips brushing over my ass, then along my spine to my shoulder. He sprawled beside me, propping his head in one hand. The other stroked up and down my back.

I turned to look at him. "How many languages do you know?"

"A little of many and a lot of a few."

"Hmm." I arched into his touch.

He kissed my shoulder again. "I'm glad you're here," he murmured. "Glad I stayed."

"I occasionally have good ideas."

"So do I." The lascivious gleam in his eyes told me exactly what he was thinking about.

He hadn't slept all night, then super-slow-fucked me for nearly two hours. He'd come three times, the first time so hard he'd *growled*. Loudly. I knew the sound must have carried out the open windows. I'd orgasmed just hearing it. And he was ready to go again. He was *always* ready. Lucky me.

I rolled to my side, facing him. "Does it take two women to wear you out?"

Gideon's face shuttered instantly. "I'm not going there."

I touched his face. "Hey. It was a joke, baby. A bad one."

He rolled to his back and grabbed a pillow, putting it between us. Then he turned his head toward me, a frown between his brows. "There used to be this . . . emptiness. In-side me," he said quietly. "You called it a void. Said you filled it. You did."

Listening, I just waited. He was talking. Sharing. It was hard for him and he didn't like it. But he loved me more.

"I was waiting for you." He brushed the hair back from my cheek. "A dozen women couldn't have done what you did. But . . . Christ." He ran both hands through his hair. "Distractions made it easier not to think about it."

"I can make that happen," I purred, wanting him to be happy and playful again. "I can make you not think about anything."

"That emptiness is gone. *You're* there."

Leaning over him, I kissed him. "I'm right *here*, too."

He shifted, rising to his knees and scooping me up, dropping me onto the pillow so that my ass was lifted into the air.

"This is how I want you."

I looked at him over my shoulder. "You remember room service is coming, right?"

"They said forty-five to sixty minutes."

"You're the boss. They won't take that long."

He moved, positioning himself between my legs. "I told them to take an hour."

I laughed. I'd thought lunch was a break. Apparently, only the phone call was.

He grabbed my butt cheeks in both hands and squeezed, kneading. "God, you have the most amazing ass. It's the perfect cushion for doing this . . ."

Holding my hips, he slid inside me. A long, slow glide. He groaned with masculine pleasure and my toes curled in my shoes.

"My God." I dropped my forehead to the bed and moaned. "You're so hard."

His lips pressed to my shoulder. He rolled his hips, stroking inside me, pushing deep enough to cause the tiniest bit of pain. "You excite me," he said roughly. "I can't turn it off. I don't want to."

"Don't." I arched my back, pushing up into his easy, measured thrusts. That was his mood today. Gentle. Indulging. Making love. "Don't stop."

His arms bracketed me, his palms pressing into the

mattress. He nuzzled against me. "I'll make you a deal, angel. I'll wear out when you do."

~~~✦~~~

"Ugh." I stared at myself in the mirror, shifting from side to side. "It's never a good idea to put on a bikini after pigging out."

I tugged at the bandeau top of the emerald green swimsuit Gideon had picked up in the lobby shop, then tried to rearrange the fit of the bottom.

He appeared behind me, looking sexy and yummy in a pair of black board shorts. His arms came around me from behind, hefting the weight of my breasts in his palms. "You look amazing. I want to peel this off you with my teeth."

"Do it." Why go to the beach? We'd been to the beach last weekend.

"Do you still want pictures of us here?" His gaze met mine in the mirror. "If not, I'm good with tossing you back in the bed and having my way with you again."

I chewed my lower lip, debating.

He pulled me back against him. Without my heels on, he could set his chin on the crown of my head. "Can't decide? Okay, we'll go down to the beach, just so you don't regret not going later. Thirty minutes . . . an hour . . . then we'll come back up until we have to leave."

I melted. He was always thinking about me and what I needed. "I love you so much."

The look that came over his face nearly stopped my heart. "You believe me," he whispered. "Always."

298 • SYLVIA DAY

Turning my head, I pressed my cheek against his chest. "Always."

～⑨～

"It's a beautiful picture," my mother whispered, keeping her voice down because the guys were all sleeping. The jet's cabin lights were dimmed, the men all reclined in their seats. "I just wish it didn't show so much of your derriere."

I smiled, my gaze on the tablet in her hand. Vientos Cruzados Barra had photographers on staff to cover the many events, conventions, and weddings that took place on the beautiful property. Gideon had arranged for one to photograph us on the beach, having them shoot from a distance so that I wasn't even aware.

The previously released photos of us in Westport had Gideon pinning me beneath him with the surf lapping at our legs. The new photos were of us in the sun, with him sprawled on his back and me lying atop him, my arms crossed over his abs and my chin on my hands. We were talking, my gaze on his face as he looked at me and ran his fingers through my hair. Yes, the Brazilian cut of my bikini meant my ass was on display, but what really stood out was the intensity of Gideon's focus on me and the easy, comfortable familiarity between us.

My mom looked at me. There was a sadness in her eyes I couldn't understand. "I had hoped you two would have a quiet, normal life. But the world isn't going to let that happen."

The photo had gone viral shortly after it was posted to a media site. Speculation was rampant. How could I be with

Gideon in Rio and be okay with him fucking two other women? Was our sex life that kinky? Or maybe it wasn't Gideon Cross in the photo at the club.

Before he'd fallen asleep, Gideon had told me his public relations team was working around the clock, fielding calls and managing his social media. As of today, the official answers were simply to confirm that I had been in Rio with Gideon. He said he'd handle the rest personally when he got home, although he was cagey about how he was going to do that.

"You're being secretive," I'd accused, without heat.

"For now," he had agreed with a faint smile.

I put my hand over my mom's. "It's going to be okay. We won't always be so interesting to people. And we're going away for a month after the wedding. That's nearly a lifetime with no news about us. The media will move on."

"I hope so," she sighed. "You're getting married on Saturday. I can't believe it. There's still so much to do."

Saturday. Only a handful of days away. I didn't think it was possible for Gideon and me to feel any more married than we already did, but it would be nice to say our vows with our families watching.

"Why don't you come over to the penthouse tomorrow?" I suggested. "I would love for you to see it and we can discuss everything that still needs to be decided. We'll have lunch in and just hang out."

Her face brightened. "What a wonderful idea! I would love that, Eva."

Leaning over the armrests, I kissed her cheek. "Me, too."

"You're not even going to take a nap?" I watched, astonished, as Gideon shifted through his closet.

He was wearing only boxer briefs, his hair towel-dried after the shower he'd taken the moment we got home. I was on the bed, feeling exhausted and wrung out even though I'd slept on the plane.

"It'll be a short day," he said, pulling out a dark gray suit. "I'll be home early."

"You're going to catch a cold if you don't get enough sleep. I don't want you sick at our wedding or on our honeymoon."

He pulled the blue tie I loved off his tie rack. "I'm not going to get sick."

I looked at the clock on his nightstand. "It's not even seven! You never go to work this early."

"I have things to do." He buttoned his shirt quickly. "Stop nagging me."

"I am *not* nagging."

He shot me an amused look. "Didn't you get enough of me yesterday?"

"Oh my God. Are you full of yourself or what?"

He sat and tugged on his socks. "Don't worry, angel. I'll give you more when I get home."

"I want to throw something at you right now."

Gideon was dressed in a flash, yet somehow looked so polished and perfect. That only soured my mood more.

"Stop scowling at me," he chastised, bending to kiss the top of my head.

"It takes me forever to look as good as you do without trying," I grumbled. "And you're wearing my favorite tie." It brought out the color of his eyes, made sure you didn't see anything else but him and how gorgeous he was.

He smiled. "I know. When I get home, would you like me to fuck you while wearing it?"

I pictured it and my scowl faded. What would it be like if he just opened his fly and screwed me with one of his power suits on? Totally hot. In more ways than one.

"We sweat too much." I pouted at the thought. "We'd ruin it."

"I've got a dozen." He straightened. "You're staying home today, right?"

"Wait. You've got a dozen of those ties?"

"It's your favorite," he replied simply, as if that explained everything. Which I supposed it did. "Home, right?" he repeated.

"Yes, my mom will be here in a few hours and I have calls to make."

He started toward the door. "Take a nap, grumpy angel. Dream about me."

"Yeah, yeah," I muttered, hugging a pillow and closing my eyes.

I dreamed of him. Of course.

◦◦◦

"Most of the RSVPs have come in already," my mom said, running her fingers over the trackpad on her laptop to show me a spreadsheet that made my eyes cross. "I didn't expect so many guests would attend on such short notice."

"That's a good thing, right?" Honestly, I hadn't a clue. I didn't even fully know who all had been invited to the reception. I just knew it was Sunday evening, at one of Gideon's hotels in the city.

We never would have gotten the space we needed otherwise. Scott never said so, but I had to think someone else's event had gotten bumped at the last minute. And the number of rooms we'd reserved to accommodate my dad's side of the family . . . I hadn't considered any of that when I picked Gideon's birthday as the date.

"Yes, it's great." My mom smiled at me, but it was a tight smile. She was stressed to the max and I felt bad about that, too.

"It's going to be wonderful, Mom. Totally amazing. And we're all going to be so happy, we won't care if something goes wrong." She flinched and I rushed on. "Which it won't. All of the staff are going to make sure they do everything right. This is their boss's big day."

"Yes." She nodded, looking relieved. "You're right. They'll want everything to be perfect."

"And it will be." How could it not? Gideon and I were already married, but celebrating his birthday was something we hadn't done together yet. I couldn't wait.

My smartphone chimed with a text message. I picked it up and read it, frowning. I reached for the TV remote.

"What is it?" my mom asked.

"I don't know. Gideon wants me to turn the TV on." My stomach tightened, worry crowding out the anticipation I'd just felt. How much more would we have to take?

I clicked on the channel he'd specified and recognized the set of a popular talk show. To my shock, Gideon was just settling into a chair at a table circled by the five female hosts— to applause, catcalls, and whistles. Think what they would about his fidelity, women couldn't resist him. His charisma and sheer sexiness were a million times more potent in person.

"My God," my mother breathed. "What is he doing?"

I turned up the volume.

As was to be expected, after congratulating him on our engagement, the hosts launched right into the topic of Rio and the infamous ménage à trois club photo. Of course, they made sure to point out that it couldn't be shown on air because it was too risqué. But they directed viewers to the show's website, which was highlighted on a banner that ran continuously along the bottom of the screen.

"Well, that's subtle," my mom snapped. "Why is he giving this any more attention?"

I hushed her. "He's got a plan." At least I hoped he did.

Holding a coffee mug branded with the show's logo between both hands, Gideon looked thoughtful as the hosts all chimed in before letting him speak.

"Should we even be having bachelor and bachelorette parties anymore?" one of the hosts asked.

"Well, that's one of the things I can clear up," Gideon interjected, before they started debating that point. "Since Eva and I married last month and I'm no longer a bachelor, it couldn't be a bachelor party."

Behind them, on a massive video screen, the show's logo gave way to a photo of Gideon kissing me after we'd said our vows.

My breath caught right along with the live audience's gasps. "Wow," I murmured. "He outed us."

I barely caught the rush of conversation that followed the reveal, too stunned by what he was doing to process everything. Gideon was such a private man. He never gave personal interviews, only ones focused on Cross Industries.

The photo of us changed to a series of shots taken inside

the same nightclub where the leggy brunettes had climbed all over him. When he glanced at the audience and suggested that some of them might be familiar with the location, there were a few shouted affirmatives.

"Obviously," he went on, looking back at the hosts. "I couldn't be in New York and Brazil at the same time. The photo that went viral was digitally altered to remove the club's logo. You can see that it's embroidered into the curtains of the VIP lounge. All it took was the right software and a couple of clicks to make it disappear."

"But the girls were there," one of the hosts countered, "and what was happening with them was real."

"True. I had a life before my wife came along," he said evenly and unapologetically. "I can't change that, unfortunately."

"She had a life before you, too. She's the Eva mentioned in, um, a Six-Ninths song." She squinted slightly. "'Golden Girl.'"

The host was obviously reading the information from a teleprompter.

"Yes, that's her," he confirmed.

His tone was neutral. He seemed unruffled. While I knew the show was never as spontaneous as it seemed, it was still surreal to see our lives used to boost the morning ratings.

A photo of Brett and me at the "Golden Girl" video launch in Times Square popped up and a portion of the song played for a moment. "How do you feel about that?"

Gideon gave them one of his rare smiles. "If I were a songwriter, I'd compose ballads about her, too."

The photo of Gideon and me in Brazil appeared on the screen. It was quickly followed by the photo of us in Westport, and a series of shots taken while we'd walked the red carpet at various charity events. In all of them, his eyes were on me.

"Ooh, he's good at this," I said, mostly to myself. My mom was busy shutting down her laptop. "He's sincere, but still aloof and confident enough to seem like the legendary Gideon Cross. And he gave them a ton of photos to work with."

It was also a good choice to go with the talk show format of multiple female hosts exploring female-focused topics. They weren't going to give him a free pass for alleged infidelity or even tiptoe around the subject. It was going to clear the air in a way an interview with a male anchor might not have.

One of the hosts leaned forward. "There's a book coming out about you, too, isn't there? Written by your former fiancée?"

A photo of Gideon and Corinne at the Kingsman Vodka party came up on the screen. A collective murmur arose from the audience. My teeth ground together. She looked stunningly beautiful, as always, and complemented Gideon's dark handsomeness so well.

I chose to believe the show had dug that image up on their own.

"Ghostwritten, actually," he answered. "By someone with an ax to grind. I'm afraid Mrs. Giroux is being taken advantage of and can't see it."

"I didn't realize that. Who's the ghostwriter?" She looked at the audience and quickly explained what a ghostwriter was.

"I'm not at liberty to say who's actually writing the book."

The host pressed the point. "But you know him? Or her? And they don't like you."

"That's correct—on both counts."

"Is it an ex-girlfriend? A former business partner?"

The one host who'd been mostly listening switched gears. "About Corinne . . . Why don't you tell us what the story is there, Gideon?"

My husband set down the mug he'd just taken a sip out of. "Mrs. Giroux and I dated in college. We were engaged for a time, but even then, the relationship wasn't going anywhere. We were immature and, truthfully, too ignorant to know what we wanted."

"That's it?"

"Being young and confused isn't very interesting or salacious, is it? We remained friends after she married. I'm sorry she feels the need to commercialize that particular time in our lives now that I'm married. I'm sure this is as awkward for Jean-François as it is for me."

"That's her husband, right? Jean-François Giroux. Do you know him?"

Corinne and Jean-François in evening wear at some event appeared on the screen. They were an attractive couple, although the contrast between the two men wasn't flattering for the Frenchman. He couldn't compete with Gideon, but then, who could?

Gideon nodded. "We're in business together."

"Have you talked about this with him?"

"No. I don't discuss it all, usually." That faint smile touched his mouth again. "I'm a newlywed. I have other things on my mind."

I clapped my hands together. "Yay! That was my idea. I told him to keep reminding people she's married and that he knows her husband." And he got a dig in about Deanna, too. Well played all around.

"You knew he was going to do this?" my mom asked, sounding horrified.

I looked at her, frowning when I saw how pale she was. Considering the tan she'd gotten over the last two weekends, that was worrying. "No. I had no idea. We talked about the Giroux thing a while ago. Are you okay?"

She pressed her fingertips into her temples. "I've got a headache."

"Hang on till this is over and I'll get you something for that." I looked back at the TV, but they broke for a commercial. I ran to the bathroom medicine cabinet and came back out rattling a little bottle of pills, surprised to find my mother packing up her stuff. "You're leaving? What about lunch?"

"I'm tired, Eva. I'm going home to lie down."

"You could take a nap here in the guest room." I figured she'd like that. After all, Gideon had precisely replicated her design of my apartment bedroom right here. A misguided but thoughtful effort to give me a safe haven in his home at a time in our relationship when I hadn't known whether I should fight for us or just run away.

She shook her head and slung the carrying strap of her laptop case over her shoulder. "I'll be fine. We covered the most important things. I'll call you later."

She air-kissed both my cheeks and left.

Sinking back onto the couch, I put the pills on the coffee table and watched the rest of Gideon's interview.

12

"Mr. Cross." Scott stood up behind his desk. "Will you be in today after all?"

I shook my head and opened my office door, waving Angus inside before me. "I just have to take care of something. I'll be in tomorrow."

I'd cleared my schedule, redistributing my meetings and appointments throughout the rest of the week. I hadn't planned to come to the Crossfire at all, but the information Angus had been sent to gather was too sensitive to risk disclosing anywhere else.

Taking a moment to close the door and make the glass opaque, I followed Angus to the seating area and dropped into a chair.

"You've had a busy few days, lad," he said, his lips twisted wryly.

"Never a dull moment." I exhaled roughly, fighting off fatigue. "Tell me you have something."

Angus leaned forward. "Little more than I had to start with: a marriage license with a fictitious hometown and Jackson Tramell's death certificate, which has Lauren Kittrie listed as his spouse. He was dead less than a year after they wed."

I homed in on the most important information. "Lauren lied about where she was from?"

He nodded. "Easy enough to do."

"But why?" Studying him, I saw the tension in his jaw. "There's something else."

"Manner of death is listed as undetermined," he said quietly. "Jackson took a bullet to the right temple."

My spine stiffened. "They couldn't decide if it was suicide or homicide?"

"Aye. It couldnae be determined conclusively one way or the other."

More questions without answers, with the biggest issue being whether Lauren had any relevance at all. Maybe we were chasing our tails.

"Fuck." I scrubbed a hand over my face. "I just want a photo, for God's sake."

"It's been a long time, Gideon. A quarter of a century. Maybe someone from her hometown would remember her, but we dinnae know where that is."

Dropping my hand, I looked at him. I knew the inflections of his voice and what they signified. "You think someone went through and tidied things up."

"It's possible. Also possible that the police report of Jackson's death was truly misplaced over the years."

"You don't believe that."

He confirmed my statement with a shake of his head. "I

brought in a lass to pose as an IRS agent looking for Lauren Kittrie Tramell. She questioned Monica Dieck, who said she hasn't seen her former sister-in-law in many years and to her knowledge, Lauren is deceased."

I shook my head, trying to make sense of it all and getting nowhere.

"Monica was scared, lad. When she heard Lauren's name she went white as a ghost."

Pushing to my feet, I began to pace. "What the fuck does that mean? None of this is getting me any closer to the truth."

"There's someone else who might have the answers."

I came to an abrupt halt. "Eva's mother."

He nodded. "You could ask her."

"Jesus." I stared at him. "I just want to know that my wife is safe. That none of this poses any danger to her whatsoever."

Angus's features softened. "From what we ken of Eva's mother, protecting her daughter has always been a priority. I cannae see her putting Eva at risk."

"Her overprotectiveness is exactly my concern. She's been tracking Eva's movements for God knows how long. I assumed it was because of Nathan Barker. But maybe he was just part of the reason. Maybe there's more."

"Raúl and I are already working on revised protocols."

I raked a hand through my hair. In addition to their security duties, they were dealing with the problem of Anne and finding whatever records her brother had kept, as well as trying to identify the photographer who took the photo of me and unravel the mystery of Eva's mother. Even with their auxiliary teams, I knew they were stretched thin.

My security detail was used to managing only my affairs.

Now I had Eva in my life, which effectively doubled their duties. Angus and Raúl were accustomed to rotating shifts, but lately they were both working nearly round the clock. They had standing orders to hire whatever support they required, but what we needed was another security chief—maybe two. Experts whose sole charge would be Eva and whom I could trust as implicitly as I did my existing team.

I'd have to make the time to get that done. When Eva and I returned from our honeymoon, I wanted everything in place.

"Thank you, Angus." I exhaled harshly. "Let's head to the penthouse. I want to be with Eva now. I'll figure out the next steps after I get some sleep."

∿

"Why didn't you tell me?"

I looked at Eva as I stripped out of my clothes. "I thought you'd like the surprise."

"Well, yeah. But still. That was *huge.*"

I could tell she was happy about the interview. The way she'd tackled me when I came home had been a good indication. She was also talking fast and hopping around all over the place. Which, come to think of it, wasn't too different from Lucky, who was darting under the bed and rolling out again, yipping happily.

Stepping out of the closet in my boxer briefs, I went to the bed and sprawled. God, I was tired. Too tired to even make a pass at my beautiful wife, who looked adorable in a strapless short romper thing. That said, I was certainly able to rise to the occasion if she propositioned me.

Eva sat on her side of the bed, then leaned over the edge to help Lucky, who tried to scramble up and couldn't quite make it. A moment later, he was on my chest, whining in protest as I held him off from slathering saliva all over my jaw. "Hey, I get it. I like you, too, but I don't lick your face."

He barked at that. Eva laughed and lay down on her pillow.

It struck me then that this was it. This was home. In a way it had never been before. Nothing had really felt like home since my dad died. But I had it back, now, better than ever.

Tucking Lucky against my stomach, I rolled toward my wife. "How did things go with your mother?"

"Good, I guess. We're pretty much ready for Sunday."

"You guess?"

She shrugged. "She got a headache during your interview. Seemed like she freaked out a little."

I studied her. "About what?"

"That you were talking about our personal stuff on television. I don't know. I don't get her sometimes."

I remembered Eva telling me about how she'd discussed Corinne's book with Monica and using the media to our advantage. Monica had cautioned her against it, told her to value our privacy. At the time, I agreed with Eva's mother and—today's interview aside—I would continue to agree with her. But in light of what little I knew about Monica's identity, it seemed probable that Eva's mother was concerned about her own privacy as well. It was one thing to appear in brief mentions in the local society papers. Quite another to gain the attention of the world.

Eva had her mother's face and some of her mannerisms.

She also had the Tramell name, which was a curious error. It would have been better cover to give her Victor's last name. Someone might be looking for Monica. If they knew at least as much as I did, having Eva's face on national television would put an X on the map.

My heart began to pound. Was my wife in danger? I had no idea what Monica might be hiding from.

"Oh!" Eva bolted up. "I didn't tell you . . . I've got a dress!"

"Jesus. You damn near gave me a heart attack." Lucky took advantage of my startled state and pounced, licking madly.

"Sorry." Eva caught up the puppy and rescued me, pulling him into her lap as she sat cross-legged beside me. "I called my dad today. My grandmother asked him if I'd want to wear her wedding dress. He sent me a picture of it, but it's been in storage so long, I couldn't really make it out. So he scanned a photo of her wearing it on her wedding day and it's perfect! It's totally what I didn't know I wanted!"

I rubbed my chest and smiled wryly. How could I be anything but captivated that she was so excited to marry me again? "I'm glad, angel."

Her eyes sparkled with excitement. "My great-grandmother made it for her, with the help of her sisters. It's a family heirloom, how cool is that?"

"Exceptionally cool."

"Right? And we're about the same height. I get my butt and boobs from that side of the family. It might not need to be altered at all."

"I love your butt and boobs."

"Fiend." She shook her head. "I feel like it'll be good for the relatives on that side to see me in it. I've been worried that they'll feel out of place, but now I'll be wearing the dress, so they have to feel like they're included in a big way. Don't you think?"

"Agreed." I crooked my finger at her. "Come here."

She eyed me. "You've got a look."

"Do I?"

"Are you still thinking about my butt and boobs?"

"Always. But for now, just a kiss will do."

"Hmm." Leaning over, she offered her mouth.

I cupped the back of her head and took what I needed.

"It's impressive, son."

I'm looking up at the Crossfire from street level, but the sound of my father's voice turns my head. "Dad."

He's dressed like me, in a dark three-piece suit. His tie is burgundy as is the handkerchief tucked into his breast pocket. We're the same height and that startles me for a moment. Why does that surprise me? The answer hovers in the back of my mind, but I can't grasp it.

His arm comes around my shoulders. "You've built an empire. I'm proud of you."

I take a deep breath. I hadn't realized how badly I'd needed to hear him say that. "Thank you."

He shifts, turning to face me. "And you're married. Congratulations."

*"You should come to the penthouse with me and meet my wife."
I'm anxious. I don't want him to say no. There are so many things I want to say to him and we never have time. Only a few min-*

utes here and there, snatches of conversation that can only scratch the surface. And with Eva there, I would have the courage to say what I needed to. "You'll love her. She's amazing."

My dad grins. "Beautiful, too. I'd like a grandson. And a granddaughter."

"Whoa." I laugh. "Let's not move too fast."

"Life moves fast, son. Before you know it, it's over. Don't waste it."

I swallow past a hard lump in my throat. "You could've had more time."

That's not what I want to say. I want to ask him why he gave up, why he checked out. But I'm afraid of the answer.

"All the time in the world wouldn't have seen me build something like this." He looks back up at the Crossfire. From the ground, it seems to reach to infinity, an optical illusion created by the pyramid at the top. "It'll be a lot of work, keeping this standing. Same with a marriage. Eventually, you'll have to put one before the other."

I think about that. Is it true? I shake my head. "We'll keep it standing together."

He slaps a hand on my shoulder and the ground reverberates beneath my feet. It starts out faintly, then builds, until glass begins to rain down around us. Horrified, I watch as the distant spire at the top explodes outward, then radiates down, windows bursting under the pressure.

I woke with a gasp, breathing hard, pushing at the weight on my chest and feeling warm fur. Blinking, I found Lucky climbing over me, low whimpers rumbling in his chest.

"Jesus." I sat up and shoved my hair back.

Eva slept beside me, curled in a ball with her hands tucked beneath her chin. Through the windows beyond her, I saw the sun was fading fast. A quick glance at the clock told me it was just past five in the evening. My alarm had been set for quarter past the hour, so I reached for my smartphone to turn it off.

Lucky shoved his head beneath my forearm. Picking him up, I held him at eye level. "You did it again."

He'd woken me from a nightmare. Who the fuck knew if he was doing it consciously or not? I was grateful either way. I gave him a brisk rubdown and slid out of bed.

"Are you getting up?" Eva asked.

"I have to go to Dr. Petersen's."

"Oh, yeah. Forgot about that."

I'd debated skipping the appointment, but Eva and I would be leaving for our honeymoon soon and I wouldn't see the good doctor for a month. I figured I could tough it out until then.

I set Lucky down on the floor and started for the bathroom.

"Hey," she called after me. "I invited Chris over for dinner tonight."

My stride faltered, then halted. Turning, I faced her.

"Don't look at me like that." She sat up, rubbing her eyes with her fists. "He's lonely, Gideon. He's on his own, without his family. It's a rough time for him. I figured I'd make something simple for dinner and we could watch a movie. Take his mind off the divorce for a while, maybe."

I sighed. That was my wife. Always circling the wagons around the lost and wounded. How could I fault her for being the woman I'd fallen in love with? "Fine."

She smiled. It was worth going along with anything, just to see that.

❧

"I just finished watching your interview," Dr. Petersen said, as he settled into his armchair. "My wife told me about it earlier and I was able to catch it on the Internet. Very well done. I enjoyed it."

Tugging up my slacks, I sank onto the sofa. "A necessary evil, but I agree, it went well."

"How's Eva?"

"Are you asking me how she reacted to seeing that photo?"

Dr. Petersen smiled. "I can imagine the reaction. How is she doing now?"

"She's okay." I was still shaken by the memory of hearing her being so violently ill. "We're good."

Which didn't change the fact that I seethed with fury every time I thought of it. That photo had existed for months. Why hold on to it, then release it now? It would have made news in May.

The only answer I could come up with was that they'd wanted to hurt Eva. Maybe put a wedge between us. They wanted to humiliate her and me.

Someone was going to pay for that. When I was done, they'd know what hell felt like. They would suffer, the way Eva and I had suffered.

"You and Eva both say things are good. What does that mean?"

I rolled my shoulders back to alleviate the tension there.

"We're . . . solid. There's a stability now that wasn't there before."

He set his tablet on the armrest and met my gaze. "Give me an example."

"The photo's a good one. There were times in our relationship when a photo like that would've really screwed us up."

"This time was different."

"Very. Eva and I discussed having my bachelor party in Rio before I left. She's very jealous. She always has been and I don't mind. In fact, I like it. But I don't like her torturing herself with it."

"Jealousy is rooted in insecurity."

"Let's change the word, then. She's territorial. I will never touch another woman for the rest of my life and she knows that. But she has an active imagination. And that photo was everything she feared in living color."

Dr. Peterson was letting me do the talking, but for a second I couldn't. I had to push the image—and the rage that it stirred—out of my mind before I could continue.

"Eva was thousands of miles away when the damn thing exploded online and I had nothing in the way of proof. I had only my word and she believed me. No questions. No doubt. I explained as best I could and she accepted it as the truth."

"That surprises you."

"Yes, it—" I paused. "You know, now that I'm talking about this, it really didn't surprise me."

"No?"

"We both had a rough moment there, but we didn't fuck it up. It was like we knew how to make it right between us. And we knew that we would. There wasn't any doubt about that, either."

He smiled gently. "You're being very candid. In the interview and now."

I shrugged. "Amazing what a man will do when faced with losing the woman he can't live without."

"You were angry about her ultimatum before. Resentful. Are you still?"

"No." My answer came without hesitation, although I would never forget how it felt when she'd forced a separation on us. "She wants me to talk, I'll talk. It doesn't matter what I throw at her, what mood I'm in when I tell her, how horrible she feels when she hears it . . . She can deal. And she loves me more."

I laughed out loud, startled by a sudden rush of joy.

Dr. Petersen's brows rose, a faint smile on his lips. "I've never heard you laugh like that before."

I shook my head, nonplussed. "Don't get used to it."

"Oh, I don't know about that. More talking. More laughter. They're connected, you know."

"Depends on who's talking."

His eyes were warm and compassionate. "You stopped talking when your mother stopped listening."

My smile faded.

"It's said that actions speak louder than words," he went on, "but we still need words. We need to speak and we need to be heard."

I stared at him, my pulse inexplicably speeding up.

"Your wife is listening to you, Gideon. She believes you." He leaned forward. "*I'm* listening and I believe you. So you're talking again and getting a different response from the one you've conditioned yourself to expect. It opens things up, doesn't it?"

"Opens me up, you mean."

He nodded. "It does. To love and acceptance. To friendship. Trust. A whole new world, really."

Reaching up, I rubbed the back of my neck. "What am I supposed to do with that?"

"More laughter is a good start." Dr. Petersen sat back with a smile and picked up his tablet again. "We'll figure out the rest."

~·~

I entered the foyer of the penthouse to the sounds of both Nina Simone and Lucky, feeling good. The puppy barked from the other side of the front door, his claws scratching madly. Smiling despite myself, I turned the knob and crouched, catching the little wriggling body as he launched himself through the opening.

"Heard me coming, did you?" Standing, I cradled him against my chest and let him lick my jaw as I rubbed his back.

I entered the living room in time to watch my stepfather push to his feet from where he'd been sitting on the floor. He greeted me with a warm smile and even warmer eyes, before he dialed it back and schooled his expression into something . . . less.

"Hi," he greeted me, closing the distance between us. He wore jeans and a polo shirt but had taken his shoes off, revealing white socks with red threading along the toes. His wavy hair, the color of a worn penny, was longer than I'd ever seen it, and a few days' growth of stubble shadowed his jaw.

I didn't move, my thoughts tumbling around themselves.

For an instant, Chris had looked at me like Dr. Petersen did. Like Angus did.

Like my father did, in my dreams.

Unable to look at him, I took a second to set Lucky down and take a deep breath. When I straightened, I found Chris holding his hand out to me.

Feeling a familiar tingle of awareness, I looked beyond Chris's shoulder and found Eva standing in the doorway to the kitchen. Her gaze met mine, soft and tender and full of love.

Something about him had changed radically. His easygoing greeting made me remember how it was between us years ago. There had been a time when Chris hadn't been so formal with me. A time when he had looked at me with affection. He'd stopped because I told him to. He wasn't my father. Would never be my father. I knew I was just the baggage that came along with him loving my mother. I didn't need him to pretend that he gave a shit about me.

Instead, it seemed, he had pretended that he didn't care.

I took his hand, then pulled him into a quick hold, slapping him firmly but gently across the shoulders before releasing him. He held on and I froze, my gaze darting to Eva.

She pretended to pour an imaginary drink for me, then retreated to get me a real one.

Chris let me go, stepping back and clearing his throat. His eyes behind his gold-framed spectacles were shiny and wet. "Casual Tuesday?" he asked gruffly, looking at my jeans and T-shirt. "You work too hard. Especially with such a cute dog and beautiful wife waiting at home for you."

Your wife is listening to you, Gideon. She believes you. I'm listening and I believe you.

My stepfather believed me, too. And it was costing him. I could see the pain he was living with, recognized it from the times I'd felt that way myself. Separation from Eva felt almost like living death, and our relationship was still new. Chris had been married to my mother for over two decades.

"I had an appointment with my therapist," I told him. The ordinary words sounded foreign to my ears, like something a mentally unstable person oversharing would say.

His throat worked on a hard swallow. "You're seeing someone. That's good, Gideon. I'm glad to hear that."

Eva appeared with a glass of wine in her hand. She passed it to me, tipping her chin up to offer her mouth. I kissed her, holding my lips to hers for a long, sweet moment.

"Are you hungry?" she asked, when I let her go.

"Starved."

"Come on, then."

I checked her out as she preceded us into the kitchen, admiring the way her capris hugged her lush ass. She was barefoot, with her blond hair swinging softly around her shoulders. Aside from something glossy on her lips, she was barefaced and breathtaking.

She'd set us up to eat at the island, putting Chris and me on the side with bar stools, while she stood opposite us and ate standing up. She was so casual and relaxed, as was the atmosphere she had created.

Three pillar candles fragranced the air with something citrusy and spicy. Dinner was a seared steak salad, with Gorgonzola, sliced red onions, red and yellow sweet peppers, and a tangy vinaigrette. Crispy bread soaked in garlic butter stayed warm in a napkin-lined basket, while a decanted bottle of red wine waited to fill stemless glasses.

I watched her as she swayed to the music while she ate and chatted with Chris about the Outer Banks beach house. I remembered for a moment how the penthouse had been before she'd started moving in. It was where I lived, but I couldn't say it was home. On some level, I must have known she was coming when I bought the place. It had waited for her, as I had, needing her to bring life into it.

"Your sister is coming with me to the dinner tomorrow night, Gideon," Chris said. "She's very excited."

Eva frowned. "What dinner?"

His brows rose. "Your husband is being honored for his generosity."

"Really?" Her eyes got big and she did a little hop. "Are you giving a speech?"

Amused, I said, "That's usually expected, yes."

"Yay!" She jumped and clapped like a cheerleader. "I love hearing you speak."

For once, I thought I might even like doing it, considering that just the thought put a fuck-me gleam in her eyes.

"And I can't wait to see Ireland," she said. "Is it black tie?"

"Yes."

"Double yay! You in a tux, giving a speech." She rubbed her hands together.

Chris laughed. "Clearly, your wife is your biggest fan."

She winked at him. "You better believe it."

I savored my wine before swallowing. "Our social calendar should be synced to your phone, angel."

Eva's smile faded into a frown. "I don't think it is."

"I'll take a look."

Settling back in his chair, Chris held his glass close to his chest and sighed. "That was wonderful, Eva. Thank you."

She waved that off. "It was salad. But I'm glad you enjoyed it."

My gaze moved from her to my stepfather. I debated saying anything, stewed over it. Things were fine the way they were. Change sometimes fucked things up that were good before.

"We should do this more often." The words were out of my mouth before I realized it.

He stared at me, then looked down into his glass. He cleared his throat. "I would like that, Gideon." He glanced at me. "I'll take you up on the offer whenever you like."

I nodded. Sliding off my stool, I grabbed his plate and my own and carried them over to the sink.

Eva joined me, handing me her plate. Our gazes met and she smiled. Then she turned to Chris. "Let's open another bottle of wine."

∽🙰∾

"We're ahead of schedule by two weeks. Barring any unforeseen events, we should be finished early."

"Excellent." Standing, I shook the project manager's hand. "You're doing good work, Leo."

Opening the newest Crosswinds resort earlier than planned offered myriad benefits, not the least of which was combining the necessary final inspections with some playtime with my wife.

"Thank you, Mr. Cross." He gathered up his materials and straightened. Leo Aigner was a stout man, with thinning blond hair and a big smile. A hard worker, he stuck rigidly to timelines and sped them up whenever he could.

"Congratulations, by the way. I heard that you got married recently."

"I did, yes. Thank you."

I walked with him to the door of my office, then glanced at my watch when he left. Eva was coming to the Crossfire at noon to have lunch with Mark and his fiancé Steven. I wanted to catch her while she was close. I needed her opinion before I proceeded with a possibility I'd been entertaining all day.

"Mr. Cross." Scott stood in the doorway, intercepting me on the way to my desk.

I shot him a questioning look.

"Deanna Johnson has been waiting at reception for half an hour. What would you like me to tell Cheryl?"

I thought of Eva. "Tell her to send Ms. Johnson in."

While I waited, I texted my wife. *Save me some time before you leave the Crossfire. I need to ask you something.*

An in-person meeting? she texted back. *Are you thinking about my butt and boobs again?*

Always, I replied.

That was how Deanna found me, smiling at my phone. I looked up as she walked in, all amusement gone in a flash. She was dressed in a white pantsuit, with a chunky gold choker around her neck; it was clear she'd taken care with her appearance. Her dark hair hung in waves around her face and shoulders, and her makeup had been applied with drama in mind.

She walked toward my desk.

"Ms. Johnson." I set my phone aside and settled into my chair before she sat down. "I don't have much time."

Her mouth tightened. She tossed her purse onto the nearest chair and remained standing. "You promised me an exclusive on your wedding photos!"

326 • SYLVIA DAY

"I did, yes." And since I remembered what I'd extracted from her in exchange, I hit the control that closed my office door.

She set her hands on my desk and leaned over it. "I gave you all the information about that sex tape of Eva and Brett Kline. I held up my end of the deal."

"While you convinced Corinne to give you what you needed to write a book about me."

Something passed through her eyes.

"Did you think I was bluffing during the interview?" I asked evenly, leaning back and tapping my fingertips together. "That I didn't know the ghostwriter is you?"

"That doesn't have anything to do with the deal we made!"

"Doesn't it?"

Deanna pushed away from the desk in a violent explosion of movement. "God, you smug son of a bitch. You don't give a shit about anyone but yourself."

"So you've said. Which raises the question—why would you trust me to follow through?"

"Total stupidity. I thought you were actually sincere when you apologized."

"I was sincere. I'm very sorry I fucked you."

Fury and embarrassment colored her face. "I hate you," she hissed.

"I'm aware. You're certainly free to do so, but I suggest you think twice before pursuing a vendetta against me or my wife." I stood. "You're going to walk out the door and I'll forget you exist—again. You don't want me thinking about you, Deanna. You won't like the direction my thoughts would take."

"I could've made a fortune with that sex tape!" she accused. "And they were going to pay me good money to write that book. Your wedding photos would've made me a mint. Now, what have I got? You've taken everything away from me. You fucking *owe* me."

I arched a brow. "They don't want you to write the book anymore? How interesting."

She straightened, visibly pulling herself together. "Corinne didn't know. About us."

"Let's be clear. There was no *us*." My smartphone chimed with a text from Raúl, letting me know that he was nearly at the Crossfire with Eva. I moved to the coatrack. "You wanted to fuck and I fucked you. If you wanted *me*, well . . . I'm not responsible for your exaggerated expectations."

"You don't take responsibility for anything! You just use people."

"You used me, too. To get laid. To try to pad your bank account." I shrugged into my jacket. "As for what I owe you for your financial losses, my wife suggested I offer you a job."

Her dark eyes widened. "You're kidding."

"That was my response, too." I retrieved my smartphone and slid it into my pocket. "But she was quite serious, so I've made the offer. If you're interested, Scott can put you together with someone in human resources."

I headed toward the door. "You can see yourself out."

Going down to the lobby was totally unnecessary. Eva had lunch plans and the few words I could trade with her wouldn't amount to a conversation of any importance.

But I wanted to see her. Touch her for just a moment.

Remind myself that the man I'd been when I'd screwed women like Deanna no longer existed. Never again would the scent of sex turn my stomach and make me scrub my skin nearly raw in the shower.

I was passing through the security turnstiles in the lobby when Raúl escorted Eva through the revolving door, then retreated to his post outside. My wife wore a wine-colored jumpsuit with sky-high heels so delicate I couldn't see how they stayed on. Her tanned shoulders were bared by thin straps, and gold hoops dangled from her ears. Sunglasses partially hid her face, drawing the eye to the plump mouth that had ringed my cock just hours ago. She carried a nude clutch in her hand and walked across the golden-veined marble with a naturally seductive sway to her hips.

Heads swiveled as she walked by. Some of those gazes lingered to admire her ass.

What would they think if they knew that deep inside her, she was still creamy with my cum? That her nipples were tender from the suction of my mouth and the plump lips of her perfect little cunt were swollen from the friction of my cock sliding through them?

I knew what I thought. *Mine. All mine.*

As if she felt the heat of that silent demand, her head turned sharply, catching me coming toward her. Her lips parted. I watched her chest lift and fall with a quick intake of breath.

Same here, angel. Like a punch in the gut every time.

"Ace."

Catching her slender waist in both hands, I pulled her into me and pressed a kiss to her forehead, breathing in the scent of her perfume. "Angel."

"This is a nice surprise," she murmured, leaning into me. "Are you heading out?"

"Just wanted to see you."

She pulled back, her eyes bright with pleasure. "You've got it real bad for me."

"It's highly contagious. Caught it from you."

"Oh, did you?" Her laughter flowed over me in a warm rush of love.

"There's the big man himself," Steven Ellison said, coming up beside us. "Congratulations, you two."

"Steven." Eva turned from me and offered the brawny redhead a hug.

He caught her in an embrace that lifted her feet from the floor. "Marriage looks good on you."

He released her and shook my hand. "You, too."

"It feels good," I said.

Steven grinned. "I can't wait. Mark's kept me waiting for years."

"You can't keep kicking my ass about that," Mark said, appearing next to us. He shook my hand, too. "Mr. Cross. Congratulations."

"Thank you."

"Are you joining us for lunch?" Steven asked.

"I wasn't planning on it, no."

"You're welcome to. The more, the merrier. We're heading to Bryant Park Grill."

I glanced at Eva. She'd pushed her sunglasses up on top of her head and eyed me expectantly. She gave a little nod of encouragement.

"I've got a lot to catch up on," I said, which wasn't a lie. I was two days behind. Considering I needed to be ahead before we left for our honeymoon, I'd planned on eating in and working.

"You're the boss," Eva said. "You can play hooky if you want to."

"You're a bad influence, Mrs. Cross."

She linked her arm with mine and pulled me toward the door. "You love it."

I held back, glancing at Mark.

"I know you're busy," he said. "But it would be nice if you could come along. I want to talk to you both about something."

With a nod, I agreed. We exited out to the street, immediately hit with the heat of the day and the sounds of the city. Raúl waited at the curb with the limo, his gaze catching mine before he opened the door for Eva. A glare turned my head, drawing my attention to the telephoto lens of a camera peering at us from a car parked across the street.

I pressed a kiss to Eva's temple before she slid into the back. She glanced at me, delighted and surprised. I didn't explain. She'd asked for more photos of us to combat the upcoming release of Corinne's book. It was no hardship to show my affection for her, regardless of whether that damned tell-all ever saw the light of day.

It was a short drive to Bryant Park. In moments, we were taking the steps up from the street and I was taking a trip back in time, remembering when Eva and I had fought in this very location. She'd seen a photo of me with Magdalene, a woman I considered a longtime family friend but who was rumored to be my lover. I'd seen a photo of Eva with Cary, a man she loved like a brother but who was rumored to be her live-in paramour.

We had both been crazed with jealousy, our relationship too new and stunted by too many secrets between us. I was already obsessed with her, my world tilting on its axis to accommodate her. Even in her fury, she'd looked at me with such love and accused me of not knowing it when I saw it. But I did know. I did see. It terrified me as nothing ever had. And it gave me hope, for the first time in my life.

She glanced at me as we approached the ivy-covered entrance to the restaurant, and I could see she remembered as well. We'd been here more recently, too, when Brett Kline had tried to win her back. She was already mine then, my rings on her fingers, our vows exchanged. We'd been stronger than before, but now . . . Now, nothing could shake us. We were anchored deep.

"I love you," she said, as we followed Mark and Steven through the door. The sounds of a popular restaurant inundated us. The clang of silverware against china, the hum of multiple conversations, the barely discernible piped music, and the bustle of a busy kitchen.

My mouth curved. "I know."

We were seated immediately and a server stopped by right away to take our drink order.

"Should we order champagne?" Steven asked.

Mark shook his head. "Come on. You know I have to go back to work."

I held my wife's hand beneath the table. "Ask again when he's working for me. We'll celebrate then."

Steven grinned. "You got it."

We placed our drink order—flat and sparkling water and one soda—and the server took off to fill them.

"So here's the thing," Mark began, straightening in his

seat. "Part of the reason Eva quit was because of the Lan-Corp proposal . . ."

She preempted him, her mouth curved in a cat-that-ate-the-canary smile. "Ryan Landon offered you a job."

His eyes widened. "How'd you know?"

She looked at me, then back at him. "You're not taking it, are you?"

"No." Mark sat back, studied us both. "It would have been a lateral move. Nothing like the bump I'll get with Cross Industries. More than that, though, I remembered you telling me that there's bad blood between Landon and Cross. I looked it up after you quit. Knowing the background, the whole thing wasn't sitting right—him declining to work with us, then trying to poach me right after."

"Could be he just wants *you*, without the agency," Eva said.

Steven nodded. "That's what I said."

As he would, I thought, because he believed in his partner. But it appeared Mark knew better. Eva glanced at me. I clearly saw the *I told you so* in her gaze. I squeezed her hand.

"You don't believe that," Mark countered, proving us both right.

"No," she agreed. "I don't. I'll be honest, I baited them. Told them Gideon and I are very fond of you and look forward to working with you again. I wanted to see if they'd bite. I figured if it was a great offer, I was doing you a favor. And if it wasn't, no harm no foul."

He frowned. "But why would you do that? Don't you want me at Cross Industries?"

"Of course we do, Mark," I interjected. "Eva was honest with them."

"I was testing the waters," she said. "I debated saying

something to you, but I didn't want you to feel awkward if he offered you a great job that you might seriously consider taking."

"So what do you do now?" Steven asked.

"Now?" Eva shrugged. "Gideon and I are planning a vow renewal ceremony and then taking off for a long honeymoon. Ryan Landon isn't a problem that's going away any time soon. He'll be around, doing his thing. I just won't underestimate him. And Mark is going to start a great new job with Cross Industries."

Eva glanced at me and I knew. Like all of my other battles, Landon wasn't going to be something I took care of on my own anymore. My wife would be there, doing what she could for me, fighting the good fight.

Mark's smile flashed white from within the frame of his goatee. "Sounds good to me."

"Do you want to play naughty secretary again?" Eva whispered.

Her hand was in mine, her other hand cupping my biceps as we entered my office. I glanced at her, enjoying the come-on, and saw the warm laughter in her eyes.

"I do have to work sometime today," I said dryly.

She winked and released me, dropping dutifully into one of the chairs facing my desk. "How can I be of service, Mr. Cross?"

I was smiling as I hung my jacket on the coatrack. "What do you think about me asking Chris to stand with me at our wedding?"

I turned just in time to see her surprise.

She blinked at me. "Really?"

"Thoughts?"

Sitting back, she crossed her legs. "I'd like to hear yours first, before I give you mine."

I joined her in the chair beside her rather than taking a seat behind my desk. Eva was my partner, my best friend. We would deal with this, and everything else, side by side.

"After Rio, I was going to ask Arnoldo, once I'd discussed it with you."

"I'd be okay with that," she said, and I could see she meant it. "It's a decision you should make for yourself and not for me."

"He understands what we have together and that it's good for both of us."

She smiled. "I'm glad."

"Me, too." I rubbed my jaw. "But after last night . . ."

"Which part of last night?"

"Dinner with Chris. It got me thinking. Things have changed. And there was something Dr. Petersen said. I just . . ."

She reached over and took my hand.

I searched for the right words. "I want someone who knows everything to be standing with me when you come down the aisle. I don't want there to be any pretense. Not for something this important. When we face each other and say our vows again, I need that to be . . . real."

"Oh, Gideon." She slipped out of her chair, crouching beside me at my knee. Her eyes were wet and luminous, like a stormy sky just after a cleansing rain. "You beautiful man," she breathed. "You don't even know how romantic you are."

I cupped her face, my thumbs brushing over the tears that slid down her cheeks. "Don't cry. I can't stand it."

She caught my wrists and surged up, pressing her mouth to mine. "I can't believe I'm this happy," she murmured, her lips whispering the words against my skin. "It doesn't seem real sometimes. Like I'm dreaming, and I'm going to wake up and realize I'm still on the floor in the lobby, looking at you for the first time and imagining all this because I want you so badly."

I pulled her up and onto my lap, holding her, burying my face in her neck. She could always say what I couldn't.

Her hands ran through my hair and over my back. "Chris will be delighted."

Squeezing my eyes shut, I held her tighter. "You did this."

She made everything possible. She made *me* possible.

"Did I?" she laughed softly, pulling back to touch my face with gentle fingertips. "It's all you, ace. I'm just the lucky girl who gets a front-row seat."

Marriage suddenly didn't seem like enough to safeguard what she meant to me. Why wasn't there something more binding than a mere piece of paper that gave me the right to call her my wife? Vows were a promise, but what I needed was a guarantee that every day of my life would have her in it. I wanted my heart to beat in rhythm with hers and stop when hers did. Inextricably entwined, so I would never live even a moment without her.

She kissed me again, softly. Sweetly. Her lips so gentle. "I love you."

I would never tire of hearing that. Never stop needing to hear it. Words, as Dr. Petersen said, that needed to be spoken and heard. "I love you."

More tears fell. "God. I'm a mess." She kissed me again. "And you have to work. But you can't stay late. I'm going to have fun helping you into your tux—and out of it."

I let her go when she slid away and stood, but I couldn't take my eyes off her.

She crossed the room and disappeared into the bathroom. I sat there, not sure I had the strength to stand yet. She weakened my knees, made my pulse race too hard and fast.

"Gideon." My mother pushed into my office, Scott hot on her heels. "I need to talk to you."

I rose to my feet and gave a nod to Scott. He retreated, closing the door. The warmth from Eva bled away, leaving me feeling empty and cold as I faced my mother.

She wore dark jeans that fit her like a second skin and a loose shirt she'd tucked in at the waist. Her long black hair was pulled back in a ponytail and her face was bare. Most who saw her would simply see a stunning woman who looked younger than her years. I knew her to be as worn and weary as Chris was. No makeup, no jewelry. It wasn't like her.

"This is a surprise," I said, moving into position behind my desk. "What brings you into the city?"

"I just left Corinne." She marched right up to my desk and remained standing, much as Deanna had only hours before her. "She's in pieces over that interview you gave yesterday. Completely destroyed. You have to go see her. Talk to her."

I stared at her, unable to comprehend the way her mind worked. "Why would I do that?"

"For God's sake," she snapped, looking at me like I'd lost my mind. "You need to apologize. You said some very hurtful things—"

"I told the truth, which is likely more than can be said about that book she's publishing."

"She didn't know you had a history with that woman . . . that ghostwriter. She told her editor she couldn't work with that person as soon as she found out."

"I don't care who writes the book. A different author won't change the fact that Corinne's violating my privacy and putting something out in the world with the potential to hurt my wife."

Her chin lifted. "I can't even talk about *your wife*, Gideon. I'm upset—no. I'm furious that you would get married without your family, your friends. Doesn't that tell you anything? That you had to do something so important without the blessing of the people who love you?"

"Are you implying that no one would've approved?" My arms crossed. "That's certainly not true, but even if it were, choosing someone to spend your life with isn't decided with a majority rule. Eva and I married privately because it was intimate and personal and didn't need to be shared."

"But you shared the news with the world?! Before you shared it with your family! I can't believe you could be so thoughtless and insensitive. You need to make things right," she said vehemently. "You have to be responsible for the pain you inflict on others. I didn't raise you this way. I can't tell you how disappointed I am."

I caught movement behind her and saw Eva fill the doorway of the bathroom, her face hard with rage, her hands clenched into fists at her sides. I gave her a curt shake of my head, my gaze narrowing with warning. She'd fought this battle enough for me. It was my turn, and I was finally ready.

I hit the controls to opaque the glass. "You don't get to lecture me about inflicting pain or feeling disappointed, *Mother*."

Her head snapped back as if I'd slapped her face. "Don't take that tone with me."

"You knew what was done to me. And you did nothing."

"We're not talking about this again." She slashed her hand through the air.

"When have we ever talked about it?" I bit out. "I told you, but at no point were you open to discussing it."

"Don't make this my fault!"

"I was raped."

The words lashed out and hung in the air, sharp as a blade and raw.

My mother jerked back.

Eva reached blindly for the doorjamb and gripped it hard.

Taking a deep breath to regain a modicum of control, I drew strength from my wife's presence. "I was raped," I said again, my voice calmer. Steadier. "For close to a year, every week. A man you invited into your home fondled me. Sodomized me. Over and over again."

"Don't." She breathed harshly, her chest heaving. "Don't say those ugly, awful things."

"It happened. Repeatedly. While you were only a few rooms away. He'd be nearly panting with excitement when he showed up. He'd stare at me with this sick gleam in his eyes. And you couldn't see it. Refused to see it."

"That's a lie!"

Fury burned through me, made me restless with the need to move. But I held my ground, my gaze moving to Eva. This time, she nodded at me.

"What's the lie, Mother? That I was raped? Or that you chose to ignore it?"

"Stop saying that!" she snapped, straightening. "I took you to be examined. I tried to find the proof—"

"Because my word wasn't enough?"

"You were a disturbed child! You lied about everything. Anything. The most obvious things."

"That gave me some control! I had no power over anything in my life—aside from the words that came out of my mouth."

"And I was supposed to just magically divine what was truth and what was a lie?" She leaned forward, taking the offensive. "You were seen by two doctors. You wouldn't let the one anywhere near you—"

"And have another man touch me there? Can you even grasp how terrifying that thought was to me?"

"You let Dr. Lucas—"

"Ah, yes. Dr. Lucas." I smiled coldly. "Where did you get his name, Mother? From the man molesting me? Or from your doctor, who was overseeing his dissertation? Either way, he steered you right toward his brother-in-law, knowing the well-respected Dr. Lucas would say anything to protect the reputation of his family."

She recoiled, stumbling back until she bumped into the chair behind her.

"He sedated me," I went on, remembering it still. The prick of the needle. The cold table. The shame as he poked and prodded a part of my body that made me tremble with revulsion. "He examined me. Then he lied."

"How would I know that?" she whispered, her eyes so strikingly blue in her pale face.

"You knew," I said flatly. "I remember your face afterward, when you told me Hugh wasn't coming back and to never bring it up again. You could barely look at me, but when you did, I saw it in your eyes."

I looked at Eva. She was crying, with her arms wrapped tight around herself. My eyes stung, but she was the one who wept for me.

"Did you think Chris would leave you?" I wondered aloud. "Did you think it was too much for your new family to take? For years, I thought you told him—I heard you mention Dr. Lucas to him—but Chris didn't know. Tell me what reason a wife would have to keep something like that from her husband."

My mother didn't speak, just shook her head over and over, as if that silent denial answered everything.

My fist hit my desk, rattling everything on top of it. "Say something!"

"You're wrong. *Wrong*. It's all twisted up for you. You don't . . ." She shook her head again. "It didn't happen that way. You're confused . . ."

Eva stared at my mother's back with a visible, heated rage. Loathing tightened her mouth and jaw. It hit me then that I could let her carry that burden for me. I had to put it down. I didn't need it anymore. Didn't want it.

I had done the same for her in a different sense, with Nathan. The action I'd taken had chased the shadows from her eyes. They lived in me now, as they should. She'd been haunted by them long enough.

My chest expanded on a deep, slow breath. When I let it out, all the anger and disgust went with it. I stood there for a long moment, absorbing the dizzying lightness I felt. There was grief, a profound anguish that burned in my chest. And resignation. A clarifying, terrible acceptance. But it weighed on me so much less than the desperate hope I'd harbored: that one day my mother would love me enough to accept the truth.

That hope was dead.

I cleared my throat. "Let's end this. I won't be going to see Corinne. And I won't apologize for telling the truth. I'm done with that."

My mother didn't move for a long moment.

Then she turned away from me without a word and walked to the door. A moment more and she was gone, lost on the other side of the frosted glass.

I looked at Eva. She started toward me and I went to her, rounding my desk to meet her partway. She hugged me so tightly I could hardly breathe.

But I didn't need air. I had her.

13

As I straightened Gideon's bow tie, I asked, "Are you sure you're okay?"

He caught my wrists and applied steady, solid pressure.

The familiar authoritative grip spurred a conditioned response. It grounded me. Heightened my awareness of him, of me. Of us. My breathing quickened.

"Stop asking." His voice was soft. "I'm fine."

"When a woman says she's fine, it means she's anything but."

"I'm not a woman."

"Duh."

A hint of a smile softened his mouth. "And when a man says he's fine, it means he is." He pressed a quick, hard kiss to my forehead and released me. Then, he went to the drawer that held his cuff links and studied the selection thoughtfully.

Gideon was long and lean in his bespoke trousers and

white formal shirt. He had on black socks, but his shoes and jacket were still waiting their turn to grace his body.

There was something about seeing him in that partially dressed state that turned me on wildly. It was an intimacy that was mine alone and I cherished it.

I was reminded of what Dr. Petersen had said. Maybe I'd have to spend some nights sleeping apart from my husband. Not forever, but for now. Still, I had these other precious pieces of him and they sustained me.

"A man. What about *my* man?" I countered, working hard not to get distracted by how hot he looked. The problem was his distance. There wasn't a trace of the razor-sharp focus on me that I was used to. Part of his mind was somewhere else, and I worried that it was a dark place where he shouldn't be alone. "That's the only one I care about."

"Angel. You've been telling me to have it out with my mother for months. I've done it. It's over and behind us."

"How do you feel about it, though? It has to hurt, Gideon. Please don't hide it from me, if it does."

His fingers drummed into the top of the built-in dresser, his gaze still focused on his damned cuff links. "It hurts. Okay? But I knew it would. That's why I put it off so long. But it's better this way. I feel . . . Fuck. It's settled."

My lips pursed. Because I wanted him to look at me when he was saying stuff like that, I untied my robe and let the silk whisper off my shoulders. I turned away to hang it by the closet door, stepping over Lucky, who'd passed out right in the middle of the floor. I arched my back as I reached for the hook, giving Gideon a prime view of the ass he loved.

As I had come to expect of my husband, he'd gifted me with a new dress for the occasion, a gorgeous dove gray gown with a beaded bodice and lightly layered diaphanous skirt that drifted like smoke when I moved.

Because of the plunging neckline—which I knew from experience would bring out his inner caveman—I'd chosen a bra designed to put my boobs on display. Together with the matching underwear, smoky eyes, and glossy lips, I looked like expensive sex.

When I faced him again, my husband was just how I wanted him—frozen in place with his eyes on me.

"I need you to promise me something, ace."

He raked me from head to toe with a scorching glance. "At the moment, I'll promise you anything."

"Just this moment?" I pouted.

He muttered something and walked over to me, cupping my face in his hands. Finally, he was with me. One hundred percent. "And the next, and the next after that." His gaze caressed my face. "What do you need, angel mine?"

I caught him by the hips, searched his eyes. "You. Just you. Happy and whole and madly in love with me." The elegant arch of his brows lifted slightly, as if being happy seemed like a dubious proposition. "You're so sad. It's killing me."

A soft sigh left him and I watched the tension drain away with it. "I don't know why I wasn't better prepared. She's incapable of accepting what happened. If she can't do it to save her marriage, she sure as hell won't do it for me."

"There's something missing in her, Gideon. Something essential. Don't you dare believe this has anything to do with you."

His mouth twisted wryly. "Between her and my dad . . . Not the greatest gene pool, is it?"

Sliding my fingers into the tailored waistband of his trousers, I yanked him closer. "Listen, ace. Your parents both buckled under pressure and put themselves first. Reality is something they can't face. But guess what? You didn't get any of their flaws. Not a single one."

"Eva—"

"You, Gideon Geoffrey Cross, are the distillation of what's best about them. Individually, they don't amount to much. But together . . . Man, did they hit it out of the park with you."

Shaking his head, he said, "I don't need this, Eva."

"I'm not bullshitting you. You don't have any problem with reality. You face it head on and tackle that bitch to the ground."

He huffed out a laugh.

"You've got a right to be hurt and pissed, Gideon. I'm pissed, too. They're not worthy of you. That doesn't make you less, it makes you *more*. I wouldn't have married you if you weren't a good man, someone I respect and admire. You inspire me, don't you know that?"

His hand slid through my hair to my nape. "Angel." His forehead touched mine.

I caressed his back, feeling the warm hard muscle beneath his shirt. "Grieve if you have to, but don't close up and blame yourself. I won't let you."

"No, you won't." He nudged my head back and kissed the tip of my nose. "Thank you."

"You don't have to thank me for anything."

"You were right. I needed to get it out and confront her. I never would have, if not for you."

"You don't know that."

Gideon looked at me with such love, my breath caught. "Yes, I do."

His smartphone chimed with an incoming text. He pressed his lips to my forehead, then moved to the dresser to read the message. "Raúl's on his way with Cary."

"I better get dressed, then. I need you to fasten me up."

"Always my pleasure."

Pulling the gown off its hanger, I stepped into it and slid my arms into the heavily beaded straps. My husband made quick work of the hook-and-eye fastening that rested just above the small of my back. I watched in the full-length mirror, biting my lower lip as the bodice tightened and settled into place where I'd thought it would. The neckline plunged to a spot halfway between my cleavage and my navel.

It was outrageously sexy, the kind of revealing style smaller-breasted women pulled off easily. On me, it was risqué, although the rest of the gown covered everything except my back and arms. I'd decided against jewelry to tone down the effect as much as I could. Still, it was a beautiful dress and we were a young couple. We could pull it off.

Gideon's gaze met mine in the mirror. I gave him my best innocent look and waited for him to see how much of my assets he'd put on display.

The storm started brewing with a faint line between his brows. That quickly progressed into a full-on scowl. He tugged at the straps from the back.

"Is there a problem?" I asked sweetly.

His gaze narrowed. Reaching around with both hands, he slid his fingers into my cleavage and tried pushing my breasts apart to hide the curves beneath the thick straps.

I hummed and leaned against him.

Taking my shoulders, he straightened me up so he could study the fit. "It didn't look like that in the photo."

Deliberately misunderstanding him, I told him, "I haven't put my heels on yet. It won't drag on the ground when I do."

"I'm not worried about the bottom," he said tightly. "We need to put something in that middle part."

"Why would we do that?"

"You know damned well why." He prowled over to the dresser and yanked a drawer open. A moment later, he came back and thrust a white handkerchief toward me. "Put that in there."

I laughed. "Oh my God. You're kidding."

But he wasn't. Reaching around from behind me, he shoved the unfolded cloth into my bodice, tucking it into either side.

"No," I told him crossly. "That looks ridiculous."

When his hands fell away, I gave him a second to see how stupid it looked. "Forget it. I'll wear something else."

"Yeah," he agreed, nodding and shoving his hands in his pockets.

I tugged the handkerchief out.

"Something like this," he murmured.

Sparks of fire shot out of his hands as he reached over my head and wrapped a dazzling diamond choker around my neck. At least two inches wide, it hugged the base of my throat and glittered as if lit from within.

"Gideon." I touched it with trembling fingers as he fastened it securely. "It's . . . gorgeous."

His arms wrapped around my waist, his lips touching my temple. "*You're* gorgeous. The necklace is just pretty."

I turned in his embrace and looked up at him. "Thank you."

The quick flash of his smile made my toes curl into the carpet.

Smiling back, I said, "I thought you were serious about my boobs."

"Angel, I take your tits *very* seriously. So tonight, when someone ogles them, they'll realize you're much too expensive and they couldn't possibly afford you."

I smacked his shoulder. "Shut up."

He grabbed my hand and pulled me to the dresser. He reached into the open drawer and pulled out a diamond cuff. I watched, stunned, as he slid it around my wrist. That was followed by a velvet box, which he opened to show me the diamond teardrop earrings inside. "You should put these on yourself."

I gaped at them, then at him.

Gideon just smiled. "You're priceless. The necklace alone wasn't going to get the message across."

Staring at him, I couldn't find the words to say anything.

My silence turned his smile into a wicked grin. "When we get home, I'm going to fuck you while you're wearing diamonds and nothing else."

The erotic image that popped into my mind sent a shiver through me.

Catching my shoulders, he turned me around and swatted my ass. "You look sensational. From every angle. Now, stop distracting me and let me get ready."

I grabbed my sparkly heels off the shoe rack and left the closet, more dazzled by my husband than by the jewels he'd given me.

❧

"You look like a million dollars." Cary pulled back from my hug and checked me out. "Actually, I think you're wearing a million dollars. Jesus. I was so blinded by your bling I almost missed that you'd let your girls come out and play."

"That's Gideon's point," I said dryly, giving a turn to set the skirt of my gown drifting around my legs. "You, of course, are gorgeous."

He gave me his famous bad-boy grin. "I know."

I had to laugh. I thought most men looked good in a tuxedo. Cary, however, looked amazing. Very dapper. Like a Rock Hudson or Cary Grant. The combination of his roguish charm and stunning good looks made him irresistible. He'd put on a little weight. Not enough to change his clothing size, but enough to fill out his face a little more. He looked good *and* healthy, which was rarer than it should be.

Gideon, on the other hand, was more . . . 007. Lethally sexy, with a refined edge of danger. He entered the living room and I could only stare helplessly, riveted by the graceful elegance of his chiseled body, that easy commanding stride which hinted at how amazing he was in bed.

Mine. All mine.

"I put Lucky in his crate," he said, joining us. "We ready?"

Cary gave a decisive nod. "Let's hit it."

We took the elevator down to the garage, where Angus waited with the limo. I climbed in first and chose the long bench, knowing Cary would sit beside me while Gideon took his usual seat in the back.

I'd had so little time with Cary lately. Fashion Week had

350 • SYLVIA DAY

kept him super busy, and since I was spending the nights at the penthouse, we didn't even have a chance for quick chats in the evening or coffee in the morning.

Cary looked at Gideon and gestured at the bar before we rolled out. "You mind?"

"Help yourself."

"Either of you want something?"

I considered. "Kingsman and cranberry, please."

Gideon shot me a warm look. "I'll have the same."

Cary poured and served, then sat back with a beer and took a deep pull straight out of the bottle. "So," he began, "I'm flying to London next week for a shoot."

"Really?" I sat forward. "That's wonderful, Cary! Your first international job."

"Yeah." He smiled into his beer, then looked at me. "I'm stoked."

"Wow. Everything has happened so fast for you." A few months ago we'd still been living in San Diego. "You're going to take the world by storm."

I managed a smile. I was truly, genuinely happy for my best friend. But I could picture a time, in the not-so-distant future, when we'd both be so busy and traveling so often we would rarely see each other. It made my eyes sting to think of it. We were closing a chapter of our lives and I mourned a little for the end, even knowing that the best was yet to come for both of us.

Cary raised his bottle in a silent toast. "That's the plan."

"How's Tatiana?"

His smile grew tight, his eyes hard. "She says she's dating someone. She moves quick when she sees something she likes, always has."

"Are you okay with that?"

"No." He started peeling the label off his beer bottle. "Some dude's blowing his load where my baby is. I think that's sick." He glanced at Gideon. "Can you imagine?"

"No one wants me imagining that," he answered, in that even tone that screamed *danger*.

"Right? It's fucked up. But I can't stop her and I'm not getting back together with her, so . . . It is what it is."

"God." I reached for his hand and held it. "That's tough. I'm sorry."

"We're being civil to each other," he said with a shrug. "She's less of a bitch when she's getting laid regularly."

"So you guys are talking a lot?"

"I check in with her every day, make sure she's got what she needs. Told her I was good for whatever—except my dick, of course." He heaved out his breath. "It's depressing. Without sex, we really don't have anything to say to each other. So we talk about work. We've got that in common, at least."

"Did you tell her about London?"

"Hell, no." Cary squeezed my hand. "Had to tell my best girl first. I'll tell her tomorrow."

I debated bringing up the question, but I couldn't help myself. "And Trey? Anything there?"

"Not really. I send him a text or photo every couple days. Stupid shit. Stuff I'd send you."

"So no dick pics?" I teased.

"Yeah, no. I'm trying to keep it real with him. He thinks I'm oversexed—which he totally doesn't mind when he's in bed with me—but whatever. I send him something every now and then, and he replies, but that's it."

My nose wrinkled. I looked at Gideon and found him typing something into his phone.

Cary took another drink, his throat working on a hard swallow. "It's not a relationship. Not even friendship at this point. For all I know, he could be seeing someone, too, and I'm the odd man out."

"Well, for what it's worth, celibacy looks good on you."

He snorted. "Because I've put on a few pounds? Happens. You eat, because you crave the endorphins you're not getting with an orgasm, and you get less exercise, because you're not practicing any mattress gymnastics."

"Cary." I laughed.

"Look at you, baby girl. You're all tight and toned from Marathon Man Cross over there."

Gideon looked up from his phone. "Come again?"

"That's what I just said, dude," Cary drawled, winking at me. "In so many words."

꿍

After waiting in a line of limos discharging their passengers, we finally pulled up to the red carpet rolled out in front of a historic brick-faced building, home to a private members-only club. Paparazzi were as thick as fall leaves on the ground, lining the velvet ropes that cordoned them off from the walkway.

Leaning forward, I looked through the open glass entrance doors and saw more photographers held back on the right side of the entrance, while logoed backdrops lined the wall on the left for event and sponsor-branded photo ops.

Angus opened the door and I could feel the momentary expectation as the paparazzi waited to see who would step out. The moment Gideon did, it was like the mother of all lightning storms, camera flashes exploding in rapid, endless succession.

Mr. Cross! Gideon! Look this way!

He held his hand out to me, the rubies in his wedding band catching the light and glittering. Holding my skirt up with one hand, I made my way over to him and set my hand in his. The moment I stepped out, I was blinded, but I kept my eyes open despite the spots dancing across my vision, a practiced smile pasted on my lips.

I straightened, Gideon's hand settled on the small of my back, and pandemonium ensued. It somehow managed to get worse when Cary appeared. The shouts became deafening. I spotted Raúl by the entrance, his hard gaze sweeping the melee. He lifted his arm and spoke into his wrist mic, coordinating with someone under his command. When he looked at me, my smile turned genuine. He gave me a brisk nod.

Inside, we were met by two event handlers, who kept the required photo op moving along quickly, then escorted us up an elevator to the ballroom floor.

We stepped into a vast space filled with New York's elite, a glamorous assembly of powerful men and perfectly presented women displayed to flattering effect by dimmed chandelier lighting and a profusion of candlelight. The atmosphere was heavily fragranced by the massive floral arrangements centering each dining table and enlivened by a society orchestra playing upbeat instrumentals through the hum of conversation.

Gideon steered me through the groups of people clustered around the dining tables, pausing often for those who stepped into our path with greetings and congratulations. My husband had slid effortlessly, seamlessly into his public persona. Splendidly handsome, completely at ease, quietly commanding, coolly aloof.

I, however, was stiff and edgy, though I hoped that practiced smile hid my nervousness. Gideon and I didn't have a good track record at events like these. We ended up fighting and leaving separately. Things were different now, but still . . .

His hand slid up my bared back and cupped my nape, kneading the tense muscles gently. He continued to speak to the two gentlemen who'd intercepted us, discussing market fluctuations, but I was instinctively certain that he was focused on me. I stood to his right and he shifted smoothly, sliding just a bit behind me so that the right side of his body touched my back from shoulder to knee.

Cary reached around my shoulder and passed me a chilled flute of champagne. "I see Monica and Stanton," he told me. "I'll let them know we're here."

I followed his direction as he closed in on where my mom stood beside her husband, her smile bright and beautiful as they talked with another couple. Stanton was elegantly handsome in his tuxedo, while my mother gleamed like a pearl in an off-white silk column dress.

"Eva!"

I turned at the sound of Ireland's voice, my eyes widening as I found her rounding the nearest table. For a moment, my brain stopped processing anything but the sight of her. She was tall and willowy, her long black hair artfully arranged in a chic updo. The side slit in her sophisticated black velvet gown showed off mile-long legs, while the single-shoulder bodice cupped breasts that were the perfect size for her slender frame.

Ireland Vidal was a stunningly beautiful girl, her thickly

lashed eyes the same striking blue as her mother's and Gideon's. And she was only seventeen. Picturing her as the woman she would become was breathtaking. Cary wasn't the only one who was going to set the world on fire.

She walked right into me, hugging me tight. "We're sisters now!"

I smiled and hugged her back, careful not to spill my champagne on her. I glanced at Chris, who stood behind her, and he gave me a grin in return. The look in his eyes when they returned to his daughter was both tender and proud. God help the guys who set their sights on Ireland. With Chris, Christopher, and Gideon watching out for her, they would have some formidable men to get through first.

Ireland pulled back and checked me out. "Wow. That necklace is amazing! And your boobs! I want a pair of those."

I laughed. "You're perfect just the way you are. You're the most beautiful woman here."

"No way. But thanks." Her face lit up as Gideon excused himself from the conversation and turned to face her. "Hey, bro."

She was in his arms in an instant, hugging him as tightly as she'd hugged me. Gideon stood statue-still for a moment. Then he hugged her back, his face softening in a way that made my heart skip a beat.

I'd spoken to Ireland briefly on the phone after Gideon's interview, apologizing for keeping the secret of our wedding and explaining why. I wanted us to be closer than we were, but I was holding off on making too many overtures. It would be so easy to become the bridge between her and Gideon, and I didn't want it that way. They needed to have their own connection, independent of anyone else.

My sister-in-law would be attending Columbia University soon, like her brothers before her. She'd be close and we'd see each other more often. Until then, I would continue to encourage Gideon to foster their budding relationship.

"Chris." I went to him and gave him a hug, pleased with the enthusiasm with which he hugged me back. He'd cleaned up since coming over to dinner, his hair freshly trimmed and his jaw clean-shaven.

Christopher Vidal Sr. was a quietly handsome man with a gentle gaze. There was an innate kindness in him that radiated in his voice and the way he looked at people. I'd thought so the first time I met him, and he'd done nothing to alter that first impression.

"Gideon. Eva." Magdalene Perez joined us, looking seductively beautiful in a sleek, emerald green gown, her arm linked with her boyfriend's.

It was good to see that Magdalene had moved on from her unrequited interest in Gideon, which had caused problems for Gideon and me when our relationship was just getting started. She'd been a bitter, nasty bitch then, spurred on by Gideon's brother's manipulations. Now that she was happy with her artist, she was serene and lovely and was slowly becoming a close acquaintance.

Greeting them both warmly, I shook Gage Flynn's hand as Gideon kissed Magdalene's proffered cheek. I didn't know Gage all that well yet, but he was obviously head over heels for Magdalene. And I knew that Gideon would've checked him out, making sure the guy was good enough for the woman who'd been a longtime friend of Gideon's family.

We were accepting their congratulations when my mother and Stanton joined us, followed by Martin and Lacey, whom we hadn't seen since the weekend in Westport. I watched with a smile as Cary and Ireland both laughed about something shared between them.

"What a beautiful girl," my mother said, sipping champagne and eyeing Gideon's sister.

"Right?"

"And Cary looks good."

"I said the same thing."

She looked at me with a smile. "You should know that we've offered to let him keep the apartment if he likes or help him find something smaller."

"Oh." My gaze went to him, catching him nodding at something Chris told him. "What did he say?"

"That you'd offered him a private apartment adjoining Gideon's penthouse." She angled toward me. "You'll all decide what works best for you, but I wanted to give him the option to stay where he is. It's always good to have options."

I sighed, then nodded.

She reached for my hand. "Now, you and Gideon are handling your public image in your own way, but you have to be aware of what those horrible gossip blogs are saying about you and Cary being lovers."

Suddenly, the frenzy on the red carpet made sense. The three of us, arriving together.

"Gideon denied that he's ever cheated on you," she went on quietly, "but he's now known to have, shall we say . . . adventurous sexual appetites. Can you imagine how rumors will fly if the three of you are living together?"

"Oh, man." Yeah, I could. The world had seen in graphic detail that my husband was up for a threesome. Not with another man in the mix, but even so. Those days were behind him, but they didn't know that—and wouldn't want to believe it anyway. It was just too salacious.

"Before you say you don't care, honey, realize that many people do. And if someone Gideon wants to do business with thinks he's morally corrupt, it could cost him a fortune."

Really. These days, not likely, but I bit my tongue instead of making a crack about my mom's concern about the bottom line. It always came down to that, in one way or another. "I hear you," I muttered.

As the time approached for the start of dinner, everyone began searching for their assigned tables. Gideon and I were at the front, of course, since he was speaking. Ireland and Chris had place cards at our table, as did Cary. My mom, Stanton, Martin, and Lacey were at the table to our right; Magdalene and Gage were further back.

Gideon pulled my chair out for me and I moved to sit, then stopped, startled by the couple I spotted a few tables away. Straightening, I looked at Gideon. "The Lucases are here."

His head went up, his gaze searching. I knew the moment he spotted them by the way his jaw hardened. "So they are. Sit down, angel."

I sat and he pushed my chair in, taking a seat beside me. He pulled out his phone and typed out a quick text.

Leaning toward him, I whispered, "I've never seen them together before."

His phone buzzed with a reply as he looked up at me. "They don't go out as a couple often."

"Are you texting Arash?"

"Angus."

"Huh? About the Lucases?"

"Fuck 'em." He slid his phone back into his jacket and leaned toward me, draping one arm along the back of my chair and the other on the table, caging me in. He put his lips next to my ear. "Next time we come to one of these, I'm putting you in a short skirt and you're going to be naked underneath."

I was grateful everyone else was looking elsewhere and couldn't possibly hear—and that the orchestra was playing a little louder to keep all the guests moving toward their seats. "You're a fiend."

His voice dropped into a seductive purr. "I'm going to slide my hand between your thighs and slip my fingers into your soft, sweet cunt."

"Gideon!" Scandalized, I glanced at him and found him watching me with a feral grin and lustful eyes.

"All through dinner, angel," he murmured, nuzzling against my temple, "I'm going to be finger-fucking you slow and easy, working that tight perfect pussy of yours until you come for me. Again and again . . ."

"Oh my God." His low, rough voice was pure sin and sex. I shivered just from that, but his dirty talk had me sagging into my chair. "What's gotten into you?"

He pressed a quick, hard kiss against my cheek and straightened. "You were all knotted up. Now, you're not."

If we'd been totally alone, I would've smacked him. I told him so.

"You love me," he shot back, turning to glance around the ballroom as servers began to bring out the salads.

"Do I?"

He focused on me again. "Yes. Madly."

No point in arguing. He was right.

∼✦∼

We were just being served dessert, a dome of chocolate cake that looked delicious, when a woman in a conservative navy gown came over to our table and crouched between Gideon and me.

"We're going to begin the program in about fifteen minutes," she said. "Glen's going to speak for a few minutes, then we'll have you come up."

He nodded. "No problem. I'm ready whenever you are."

She smiled and I could tell she was a little flustered being that close to him. She had to be at least his mother's age, but then women of all ages appreciated a gorgeous man.

"Eva." Ireland leaned toward me. "You want to take a break before he goes up?"

I understood what she meant. "Of course."

Gideon and Chris pushed back from the table and pulled out our chairs. Since I'd lost all my lip gloss while eating and drinking, I pressed a kiss to my husband's jaw.

"I can't wait to hear you talk," I told him, my smile wide with anticipation.

He shook his head. "The things that turn you on."

"You love me."

"I do. Madly."

Following Ireland, I weaved through the tables, passing directly by the Lucases. They watched us, looking cozy, with Dr. Terrence Lucas's arm slung around his wife's shoulders.

Anne caught my gaze and flashed a sharp smile that made my skin crawl.

I reached up and smoothed my middle finger over my brow in a subtle but obvious *fuck you*.

Ireland and I had moved a few tables farther when she abruptly stopped in front of me.

I bumped into her back. "Sorry."

When she didn't continue forward, I angled around her to see what was blocking our way. "What's going on?"

She turned to look at me. Her eyes were bright with tears. "It's Rick," she said, her voice wavering.

"Who?" My brain scrambled to catch up. She looked so hurt. And lost. The connection suddenly clicked. "Your boyfriend?"

She turned her head forward again and I tried to track her attention, searching the packed tables for . . . someone. "Where? What does he look like?"

"Right there." She gave a hard jerk of her chin and I spotted tears running down her face. "With the blonde in the red dress."

Where? I found a few possibilities, then zeroed in on the youngest couple. One look at him and I knew the type. I used to fall for them, too. Confident, sexually experienced, all the right lines. I felt a bit sick thinking about how many guys like that I'd once let use me.

Then I got pissed. Rick was giving the girl plastered to his side a cocky, sexy smile. They certainly weren't just friends. Not when they were both eye-fucking each other.

I caught Ireland by the elbow and guided her forward. "Keep walking."

362 • SYLVIA DAY

We got to the ladies' room. The sudden quiet when we stepped inside made it possible to hear her sobbing. I pulled her aside in the vanity area, thankful we were the only ones there, and handed her some tissues I pulled out of the box on the counter.

"He told me he had to work tonight," she said. "That's why I said yes when Dad asked me if I wanted to come."

"This is the guy who won't tell his parents about you because of Gideon's father?"

She nodded. "They're out there. Sitting with him."

It was coming back to me, that conversation we'd had during the launch of the Six-Ninths music video. Rick's grandparents had lost a chunk of their wealth to Geoffrey Cross's Ponzi scheme. They thought it was "convenient" that Gideon was one of the wealthiest men in the world now, even though it was evident to anyone who looked that he'd built his empire with his own hard work and capital.

But then, Rick was probably just making excuses to juggle multiple dates. After all, his parents were here and Gideon was the star attraction. Made me question whether the animosity he'd told her about was bullshit.

"He told me he'd broken up with her months ago!" she cried.

"The blonde?"

Sniffling, she nodded again. "I just saw him last night. He didn't say anything about getting the night off and coming here."

"Did you mention that you would be here?"

"No. I don't talk about Gideon. Not with him, anyway."

Was Rick just a young, dumb kid getting his rocks off with every pretty girl who'd let him? Or was he screwing with Gideon's sister as some sort of twisted payback? In any case, the guy was a douche.

"Don't cry over that loser, Ireland." I got her more tissue. "Don't give him the satisfaction."

"I just want to go home."

I shook my head. "That's not going to help. Honestly, nothing's going to help. It's going to hurt for a while. But you can get back at him if you want to. That might feel good."

She looked at me, tears still streaming. "What do you mean?"

"You've got one of the hottest male models in New York sitting by you. Just say the word and Cary will become your very attentive, very crazy-about-you date." The more I thought of it, the more I liked it. "Together you can run into Rick and oops . . . well, *hellooo*. Fancy seeing you here. But what can he say? He's got the blonde. And you get to walk away with an even score."

Ireland started shaking. "Maybe I should just talk to him . . ."

Magdalene stepped into the ladies' room and paused, assessing the situation. "Ireland. What's wrong?"

I kept my mouth shut, since it wasn't my story to share.

Ireland shook her head. "It's nothing. I'm okay."

"All right." Magdalene looked at me. "I won't pry, but you should know that I'd never share anything with your brothers if you told me not to."

It took her a moment, and then Ireland spoke through her tears. "This guy I've been seeing for a couple months now . . . he's out there with someone else. His old girlfriend."

Personally, I suspected Rick had never broken up with that girlfriend to begin with and had been stringing Ireland along on the side, but then I was cynical about things like that.

"Oh." Magdalene's face softened in sympathy. "Men can be such assholes. Look, if you want to slip out without him noticing, I'll order a car for you." She snapped open her clutch and took out her smartphone. "On me. How's that?"

"Hang on," I interjected. I laid out my plan.

Magdalene's brows rose. "Devious. Why get mad when you can get even?"

"I don't know . . ." Ireland glanced at the mirror and cursed. She grabbed more tissues and worked on fixing her eye makeup. "I look like shit."

"You look a million times better than that tramp out there," I told her.

She gave a watery laugh. "I hate her, too. She's such a bitch."

"Bet she's admired some of Cary's Grey Isles ads," Magdalene said. "I know I have."

That did the trick. While Ireland wasn't ready yet to completely write off Rick, she was certainly open to making his date envious.

The rest would come in time. Hopefully.

Then again, there were some lessons we women had to learn the hard way.

❧

We made it back to our table just as a gentleman I assumed was Glen headed up the stairs onto the stage and crossed over to the lectern. I knelt by Cary, setting my hand on his arm.

He glanced down at me. "What's up?"

I explained what I wanted him to do and why.

His grin flashed white in the dimmed lighting. "Sure thing, baby girl."

"You're the best, Cary."

"So they all say."

Rolling my eyes, I stood and headed back to my chair, which Gideon pulled out for me. My cake was still there and I eyed it eagerly.

"They tried to take that," Gideon murmured. "I defended it for you."

"Aww. Thank you, baby. You're so good to me."

He put his hand on my thigh beneath the table and gave it a soft squeeze.

I watched my husband while I ate, admiring Gideon's air of calm relaxation as we both listened to Glen talk about the importance of the work his organization did in the city. Whenever I thought about giving speeches on behalf of Crossroads, I got butterflies in my stomach. But I'd eventually get the hang of it, figure things out. I would learn what I needed to know to be an asset to both my husband and Cross Industries.

We had time and I had Gideon's love. The rest would fall into place.

"It is our pleasure to honor a man who truly needs no introduction—"

Putting my fork down, I sat back and listened as Glen extolled my husband's many accomplishments and his generous commitment to causes that benefited victims of sexual abuse. It didn't escape my notice that Chris was watching Gideon with a new understanding in his gaze. And pride. The look he gave my husband was no different from the one I'd seen him give Ireland.

The room exploded into applause as Gideon rose lithely to his feet. I stood, too, along with Chris, Cary, and Ireland. The rest of the room followed suit, until a full standing ovation welcomed Gideon to the stage. He glanced at me before he walked away, his fingers brushing the ends of my hair.

Seeing him traverse the stage was its own pleasure. His stride was smooth and unhurried, but it commanded attention. Gracefully powerful, he moved so beautifully it was a joy to watch him.

He set the plaque they'd given him atop the lectern, his tanned hands in notable contrast to the white of his cuffs. Then he began speaking, his dynamic baritone smooth and cultured, making each word a separate caress. There was no other sound in the room, everyone riveted by his dark good looks and consummate oration.

It was over too quickly. I was on my feet again the moment he picked up the plaque, my hands clapping so hard my palms hurt. They directed him to the side of the stage, where a photographer waited with Glen. Gideon spoke to them, then looked at me, beckoning me to him with an outstretched hand.

He met me at the bottom of the stairs, offering his arm to help me navigate the ascent in my dress and heels.

"I am so hot for you right now," I told him softly.

He laughed. "Fiend."

We danced for an hour after the dinner was over.

Why didn't I dance with my husband more often? He was as skilled and sexual on the dance floor as he was in bed, his body moving with fluid strength, his lead confident and expertly assertive.

Gideon was intimately familiar with how we flowed together and used that to his advantage, taking every opportunity to slide his body against mine. I was wildly aroused and he was aware, his gaze on my face both hot and knowing.

When I could tear my attention away from him, I spotted Cary dancing with Ireland. He had scoffed when I first asked him to take dancing lessons with me, but he'd come around and quickly become our instructor's favorite. He was a natural and he easily led Ireland, despite her inexperience.

A flamboyant dancer, Cary claimed a wide space on the floor, which made him and Ireland the focus of much attention. He, however, only had eyes for his partner, playing the part of a completely spellbound date to perfection. Even heartbroken, Ireland couldn't help but be charmed by his unwavering, focused attention. I saw her laugh often, her cheeks prettily flushed with exertion.

I'd missed that *oops* moment with Rick I'd hoped to witness, but I saw the result. He was dancing with his girlfriend, woefully unable to compete with Cary in either skill or looks. There was no more smiling or eye-fucking, since both he and the blonde kept glancing at Cary and Ireland, who were clearly having far more fun.

Terrence and Anne Lucas danced, too, but were wise enough to stay on the other side of the dance floor.

"Let's go home," Gideon murmured, as the song ended and we slowed to a halt, "and put some sweat on those diamonds."

I smiled. "Yes, please."

We went back to our table to retrieve his plaque and my clutch.

"We'll head out with you," Stanton said, joining us with my mother beside him.

"What about Cary?" I asked.

"Martin will take him home," my mother answered. "They're all still enjoying themselves."

It took us just as long to leave as it'd taken us to arrive, with so many people catching Gideon and Stanton for the first time all evening. I could only say thank you to congratulations, but my mother occasionally spoke with authority, adding brief but incisive comments to things Stanton discussed. I envied her that knowledge and was inspired by it. We'd have to talk about that when the time presented itself.

The plus side of being delayed for so long was that it gave time for the cars to be brought around. When we finally made it down to street level, Raúl informed us that the limo was only a block away. Clancy shot me a quick smile before he told my mom and Stanton their car was pulling up now.

Paparazzi waited outside. Not as many as before, but more than a dozen.

"Let's get together tomorrow," my mom said, giving me a hug in the lobby.

"Sounds good." I pulled back. "I could use a day at the spa."

"What a lovely idea." Her smile was brilliant. "I'll make the arrangements."

I hugged Stanton good-bye; Gideon shook his hand. We stepped outside and the camera flashes burst around us. The city welcomed us outdoors with the sounds of late-evening traffic and the gentle warmth of the evening. The humidity was slowly receding as summer gave way to fall and I looked forward to spending more time outdoors. Autumn in New York was a unique enchantment, something I'd only enjoyed previously during short visits.

Get down!

The shout barely registered before Gideon tackled me. A loud crack of sound jolted through me, reverberating off the brick and ringing in my ears. Deafeningly close . . . Jesus. Right beside us.

We hit the carpeted pavement hard. Gideon rolled, covering me with his body. More weight as someone threw themselves over Gideon. Another bark of noise. Then another. Another . . .

Crushed. Too heavy. Breathe. My lungs couldn't expand. My head pounded. *Oxygen. God.*

I struggled. Clawing at the red carpet. Gideon clutched me tighter. His voice was harsh in my ear, the words lost beneath the frantic buzzing in my head.

Air. Can't breathe . . . The world went black.

14

"Christ. Eva." I ran frantic hands over her limp form, searching for injury as the driver hit the gas pedal hard and the limo lurched forward, slamming me back into the seat.

My wife lay deathly still across my lap, unresponsive to my desperate examination. No blood on her gown or skin. A pulse, hard and quick. Her chest lifting and falling with each breath.

Relief hit me so hard I felt dizzy. I pulled her up tight against me, cradling her close. "Thank God."

Raúl barked orders into the mic at his wrist. The moment he shut up, I demanded, "What the fuck happened?"

He dropped his arm. "One of the photographers had a gun and opened fire. Clancy got him."

"Was anyone hurt?"

"Monica Stanton went down."

"What?" My slowing heartbeat lurched back into a

pounding rhythm. I looked down at my wife as she slowly came to, her eyelids fluttering. "Jesus. How bad?"

He exhaled harshly. "I'm waiting for word. It didn't look good. You grabbed Mrs. Cross and Mrs. Stanton moved into the way."

Eva.

I held my wife tighter, running my hand over her hair as we sped through the city.

⁓♉⁓

"What happened?"

Eva's soft question as we turned the corner that led to the garage knotted my stomach. Raúl looked at me, his face grim. Only moments before he'd taken a call and met my gaze, confirming my worst fear with a shake of his head and a quietly voiced *I'm sorry.*

My wife's mother was dead.

How was I supposed to tell Eva? And after I did, how could I keep her safe until we knew what the hell was going on?

In my jacket pocket, my phone buzzed constantly. Calls. Messages. I needed to get to them all, but my wife came first.

We pulled into the garage, driving past the guard in the glass cubicle. My foot tapped restlessly on the floorboard. I wanted out of the car. I needed my wife locked down.

"Gideon?" She clutched at my jacket. "What happened? I heard gunshots—"

"False alarm," I said gruffly, my grip on her too tight. "A car backfired."

"What? Really?" She blinked up at me, wincing as I pulled her even closer. "Oww."

"I'm sorry." I'd taken her down hard, unable to break the fall for her without exposing her to danger. It had been instinctual, an abrupt response to the urgency in Raúl's voice. "I overreacted."

"For real?" She tried to sit up. "I thought I heard multiple shots."

"The death of a few cameras, maybe. A few people got startled, dropped their gear."

The car slowed to a halt and Raúl leapt out, extending his hand to Eva to help her. She climbed out slowly and I was directly behind her, scooping her up into my arms the moment I straightened.

I strode to the garage elevator, waited while Raúl typed in the code. One of his team stood behind us, facing the other direction, his hand in his jacket on his gun as he surveilled.

Would he be enough if there was another shooter lying in wait?

"Hey, I can walk," Eva said, still punchy, her arms around my shoulders. "And you need to answer your phone. That thing's going crazy."

"Give me a minute." I stepped into the elevator. "You passed out. Scared the shit out of me."

"I couldn't breathe."

Kissing her forehead, I apologized again. I wouldn't feel safe until we stepped into our living room. I glanced at Raúl. "I'll be out shortly."

I took my wife directly to the bedroom, laying her down

atop the comforter. Lucky barked in his crate, pawing at the door.

"That was so weird." Eva shook her head. "Where's my clutch? I want to call Mom. Did Clancy freak out, too?"

My gut knotted. I'd promised to never lie to my wife and I knew this lie was going to hurt her badly. Hurt us. But . . . *God.* How the fuck did I tell her? And if I did, how could I keep her home when she'd want to go out and see the truth for herself?

Lucky's plaintive whines only ratcheted up my anxiety.

"I think we left your purse in the car." I brushed the hair back from her forehead, fighting the tremor that wanted to rack my entire body. "I'll have someone get it and bring it up."

"Okay. Can I use your phone for now?"

"Let's get you settled first. Are you hurting? Bruised?" I shot a glare at Lucky, but that only made him paw the metal bars more furiously.

She poked at her hip and winced. "Maybe."

"All right. We'll take care of that."

I went to the bathroom, pulling out my phone to turn it off. The screen was an endless scroll of missed calls and texts. I watched it go black, shoved it into my pants pocket, and then turned on the taps in the bathtub. Anyone I'd want to hear from could reach Raúl or Angus.

I tossed a handful of Epsom salts into the steaming water; I knew a bath was a risk considering how rare it was for me to not join Eva when she took one. Still, hot soaks relaxed her, made her calm. I suspected she took naps during the day to make up for the hours our sex life took out of the nights, but she was running a sleep deficit after the weekend.

If I could just get her to wind down and get in bed, she might drift off. It would buy me some time to figure out what had happened, what risk remained, talk to Dr. Petersen . . .

Fuck. And Victor. I had to call Eva's dad. Get him on a flight to New York as soon as possible. Cary. He should be here, too. Once I had more facts and a support system for my wife, then I could tell her. Just a few hours. That was all I needed.

I struggled to ignore the sick fear that Eva wouldn't forgive me for the delay.

She was letting Lucky out when I stepped back into the bedroom. A laugh escaped her at the puppy's enthusiasm. The joyous sound, one I loved so much, pierced me like a knife in the chest.

Kissing Lucky's head, she looked at me with bright eyes. "You should put him on his puppy pad. He's been locked up awhile."

"I'll take him."

She rubbed Lucky's head before passing him over. "I hear a bath running."

"A soak might do you good."

"Limber me up?" she teased. The look in her eyes . . . It killed me. I almost told her, but I couldn't get the words past the lump in my throat.

Instead, I turned away and headed down the hallway to the half bath off the living room, where Lucky's patch of fake grass was. I set him down on it, ran my hands through my hair.

Think, damn it. God, I needed a drink.

Yes. A drink. Hard liquor.

I went to the kitchen, tried to think of something strong

that Eva would actually drink. A digestif, maybe? The house phone. Shit. I went to turn off the ringer and saw that some-one had already thought of it. Turning back around, I spot-ted the coffeemaker.

Something hot. Relaxing. No caffeine.

Tea. I went the pantry and searched, shoving around the items on the shelves looking for a box of tea Angus kept at the penthouse. Some herbal crap he said smoothed the rough edges. I found it and focused, filling a mug from the instant hot water tap. I dropped two tea bags into it, a liberal pour of rum, then a scoop of honey. I stirred, spilled onto the counter. More rum.

Tossing the tea bags into the sink, I headed back to my wife.

For an instant, when I didn't find her in the bedroom, I panicked. Then I heard her in the closet and my breath left me in a rush. I set the mug down by the bath, turned the water off, and went to her. I found her sitting on the bench, taking off her shoes.

"The dress is ruined, I think," she said, as she stood in her bare feet, showing me the tear along the left side.

"I'll buy you another."

She flashed me a big smile. "You're spoiling me."

It was fucking torture. Every second. Every lie I told. Every truth I left unsaid.

I was flayed by the love in her eyes. The utter trust. Sweat slid down my back. I yanked my jacket off and tossed it aside, clawing at my bow tie and collar until they both came apart and let me breathe.

"Help me out of this." She turned her back to me.

I unfastened the gown and pushed it off her shoulders,

letting it fall to a puddle on the floor. Then I unhooked her bra, hearing her sigh with pleasure as its constriction eased.

Looking her over, I cursed silently at the bruise already shadowing her hip and the abrasions on her arm from the red carpet.

She yawned. "Wow. I'm tired."

Thank God. "You should sleep, then."

She shot me a heated look over her shoulder. "I'm not *that* tired."

Jesus. Being gutted couldn't hurt worse. I couldn't touch her, make love to her . . . not with my deceit between us.

I swallowed hard. "All right, then. I've got to see to some business first. And get your purse. I made a hot toddy for you. It's by the bathtub. Just relax and I'll join you as soon as I can."

"Is everything all right?"

Unable to lie any more than I already had, I told her an irrelevant truth. "I've missed a lot of work this week. Some pressing things need to be dealt with."

"Sorry. I know that's my fault." She kissed my jaw. "Love you, ace."

Grabbing a robe off the hooks, she slid into it and walked out. I stood there, surrounded by the smell of her, my hands still tingling from the feel of her, my heart pounding with fear and self-loathing.

Lucky raced in so fast, he ricocheted off the door before barreling into my feet. I picked him up, rubbing the top of his head.

This was one nightmare he couldn't wake me from.

Raúl waited in my home office, talking briskly on his phone. I joined him, closing the door behind me.

He ended the call and stood. "The police are on scene. The gunman's in custody."

"Monica?"

"They're waiting for the medical examiner."

I couldn't imagine it. I went to my desk, sat heavily in the chair. My gaze went to the photos of Eva on the wall.

"The detectives have been told that you and Mrs. Cross will be here at home when it's time to get your statements."

I nodded, and prayed for them to wait until morning to make that house call.

"I took the phone off the hook in the kitchen when we arrived," he said quietly.

"I noticed. Thank you."

There was a knock at the door. Tensing, I expected Eva to walk in. I exhaled in relief when it was Angus instead.

"I'm going to head back," Raúl said. "I'll keep you posted."

"I need Eva's purse from the car. And Cary. Get him here."

He nodded and left.

Angus settled into the seat Raúl had just vacated. "I'm sorry, lad."

"So am I."

"I should've been there."

"And have someone else I love in the line of fire?" I pushed to my feet, too restless to sit. "It's a blessing you were at the Lucases'."

He stared at me a moment, and then his gaze dropped to his hands.

It took me a second to realize what I'd said. Another to

know that I hadn't told him I loved him before now. I hoped he'd known anyway.

Taking a deep breath, his chin lifted and he looked at me again. "How's Eva?"

"I have to check on her. She's taking a bath."

"Poor lass."

"She doesn't know." I rubbed the back of my neck. "I haven't told her."

"Gideon." His eyes were wide with the same dismay I felt. "You cannae—"

"What good would it do?" I snapped. "We don't have answers. Her mother's gone. I can't have her going back to the scene and seeing . . . that. Why torture her or put her at risk? Christ, it could've been her! It could still be her if we don't keep her safe."

He watched me pace, with eyes that had seen—and still saw—too much.

"I'm going to make some calls." I pulled out my phone. "I need to get a handle on the situation before I tell her. Try to cushion the blow as much as I can. She's been through so much—" My voice broke. My eyes burned.

"What can I do to help?" he asked softly.

I pulled myself together. "I need a jet available for Eva's father. I'm going to call him now."

"I'll see to it." He stood.

"Give me a few minutes to break the news to him, then text him the info when you have it."

"Consider it done."

"Thank you."

"Gideon . . . You should know my search of the Lucas residence was successful." Reaching into his pocket, he pulled out a flash drive no bigger than a dime. "She kept this in a bedroom safe, buried beneath her jewelry in a box. She scanned all his notes."

I looked at him blankly. Anne and Hugh were the least of my concerns at the moment.

"It's all lies," he continued. "He mentioned nothing of what really went on. What you may find of interest, when the time comes, is what he had to say about Christopher."

Setting the drive on my desktop, Angus left the room.

I stared at it. Then I went to my desk, opened a drawer, and swept the drive into it with a brush of my hand.

Turning my phone back on, I saw that there were texts and voice mails from Cary, Magdalene, Clancy, Ireland, Chris . . .

Overwhelmed, I went to the home screen.

I pulled up Dr. Petersen's office in my contacts and dialed. Going through the automated menu, I selected the after-hours emergency switchboard and told the answering operator that it was very much an emergency—a death was involved and the doctor needed to call me back as soon as he could.

The entire interaction was cold and clinical, especially for something so desperately personal. The grim process seemed like a terrible insult to the vibrantly beautiful wife and mother who was no longer with us. And yet I found myself wishing the next call I had to make could be accomplished with so little emotion.

As the line rang on the other end, I sank into my chair. The last time I'd talked to Victor had been the call I had placed from Rio de Janeiro, when I explained that the photo of me with two women was taken before I ever met his daughter. He had received that information with chilly reserve, letting me know without saying it that I wasn't good enough for Eva. I couldn't disagree. Now, I had to tell him that the other woman he cared for had been taken from him again—this time, forever.

Eva believed her father was still in love with her mother. If so, the news would level him. I could still taste the bile at the back of my throat and feel the icy panic that had blanked my mind in those first few moments after the shooting. There would be nothing for me without Eva.

"Reyes," Victor answered, sounding cool and alert. There was noise in the background, traffic maybe. Distant music. I glanced at my watch, realized he might be on duty.

"It's Cross. I need to tell you something. Are you alone?"

"I can be. What's wrong?" he demanded, picking up on the gravity of my tone. "Has something happened to Eva?"

"No, it's not Eva." Just get it out. Blunt and quick. That's how I'd want to be told that my life was over. "I'm sorry. Monica was killed tonight."

There was a terrible pause. "What did you just say?"

My head fell back against the chair. He'd heard me the first time, I could tell by his voice. But he couldn't believe it. "I'm very sorry, Victor. We don't know much more than that at this time."

From his side of the call, I heard a car door open, then slam shut. There was a brief spate of transmissions from a police scanner, then eerie quiet followed and stretched out for long minutes. Still, I knew he was there.

"It happened barely an hour ago," I explained quietly, trying to bridge that silence. "We were all leaving an event. A gunman in the crowd opened fire."

"Why?"

"I don't know. But the shooter was apprehended. We should have more details soon."

His voice strengthened. "Where's my daughter?"

"She's home with me. She won't leave here until I'm certain it's safe for her to do so. I'm making flight arrangements for you now. Eva will need you, Victor."

"Let me talk to her."

"She's resting. You'll get a text with the information for the flight as soon as it's confirmed. It'll be one of my jets. You can speak with her in the morning when you get here."

Victor exhaled roughly. "All right. I'll be ready."

"I'll see you shortly."

Hanging up, I thought of the other man who was a father figure for Eva. I couldn't think about what Stanton was going through; it shattered my mind. But I felt for him and was deeply sorry that anything I could offer would be inadequate.

Still, I reached out, typing a quick text. *If I can be of service in any way, please let me know.*

I left my office and went to the master bathroom. I paused on the threshold, everything inside me raw and aching at the sight of Eva stretched out in the steaming water with her eyes closed. Her hair was clipped up in a sexy, wild mess. The diamonds glittered on the counter. Lucky pawed at my shins.

"Hi," she murmured, her eyes still closed. "You take care of everything?"

"Not yet. Right now, I need to take care of you." I went to her, saw the toddy was half gone. "You should finish your drink."

Her eyes opened slowly, dreamy and soft. "It's strong. I've got a buzz."

"Good. Now drink the rest."

She complied. Not out of obedience but in the way a woman with a hidden agenda pretended to follow an order: because it suited her.

"Are you coming in?" she asked, licking her lips.

I shook my head. She pouted.

"I'm done then." She rose from the tub, rivulets of water sliding over her flushed curves. She gave me a seductive smile, knowing what she was doing to me. "Sure you won't change your mind?"

My throat worked on a hard swallow. "I can't."

With weighted steps, I grabbed a towel and handed it to her. I turned away, tormented by the sight of her, and collected first-aid items, setting the tubes and packets on the counter.

She came to me, leaning into my side. "Are you okay? Still thinking about your mom?"

"What? No." I groaned, my head bowed. "When you passed out . . . Fuck. I've never been so scared."

"Gideon." She slid into me, hugging me. "I'm okay."

Sighing, I gave her a quick squeeze and let her go. It pained me too much to hold her, knowing what had been left unspoken. "Let me take a look and make sure."

Lucky sat with his head to the side, watching me curiously as I inspected Eva's arm. I cleaned it with an antibiotic wipe before smoothing ointment over the angry red scrape. I taped gauze over it to keep it protected. The livid bruise on her hip got a generous application of arnica, my fingers lightly swirling over the darkening skin until the gel was fully absorbed.

My touch and focus aroused her, despite my best efforts.

Squeezing my eyes shut, I straightened. "Off to bed with you, Mrs. Cross."

"Umm . . . yes, let's go to bed." Her hands went to my shoulders, her fingers running down the untied ends of my bow tie. "I like your collar open like this. Very sexy."

"Angel . . . You're shredding me." I caught her hands. "I've still got some things to handle."

"Okay. I'll behave. For now."

With her hand in mine, I led her into the bedroom. She protested when I pulled out a Cross Industries T-shirt and slipped it over her head.

"What about the diamonds?" she asked.

She might never wear them again after this night. Where the fuck was Dr. Petersen? I needed his help to say the right things in the right way when the time came.

My fingers brushed her cheek, the only touch I would allow myself. "This will be more comfortable for now."

I tucked her into bed, smoothing her hair back from her cheeks. She was going to sleep believing her world still had her mother in it and that her husband would never lie to her.

"I love you." I pressed a kiss to her forehead, wanting those words to echo in her dreams.

It was all too possible that she wouldn't believe them once she was awake.

Leaving Eva to rest, I shut the bedroom door and headed to the kitchen for a drink, something strong and smooth that might ease the cold knot in my gut.

I found Cary in the living room, sitting on the sofa with

his head in his hands. Angus sat at the far end of the dining table, talking quietly on his phone.

"Would you like a drink?" I asked Cary, as I passed him.

His head came up and I saw the tears. The devastation. "Where's Eva?"

"She's trying to sleep. It's best that she does." I entered the kitchen, grabbed two tumblers and a bottle of scotch, and poured two hefty rations. I slid one over when he joined me at the island.

I tossed mine back, gulping down the contents. Closing my eyes, I felt the burn. "You'll stay in the guest room." My voice was roughened by the liquor's bite. "She's going to need you in the morning."

"We're going to need each other."

I poured another glass for myself. "Victor's coming."

"Fuck." Cary swiped at his damp eyes. "Stanton, man . . . He aged right in front of me. Like thirty years just ran through him while I was standing there." He lifted his tumbler to his lips with a violently shaking hand.

My phone buzzed in my pocket and I pulled it out, answering it even though I didn't recognize the number. "Cross."

"Gideon. It's Dr. Petersen. I got your message."

"Just a minute." I pressed the phone to my chest and looked at Cary. "I have to take this."

He waved me off, his gaze locked into the amber liquid in his glass.

I went to the bedroom and cracked open the door, relieved to find Eva fast asleep with the dog curled up next to her. Backing out, I shut myself in my office. "I'm sorry. I needed to step away for privacy."

"That's fine. What's happened, Gideon?"

Sinking into my desk chair, I dropped my head into my hand. "It's Eva's mother. There was an incident tonight. She was killed."

"Monica . . ." He took a deep breath. "Tell me what happened."

I remembered then that Monica was—had been—a patient of Dr. Petersen, too. I relayed the same information I'd passed to Victor. "I need you to come to my home. I need your help. I don't know how to tell Eva."

"How to . . . ? I'm sorry, Gideon. It's late and I'm confused. I assumed she was with you when it happened."

"She was right by my side, but I knocked her down to get her out of the way. Knocked the breath right out of her. She passed out and when she came to, I told her it was a false alarm."

"Oh, Gideon." He sighed heavily. "That wasn't wise."

"It was the right decision. There's nothing she can do about what happened."

"You can't protect her from everything, and lying is never a solution."

"I can protect her from being a target!" I surged to my feet, furious that his reaction and Angus's reflected my worst fears about how Eva would respond to the choice I'd made. "Until I know what the threat is, I won't have her out in the open, which is exactly where she'd want to be!"

"That's her choice to make."

"It would be the wrong one."

"Regardless, it's a decision she has a right to come to on her own."

I shook my head, even though he couldn't see it. "Her safety is nonnegotiable. She worries about everyone else. It's my job to worry about her."

"You could tell her your concerns," Dr. Petersen said, his voice low and soothing. "Explain them to her."

"She wouldn't put her safety first. She'd want to be with Stanton."

"Being with others who share her grief can—"

"He's standing over her mother's corpse on a city sidewalk right now!"

The words and the image they evoked were vile. My stomach churned, revolting against the liquor I'd poured into it. But I needed someone to grasp the full extent of the horror and understand why I'd made *my* decision. To give me some hope that Eva would understand.

"Don't tell me what would be best for her right now," I said coldly. "I won't let her go there. She would be haunted for the rest of her life if she saw . . . that."

He was quiet. Then, "The longer you wait, the more difficult this will be for both of you."

"I'm going to tell her as soon as she wakes up. You're going to come over here and help me do that."

"Gideon—"

"I've talked to her father in California. He'll be on his way soon. And Cary's here." I paced. "They've got some time to deal with it, so when Eva sees them, they'll be able to give her the support she needs. You'll be able to help her, too."

"You're not seeing that Eva's biggest source of strength and comfort is *you*, Gideon. And by failing to disclose something of this magnitude and being dishonest about it initially, you've put her most depended-upon foundation on shaky ground."

"You think I don't know that?!" I stopped in my tracks,

directly in front of the photo collage of my wife. "I'm . . . Jesus. I'm terrified she won't forgive me."

Dr. Petersen's silence allowed those words to hang in the air, mocking my helplessness.

I looked away from the images of my wife. "But I would do it again. This situation, these stakes . . ."

"All right. You'll need to talk to her about all of this as soon as she wakes up. Be frank about what you're feeling, and focus on that rather than logic or your rationale. She may not agree with you or see your point, but understanding the emotional impetus behind your actions will help."

"Do you?" I challenged.

"I do, yes. Which isn't to say I wouldn't have recommended a different course of action, but I understand. I'm going to give you another number where you can reach me directly."

Grabbing a pen off my desk, I wrote it down.

"Talk to Eva. Afterward, if you still want me there, I'll come by. I can't promise to respond immediately," he went on, "but I'll come as soon as I can."

"Thank you." I ended the call and took a seat at my desk. There was nothing more for me to do but wait. Wait for Eva to wake up. Wait for the police. Wait for the visitors who would come and call, friends and family who would be as ineffectual as I was.

I woke my computer and sent an e-mail to Scott, telling him to clear my calendar for the rest of the week and to get in touch with the wedding planner. Informing her and others was most likely moot, considering the paparazzi were already there at the time of the shooting. There was no way to have even a single day of private grieving.

388 • SYLVIA DAY

The thought of what had to have been posted online already filled me with helpless fury. Graphic crime-scene photos. Conspiracy theories and wild speculation. The world would be looking in our windows for months to come.

I pushed the thoughts aside.

I forced myself to think of the things that would alleviate Eva's stress. I already had plans to talk to Victor, and we would discuss his family then, since they were scheduled to arrive on Friday.

My phone was in my hand before I realized it. I checked my missed calls and scrolled through my texts. There was nothing from my mother, although I had to think Chris or Ireland would have said something to her by this point. Her silence didn't surprise me as much as the text from Christopher.

Please give my condolences to Eva.

I stared at the text for a long while, tapping the screen when it dimmed to keep it lit up and in front of me. It was the word *please* that struck me. Such an everyday courtesy, but not one Christopher used with me.

I thought of the people I'd called on Eva's behalf. Cary, who was like a brother to her. Victor, her father. Who would Eva call if our situations were reversed? Chris? Certainly not my brother.

Why? All these years I'd wondered about that. Christopher could have meant much more to me, a link to the new family my mother had created.

Opening the drawer, I stared at the tiny flash drive that Angus had retrieved from the Lucases' home. Did it hold the answer?

Would it matter now if it did?

The moment I dreaded came much too quickly. I lay on the bed with my eyes closed, feeling the bed shift as Eva turned over, hearing her soft sigh as she settled into the new position. She would drift back into sleep if I let her. I could give her a few more hours of peace.

But Victor's flight was on the ground in New York. The police could arrive here at any moment. Reality was going to intrude no matter how badly I wanted to hold it at bay, which meant the time I had left to break the news to my wife was winding down.

I sat up and scrubbed a hand over my face, feeling the burn of the stubble that shadowed my jaw. Then I touched her shoulder, rousing her as gently as I could.

"Hey." She rolled toward me, her eyes slumberous. "You're still dressed. Did you work all night?"

I stood and turned the bedside light on, unable to discuss the situation without being on my feet. "Eva. We need to talk."

Blinking at me, she pushed up onto her elbow. "What's wrong?"

"Splash some water on your face while I fix you a cup of coffee, okay? And wait here in the bedroom until I bring it to you."

She frowned. "You sound serious."

"I am. And you need to be awake."

"Okay." Tossing back the comforter, Eva got out of bed.

I grabbed Lucky and shut the bedroom door behind me, dropping him off in the bathroom before I fixed coffee for both me and Eva. New day, same routine. A few more minutes of pretending nothing had changed amounted to a different kind of lie.

When I returned to the bedroom, I found Eva pulling on a pair of pajama pants. She'd pulled her hair back in a short ponytail and there was a spot of toothpaste on her T-shirt. Normal. For the moment, she was the wife I loved beyond all reason.

She took the mug from me and breathed in the aroma, her eyes closing in pure pleasure. It was so like her, so very Eva, that my chest hurt.

I set my coffee aside, my stomach suddenly too knotted to contemplate putting anything into it. "Sit in that chair over there, angel."

"You're starting to freak me out."

"I know. I'm sorry." I touched her cheek. "I don't mean to drag this out. If you sit down, I'll explain."

Eva settled into the reading chair beneath the arched windows. The sky was turning from night to bluish gray. I turned on the light beside her, then grabbed the other chair and placed it in front of her. Holding out my hand for hers, I sat, squeezing her fingers gently.

I took a deep breath. "I lied to you. I'm going to defend that decision when I'm done, but for now . . ."

Her gaze narrowed. "Spit it out, ace."

"You were right about the gunshots you heard. One of the photographers opened fire on us last night. Your mother was hit." I paused, struggled to say the words. "She didn't make it."

Eva stared at me, her eyes big and dark in her suddenly pale face. Her hand was trembling violently when she put her coffee on the end table. "What are you saying?"

"She was shot, Eva." I tightened my grip on her abruptly cold hands, sensing her panic. "It was fatal. I'm sorry."

Her breathing picked up.

"I don't have any answers to give you right now. They have the shooter in custody and Raúl has told me that Detectives Graves and Michna were assigned to the case."

"They're homicide cops," she said, her voice flat.

"Yes." They'd been the ones to investigate Nathan Barker's death. I knew them better than I wished.

"Why would someone want to kill my mother?"

"I don't know, Eva. It might have been random. Could be he missed his target. We could call Graves or Michna—you still have their cards, right? They might not tell us anything, but I'm expecting them to come by and take our statements."

"Why? I don't know anything."

The fear I'd been fighting all night swamped me. I'd expected anger and tears. A violent explosion of emotion. Instead, she seemed disoriented. Almost lifeless.

"Angel." I released one of her hands to cup her face. "Cary's here, in the guest room. Your father is en route from the airport. He'll be here soon."

"Dad." A lone tear slid down her face. "Does he know?"

"Yes. I told him. Cary knows, too. He was there."

"I need to talk to him. She was like a mother to Cary."

"Eva." I slid to the end of my seat and gripped her shoulders. "You don't need to worry about anyone else right now."

"Why didn't you tell me?" She looked at me blankly. "Why lie to me?"

I started to explain, then hesitated. Finally, "To protect you."

Her gaze left my face, drifted off to the side. "I think I

knew something bad happened. I think that's why I'm not surprised. But when we left . . . Was she . . . ?"

"She was already gone, Eva. I won't lie to you again—I didn't know whether anyone had been hit when I got you out of there. The most important thing was to get you somewhere safe. After that—"

"Never mind."

My chest expanded, my lungs shuddered. "There was nothing you could do."

"It doesn't matter now anyway."

"You're in shock, Eva. Look at me." When she didn't, I scooped her up and pulled her onto my lap. Her entire body was cold. I hugged her close, trying to warm her, and she shivered.

Standing, I took her to the bed and yanked the comforter back. I sat on the edge of the mattress and pulled the blankets around us, covering her from the shoulders down. Then I rocked her, my lips pressed to her forehead.

"I'm so sorry, angel. I don't know what to do. Tell me what to do."

She didn't answer me and she didn't cry.

∽

"Have you slept at all?" Chris asked softly. "Maybe you should lie down for an hour or so."

I looked across my desk, startled to see my stepfather standing in front of me. I hadn't heard him come in, my thoughts somewhere else as I stared sightlessly out the window.

Victor and Cary were in the living room with Eva, the two men barely able to talk, stunned with grief. Angus was somewhere in the building, working with the lobby staff to manage the throng of photographers and reporters camped outside the main entrance.

"Did you speak to Eva?" I rubbed my stinging eyes. "Her father and Cary are wrecks, and she's . . ."

Christ. What was she? I hadn't a clue. She seemed . . . detached. As if she weren't connected at all with the anguish and powerless anger pouring from two people she loved deeply.

"She's numb." He took a seat. "It will hit her, eventually. For now, she's dealing with it the only way she knows how."

"'Eventually' isn't quantifiable! I just need to know when . . . how . . . what to do."

"That's why you need to take care of yourself, Gideon." His soft gaze searched my face. "So you can be strong for her when she needs you to be."

"She won't let me comfort her. She's too busy worrying about everyone else."

"It's a distraction, I'm sure," he said quietly. "Something to focus on besides her own loss. And if you'll take my advice, right now you need to focus on *you*. It's obvious you've been up all night."

I gave a humorless laugh. "What gave me away? The tux?"

"The bloodshot eyes, the morning stubble. You don't look like the husband Eva counts on to keep it together and do everything he can."

"Damn it." I stood. "It just seems . . . wrong to act like nothing happened."

"That's not what I meant. But life has to go on. And for Eva—that's going to happen with you. So be *you*. Right now, you look as shaky as they do out there."

I was. The fact that Eva wasn't turning to me for comfort . . . It was everything I had been afraid of.

But I knew he was right. If I didn't look like I could support her, how could I expect her to lean on me?

Chris rose to his feet. "I'll make a pot of coffee while you're in the shower. I brought food, by the way. Some pastries and sandwiches from a bakery your brother recommended. It'll be lunchtime soon."

I couldn't imagine eating anything, but it was thoughtful of him. "Thank you."

He walked with me to the door. "I'm staying in the city now, as you know. Christopher is going to manage things at work for the next few days so I can help you out here. If you need anything—at any time, doesn't matter—just call me."

I halted. My chest was too tight. I fought for every breath.

"Gideon." Chris put his hand on my shoulder. "You're both going to get through this. You have family and friends looking—"

"What family?"

His arm fell to his side.

"No, don't," I said, hating that he'd pulled away. Hating that I'd put that look of hurt on his face. "Look, I'm glad you're here. I didn't expect it, but I'm glad. . . ."

He pulled me into a firm embrace. "Then learn to expect it," he said gruffly. "Because I'm not backing off this time, Gideon. We're family. Maybe now we can start to think about what that means to all of us. You and me. Your mother, Christopher, and Ireland."

Head bowed against his shoulder, I fought for some measure of composure. I was tired. Weary to my bones. My brain wasn't processing anything well. That had to be why I felt . . . Fuck. I didn't know what I felt.

Eva's father and Cary were devastated. Stanton . . . I couldn't even begin to imagine how shattered he must be. Whatever I was feeling didn't matter much in comparison.

Stressed, my mind straying, I spoke without thinking. "Christopher would need a complete personality transplant to ever be family to me."

Chris stiffened and pulled away. "I know you and Christopher don't get along, but—"

"Through no fault of mine. Let's be clear about that." I tried to fight the question, tried to swallow it back unsaid. "Has he ever discussed with you why he hates me?"

For fuck's sake. *Why?* Why did I have to ask? It shouldn't matter. Not after all these damn years.

Chris pulled away, shaking his head. "He doesn't hate you, Gideon."

I straightened, willing myself not to shake—from exhaustion or emotion, I couldn't tell. The past was behind me. I'd left it back there, shoved in a box where it belonged. I had Eva now—

Damn it. I hoped I still had Eva.

My wife had never pushed me to deal with Christopher, as she had with the rest of my family. My brother had gone too far in her eyes, used Magdalene too callously, which Cary had caught on video. Maybe Eva wouldn't care if I resolved my relationship with Christopher. . . .

But maybe she'd be proud of me for trying.

And if she was, if it proved to her that I was different, that I'd changed in the way she needed me to . . . *Son of a bitch.* I had just backtracked on all the progress we'd made by not telling her about Monica's death the moment I knew. If mending things with my family now would somehow help her forgive me for the lie I'd told, then it was worth whatever it cost me to make the effort.

I forced my hands to relax. When I spoke, my voice was low and even. "I need to show you something."

I gestured for my stepfather to sit at my desk. When he slid the chair forward, I shook the mouse to wake the monitor. Hugh's handwritten notes filled the screen.

Chris's eyes darted from side to side, quickly reading. I knew the moment he understood what he was looking at. His spine stiffened.

"I don't know how much of this is true," I cautioned. "Hugh's notes about his sessions with me are all lies. This reads like he was building a profile of me to use as a defense, in case we ever filed charges against him."

"We should have." The words were bitten out between clenched teeth. "How did you get these?"

"It doesn't matter. What's important is that he has notes from four different sessions with Christopher. One of them was supposedly a group session with me. Either that's a fabrication or I've forgotten."

"Which do you think it is?"

"I really can't say. There are . . . chunks of my childhood I can't remember." I recalled more in dreams than I did when awake.

Chris swiveled in the chair to look at me. "Do you think he molested your brother?"

It took a beat for me to shove the memories away and

respond. "I don't know—you'll have to ask Christopher—but I doubt it."

"Why?"

"The dates and times on Hugh's notes put Christopher's sessions directly following mine. If those time stamps are correct—which would be wise if he was covering his tracks—then he wouldn't have it in him." My arms crossed. Trying to explain brought back all the bitterness. And loathing—for both Hugh and myself. "He was a sick piece of shit, but—listen, there's no tidy way to say this. He never had anything left after he was done with me."

"My God . . . Gideon."

I turned my gaze away from the shock and simmering fury in his eyes. "Hugh told Christopher he was seeing me because you and Mom were afraid I would kill him."

Thinking of the other people in the penthouse was the only thing that restrained me from punching a wall. God knew I'd lashed out with my fists more than once as a kid.

Remembering what I could of that time, I could see how easily Hugh's brainwashing might have taken root in the mind of a small boy whose older brother frequently had fits of rage and destruction.

"Christopher wouldn't believe that," he asserted.

My shoulders lifted in a weary shrug. "Christopher told me once, recently, that I'd wanted him dead since the day he was born. I had no idea what he was talking about, but now . . ."

"Let me read," he said grimly, turning back to the monitor. "Go take that shower. We'll have some coffee when you get out. Or something stronger."

I started to leave the room but paused before I opened the door. Looking back at Chris, I saw him focused tautly on the words in front of him. "You didn't know Hugh like I did," I told him. "How he could twist things around . . . make you believe things . . ."

Chris's gaze came up and held mine. "You don't have to convince me, Gideon. Your word is enough."

I glanced away quickly. Did he have any clue what those four words meant to me? I couldn't tell him; my throat was too raw.

With a nod, I left him.

～∽∽～

It took longer than it should have to put some goddamned clothes on. I chose with Eva in mind. The gray slacks she loved. A black V-neck T-shirt. Done.

There was a knock at the door. "Come in."

Angus filled the frame. "The detectives are on their way up."

"All right." I walked with him down the hall to the living room.

My wife sat on the couch, bundled in sweatpants and a baggy sweater with socks on her feet. Her head rested on Victor's shoulder, his cheek against the crown of her head. Her fingers stroked through Cary's hair as he sat on a pillow by her knee. Couldn't get more connected than that. The television was on, tuned to a movie none of them were watching.

"Eva."

Her gaze slid slowly over to me.

I held out my hand to her. "The police are here."

Victor straightened, jarring my wife into sitting up. A brisk rap on the foyer door had everyone on alert.

Stepping closer to the couch, I kept my arm extended. Eva slowly disentangled herself and stood, her face still far too pale. She put her hand in mine and I exhaled a sigh of relief. I pulled her close, draping my arm over her shoulders and pressing a kiss to her forehead.

"I love you," I said softly, walking her toward the door.

Her arms came around my waist and she leaned into me. "I know."

I turned the knob. "Detectives. Please, come in."

Graves entered first, her sharp blue eyes going immediately to Eva. Michna followed, his height advantage over his partner allowing him to lock eyes with me.

He gave me a brisk nod. "Mr. Cross."

Eva stepped away from me as I closed the door.

"We're very sorry for your loss, Mrs. Cross," Graves said, in that way cops had that told you they said those words too often.

"You may remember Eva's father, Victor Reyes," I said. "And the tall Scotsman over there is Angus McLeod."

The detectives both nodded, but Graves took the lead, as usual. "Detective Shelley Graves and my partner, Detective Richard Michna." She looked at Cary, whom she'd spoken with just hours before. "Mr. Taylor."

I gestured toward the dining table. "Let's have a seat."

My wife smoothed her hair back with unsteady hands. "Can I get you both some coffee? Or water?"

"Coffee would be great," Michna said, pulling out a chair for himself.

"I'll get it," Chris interjected, entering the room from the hallway. "Hello. I'm Gideon's stepfather, Chris Vidal."

Acknowledged by the detectives, he passed through to the kitchen.

Graves took the seat beside her partner, setting a battered leather satchel on the table at her elbow. Where she was reed thin, he was portly. Her hair was brown and curly, held back in a ponytail as severe as her foxlike face. Michna's hair was both graying and thinning, bringing more focus to his dark eyes and rugged features.

Graves eyed me as I pulled a chair out for my wife. I met her look and held it, seeing the dark knowledge of my crime. In return, I let her see my resolve. Yes, I'd done some immoral deeds for the sake of protecting my wife. I owned those decisions, even the ones I'd take to my grave.

I sat next to Eva, pulling my chair close and taking her hand in my own. Victor settled on the other side, with Cary beside him. Angus stood behind me.

"Can you both run through your evening, starting with when you arrived at the event?" Michna asked.

I went first, painfully aware of Eva's attention to every word I said. Only the last few moments were lost to her, but I knew those minutes were vital.

"You didn't see the shooter?" Grave pressed.

"No. I heard Raúl shout and I got Eva on the ground. It's protocol for the security team to evacuate at the first sign of trouble. They escorted us away in the opposite direction and I didn't look back. My focus was on my wife, who was unconscious at the time."

"You didn't see Monica Stanton go down?"

Eva's hand tightened on mine. I shook my head. "No. I

had no idea anyone had been injured until several minutes after we left the scene."

Michna looked at Eva. "At what point did you lose consciousness, Mrs. Cross?"

She licked lips that were starting to crack. "I hit the sidewalk pretty hard. Gideon rolled over me, holding me down. I couldn't breathe, and then someone covered Gideon. They were both so heavy . . . I thought I heard two, maybe three shots. I'm not sure. When I came to, I was in the limo."

"Okay." Michna nodded. "Thank you."

Graves unzipped the satchel and pulled out a file folder. Opening it, she pulled out a mug shot and set it on the table facing us. "Do either of you recognize this man?"

I bent closer. Blond with green eyes. A trimmed beard. Average looking.

"Aye," Angus said, drawing my head around to look at him. "He's the chap we ran off in Westport, the one who was taking pictures."

"We're going to need a statement from you, Mr. McLeod," Michna advised.

"Of course." He straightened, his arms crossing. "He's the one who shot Mrs. Stanton?"

"Yes. His name is Roland Tyler Hall. Have you ever had contact with this man, Mr. Cross? Ever recall speaking with him?"

"No," I replied, searching my memory and coming up blank.

Eva leaned forward. "Was he stalking her? Some kind of obsession?"

Her questions were softly voiced, her muted grief edged with an icy fury. It was the first spark I'd seen in her since I broke the news. And it came at the moment that I remembered what else I was keeping from her: her mother's shadowy past. A tangled history that could be the reason Monica was dead now.

Graves began sliding out images, starting with the Westport photos. "It's not your mother Hall was fixated on."

What? The dread I felt reversed back into the fear that had plagued me all night.

There were so many images, it was hard to focus on any single one. Numerous pictures taken of us outside the Crossfire. Some from events, which looked like standard paparazzi shots. Others caught us out on the town.

Eva reached for the corner of one and slid it out, gasping at the image of me dipping her into a passionate kiss on a crowded city sidewalk outside a CrossTrainer gym.

The photo had been the first of us to go viral. I had responded to press inquiries with the confirmation that she was the significant woman in my life, and she'd opened up to me about Nathan and her past.

There was another widely seen image of us, capturing us arguing in Bryant Park. Another picture of us in the park on a different day showed us embracing. I hadn't seen that one before.

"He didn't sell all of these," I said.

Graves shook her head. "Most of the photos Hall took for himself. When money ran low, he'd sell a few. He hasn't worked in months and lives out of his car."

Sliding the top layer of pictures around to expose the ones underneath, I realized that many of the times Eva and I had spotted a photographer, it had been Hall holding the camera.

I sat back, releasing Eva's hand to put my arm around her and pull her close. Hall had been so near to my wife, and we hadn't even known it.

"Let me see those," Victor said.

I pushed them down the table, the top layer sliding over first. The images left behind had me straightening in my chair. I pulled out the highly publicized picture of Magdalene and me that helped trigger the infamous fight with Eva in Bryant Park. And another of me and Corinne at the Kingsman Vodka party.

My breathing quickened. I released Eva, sliding to the edge of my chair to sift through the images with both hands.

Cary leaned forward to look over Victor's shoulder. "Was this guy just a really bad shot? Or did he confuse Monica for Eva?"

"He wasn't stalking Eva," I said tightly, the horrific realization sinking in. I pulled out the photo from the nightclub of me and two women. Taken in May, it preceded Eva's arrival in New York.

Graves met my questioning gaze with a nod. "Hall is obsessed with *you*."

Which meant I hadn't just hidden what I knew of Monica's life, I was also indirectly responsible for her death.

15

Moving closer to the table, I set my hand on Gideon's back and felt the tension there. His skin was so warm beneath the soft cotton of his T-shirt, the muscles stretched tight.

Chris came in from the kitchen with a tray bearing four steaming mugs of coffee, a small cup of half-and-half, and sugar in a bowl. He set it down near Michna, since the rest of the dining table was covered in pictures.

The detectives thanked him and each took a mug. Graves took her coffee black. Michna added a splash of cream and a sprinkling of sugar.

I'd only seen Michna in the course of the investigation into Nathan's death. I knew Graves more personally; I'd sparred with her during Parker's Krav Maga classes. I believed Graves liked me or was at least sympathetic. And I was certain it was Gideon's love for me that swayed her into closing Nathan's case while she still had questions.

It comforted me to have them in charge.

"I want to be sure I understand," I said, pushing through the grief that had fogged my mind all day. "This man was stalking Gideon?"

My dad shoved the photos away. "Was Hall targeting my daughter or Cross?"

"Hall believes Cross betrayed him," Graves answered, "by getting married."

I stared at her. She wore no jewelry or makeup, yet she was fiercely compelling. Pummeled by the realities of her job, she still had a passion for justice—even if it came outside the law. "If he couldn't have Gideon, no one could?"

"Not quite." She looked at Gideon. "Hall believes he has an 'entwined destiny' with you—some kind of cosmic pact—and that your marriage breaks this pact between you. Killing you is the only way to prevent his life from going in a direction he doesn't want to go."

"Is that supposed to make sense?" Cary asked, setting his elbows on the table and gripping his head in both hands.

"Hall's fixation isn't sexual," Michna elaborated, looking rumpled and tired from pulling an all-nighter. Still, he was keenly and disconcertingly observant. His partner zeroed in; he assessed the periphery. "It's not even romantic. He claims he's heterosexual."

Graves pulled another photo out of the file and set it atop the others. "You both know this woman."

Anne. My palms were suddenly damp. Gideon's body tautened like a bow.

"Fuck me," Cary muttered, his fisted hands dropping to the table with a thud that made me jump.

"I saw her last night," Chris said, taking a chair by

Gideon. "She was at the dinner. Hard to miss that bright red hair."

"Who is that?" my dad asked, his voice firm and flat.

"Dr. Anne Leslie Lucas," Graves replied. "She's the psychiatrist who was treating Hall, although she met with him at a second office away from her primary practice, using the alias Dr. Aris Matevosian."

Gideon's breath hissed out between his teeth. "I know that name."

Graves zeroed in, her gaze sharply focused. "How?"

"Just a moment. I'll show you." He pushed back from the table and headed down the hallway.

I watched him go, saw Lucky scampering after him. The puppy had been sticking close to me for most of the morning, as if he thought I needed him more than Gideon did right now. Something had changed. And since Lucky's emotional barometer was more accurate than mine at the moment, I needed to pay attention to that.

"Will someone explain who Dr. Lucas is," my father demanded, "and her relevance to Hall and Monica?"

"We'll let Cross fill us all in on that," Michna said.

"They had a sexual relationship awhile back," I interjected, wanting to take the burden of telling the story off Gideon's shoulders. He was ashamed of what he'd done, I knew that.

I pulled my knees up to my chest and wrapped my arms around them, trying to get warm. I knew I had to choose my words carefully. Telling the whole truth would be difficult, considering the unflattering picture of my husband my father would see.

"She got wrapped up in it," I went on, "and wanted to

leave her husband, so Gideon broke it off. She hasn't been able to move on or get past it. She showed up at my building once, and tried approaching Cary a couple times, wearing a wig, pretending to be someone else."

Graves watched me with a sharp, savvy gaze. "We reviewed her complaint. You and Cross confronted her, separately, on two different occasions."

"Damn it, Eva." My dad glared at me, his eyes bloodshot and red rimmed. "You know better."

"Know what?" I shot back. "I still don't understand what this all means. She was harassing my best friend and my husband. I told her to back off."

Gideon returned and held out his phone, showing a picture he'd taken.

Michna examined the image. "A prescription for Corinne Giroux written by Dr. Aris Matevosian. Why do you have this?"

"There was a time, a couple months ago," Gideon said tonelessly, resuming his seat beside me, "when Corinne became erratic. I discovered she'd been seeing a therapist who prescribed antidepressants, which were causing her mood swings. I took a picture of the label so I'd know who to contact if she continued having problems."

Gideon put his arm around me, urging me to lean into him. The moment I was pressed against him, I felt him sag heavily into the chair, as if holding me was a major relief. I slid my arm around his waist, felt his lips press against my forehead.

His chest rumbled beneath my ear as he spoke. "So Anne was Hall's therapist," he said, his voice rough with fatigue. "Why the alias?"

"She thought she was smart," Grave said bluntly. "We're smarter. And we have Hall, who is very disturbed but also very cooperative. He confessed the minute we sat down with him. He was also clever—or paranoid—enough to secretly record all of his sessions with Dr. Lucas, which we recovered during a search of his vehicle."

"Did she put him up to this?" I asked, wanting to be sure there was no misunderstanding.

"I don't think Hall was ever playing with a full deck," Michna said, "but he used to have a job, a place to live, and no particular interest in Cross. Anne Lucas did a number on him."

Graves started gathering up the photos with the help of her partner. "He mentioned to her that he dropped out of school after the Cross Ponzi scheme wiped out his grandparents. It wasn't something he held a grudge over, but she got him thinking that his life and Cross's are paralleled in some way."

"Can she go to jail for that?" I hung on tighter to Gideon. "What she did—that's part of the reason my mom's . . . gone. She can't just get away with that, right?"

"We picked her up about an hour ago." Graves held my gaze and I saw her determination. "When her lawyer shows up, we'll take a crack at her."

"The DA's office will determine the full extent of the charges," Michna said, "but Hall's recordings, plus security footage of both Lucas and Hall entering and leaving her secondary office, gave us probable cause."

"You'll keep us posted," my father said.

"Of course." Graves tucked everything back in her satchel, then shot a look at Gideon. "Did you see Dr. Lucas at the dinner?"

"Yes," he answered, his hand stroking up and down my arm. "Eva pointed her out to me."

"Did either of you speak with her at all?" Michna asked.

"No." Gideon looked down at me with a question in his eyes.

"I flipped her the bird from a distance," I confessed, the memory of her drifting through my blurry mind. "She had this smirk on her face. Maybe that's why she was there, so she could see what happened."

"Angel." Gideon enfolded me, wrapping me into his warmth and the scent of his skin.

"All right. We've got what we need for now," Graves said briskly. "We'll just take Mr. McLeod's statement regarding the Westport incident and be on our way. Thank you for your time."

Dismissed, we all pushed back from the table.

"Eva." Graves waited until our gazes met. For a moment, she wasn't just a cop. "I'm very sorry for your loss."

"Thank you." Self-conscious, I looked away from Graves.

Did she wonder at my dry eyes? God knew I did. As crazy as my mother drove me at times, I loved her. Didn't I? What kind of daughter didn't feel anything when her mom died?

Angus took Gideon's abandoned chair and began recounting what had happened in Westport.

Gideon took my hand and led me a few feet away. "I need some time with you."

Frowning, I nodded. "Yeah, of course."

He drew me along with him toward our bedroom.

"Cross."

We both turned at the sound of my father's voice. "Yes?"

Dad stood by the living room, his face hard and his gaze heated. "We have to talk."

"Agreed," Gideon said with a nod. "Just give me five minutes with my wife."

He kept going, not giving my dad a chance to object. I followed along to our bedroom, Lucky racing ahead of us. I watched Gideon as he shut the door with the three of us inside. Then he faced me, his gaze searching.

"You should take a nap," I told him. "You look tired." And that troubled me. I couldn't recall when I'd ever seen him so wiped out.

"Do you see me?" he asked hoarsely. "Are you looking at me and *seeing* me?"

My frown deepened. I looked him over from head to toe. *Oh. He'd dressed for me. Thinking of me.* "Yes."

He reached out and touched my face. His tormented gaze held mine. "I feel like I'm invisible to you."

"I see you."

"I . . ." He breathed hard, his chest working as if he'd just run miles. "I'm sorry, Eva. Sorry about Anne . . . about last night . . ."

"I know." Of course I knew that.

He was so upset. Much more than I was. Why? My self-control was never as good as his. Except for now. From the moment I learned the truth, I'd felt an icy resolve form somewhere deep inside me. I didn't understand it, but I used it. To deal with the police. And my dad and Cary, who needed me to be strong for them.

"Damn it." He came to me and cupped my face in his hands. "Yell at me. Hit me. For God's sake—"

"Why?"

"Why?" He stared at me as if I were crazy. "Because this is my fault! Anne was my problem and I didn't manage her. I didn't—"

"You're not responsible for her actions, Gideon," I said crossly, frustrated he would think that way. "Why would you believe you were? That doesn't make any sense."

His hands went to my shoulders and he gave me a little shake. *"You're* not making sense! Why aren't you mad that I didn't tell you about your mother? You lost it when I hired Mark and didn't tell you. You left me—" His voice broke. "You're not leaving me over this, Eva. We'll work through it . . . we'll figure out how to get past it."

"I'm not leaving you." I touched his face. "You need to sleep, Gideon."

"God." He caught me up and took my mouth, his lips slanting over mine. I put my arms around him, stroking his back to try to calm him down.

"Where are you?" he muttered. "Come back to me."

Cupping my jaw, he pressed gently with trembling fingers, urging my mouth to open. The moment it did, his tongue swept inside, licking desperately. With a groan, he pulled me up hard against him, urgently fucking his tongue into my mouth.

Heat bloomed inside me. The warmth of his feverishly hot skin penetrated my clothes, sinking into my flesh. Desperate for something to thaw me, I kissed him back, my tongue stroking his.

"Eva." Gideon released me, his hands moving over me, sliding over my back and arms.

I pushed up onto the tips of my toes, deepening the contact of our mouths. My hands slid beneath his shirt and he hissed, arching into me and away from the chill of my fingers. My touch followed, caressing his skin, seeking that warmth.

"Yes," he gasped into my mouth. "God, Eva. I love you."

I licked across his lips, sucked his tongue when he licked me back. The sound he made was both pain and relief, his hands cupping my buttocks and pulling me up against him. I clung to him, lost in him. He was what I needed. I couldn't think about anything else when he was holding me.

"Tell me you love me," he breathed. "That you'll forgive me. Next week . . . next year . . . someday . . ."

"I love you."

He tore his mouth away, hugging me so tightly it was hard to breathe. My feet dangled above the floor, my temple pressed to his.

"I'll make it up to you," he vowed. "I'll find a way."

"Shh . . ." It was there, in the back of my mind, the dismay. The hurt. But I didn't know whether it was because of Gideon or my mom.

I closed my eyes. Focused on the adored, familiar scent of him. "Kiss me again."

Gideon turned his head, his lips finding mine. I craved deeper, harder, but he denied me. As ferociously passionate as his first kisses had been, this one was soft. Tender. I whimpered a protest, my hands pushing into his hair to pull him closer.

"Angel." He nuzzled against me. "Your dad's waiting."

Oh, God. I loved my dad, but his agony and helpless rage were pouring off him, battering me. I didn't know how to comfort or soothe. There was a void inside me, as if I had nothing left to give anyone. But everyone needed me.

Putting me back on my feet, Gideon searched my face again. "Let me be here for you. Don't shut me out."

"I'm not trying to." I looked away, toward the bathroom. *There's a towel on the floor. Why is it there?* "There's something wrong."

"Yes. Everything," he said tightly. "It's all fucked up. I don't know what to do."

"No. Wrong inside me."

"Eva. How can you say that? There's nothing wrong with you." He cupped my face again, brought it around.

"You nicked yourself." I touched the little spot of dried blood on his jaw. "You never do that, either."

"What's going on in that head of yours?" He wrapped himself around me. "I don't know what to do," he said again. "I don't know what to do."

❧

Gideon kept my hand in his as we returned to the living room.

My father looked over from where he sat on the couch, then stood. Worn jeans. A faded UCSD T-shirt. The shadow of stubble on his strong square jaw.

Gideon had shaved. Why hadn't I processed that when I noticed the cut from the razor? Why hadn't I noticed that he'd changed out of his tux?

Some things came to me with strange clarity. Others were lost in the fog in my mind.

The detectives were gone. Cary was curled up against the armrest of the couch, fast asleep, his mouth hanging partway open. I could hear him snoring softly.

414 • SYLVIA DAY

"We can step into my office," Gideon said, releasing my hand to gesture down the hallway.

With a curt nod, my dad rounded the coffee table. "Lead the way."

Gideon started walking. I fell into step behind him.

"Eva." My dad's voice stopped me and I turned around. "I need to speak to Cross alone."

"Why?"

"I've got things to say that you don't need to hear."

I shook my head slowly. "No."

He made a frustrated noise. "We're not arguing about this."

"Dad, I'm not a child. Anything you have to say to my husband has something to do with me and I think I should be involved."

"I have no objection," Gideon said, returning to my side.

My father's jaw tensed, his gaze darting back and forth between us. "Fine."

We all went to Gideon's office. Chris was sitting at Gideon's desk, talking on the phone. He pushed back and stood when we came in. "Whenever you're done for the day," he said to whomever he was talking to. "I'll explain when I see you. All right. Talk to you then, son."

"I need my office a minute," Gideon told him when he hung up.

"Sure." His concerned gaze raked all three of us. "I'll pull out some plates and things for lunch. We all need to eat something."

Chris left the room, which drew my eye to my dad, who was staring at the massive collage of photos on the wall. The one in the center was of me, sleeping. It was an intimate image; the kind of picture a man took to remember the things he had done with his lover before she'd fallen asleep.

I looked at the other photos, noted one of me and Gideon at an event that I now knew had been captured by Hall. I turned my head away, feeling a prickle running down my spine.

Fear? Hall had taken my mother from me, but who he'd really wanted was Gideon. I could be mourning my husband now. My stomach cramped at the thought, hunching me over.

"Angel." He was near me in an instant, urging me to sit in one of the two chairs facing his desk.

"What's wrong?" My dad hovered, too, his eyes wild. I couldn't recognize my own feelings, but I saw his. He was frightened for me, more anxious than was warranted.

"I'm okay," I assured them, even as I reached for Gideon's hand and held on tight.

"You need to eat," Gideon said.

"So do you," I countered. "The sooner you two get done, the faster we can do that."

Just the thought of food made me queasy, but I didn't say that. They were both already too worried about me.

My dad straightened. "I spoke to my family," he told Gideon. "They still want to come and be here for Eva. And me."

Gideon half-sat on the edge of his desk, one hand running through his hair. "Okay. We were going to fly them direct to North Carolina. We'll have to adjust the flight plan."

"I would appreciate that," my dad said, grudgingly.

"It's fine. Don't worry about it."

"Then why do you look worried?" I said to Gideon, seeing his frown.

"It's just . . . It's a madhouse on the street right now. We can bring your family in through the garage, but if word gets out that they're in town, they may have to deal with media and photographers at their hotel or anywhere else they may go in the city."

"They're not coming to sightsee," my dad snapped.

"That's not what I meant, Victor." Gideon sighed wearily. "I'm just thinking out loud. I'll work it out. Consider it taken care of."

I pictured how it must be downstairs outside the lobby, imagined my grandmother and cousins wading through a gauntlet like that. I shook my head and had a moment of clarity. "If they want to come, we should go to the Outer Banks like we planned. We already have the rooms reserved for them. It'll be quiet and private."

Suddenly, I longed to be at the beach. Feeling the wind in my hair, the surf lapping at my bare feet. I'd felt alive there. I wanted to feel alive again. "We had catering arranged. We'd have food and beverages for everyone."

Gideon looked at me. "I had Scott talk to Kristine. We pulled out of everything."

"It can't have been more than a few hours ago. The hotel probably hasn't filled the room block in that short of time. And the caterer already has the things well under way at this point."

"You really want to go to the beach house?" he asked me quietly.

I nodded. There were no memories of my mom there, as there were in the city. And if I wanted to step outside and take a walk, no one would bother me.

"Okay, then. I'll take care of it."

I looked at my dad, hoping that plan was good with him.

He stood beside me, his arms crossed and his gaze on his feet.

Finally, he said, "What happened changes everything. For all of us. I want to move to New York."

Taken aback, I glanced at Gideon, then back at my dad. "Really?"

"It's going to take some time for me to deal with work and selling my house, but I'm going to get the ball rolling." He looked at me. "I need to be closer than the other side of the damn country. You're all I've got."

"Oh, Dad. You love your job."

"I love you more."

"What will you do for work?" Gideon asked.

There was something in his tone that drew my attention to him. He'd twisted a bit to face us better, drawing one thigh up to the desktop and resting his crossed hands atop it. He watched my father avidly. There wasn't any of the surprise on his face that I felt.

"That's what I wanted to talk about," my father said, his handsome face grim.

"Eva needs a dedicated security chief," Gideon said preemptively. "I've got Angus and Raúl stretched to their limits and my wife needs her own security team."

My mouth fell open as I registered what my husband had said. "What? No, Gideon."

His brows rose. "Why not? It would be ideal. There's no one I could trust more to protect you than your own father."

"Because it's . . . weird. Okay? Dad's his own man. It would be awkward to have my father on my husband's payroll. It's just . . . not right."

"Angus is the closest I've had to a father," he pointed out, "and he works the same job." His gaze lifted to my dad. "I don't think any less of him. And Chris, as the head of a company in which I have controlling interest, also could be said to work for me."

"That's different," I said stubbornly.

"Eva." My dad set his hand on my shoulder. "If I can handle it, you should be able to."

I turned wide eyes to him. "Are you serious? Were you thinking about this before he brought it up?"

He nodded, still somber. "I've been thinking about it since he called me about . . . your mom. Cross is right: There's no one I trust more than myself to keep you safe."

"Safe from what? What happened last night . . . It's not an everyday thing." I couldn't think differently. Living with the fear that Gideon might be in danger at any given moment? It would drive me insane. I certainly couldn't live with putting my dad in the line of fire.

"Eva, I've seen you more on television, the Internet, and in magazines than I have in person this entire last year and you were living in San Diego for most of that time." His face hardened. "God willing you'll never be at risk, but I can't take that chance. Besides, Cross is planning on hiring someone anyway. Might as well be me."

"Were you?" I demanded, rounding on Gideon.

He nodded. "Yes. It's been on my mind."

"I don't like it."

"I'm sorry, angel." His tone of voice told me I'd just have to suck it up.

My dad's arms crossed. "I won't accept any perks or compensation outside the scope of what you're paying your other men."

Gideon unfolded and rounded his desk, opening a drawer to withdraw a paper-clipped sheaf of paper. "Angus and Raúl both agreed to let me share their salaries with you. I've also laid out what you can expect, to start."

"I can't believe this," I complained. "You were this far along and didn't say anything to me?"

"I worked on it earlier this morning. It hasn't come up before now and I wasn't going to say anything unless your father mentioned moving to the city."

And that was Gideon Cross: He never missed a trick.

My dad took the papers, perused the top sheet, then looked at Gideon incredulously. "Is this for real?"

"Consider that Angus has been with me for more years of my life than not. He also has considerable covert and military training. In short, he's earned it." Gideon watched as my dad flipped the page. "Raúl has been with me a shorter amount of time, so he's not where Angus is—yet. But he also has a broad range of training and skills."

My dad exhaled in a rush when he flipped to the next page. "Okay. This is . . ."

"More than you were likely expecting, but that spreadsheet gives you the info you need to gauge the offered compensation compared to my other chiefs. You can see that it's fair. It's predicated on the expectation that you will consent to further training and attain the necessary permits, licenses, and registrations."

I watched my dad's shoulders go back and his chin lift, the stubborn line of his mouth softening. Whatever he saw, he was taking as a challenge. "All right."

"You'll note that a housing allowance is included," Gideon continued, in full-on mogul mode despite his matter-of-fact tone. "If you would like, there's a unit next door to Eva's former apartment that's available and furnished."

I caught my lower lip between my teeth, knowing he was talking about the apartment he'd kept while Nathan was a threat. We had met there clandestinely for weeks while keeping up the façade that we were no longer together.

"I'll think about it," my dad said.

"Another thing to think about," Gideon began, "is the reality of your daughter being my wife. Certainly we would be mindful of your personal role in Eva's life and be respectful of that. But respecting your place as her father means we won't be brazen. It doesn't mean we won't be intimate."

Oh my God. My shoulders hunched with embarrassment. I glared at Gideon. So did my dad.

It took my father a long minute to unclench his jaw and respond. "I'll keep that in mind while I'm thinking things over."

Gideon gave a brisk nod. "All right. Was there anything else we needed to cover?"

My dad shook his head. "Not right now."

I crossed my arms, knowing I'd have more to say at some point.

"You know where to find me, angel, when you're ready to tear into me." My husband offered his hand to me. "In the meantime, let's get some food into you."

Dr. Petersen showed up around three, looking a little rattled. Getting through the throng on the sidewalk to enter the lobby had obviously been a trial. Gideon introduced him to everyone as I watched, trying to judge his reaction to meeting the people he'd heard such intimate things about.

He spoke to me briefly, offering his condolences. He'd liked my mother and often was somewhat indulgent about her neurotic behavior, to my frustration. I could tell he was affected by her loss, which made me wonder how I came across to him. Evidently, he couldn't quite tell. I struggled to answer his questions about how I was doing.

He talked with Gideon for a much longer time, retreating with my husband to the dining room, where they spoke in hushed tones.

But not for long. Gideon turned toward me and I understood their talk was over. I accompanied Dr. Petersen to the foyer and saw him out, but not before I spotted my clutch on an end table.

When I retrieved my phone, I saw the dozens of missed calls and texts. Megumi, Will, Shawna, Dr. Travis . . . even Brett. I opened my messages and started to send out replies when the phone vibrated in my hand with an incoming call. I saw the name of the caller, looked up at Cary and found him talking with my dad, then headed down the hall to the bedroom.

Through the slender windows, I could see how far the afternoon had progressed. It would be dark in a few hours and the first day without my mom would be over.

"Hi, Trey."

"Eva. I . . . I probably shouldn't be intruding at a time like this, but I saw the news and I was calling you before I thought about it being a bad idea. I just wanted to tell you how sorry I am."

I took a seat in one of the reading chairs, refusing to

think about what the headlines might be shouting right now. "I appreciate you thinking of me."

"I can't believe what happened. If there's anything I can do, please let me know."

I let my heavy head fall back against the seat and closed my eyes. I recalled Trey's handsome face, his kind hazel eyes and the little bump on his nose that told me it'd once been broken. "Look, Trey, I don't want to lay a guilt trip on you, but you should know that my mother meant a lot to Cary. She was like a surrogate mom to him. He's really hurting a lot right now."

He sighed. "I'm sorry to hear that."

"I meant to call you . . . before." I curled my legs up beneath me. "To see how you're doing, but also—well, there's more. I wanted to tell you that I know you have to do what's best for you. That said, if you're thinking at all that you might want something with Cary, you should make up your mind quickly. The door is closing."

"Let me guess. He's seeing someone," he said flatly.

"No, just the opposite. He's taking some time for himself and reevaluating what he wants. You know he broke it off with Tatiana, right?"

"That's what he says."

"If you don't trust him to tell the truth, it's good you broke things off."

"I'm sorry." He made a low frustrated noise. "That's not what I meant."

"Cary's healing, Trey. Pretty soon, he's going to be ready to move on. It's just something you need to think about."

"All I've done is think about it. I still don't know what the answer is."

I rubbed the space between my brows. "Maybe you're asking the wrong question. Are you happier with him or without him? Figure that out and I think the rest will become clear."

"Thank you, Eva."

"For what it's worth, you and I kinda took the same route. Gideon and I always said we were going to make it work, but that was . . . I don't know . . ." I searched through my brain fog. "Bravado. Stubbornness. That was part of our problem, we knew it was a house of cards. We weren't taking the steps to make us solid. Does that make sense?"

"Yeah."

"But we both made big changes, just like Cary has for you. And big concessions."

I felt my husband enter the room and opened my eyes.

"It was worth it, Trey," I said softly. "It's not wishful thinking anymore. We'll still hit bumps, people will throw us some curve balls, but when we say we're going to get through anything, it's nothing but the truth."

"You're telling me to give Cary another chance."

I reached out to Gideon, felt a soft stirring in my chest as he came to me. "I'm saying I think you'll like the changes he's made. And if you meet him halfway, you might find it's worth the trip."

Chris left for the evening shortly after six to have dinner with Christopher. For some reason, he and Gideon exchanged a long look as my husband showed him out. I let it go without asking for an explanation. Their relationship had shifted.

The wariness they used to regard each other with was gone. There was no way I was going to question it or make Gideon think too hard about it. It was time for him to make some decisions with his heart.

My dad and Cary left around nine, heading back to my old apartment, since there was room for both of them there and not enough in the penthouse.

Would my dad stay in the bedroom where he'd last made love to my mother? How would he bear it, if he did? When Gideon and I had been apart, I'd had to stay at Stanton's. My room had too many memories of Gideon and the last thing I needed was to be tormented with reminders of what I wanted more than anything, yet feared I couldn't have.

Gideon went around the penthouse, turning off lights, Lucky following him every step of the way. I watched my husband move, his tread heavier than usual. He was so tired. I had no idea how he'd managed to get through the day, considering how busy he'd been in the morning's aftermath—coordinating with Kristine, answering the occasional call from Scott, and catching Arash up on the visit with the police.

"Angel." He held his hand out to me.

I stared at it a moment. All day long, he'd offered me his hand. Such a simple thing, really, but it was powerful. *I'm here*, it said. *You're not alone. We can do this together.*

Rising from my seat on the sofa, I linked my fingers with his and let him lead me to the bedroom and into the bathroom. There, I went through nearly the same routine as he did. Brushing my teeth, washing my face. He added the step of taking one of the pills Dr. Petersen had prescribed. Then I followed him into the bedroom and let him undress me, before sliding another T-shirt over my head. He tucked me in with a soft, slow kiss.

"Where are you going?" I asked, when he walked away.

"Nowhere." He stripped with brusque efficiency, leaving his boxer briefs on. Then he joined me in bed, helped Lucky scramble up, then turned off the light.

Rolling toward me, he caught me around the waist and pulled me back against him, spooning behind me. I moaned softly at the heat of his body and shivered as it combated the chill in my bones.

I closed my eyes, focusing on the sound and feel of him breathing. Within a few moments, the tempo fell into the rhythmic evenness of sleep.

The wind whips through my hair as I walk along the shore, my feet sinking into the sand as the surf erodes every step. Ahead of me, I see the weathered shingles of the beach house Gideon bought for us. It sits perched above the tide on tall stilts, its many windows gazing far out over the water. Gulls circle and cry out above me, their quick dips and arrested hovering like a dance in the salt-tinged breeze.

"I can't believe I'm going to miss the reception."

I turn my head and discover my mother walking beside me. She's wearing the same elegant formal gown I last saw her in. She's so beautiful. Truly breathtaking. My eyes burn to look at her.

"We're all going to miss it," I tell her.

"I know. And I worked so hard on it." She glances at me, the ends of her hair fluttering along her cheek. "I did manage to work some touches of red in."

"Did you?" That makes me smile, despite my pain. She does love me the best way she knows how. Just because it's not always the way I want her to doesn't mean it's not precious for what it is.

"It really is a garish color for a wedding, though. It was difficult."

"It's kinda your fault, you know, for buying that red dress I wore the first night Gideon took me out as his date."

"Is that what inspired you?" She shakes her head. "Next time, you should pick a softer accent color."

"There won't be a next time. Gideon is it for me." I pick up a shell, then toss it back into the water it came from. "There were times I wasn't sure we'd make it, but I don't worry about that anymore. We were our own worst enemy, but we let go of the baggage weighting us down."

"The first few months are supposed to be the easy part." My mom dances a little ahead of me and gives a graceful twirl. "The courtship. Fabulous trips, sparkling jewels."

I snort. "It wasn't easy for us. The beginning was the rockiest. But it gets smoother every day."

"You'll have to help your father find someone," she says, the girlish delight faded from her voice. "He's been lonely for so long."

"You're a hard act to follow. He still loves you."

She shoots me a sad smile, then looks out over the water. "I had Richard . . . He's such a good man. I wish he'd be happy again."

I think of my stepfather and worry. My mother was everything to him. What will give him joy now that she's gone?

"I'll never be a grandmother," she says thoughtfully. "I died young and in my prime. That's not so terrible, is it?"

"How can you ask me that?" I let the tears flow. I searched my soul all day because I couldn't cry. Now that they're here, I welcome them. It feels as if a dam has burst.

"Don't cry, honey." *She stops and hugs me, filling the air I breathe with the scent of her perfume. "You'll see that—"*

I woke with a gasp, my body racked by a hard jerk of surprise. Lucky whimpered and pawed at me, kneading into my stomach. I stroked his velvety head with one hand and swiped at my eyes with the other, but they were dry. The pain of my dream was already fading into a distant memory.

"Come here," Gideon murmured, his voice a rough warm beacon in our moonlit bedroom. His arms came around me, pulling me back against him.

Turning into him, I sought his mouth and found it, sinking into him with a lush, deep kiss. Surprise held him motionless a moment, and then his hand was cupping the back of my head, holding me in place as he took over.

I tangled my legs with his, feeling the coarse brush of hair, the deliciously warm skin, and the powerful muscles underneath. The soft, rhythmic stroking of his tongue soothed and aroused me. No one kissed like Gideon. The coaxing demand of his mouth was searingly sexual, yet it was also tender. Reverent. His lips were both firm and soft, and he used them to tease, to brush gently against my own.

Reaching between us, I cupped his penis in my hand, stroking with a demand that answered his. He swelled to my touch, lengthening until the broad head pushed up beneath the elastic of his waistband. He groaned, his hips thrusting into my caress.

"Eva."

I heard the question in the way he said my name.

"Make me *feel*," I whispered.

His hand slid beneath my shirt, his fingers drifting

feather-light across my belly until he palmed my breast. He squeezed, plumping the aching flesh before his clever fingers gripped my nipple. With a decadent knowledge of my body, Gideon rolled and tugged the hard, tight point of my breast, the relentless pressure and pulling sending pulses of need through my entire body.

I moaned, aroused. Desperate. My legs tightened around his so I could rub my damp sex against his thigh.

"Does your pretty cunt ache, angel?" He nibbled at the corner of my lips, the words a seduction all their own. "What does it need? My tongue . . . my fingers . . . my cock?"

"Gideon." I whimpered shamelessly when he pulled away, my arms reaching for him as he rose above me. He hummed a soft sound of reassurance and dropped Lucky carefully to the floor. Then his hands were at my hips, pulling my underwear down to my knees.

"You haven't answered me, Eva. What do you want me to put into your greedy little cunt? All of the above?"

"Yes," I gasped. "Everything."

A moment later my legs were in the air and his dark head was lowering to the sensitized flesh between my thighs.

I held my breath, waiting. Folded as I was, I couldn't see . . .

The hot, wet velvet of his tongue slid between the tender folds of my sex.

"Oh, God!" I arched into a rigid bow.

Gideon purred. I struggled, trying to lift my hips up to the ecstasy of his wicked mouth. Gripping my thighs, he held me in place, tasting me at the pace he wanted, licking over and around the slick opening . . . taunting me with my hunger to feel his tongue inside me. His lips circled my throbbing clit, his mouth suckling, the flat of his tongue rubbing across that sensitive pleasure point.

"Please . . ." I didn't care that he made me beg. The more I gave him, the more he gave back to me.

But he made me wait as he savored me, his hair caressing the tender skin at the back of my thighs, his tongue massaging my clit with the faintest of pressures.

I pressed my hands to my face. "That feels so good . . . Don't stop . . ."

My mouth fell open when he licked lower, dipping the merest fraction into the trembling clutch of my body . . . then lower still, rimming the rosette that quivered beneath the silky caress.

"*Oh!*" I gasped, half mad with the barrage of sensation after hours of numbness.

His growl shivered through me. My body jerked as he finally gave me what I wanted, his stiffened tongue pushing into my slick heat with a slow, delicious thrust.

"Yes," I gasped. "Fuck me."

His mouth was exquisite, the source of all pleasure and torment, his tongue wicked in its sensual assault, plunging between the clenching delicate muscles.

Gideon ate me with tautly driven focus, so avid and greedy that I writhed with the incredible ecstasy pulsing through my body. There was pressure, and then his thumb slid into my rear and began fucking the tender opening. The fullness there contrasted with the rhythmic thrusts of his tongue. My core tensed. I hovered tautly, on the precipice of orgasm . . .

I screamed his name, my body on fire, my skin hot and damp. I was alive with pleasure, burning with it. The climax shattered me, broke me into pieces. But Gideon wouldn't relent, his tongue sliding up to lash my clit. One orgasm rolled into the next.

Sobbing, coming hard and endlessly, I pressed my fists to my eyes. "No more," I pleaded hoarsely, my limbs trembling hard as my core spasmed with yet another rush. "I can't take any more."

I felt the mattress dip as he moved, one hand holding my ankles. I heard the snap of his waistband as he shoved his boxer briefs down.

"How do you want it?" he asked darkly. "Slow and sweet? Fast and rough?"

Oh God . . .

I forced my answer past dry lips. "Deep. Hard."

He came over me, pushing my legs back until I was bent in half.

"I love you," he vowed fiercely, gruffly.

The lush crest of his thick cock surged into my sex, stroking over tissues already swollen and tender.

Folded as I was, my legs bound by my underwear around my knees, it was tight inside me and he was so big. I was stretched by his girth, my sensitive flesh stinging from the forcefulness of his possession. And he still had more to give.

Groaning my name, Gideon swiveled his hips, pulling out, pushing in, working the heavy shaft deeper. "Are you feeling this, angel?" he demanded, his voice gruff with desire.

"You're all I feel," I moaned, needing to move, to take more. But he kept me restrained, his body fucking me with destructive expertise.

The feel of him . . . so hard . . . the relentless, leisurely thrusts . . .

My fingers grasped at the sheets. My sex rippled frantically around him, grasping at the wide head of his penis with ravenous greed. Every withdrawal left me empty, every thick hot slide forced pleasure through my veins like a drug.

"Eva. Christ."

Gideon loomed over me in the moonlight, a darkly sexual fallen angel. His beautiful face was hard with lust as his eyes gleamed down at me. His arms strained with unappeased need, his torso chiseled by the tension in his muscles. "You keep sucking on my dick with that tight cunt of yours and you'll make me come. Is that what you want, angel? You want me to fill you up before you take it all?"

"No!" I exhaled in a rush, willing my core to relax its eager tightening. He rolled his hips, stroking into me, his breath hissing as I took more of him.

"God, Eva. Your cunt loves my cock."

Reaching for the headboard, Gideon stretched over me, my legs trapped between us. Fully exposed and tilted back for his pleasure, I was helpless to do more than watch as he straightened his hips and sank the last few inches of his penis into me.

The sound that left me was a harsh wail, the pleasure so intense it hurt. Distantly, I heard Gideon curse, felt his powerful body shudder.

"You good?" he bit out, his teeth grinding.

I tried to catch my breath, my lungs expanding as much as they were able.

"Eva." He growled my name. "Are. You. Good?"

Unable to speak, I reached for his hips, my fingers catching in his boxer briefs. I had a moment to think how hot that was, that he hadn't bothered to undress either one of us . . .

Then he started fucking, his hips pistoning in a relentless tempo, his long thick cock plunging and withdrawing from root to tip in rapid-fire thrusts. Supporting his weight entirely with his arms and the tips of his toes, he powered into me, his rigid penis nailing me straight into the mattress.

I came so hard my vision went black, my body seized with pleasure so intense I was locked in it, suspended in the powerful waves of erotic sensation.

I was inundated by the ferocious surge of my climax. My skin tingled from head to toe. Gideon paused on a downstroke, grinding into me, giving my body the steely length of his penis to grasp. My sex spasmed ecstatically around that delicious hardness, gripping him hungrily.

"Fuck," Gideon bit out, "you're milking my dick so hard."

I shook violently, fighting to breathe.

The moment I sagged into the mattress, replete, Gideon pulled his cock out of my trembling slit and left the bed.

Bereft, I lifted a hand to him. "Where are you going?"

"Hang on." He shoved his boxer briefs all the way off.

He was still hard, his cock rising high and proud, slick from my orgasm—but I wasn't wet with his.

"You didn't come." I was too languid to help when he stripped me of my underwear. Sliding a hand beneath my back, he lifted me and whipped my shirt over my head.

His lips brushed over my brow. "You wanted fast and rough. I want slow and sweet."

He levered over me again, this time settling into the cradle of my open arms and legs. The moment I felt his weight, his heat, his desire, I realized how much I wanted slow and sweet, too. The tears came then, finally, freed by the heat of his passion and the warmth of his love.

"You're everything to me," I cried, the words choked with tears.

"Eva."

Shifting his hips, Gideon tucked the tip of his penis into my cleft and pushed forward gently, taking time and care to fill me. His lips moved against mine, the stroke of his tongue somehow more erotic than the slide of his cock.

"Hold me," he whispered, his arms curved beneath my shoulders and his hands cupping the back of my head.

I tightened my grip on him. His buttocks flexed against my calves as he drove into me, his sweat slicking my palms as I caressed his back.

"I love you," he murmured, his fingertips brushing my tears. "Do you feel it?"

"Yes."

I watched the pleasure drift over his face as he moved within me.

I held him as he groaned, his body quivering in orgasm.

I kissed the tears away when he cried silently along with me.

And I let go of my grief in the shelter of his arms, knowing that whether in joy or pain, Gideon was one with me.

❧

"I can't get over this place." Cary set his hands on the railing that surrounded the wraparound deck and looked out over the water. Sunglasses shielded his eyes while the wind played with his hair. "This house is awesome. I feel like we're miles from anyone. And the view . . . un-fucking-believable."

"Right?" I leaned my butt against the railing, facing the house. Through the wall of sliding glass doors, I watched the Reyes family swarm like bees around the kitchen and great room, with Gideon held captive by my grandmother and both of my aunts.

For me, the joyous mood was tinged with poignancy. My mother had never been a part of this extended group, and now she would never have a chance. But life went on.

Two of my younger cousins chased Lucky around the sofas, while the three older ones played video games with Chris. My uncle Tony and my dad were talking in the reading nook, while my dad bounced his fussy baby niece on his knee.

Gideon was a man who feared family in a way he feared little else, and his heartbreaker of a face reflected bemusement and dismay whenever he surveyed the chaos around him. Since I knew him well, I also saw the hint of panic in his eyes, but I couldn't save him. My grandmother wasn't letting him out of her sight.

Cary looked over to see what had drawn my attention. "I'm waiting for your man to sneak out and run like hell."

I laughed. "That's why I asked Chris to come, so Gideon could have some support."

Our group—Gideon, me, Cary, my dad, and Chris—had arrived at the beach around ten in the morning. It was a little after noon when my dad's family was brought over from their hotel with groceries in tow, so that my grandmother could whip up her famous posole. She said it was known to soothe even the most wounded souls. Whether that was true or not, I knew firsthand that her rendition of the classic Mexican soupy stew was delicious.

"Chris is leaving him to fend for himself," Cary drawled, "like you did."

"What can I do? Oh my God." I grinned. "My nana just handed him an apron."

I'd been a little nervous when everyone showed up. I hadn't spent much time with my dad's family when I was little and had only made a couple trips out to Texas with him after I started at UCSD. Every time I visited with them, the Reyeses had been a bit reserved with me, which made me wonder if I looked too much like the woman they all knew had broken my dad's heart. They had met my mother once and hadn't approved, saying my dad was reaching too high and that his love for her wouldn't end well.

So when my grandmother had marched right up to Gideon the moment she arrived and cupped his face in her hands, I'd held my breath right along with him.

My grandmother had brushed his hair back from his face, turned his head from side to side, and pronounced that she saw a lot of my father in him. Gideon had understood the Spanish and replied in her native tongue—he took her statement as a high compliment. My grandmother had been delighted. She'd been speaking to him in rapid-fire Spanish ever since.

"Trey called me yesterday," Cary tossed out casually.

I looked at him. "Did he? How'd that go?"

"Did you say something to him, baby girl, to get him to reach out?"

Trying to look innocent, I asked, "Why would you think that?"

He shot me a knowing look, his mouth twisted wryly. "So you did."

"I just told him you're not going to wait around forever."

"Yeah." He tried looking innocent, too. I had to hope I pulled it off better than he did. "You know I'm not above taking a pity fuck, right? So thanks for hooking me up."

I gave him a gentle shove on the shoulder. "You're full of shit."

Something had shifted for Cary in the last few weeks. He hadn't turned to his usual self-destructive coping mechanisms and since things were going good for him without them, I was holding out hope that he wouldn't backslide.

"True." He flashed his brilliant grin and it was genuine, rather than the cocky façade I knew too well. "Although banging Trey is certainly something tempting to think about. Figure it's probably tempting for him, too, so I should use that to my advantage."

"Are you going to see each other?"

He nodded. "He's going to come with me to the memorial at Stanton's on Monday."

"Oh." I sighed, hurting. Clancy had called Gideon and passed on that information earlier in the morning.

Should I have tried to handle the memorial myself and spare Stanton? I just didn't know. I was still trying to accept the fact that my mom was really gone. After I'd cried for hours the night before, heavy guilt had settled in. There were so many things I'd said to my mother that I regretted and could no longer take back, so many times I'd thought of her with frustration and disrespect.

Ironic, in retrospect, that her chief fault was loving me too much.

As my stepfather had loved her—inordinately.

"I've tried calling Stanton," I said, "but I just get his voice mail."

"Me, too." Cary rubbed at his unshaven jaw. "I hope he's okay, but I realize he's probably not."

"I think it might be a while before any of us are okay."

We settled into comfortable silence for a moment. Then Cary spoke. "I was talking to your dad this morning, before we headed to the airport, about his plans to move to New York."

My nose wrinkled. "I would love to have him near, but I can't help thinking how bizarre it would be if he worked for Gideon."

He nodded slowly. "You have a point."

"What do you think?"

He shifted his body to face me. "Well, just the pregnancy part of having a kid has changed my life, right? So, multiply that by twenty-four years in your case, and I'd say a loving parent would do just about anything to make things better for their child."

Yep, something had definitely shifted for Cary. Sometimes, you just needed a hard jolt to bump you in the right direction. For Cary, that was the thought of being a father. For me, it had been meeting Gideon. And for Gideon, it had been the possibility of losing me.

"Anyway," Cary went on, "he was saying that Gideon offered him a housing allowance and he was thinking he'd like to stay in the apartment with me."

"Wow. Okay." There was a lot to process there. One, my

dad was obviously taking the idea of working for Gideon in New York seriously. Two, my best friend was thinking about living separately from me. I wasn't sure how I felt about that. "I'd been worried Dad would have a hard time using that room after him and my mom . . . you know."

I didn't think I could stay in the penthouse if I didn't have Gideon. Too much had happened between us there. I didn't know if I could handle remembering what I no longer had.

"Yeah, I'd wondered about that, too." Cary reached out and touched my shoulder, a simple comforting touch. "But you know, memories are all that Victor has ever really had of Monica."

I nodded. My dad had to have wondered more than once over the years if the love had always been one-sided. After that afternoon with my mom, maybe he realized that wasn't true. That'd be a good memory to hold on to.

"So you're thinking about staying there," I said. "Mom told me she'd offered you that option."

He gave me a smile tinged with melancholy. "I'm considering it, yes. Kinda makes it easier if your dad's going to be there, too. I warned him it was likely there'd be a baby around now and then. I got the impression he might like that."

Looking back into the house, I saw my dad making silly faces to amuse my baby cousin. He was the only one of his siblings to have just one child, and I was an adult.

I frowned as I watched Gideon walk to the front entrance. Where was he going with an apron tied around his denim-clad hips? He opened the front door and stood unmoving for a long minute. I realized someone must have knocked, but I couldn't see because Gideon was blocking my view. Finally, he stepped aside.

Cary looked over to see where my attention was and scowled. "What's he doing here?"

As Gideon's brother walked in, I wondered the same thing. Then Ireland appeared behind him, holding a gift bag.

"What's up with the gift?" Cary asked. "An unreturnable wedding present?"

"No." I noticed the design on the bag, which was definitely too colorful and festive for a wedding. "It's a birthday present."

"Oh, shit," Cary muttered. "I totally forgot about that."

When Gideon closed the door without his mother making an appearance, I realized Elizabeth was a no-show on her firstborn's birthday. A potent mix of sympathy and pain swamped me and caused my fists to clench.

What the fuck was *wrong* with that woman? Gideon hadn't heard from his mother since confronting her in his office. Considering what the day was, I couldn't believe she could be so thoughtless.

It made me realize I wasn't the only one who'd lost a mother in the past few days.

Chris stood and went to his children, hugging Christopher while Ireland hugged my husband. She smiled up at him, offering the bag. He took it and turned, gesturing toward where I stood on the deck.

Fresh and lovely in a delicately printed sundress, Ireland joined us outside. "Wow, Eva. This place is choice."

440 • SYLVIA DAY

I hugged her. "You like it?"

"What's not to like?" Ireland hugged Cary, and then her lovely face sobered. "I'm really sorry about your mom, Eva."

The tears that were no longer very far away stung my eyes. "Thank you."

"I can't even imagine," she said. "And I don't even like my mom right now."

Reaching out, I touched her arm. Regardless of how I felt about Elizabeth, I wouldn't wish the regret I had on anyone, especially Ireland. "I hope you work out whatever it is. If I had my mom back, I'd take back a lot of the things I said and did."

And because saying that aloud made me feel like crying, I excused myself quickly and headed toward the stairs, running down them to the beach, then out to the water. I stopped when my ankles were submerged, letting the sea breeze blow the tears away.

Closing my eyes, I willed the grief back into the box I'd put it in for the day. It was Gideon's birthday, an occasion I wanted to celebrate because it'd seen him enter the world and, eventually, my life.

I jumped when warm muscular arms slipped around my waist, gathering me back against a familiar hard body.

Gideon set his chin on the crown of my head. I felt his chest expand and contract on a deep sigh when I wrapped my arms over his.

When I pulled myself together enough to speak, I said, "I'm surprised my nana let you escape."

He gave a short laugh. "She says I remind her of your dad—well, she reminds me of you."

Which made it apt, I supposed, that I'd been named after her. "Because I won't let you out of my greedy clutches?"

"Because even though she scares me, I can't seem to walk away."

Touched, I turned my head and rested my cheek against his heart, listening to its strong and steady beat. "I didn't know your brother and sister were coming."

"I didn't, either."

"How do you feel about Christopher being here?"

I felt him shrug. "If he's not acting like a dick, I don't care."

"Fair enough." If his brother's unexpected appearance didn't trouble Gideon, I wouldn't let it bother me.

"I've got some things to share with you," he said. "About Christopher. But now's not the time."

I opened my mouth to contradict that, but caught myself. Gideon was right. We should have renewed our vows today, surrounded by friends and family. We should be celebrating his birthday and being so joyful there wasn't any room for sorrows and regrets. Instead, the day was shadowed by sorrow we had to hide. Still, there was no point in adding any more unpleasantness.

"I have something for you," I told him.

"Umm . . . I'm tempted, angel, but we have too many people here."

It took me a beat to understand he was teasing me. "Oh my God. You fiend."

I reached into my pocket and wrapped my fingers around his gift, which was safely shielded by a black velvet drawstring bag. It had a nice gift box, too, but I'd elected to carry the present in my pocket, hoping to be spontaneous and give it to him when the moment was right. I didn't want to give it to him along with his other presents.

Turning to face him as I pulled the gift out, I offered it on both open palms. "Happy birthday, ace."

His gaze lifted from my hands to my face. There was a brightness to his eyes I saw only when I gave him something. It always made me want to give him more, give him everything. My husband so deserved to be happy. It was my life's mission to make sure he always was.

Gideon took the pouch and untied the drawstring.

"I just want you to know," I began, trying to cover my nervousness, "that it's crazy difficult buying a gift for someone who has everything, including a good chunk of the island of Manhattan."

"I wasn't expecting anything, but I always love what you give me."

I blew out my breath. "Well, you may not want to use it, which is totally fine. I mean, don't feel obligated to—"

The platinum Vacheron Constantin pocket watch slid out into his waiting palm, the polished case twinkling when the sunlight hit it. Biting my lower lip, I waited for him to open it and look inside.

Gideon read the engraved words aloud. "*Yours for all time, Eva.*"

"It can hold a little picture over the inscription. I'd planned for that to be a photo from the renewal ceremony, but . . ." I cleared my throat when he looked at me with such love, it made everything flutter inside me. "It's old school, I know. I just thought, since you wear vests, that it might be something you could use. Although I know you wear a watch on your wrist, so probably not. But—"

He kissed me, shutting me up. "I'll treasure this. Thank you."

"Oh." I licked my lips, tasting him. "I'm glad. There's a fob that goes with it, in the box."

Placing the pocket watch carefully into its pouch, he tucked it into his pocket. "I have something for you, too."

"Keep it clean," I teased him back. "We've got an audience."

Gideon looked over his shoulder and saw how many of our family members had stepped outside onto the deck. The caterer had stocked the outside kitchen with beverages and easy finger foods, and people were starting to poke through it all while the pork for the posole cooked in the oven.

He held out his fist, then opened it to show me the gorgeous wedding band in his palm. Large round diamonds in a channel setting circled the entire band, shooting multi-hued sparks.

My fingers covered my mouth, my eyes watering all over again. The salt-flavored breeze danced around us, carrying the plaintive cries of seagulls soaring over the waves. The rhythmic surge of the tide against the shore lapped over my feet, anchoring me in the moment.

I reached for the ring with trembling fingers.

Gideon's hand closed up and he grinned. "Not yet."

"What?" I pushed at his shoulder. "Don't tease me!"

"Ah, but I always deliver," he purred.

I glared at him. The wicked smirk faded.

His fingers brushed over my cheek. "I'm so proud to be your husband," he said solemnly. "It's my greatest accomplishment to have been found worthy of that honor in your eyes."

444 • SYLVIA DAY

"Oh, Gideon." How he dazzled me. I was so over-whelmed by him, so filled by his love. "I'm the lucky one."

"You've changed my life, Eva. And you did the impossi-ble: you transformed me. I like who I am now. I never thought that would happen."

"You were always wonderful," I said fervently. "I loved you when I saw you. I love you more now."

"There aren't words to tell you what you mean to me." He opened his hand again. "But I hope that when you see this ring on your hand, you'll remember that you shine as brightly as diamonds in my life and you're infinitely more precious."

Pushing onto my toes, fighting the sinking of the wet sand, I sought out his mouth and nearly sobbed with joy when he kissed me. "You're the best thing that ever happened to me."

He was smiling as he took my hand and slid the ring on my finger, nestling it next to the beautiful Asscher diamond he'd given me at our wedding.

Applause and cheers jolted both of us. We looked at the house and saw our families lined up along the railing, watch-ing us. The children were already running down the stairs, chasing Lucky, who was eager to get to Gideon.

I understood that feeling all too well. For the rest of our lives, I would always run to him.

Taking a deep cleansing breath, I let the hope and the joy push the guilt and grief away, just for a moment.

"This is perfect," I murmured, the words lost in the wind. No dress, no flowers, no formality or ritual. Just Gideon and me, committed to each other, with those who loved us nearby.

Gideon caught me up and spun me, making me laugh with pure pleasure.

"I love you!" I shouted, for all the world to hear.

My husband set me down and kissed me breathless. Then, with his lips to my ear, he whispered, "Crossfire."

16

IT WAS DIFFICULT to watch Eva trying to console Richard Stanton, who was a shell of the man we'd spent the weekend with in Westport. He had been vibrantly alive then, seemingly younger than his years. Now, he looked frail and stooped, his broad shoulders weighted by grief.

A profusion of white flower arrangements covered every available surface in Stanton's sprawling penthouse living room, heavily perfuming the air. Photos of Monica were sprinkled liberally around the bouquets, showing Eva's mother in the best moments of her time with Stanton.

Victor sat with Cary and Trey in a smaller area tucked away from the main floor. When we first arrived, there had been a moment when Eva's father and Stanton stood frozen and staring at each other. I suspected each of them resented what the other man had possessed of Monica: Victor had her love, Stanton had the woman herself.

The doorbell rang. My gaze followed Eva and Martin as they walked together to answer it. Stanton didn't move from his wingback chair, his thoughts clearly turned inward. I'd felt his pain when he first opened the door to us, his body visibly jerking at the sight of Eva.

It was good that my wife and I were leaving for the airport directly after. For a month, we'd be away from the city and out of the spotlight. Hopefully, by the time we returned, Stanton could bear the sight of the daughter who looked so much like her mother, the woman he'd loved.

"Cross."

Turning my head, I found Benjamin Clancy. Like Detective Graves, Clancy's eyes held the knowledge of what I'd done to eliminate Nathan Barker as a threat to my wife. Unlike Graves, Clancy had helped cover up my involvement, staging the scene of the crime and another unrelated scene to cast blame onto a dead man who'd paid for his own crimes with his life and wouldn't pay further for mine.

My brows rose in silent inquiry.

"I need a minute." He gestured to the hallway beyond him without waiting for my agreement.

"Lead the way."

I followed him to a library, taking in the shelves of books that lined the walls. The room smelled of leather and paper, the color palette a masculine blend of cognac and evergreen. Four distinct seating areas and a fully stocked bar invited guests to get comfortable and linger.

Clancy shut the door behind us and sat in one of the two club chairs facing the unlit fireplace. I took the other.

He got right to the point. "Mrs. Stanton left behind over

twenty-five years' worth of handwritten journals and a backup computer drive with electronic journal entries. She asked that I pass them along to Eva in the event of her death."

Keeping my curiosity to myself, I said, "I'll make sure she gets them."

He sat forward, setting his elbows on his knees. Ben Clancy was a big man, his biceps and thighs thick with muscle. He wore his dark blond hair in a severe military cut and his eyes had the flat, cold lethality of a great white shark—but they warmed when he looked at Eva, like the loving glance of a very protective older brother.

"You'll need to judge the best time to give them to her," he said. "And you may decide she should never see them."

"I see." So I'd have to go through them. It made me uncomfortable to think of doing so.

"Regardless," Clancy went on, "you now have a new financial responsibility that you'll have to take over on Lauren's behalf. It's not inconsiderable, but you won't have any trouble managing it."

I'd stiffened at the name he used, then grown more alert as he continued.

Nodding, he said, "You started researching her story after the Tramells died."

"But you'd cleaned most of it up." Out of the entire conversation thus far, that was the one thing that made sense.

"What I could. I dug into her past when Mr. Stanton became serious about their relationship. When I confronted her, she told me what I'm about to tell you—none of which is known to Mr. Stanton. I'd like to keep it that way. He was happy. Who she was didn't affect him, so he doesn't need to know."

Whatever it was, Clancy had been swayed. Whether I would be, remained to be seen.

Clancy paused a moment. "You'll get more out of the journals. I haven't read them, but Lauren's story is certainly more compelling than the dry facts I'll give you."

"I understand. Go ahead."

"Lauren Kittrie was raised in a small town on the outskirts of Austin, Texas. Her family was poor. Her mother abandoned her and her twin sister with their father, who worked as a hand on a local ranch. He was a busy man, not much interested in or capable of raising two beautiful headstrong girls."

Sitting back, I took a page from Eva's book and tried to picture two teenage Monicas. The image was more than striking.

"As you can imagine," he continued, "they got noticed. Toward the end of high school, they'd caught the attention of a group of wealthy college students from Austin. Punks, with a dangerous sense of entitlement. The leader was Jackson Tramell."

I nodded. "She married him."

"That was later," he said flatly. "Lauren was savvy about men from the outset. She wanted out of the life her parents had, but she knew trouble when she saw it. She rebuffed him, many times. Her sister, Katherine, wasn't as smart. She thought Tramell could be her ticket out."

Unease caused me to sit back. "How much of this do I need to hear?"

"Against Lauren's advice, Katherine went out with him. When she didn't come home either that night or the next day, Lauren called the police. Katherine was discovered by a local farmer in his field, barely conscious thanks to a toxic combination of street drugs and alcohol. She'd been violently assaulted. Although it wasn't proven, it was suspected that multiple individuals were involved."

"Jesus."

"Katherine was in bad shape," Clancy went on. "The hallucinogenic drugs in her system combined with the physical trauma of gang rape caused permanent brain damage. She needed round-the-clock care for an indefinite period of time, something their father couldn't afford."

Restless, I went to the bar, then realized a drink was the last thing I wanted.

"Lauren went to the Tramells, confronted them about their son and what she suspected he'd done. He denied it and no one was able to prove a connection to him, owing to a lack of physical evidence at that time. But he saw an opportunity and took it. Lauren was the one he'd wanted, so he got his parents to cover the expenses of basic care for Katherine in return for Lauren herself and her silence about the assault."

Turning to face him, I stared. Money could hide a multitude of sins. The fact that Stanton had effectively hidden Eva's past with sealed court files and nondisclosure agreements proved that. But Nathan Barker's father had let him pay for his crimes. The Tramells had gone out of their way to conceal their son's.

Clancy straightened in his chair. "Jackson wanted sex. Lauren negotiated with his parents to secure marriage, which she thought would provide some sort of guarantee that Katherine would always be looked after."

I changed my mind about the drink and filled a tumbler to the halfway point with scotch.

"For a span of months, the situation between Lauren and Jackson was stable. They lived—"

"Stable?" A harsh laugh tore at my throat. "She just about sold herself to the man who orchestrated the gang rape of her twin sister. My God . . ."

I tossed back the liquor.

Monica—or Lauren—had been stronger than any of us had given her credit for. But was it worth it to Eva to learn that, considering the horror of the rest of it?

"The situation was stable," Clancy reiterated, "until she met Victor."

I caught his gaze. Just when you thought a situation was as bad as it could be, there was always worse.

His jaw tightened. "She became pregnant with Eva. When Jackson found out the baby wasn't his, he tried to take care of it—with his fists. Although they lived in his parents' home, the older Tramells never interceded during arguments between the two. Lauren feared for the life of her child."

"She shot him." I ran my hands through my hair, wishing I could scrape the image out of my mind as easily. "The undetermined manner of death—she killed him."

Clancy sat quietly, letting me absorb that revelation. I wasn't the only one who'd killed to protect Eva.

I began to pace. "The Tramells helped Lauren get away with it. They had to. Why?"

"During the time Lauren was with Jackson, she quietly documented anything and everything she could use against him later. The Tramells valued their reputation—and the reputation of their debutante daughter, Monica—and they just wanted Lauren, and all the problems she'd caused, gone.

Lauren left with the clothes on her back and the understanding that, moving forward, Katherine's care was entirely her responsibility."

"So it was all for nothing," I muttered. "She was right where she started."

Then all the information clicked into place. "Katherine's still alive."

Which explained Monica's marriages to wealthy men and her preoccupation with money. All these years, she had to know how shallow her daughter thought she was, but she'd lived with it, instead of telling the truth.

Of course, I'd hoped Eva would never learn what I had done to Nathan. I feared she would think I was a monster.

Clancy rose swiftly to his feet, despite his bulk. "And as I mentioned at the outset, Katherine's care is now your financial responsibility. Whether you disclose any of this to Eva is something you'll have to weigh."

I studied him. "Why are you trusting me with this?"

He straightened his jacket. "I saw you throw yourself over Eva when Hall opened fire. That, along with how you dealt with Barker, tells me you'll do anything to protect her. If you think it's in her best interests to know, you'll tell her when the time is right."

With a brusque nod of his head, he left the room.

I lingered, gathering my thoughts.

"Hey."

Pivoting at the sound of Eva's voice, I faced the doorway and watched her come toward me.

"What are you doing here?" she asked, looking starkly beautiful in a simple black dress. "I was looking all over for you. Clancy had to tell me where you were."

"I had a drink," I told her, giving her a partial truth.

"How many drinks?" The slight twinkle in her eye told me she wasn't upset about it. "You've been in here awhile, ace. We have to take Dad to the airport."

Startled, I glanced at my watch, realized I'd been lost in my own reflections for some time. It was an effort to come back to the present and stop mulling over Lauren's tragic history. I couldn't change the past.

But what I had to do was clear enough. I would see to her sister's welfare. I would take care of her beloved daughter. In those ways, I would honor the woman Monica had been. And one day, if it seemed like the right thing to do, I'd introduce her to Eva.

"I love you," I told my wife, taking her hand in mine.

"You okay?" she asked, knowing my moods so well.

"Yes." I touched her cheek and gave her a soft smile. "Let's go."

Epilogue

"What an odd choice for a honeymoon hotel."

I turn my head to find my mom stretched out on the lounger beside me on the deck. She's wearing a purple bikini, her skin lightly tanned and firm, her nails painted an elegant nude.

Happiness fills me. I'm so glad to see her again.

"It's a private joke," I explain, taking in the view of the Pacific Ocean glittering beyond the emerald ribbon of forest in front of us. "I told Gideon I have a Tarzan fantasy, so he found us a luxury tree house."

I'd been delighted when I first saw the hotel suite suspended high above the ground in the arms of an ancient banyan tree. The panoramic views from its deck are indescribably beautiful, something Gideon and I enjoy whenever we step outside our leafy bower.

"So you're Jane . . ." My mother shakes her head. "I won't even comment."

I grin, glad I can still shock her speechless on occasion.

With a sigh, she leans her head back and closes her eyes,

sunbathing. "*I'm so glad your father has decided to move to New York. It gives me peace of mind to know he'll be there for you.*"

"*Yeah, well . . . I'm getting used to the idea.*"

It's harder accepting that my mom was a completely different person than who I'd thought she was. I debate bringing all of that up. I don't want to mar the joy of spending time with her again. But her journal entries were written as letters to me and I can't help the need to respond.

"*I've been reading your diaries,*" *I say.*

"*I know.*"

Her answer is casual. I feel anger and frustration but push them away. "*Why didn't you share any of your past with me before?*"

"*I meant to.*" *Her head turns toward me.* "*When you were little, I planned to one day. Then Nathan . . . happened, and you were recovering from that. And you met Gideon. I always thought there would be time.*"

I know that's not completely true. Life continues. Something would always serve as an excuse to wait longer. My mom hadn't held out for a time when I could accept all she'd done for the sake of her sister; she'd waited until she could.

It took a strong woman to make the choices and take the actions she had. It was good to know that about her, but more so to understand the source of her fragility. My mother had been a woman tormented by the path her life had taken. Killing Jackson had haunted her, because she'd hated him so desperately and felt joy when he was dead, even as she felt horror for the murder itself.

Leaving my father behind had destroyed a vital part of her, as had living as if her sister, Katherine, didn't exist. My mother had been separated from two pieces of her heart yet somehow managed to go on. Her overprotectiveness made sense to me now—she could not have imagined surviving if she lost me, too.

"*Gideon says we'll go see Katherine when we get back,*" I tell her. "*We're thinking about moving her closer, so she can be part of our lives.*" I'm bracing myself for that, knowing my aunt is my mother's twin.

My mom looks at me with a sad smile. "*She'll be happy to see you. She's been hearing about you for years.*"

"*Really?*" I know from the journals that my mom could rarely see Katherine in person, since my mom's husbands preferred to keep their lovely wife close. She'd had to settle for mailed letters and cards, since e-mails and calls left a trail.

"*Of course. I can't help but brag. I'm so proud of you.*"

Tears fill my eyes.

She tilts her face up to the sun. "*For so long, I was angry at the damage that had been done to Kathy—I never got back the sister I knew. But then I realized her mind protected her from that one night of hell. She doesn't remember it. And as simple as her thoughts are now, she finds a childlike joy in everything.*"

"*We'll take care of her,*" I promise.

My mom holds out her hand and I take it. "*Do tree houses have champagne?*" she asks.

I laugh and squeeze her fingers. "*Sure.*"

I woke slowly, drifting lazily upward from the depths of sleep into full awareness. Dappled sunlight filtered through the mosquito netting cocooning the bed. I stretched, my arm sliding over to search for my husband, but he wasn't lying beside me.

Instead, I found Gideon standing at the window in the rustic nook he was using as an office, talking on the phone. For a moment, I just soaked up the sight of him. Disheveled and unshaven, he was so totally sexy I could hardly stand it.

The fact that Lucky sprawled at his feet only added to the yumminess.

Gideon was wearing nothing but shorts, with the zipper tugged up and the button undone so I could see that he was commando. It was about as far as he got when it came to dressing on our honeymoon. Some days, the only thing he wore was sweat, which looked and smelled so damn hot on him I made sure he worked up more of it.

As for me, I'd been surprised to find my packing augmented with a lot of strapless tube dresses and a noticeable lack of underwear. At any moment, I could find myself bent over, my skirt flipped up, and some part of my husband's anatomy sliding into me. We'd been on our honeymoon for two weeks and in that time, Gideon had trained my body to anticipate his lust. He could arouse me in moments, satisfy us both nearly as quickly.

It was deliciously, insatiably hedonistic.

In between bouts of crazed monkey sex, we'd spent time talking and making plans for when we returned to the world. We watched movies and played card games, with Gideon teaching me how to play well. He did occasionally have to work and when he did, I read the diaries my mother left behind for me. It had taken him a couple of days to tell me about them, but when he did, it was the right time.

We talked about those a lot, too.

"The demand is unreasonable," Gideon said into his phone, eyeing me in my short silk robe. "There's wiggle room elsewhere. They need to be redirected to those fluid points."

Blowing him a kiss, I backed out and headed to the kitchen.

I looked out onto the deck while the coffee brewed, at the

copse of trees beyond that, and the ocean beyond that. Maybe we'd go to the beach today. We had a spot that was ours alone. For now, just being with each other was all we wanted.

A tingle raced down my spine as I heard Lucky's paws hurrying across the hardwood floors. He would be following alongside Gideon, whom he worshipped. My husband was more than a little fond of Lucky, too. The nightmares were coming less and less frequently, but when they did, Lucky was handy to have around.

"Good morning," Gideon murmured, his arms encircling me.

I leaned into him. "I think it's technically afternoon."

"We could go back to bed until evening," he purred, nuzzling my neck.

"I can't believe I haven't bored you yet."

"Angel, if you're bored, I'll put more back into it."

I shivered at the image that came to mind with those words. Gideon was a vigorous lover on an average day. Since we'd been on our honeymoon, he had been even more so. I could swear his body was even more lean and ripped now than before, just from the exercise he got making love to me. Certainly I was happier with my body than I'd been in years.

"Who was on the phone?" I asked.

He took a deep breath. "My brother."

"Really? Isn't that the third time in the last couple of weeks?"

"Don't be jealous. You're much sexier than he is."

I bumped him with my elbow.

Gideon had told me about Hugh's files and that Chris had talked to Christopher. What was said during that con-

versation, we didn't know. That was something private between father and son. But whatever it was, Christopher had
e-mailed Gideon twice—three times now—asking for advice.

"Is it always business he wants to talk about?"

"Yeah, but the stuff he's asking . . . He already knows the
answer."

"Anything personal?"

Gideon had been assured by Chris that nothing of his
abuse had been relayed to his brother, and my husband
wasn't inclined to change that. Christopher had caused a lot
of damage over the years, and without an apology, Gideon
wasn't writing a blank check of forgiveness any time soon.

He shrugged. "Are we having fun . . . How's the
weather . . . That sort of thing."

"He's reaching out in his own way, I guess." I shrugged it
off, too. "Wanna head down to the beach?"

"We could . . ."

Turning in his arms, I looked up at him. "Something else
on your mind?"

"I'd like to run a couple of things by you before I put
work aside for the day."

"Okay. Let me caffeinate first."

I was smiling as we fixed our coffee. Once we reached his
office, he woke up his laptop.

The image on the screen was self-explanatory. I pulled
out the chair and sat. "More GenTen creative?"

I'd seen a dozen different ad concepts so far. Some of the
messaging was clever, some was too clever, and some was
just pedestrian.

"Refinements to the last round," he explained, setting

one hand on the back of the chair and the other on the desk, surrounding me with warm skin and delicious masculine scent. "And some new directions."

Scrolling through the deck, I nodded at most, but one made me shake my head. "That's a no."

"I don't like it, either," Gideon agreed. "But why doesn't it work for you?"

"I think it's sending the wrong message. You know, the overwhelmed wife/mother/businesswoman can only find quiet time by distracting the family with the GenTen." I looked at him. "Women are capable of wearing those various hats easily. Let's show her playing the games with the family or enjoying the GenTen for herself."

He nodded. "I said I wouldn't ask again, but since we're discussing women having it all . . . Are you still feeling good about leaving your job?"

"Yes." There was no hesitation before answering. "I still want to work," I qualified, "and helping you with things you don't need help with isn't going to satisfy me for long. But we'll find a place where I fit."

His mouth quirked wryly. "I do appreciate your take or I wouldn't ask for it."

"You know what I mean."

"I do." He swiped and tapped on the trackpad, bringing up a presentation. "These are a few of the projects currently taking priority. When you have time, look them over and let me know which ones interest you most."

"They all interest you, right?"

"Of course."

"Okay." I'd make a few lists, order them by interest, and knowledge base, and skill set. Then cross-reference. Most important, I would discuss everything with Gideon. That was what I enjoyed most about sharing his work with him—exploring that fascinating razor-sharp mind of his.

"I don't want to tie you down," he said quietly, his hand moving to my shoulder and brushing down my arm. "I want you to soar."

"I know, baby." I caught his caressing hand and kissed the back of it. The sky was the limit with a husband who loved you like that.

❧

The sun dipped below the edge of the horizon, setting fire to the ocean.

Gideon refilled our flutes with champagne, a small splash of the golden liquid escaping the rim as the yacht rocked gently on the waves.

"This is nice," he said, giving me a slow, easy smile.

"I'm glad you like it."

It amazed me to see him so happy and relaxed. I'd always thought of Gideon Cross as a tempest. Lightning and thunder, fiercely beautiful power that could be both dangerous and compelling. Barely contained, like the vortex of a tornado.

I would describe him as the calm after a storm now, which only made him an even greater force of nature. We were both . . . centered now. Feeling confident and committed. Having each other made everything achievable.

All of which had led me to thinking about a dinner cruise.

"Come here, angel." Standing, he held his hand out to me.

We carried our champagne from the candlelit dining table to the luxurious chaise longue for two. We settled there, tangled with each other.

His hand stroked up and down my back. "I'm thinking of blue skies and smooth sailing."

I smiled. So often our thoughts followed similar paths.

Reaching up, I cupped his nape, running my fingers through the rough silk of his hair. "We're getting the hang of this."

Gideon dipped his head down to kiss me, his mouth moving gently, his tongue licking leisurely, reaffirming the bond between us that grew stronger every day. The ghosts of our pasts seemed like faint shadows now, beginning to dissolve even before we'd renewed our vows.

One day, they would vanish forever. Until then, we had each other. And that was all we needed.

Author's Note

Dear Friends,

It's always difficult to say good-bye at the end of a journey, and to part ways with companions you've come to love. Saying farewell to Gideon and Eva is bittersweet. I've spent many years with them and hundreds of thousands of words (*One with You* is the longest novel I've written in a career that spans a dozen years!), and yet now that Crossfire is over, I know Eva and Gideon are ready and able to go forward with their lives on their own. Whatever help they needed from me, they don't require it any longer.

Now it's time to introduce you to Kane Black, whose epic and all-consuming love for Lily has touched me uniquely. Unlike the Crossfire series, which spans only a few months, the Blacklist series follows Kane and Lily over a number of years. The Kane who first falls in love with Lily isn't the man who fights to win her back, but I love both the younger and the wiser versions of him equally. I know you will, too.

Enjoy Kane in the pages that follow. His story is just beginning. . . .

With love,
Sylvia

Turn the page for a sneak peek at Sylvia Day's next

So Close

Copyright © 2016 by Sylvia Day, LLC.

1

THE MOMENT THE SLEEK BRUNETTE walks in the door, I know my employer will seduce her. She's arrived on the arm of another man, but that's irrelevant. She'll succumb; they all do.

The lady's resemblance to the photos Mr. Black treasures is unmistakable. She is categorically his type: shiny black hair, bright green eyes, pale skin, and red lips.

I greet them both with a slight tip of my head. "Good evening. May I take your coats?"

The gentleman assists her as I cast a glance at the living room, assuring myself that the staff is present but unobtrusive, supplying canapés and beverages, while clearing away the discarded glasses and plates.

Manhattan sprawls in a blanket of twinkling lights beyond the floor-to-ceiling windows of the penthouse. The event is a black-tie reception in honor of a new start-up. Mr. Black celebrates often, surrounding himself with people as if that will bring the life to him that he lacks within himself.

His home is an excess of glass, steel, and leather, lacking all color and warmth. Still, it's a comfortable space if not inviting, filled with oversize pieces carefully positioned to leave the vast room open and airy. The ideal showcase for the roiling storm of power my employer exudes.

I wonder if his preference for black and white is a reflection of his view on the world. Colorless. Lifeless.

I look for a moment at Mr. Black, searching for his reaction to the latest arrival. I see what I expected: a sudden stillness in his restless energy as he catches sight of her, followed by an avid gaze. As he studies her, his jaw tightens. The signs are subtle, but I sense his terrible disappointment and the resulting surge of anger.

He'd hoped it was her. *Lily.* The woman whose image graces all of his most private rooms.

I don't know Lily; she was gone from his life before my services were acquired. I know her name only because he spoke it once, on a tormented night, when he was wild with drink and half mad. And I know the hold she has on him; I can feel it when I look at the massive photo canvas of her that hangs over his bed.

Her images are the only spots of color in the entire residence, but that isn't what makes them so striking. It's her eyes, and the utter trust and fierce longing one sees there.

Whoever Lily was, she'd loved Kane Black with everything she had.

"Thank you," the brunette says as her escort hands me her coat. She's speaking to me, but Mr. Black has already captured her attention and her gaze is on him. He is impossible to ignore, a dark tempest checked only by a remarkable force of will.

He's recently been named Manhattan's most eligible bachelor, as the previous holder of that title just announced his elopement on national television. Mr. Black is not yet thirty and already wealthy enough to afford me, a seventh-generation factotum of impeccable British lineage. He is a charismatic young man, the sort women are drawn to without any thought of self-preservation. My daughter assures me that he is blessed with uncommon masculine beauty and something she claims is even more compelling: raw, animal magnetism. She says his air of unattainability is utterly irresistible.

I'm afraid, however, that it's more than an affectation. His many sexual liaisons aside, Mr. Black is taken in the most profound sense of the word.

His heart was given to Lily and he lost it when he lost her. All that's left is the shell of a man I love as if he were one of my own sons.

"Did you show her out?"

Mr. Black enters the kitchen the next morning dressed for the day in an immaculate hand-tailored business suit and pristinely knotted tie, neither being an article of clothing he owned prior to my employ. I'd schooled him in the fine art of bespoke clothing for gentlemen, and he had absorbed the information with a thirst for knowledge I learned was unquenchable.

Judging by his exterior, one could scarcely see the

uncultured young man who'd hired me. He's been transformed, a task he attacked with single-minded ferocity.

I turn and set his breakfast on the island, positioning it
perfectly between the silverware I've already set out. Eggs,
bacon, fresh fruit—his staples. "Yes, Ms. Ferrari left while
you were in the shower."

One dark brow lifts. "Ferrari? Really?"

I'm not surprised that he never asked her for her name,
only saddened. Who they are means nothing to him. Only
that they look like Lily.

He reaches for the coffee I set in front of him, his mind
clearly running through his plan of attack for the day, his latest lover dismissed from his thoughts forever. He rarely sleeps
and works far too much. There are deep grooves on either side
of his mouth that should not be there on one so young. I've
seen him smile and have even heard him laugh, but the
amusement never reaches his eyes.

I mentioned once that he should try to enjoy all that he's
accomplished. He told me he'd enjoy life better when he was
dead.

"You did an excellent job with the party last night,
Witte," he says, rather absentmindedly. "You always do, but
still." His mouth curves on one side. "Never hurts to say I
appreciate you, does it?"

"No, Mr. Black. Thank you."

I leave him to eat and to read the day's paper, heading
down the hallway to the private side of the residence he
shares with no one. The darkly beautiful Ms. Ferrari spent
the night in the opposite end of the penthouse, a space free
from the visual specter of Lily.

I pause on the threshold of the master suite, sensing the

lingering humidity of a recent shower. My eyes are drawn to the massive canvas hanging on the wall directly in front of me. It's an intimate picture. Lily lies on a disheveled bed, her slender limbs tangled in a white sheet, her long dark hair fanned across a rumpled pillow. Her sensual yearning is intensely evident, her lips reddened and swollen from kisses, her pale cheeks flushed, her adoring eyes heavy-lidded with desire.

How did she die? A tragic accident? An insidious disease?

She was so young, barely a woman. I wish I'd known my employer when he was with her. What a force of nature he must have been then.

I can't help but grieve. Such a shame that two such bright flames would be snuffed out before their prime.

❧

As I merge the Range Rover into traffic, I hear Mr. Black relay clipped orders into his mobile. It's barely eight in the morning and he's already deep into managing the various spokes of his growing conglomerate.

Manhattan teems around us, the brimming stream of cars flowing in every direction. In places, bags of rubbish are piled several feet high on the pavements, waiting to be hauled away. I was put off by the sight when I first came to New York, but now it's just part of the milieu.

I've come to enjoy this city I now reside in, so different from the rolling green dales of my homeland. There is nothing one can't find on this small island, and the energy of the people . . . the diversity and complexity . . . is unrivaled.

My eyes shift back and forth from the traffic to the pedestrians. Ahead of us, the one-way street is blocked by a delivery lorry. On the left pavement, a bearded man deftly handles a half-dozen leashes as he takes a group of excited canines on their morning walk. On the right side, a mother dressed for a run pushes a jogging pram ahead of her toward the park. The sun is shining, but the towering buildings and thickly leafed trees shadow the street. Horns begin to blare as the traffic delay stretches.

Mr. Black continues his business dealings with self-assured ease, his voice calm and assertive. The cars begin to creep forward, then pick up speed. We head downtown. For a short time, we are blessed with green lights in succession. Then our luck runs out and I'm stopped by a red light.

A flood of people hurry by in front of us, most with heads down and a few with ear buds that, I suppose, offer some respite from the cacophony of the busy city. I glance at the time, making sure we're on schedule.

A sudden pained noise sends ice through my veins. It's a half-strangled moan that is vaguely inhuman. Turning my head swiftly, I glance at the backseat, alarmed.

Mr. Black sits still and silent, his eyes dark as coal, his tanned skin drained of all color. His gaze is sliding along the pedestrian crossing, following. I look that way, seeking.

A slender brunette hurries away from us, trying to beat the light. Her hair is short, cut high at the nape in a bob that lengthens at the sides to cup her jaw. It's not Lily's luxuriant mane, not at all. But when she turns to walk down the pavement, I think it might be her face.

The back door swings open violently. Mr. Black leaps out

just as the light turns green. The taxi driver behind us lays on his horn but I hear my employer shout over it.

"Lily!"

Her gaze darts toward us. She stumbles. Freezes in place.

Her face pales like Mr. Black's. I see her lips move, see the name escape her. *Kane.*

Yes, the world knows his handsome face and what he has accomplished, but her shocked recognition is intimate and unmistakable. As is the desperate pining she cannot hide.

It is *her.*

Mr. Black glances toward traffic, then lunges between moving cars, nearly causing an accident. The barrage of honking becomes deafening.

The harsh sound visibly jolts her. She surges into a run, pushing her way through the throng on the sidewalk in obvious panic, her emerald green dress a beacon in the crowd.

And Mr. Black, a man who attains without pursuit, gives chase.